A COVENANT KEEPER NOVEL

KAHTAR

WARRIOR OF THE AGES

S.R. KARFELT

INDIGO
Livonia, Michigan

KAHTAR—WARRIOR OF THE AGES

Published by Indigo
an imprint of BHC Press

Library of Congress Control Number:
2017945125

ISBN-13: 978-1-946848-44-4
ISBN-10: 1-946848-44-1

Also available in ebook

Visit the publisher at:
www.bhcpress.com

PRAISE FOR
"KAHTAR—WARRIOR OF THE AGES"

S.R. Karfelt's *Kahtar—Warrior of the Ages* presents a fascinating twist on immortality that opens the doors for deep philosophical ponderings and wildly intriguing storylines—doors through which Karfelt boldly and masterfully charges. Add fully fleshed-out characters worthy of cheering or booing and you have a story that's impossible to put down. *Kahtar—Warrior of the Ages* is a wonderful tale, brilliantly told.

~ Robert Liparulo, author of the "Dreamhouse Kings,"
"The 13th Tribe" and "The Judgment Stone" ~

Gritty characters and a compelling story. S. R. Karfelt is a fabulous new voice in the paranormal genre.

~ Heather Burch, bestselling author of the Halflings Series ~

A well crafted story that captures your imagination from page one. A story arc designed to snatch you and whisk you through the portal into the ever place of the *Kahtar—Warrior of the Ages*. Well developed characters are the heart and soul of this tale, these people will become your friends as you cheer them on. Swords, bombs, cars, intrigue, rival clans, love, this story has it all. The ending was satisfying and unpredictable. I found myself luxuriating in the final words, soaking up every last detail. A wild ride left me craving more.

~ LaDonna Cole, author of "The Torn" ~

What is there to say about S.R. Karfelt's *Kahtar—Warrior of the Ages*? Sheer genius, that's what…Falling deeply in love with the characters was something I didn't know to expect. I ping-ponged between Kahtar—our immortal hero—and Beth—the woman who would ruin everything he's worked for. Several times I stopped to ask myself "Whose side am I on, anyway?" only to dive back in for more.

~ Kelsey Keating, author of "A Stolen Kiss" ~

This was the fourth time that I have read *Kahtar—Warrior of the Ages* all the way through…and it still moves me…I am still fascinated by the background to the book, the Covenant Keepers, Old Guard, ilu, Orphans, and so on… (hard to realise that this is Karfelt's first book, it seems so skillfully done) but the characters, the plot, the themes, are all quite mature. Ultimately, the result for me is that this book definitely meets my criterion of success, and has been a pleasure to read.

~ Elsie Wilson, reviewer, Elsie's Stuff and Nonsense ~

S.R. Karfelt pushes the boundaries and makes you question your very way of living. With *Kahtar—Warrior of the Ages*, I was immediately immersed in an intense, wild ride, cheering and weeping with Kahtar and Beth. Gasping for air, the ending came all too soon!

~ Robin Harnist, editor ~

With a seasoned writer's prowess, the author sets up the conflict…immediately and escalates the tension with every scene. I hardly ever read a trade-length book in two days, but I confess this one had me at first encounter…. Look for more from this emerging and talented…author.

~ Kathleen L. Maher, historical romance writer ~

ALSO BY S.R. KARFELT

The Covenant Keeper Novels
Heartless—A Shieldmaiden's Voice
Forever—The Constantines' Secret

Other Novels
Bitch Witch

Non Fiction
Nobody Told Me—Love in the Time of Dementia

Multi-Author Collections
A Winter's Romance
In Creeps the Night
Through the Portal
Call of the Warrior

For
The Ragged Edge Writers for telling me I could,
Bailey for telling me I should,
And Lindsay, for being the first to say I had.

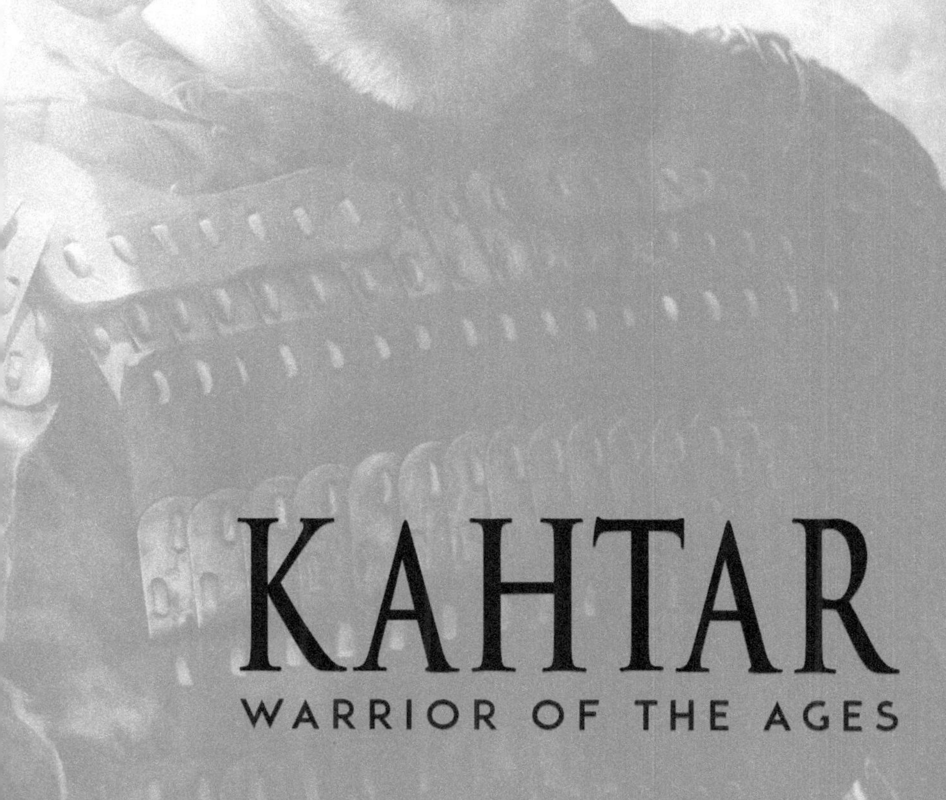
KAHTAR
WARRIOR OF THE AGES

CHAPTER
ONE

IMMORTALITY PROBABLY MADE a man patient. Part-time immortality, the kind that Kahtar had been inflicted with, didn't. Crammed inside his squad car in what was possibly the hottest May Day in his existence reminded him of being locked inside an iron maiden. Except those weapons of torture had been wooden coffins, not metal, though if memory served they had better ventilation.

Across a clearing framed by spindly trees, his rookie sat inside a second patrol car. Kahtar watched Honor Monroe gaze at himself in the rearview mirror, both hands twisting his spiky hairdo to perfection, and paying no attention to his surroundings. The kid had no idea how close he was to being shaved bald. Not that there was anything dangerous around for miles, but still.

Closing his eyes to shut out the visual of Honor now picking at his teeth, Kahtar gripped the steering wheel and stilled. Military crew-cut almost flush with the ceiling, it brushed against the fabric with each breath. His mind sharpened and focused, flying outward like a stealth aircraft, scanning with a precision beyond the capability of any man-made radar. The beating wings of buzzing insects, larvae crawling through rotting wood, the clear air rife with invisible particles filled his senses. His scan moved up through the blossoming trees before plunging down, far beneath the mulch of last year's fallen leaves. Kahtar forced his mind through the forest floor. It took years to learn to identify what was in the ground, but he'd had plenty of time to perfect the skill.

Abruptly pulled from the depths of the earth by another warrior's scan crossing into his, it felt like a shard of glass plunged deep into his brain. Pressing his fingers against his skull he tried to ease the dark shadow. The interfering scan lifted as the culprit approached.

"Hoy!" His entirely too enthusiastic rookie rounded the patrol car, hair artfully arranged, teeth apparently picked. "Sorry about that! Not used to being around my own kind anymore!"

A tour of duty in the Middle East might have made the man forget his manners, but it hadn't dimmed his chipper demeanor. Honor Monroe approached police work with the same animation he gave a game of stickball. His hand smacked against the windshield, and the kid peered at him, shouting through the glass.

"Chief? We're partners today. Real cops sit in the same car with their partners."

Kahtar glared into Honor Monroe's bright eyes. "Monroe, I doubt your own mother would sit in a car with you all day." For emphasis Kahtar rolled the window up. Honor wisely hurried towards his own squad car. The kid had a lot to learn. It was very tempting to scan right through his head, but Kahtar resisted the impulse to make him cry on his first day playing cops.

Closing his eyes to focus, Kahtar's scan resumed, moving down the country road. Scanning asphalt felt almost poisonous, he could practically smell it, taste tar on his tongue. Simultaneously, he shoved his mind east and west, following the road in both directions at once. From one edge of his scan came movement, a vehicle from the west. It blew through his mind, instantly engulfed by his mental radar. He digested every minute detail: *3,109 pounds of metal and synthetic substances, one 140 pound human being, vehicle speed fluctuating between 65 and 70 mph.* For today, barely speeding was still speeding because Honor Monroe's scan still hovered dangerously near, and Kahtar was in no mood to have it bite into his head again. Besides, the more unpleasant he could make a trip to the village of Willowyth, the less likely people were to want to return.

Turning the key, Honor's second voice, somehow as enthusiastic as his real voice, sounded in Kahtar's mind. *"Chief? I feel it too! The car's yellow!"*

Ignoring Honor, he edged the patrol car to the roadway. The speeding car appeared atop a little knoll, a bright yellow Saab convertible. Honor Monroe insisted he could scan color, and although often wrong, he did seem to have some sort of extra gift. Honor's annoyingly enthusiastic second voice sounded very faintly as Kahtar pulled onto the highway behind the Saab. *"I was right, wasn't I?"*

"Just stay out of trouble. I'll be fifteen minutes, tops." He wondered if his second voice sounded as annoyed as he felt.

KAHTAR TRAILED THE yellow convertible, wondering how the woman inside could possibly see to drive while her hair whipped around her head in the wind like a dozen albino bats. It took flashing lights, a siren and a mile of riding her bumper before she noticed him.

The Saab came to a stop at the edge of a residential street with one wheel propped up on the sidewalk. Following merciless police protocol, he waited several menacing minutes before unfolding his nearly seven-foot frame from the squad car and slowly approaching. The bass of her music forced its own rhythm into his heart, but it wasn't nearly as intrusive as the profane lyrics.

Nobody played bad cop as well as he did, and ruining the morning of a vulgar stranger had potential to cheer him up.

"Shut. It. Off."

With an open palm the blonde obediently smacked a dial and silenced her radio. Despite miles of whipping wind her curtain of silky hair fell obediently into place as she looked attentively up at him.

"I drove behind you for miles before you even...." Kahtar's lecture evaporated, as stunned, he momentarily lost the ability for any coherent speech.

Covenant Keepers never forgot the touch of another's heart and though he didn't know hers, images flashed through his mind unbidden as her heart unexpectedly touched his: *A pristine stream on The Fortunate Isles, a fresh squeeze of lemon in tea, the way snow used to taste before the Industrial Revolution.* This woman was one of his kind; as much Covenant Keeper as he was. The gale force of her impossibly familiar heart slapped right against his, announcing that truth as intensely as if he'd known her all his life.

Standing in the humid spring day and gaping like a suffocating fish, he basked in her heart skipping around his like the dappled summer sunshine shining through the Buckeye blossoms above them. The pretty blonde Covenant Keeper looked him up and down with wide eyes the exact same shade of blue as her dress.

The look on her face incredulous, she asked bluntly, "What are you supposed to be?"

Kahtar had almost forgotten the thrill of being pleasantly surprised. Gazing down at the strange Covenant Keeper, he explained his guise.

"I'm supposed to be a Willowyth cop, the Police Chief to be precise. You're Clan Huron, aren't you?" He leaned against the convertible, studying the open-hearted woman.

Shading her eyes with a hand, her expression confused, she said, "No, sorry, I'm not Clan. My name is Beth White."

Kahtar straightened, surprised by the answer. Freed from his weight the sports car shifted slightly.

Beth reached into the backseat to tug an enormous silver pocketbook onto her lap. She scratched her lightly freckled nose, a slight crease between her brows as she squinted up at him. "Okay, look, I don't have an Ohio license, but I do have an International Driving Permit and a Greek license. At least I did...." When he didn't respond, she started fishing through her bag with one hand, occasionally shooting a concerned glance up at him.

"What are you playing at? Did Honor put you up to this?" It was the first random thought that popped into his mind, and he was surprised to hear himself voice the ludicrous idea.

She scratched her nose again. "Um, my permit expired two years ago. Is this really going to be a big deal? It's hardly dishonorable to get behind on paperwork!"

She was sincere and frank about the stupid papers, as though she didn't recognize him as one of her own, as though he was a regular cop pulling over a speeder.

"Beth White? Surely you recognize me?"

Perfectly arched eyebrows rose as she looked him up and down a bit more slowly than was polite. "Sorry. I make it a point to remember all the Avengers I've ever met," she blurted, then bit her lip.

Kahtar blinked and his heart skipped a beat. For one wild moment he thought she knew his secret. His mind reeled.

"That's what we like to call a joke. Are you all right?" Beth held out her paperwork, and even in his semi-stunned state he noted the worn passport and laminated card were genuine documents. "I do have American insurance. Are you okay? Officer…Officer?"

It took less than a heartbeat to realize she didn't know his secret, and for the strange space of another beat he wasn't sure if he was disappointed or relieved. That she was not from any neighboring clan was now obvious. Her behavior was off-the-chart odd for any Covenant Keeper. Internal alarms began to sound even while her heart continued to leapfrog around his like a friendly puppy. Kahtar tried to make sense of her and his mind flew through several highly improbable scenarios, distracted by the touch of that heart.

The touch of her heart reminded him of running through fields when he had been a boy in a clan in Malaysia, or a time when he'd been a boy during the Middle Ages, memories of joy. With effort Kahtar forced his attention away from old memories and blinked. She stared at him and judging by the frank concern in her blue eyes, she was bewildered by his behavior too.

Hiding behind the guise of an officer of the law, Kahtar took her paperwork and glanced at it. As he read her name, the answer to her behavior finally dropped into his mind. Beth White wasn't an alias. It was her name.

Beth was not the name of a Covenant Keeper. Orphan. Beth White was an Orphan of the Inquisition. A Covenant Keeper without a clan, without a home. A descendant of a Covenant Keeper lost to her own, perhaps generations ago. Pangs of disappointment rippled in Kahtar's heart. This woman didn't know her own when one of them stood right in front of her because she didn't know herself.

"Hey, Chief?" Beth White interrupted his reverie. "Are you sure you're all right?"

And this is the part where I chase her away. It was as simple as that. She belonged to another world and as far from Willowyth as possible. Meeting her eyes, he glared with hostility usually reserved for opponents on the battlefield. Many sins darkened his soul, but no one could ever accuse him of not doing his duty. Bending down so that he was level with her eyes, he growled, "Keep right on moving, Beth White, or I will arrest you. I don't like you, and if I ever see you again, you will regret it."

LIAR, BETH THOUGHT. Despite his bipolar-on-crack behavior, the Zeus-like cop definitely liked her. Granted, he'd thought she was somebody else at first, whoever Clan Huron was. He'd realized his mistake quickly though. Then like a Greek god suffering from a head injury, he'd gone from bad cop to good cop to nutter cop and back to bad in the course of a few minutes. Still. He definitely liked her.

Peeking in her rearview mirror, she watched him stalk back to the cruiser. Boldly adjusting the mirror to get a better look, she bit back a sigh. There was something about him that made her want to like him too, but who could like a whack like that? Starting her car, she kept an eye on the mirror, her hand on the gear when she saw it. A light she'd seen thousands of times in dreams, danced in a brief sparkling column near the back of the police car. She sucked in breath as it vanished. Something tingled through her. Not fear—a thrill. Always, since she'd been a child, she'd known those lights existed. The memory of what they were was elusive, like trying to catch a thought that raced away faster as you reached for it.

The cop pivoted to look at her and their eyes met in the mirror. His were steely, hiding something. They held her gaze a brief second, but that was all Beth needed to see to understand the truth. The Police Chief hoped she hadn't seen the light. That light meant something had happened, something serious, something he didn't want her to know about. He wanted her to leave and instinctively she cooperated. Giving him half of what he wanted, she shoved the car into gear and pressed a toe of her favorite lemon colored stiletto pumps against the gas pedal, leaving a spray of gravel in her wake. That cop, however, would quite possibly see her again. She wasn't going anywhere—Willowyth was right where she belonged. And if that was in his way, that was just too bad for him.

THE OLD GUARD'S second voice seared through Kahtar's brain. *"Honor Monroe critically injured."* Anger and frustration wrestled with disbelief as Kahtar sent a battle cry. Like a wave it moved silently from his mind, echoing towards the consciousness of nearby warriors. It consisted of only one word. **Pray.** That was where Honor's only hope lay, in the healing prayers of his fellow warriors.

Jumping into his squad car, Kahtar turned it in the opposite direction of the departing Orphan. Racing over miles of country road, frustration won as his leading emotion. The slow means of transportation the car provided was infuriating, although the speedometer edged into the red zone. Putting miles between the Orphan and Old Guard was mandatory. It would be nothing short of a miracle if Beth White hadn't noticed the Old Guard shimmering his warning message. For her sake, he hoped she hadn't.

Scanning the abandoned roadway, and then into the empty sky, Kahtar braked hard. The cruiser's tires shrieked in protest, leaving a rubber trail the back end spun into the wrong lane. Unpleasant burning smells filled the car as he backed recklessly into the woods, right over weedy shrubs and through bramble, hiding the vehicle out of sight from both road and sky. Turning the key and tossing the door open, he shouted, "Old Guard!"

The shimmering column of light appeared again briefly, solidifying into a man that stood considerably taller and broader than Kahtar's ample mass. His hand grabbed Kahtar's upper arm, and before the door stopped swinging, both men vanished.

CHAPTER
TWO

THE OLD GUARD reappeared with Kahtar inside a spartan surgery, bright lights and antiseptic in the air. Pulling free, Kahtar stepped towards his rookie.

Honor Monroe lay face down, unconscious, on a white marble table. A gunshot through the chest had left a massive exit wound, the hole in Honor's back horrifying and large. Blood pooled inside the wound, running over flesh and onto the marble table. It dripped over the side, splashing onto the cream colored floor that absorbed it sponge-like. The remnants of Honor's navy blue police shirt lay on the floor. Dozens of Warriors of ilu had clustered in the room. Several surrounded the head of the table, their healing hands touching Honor. The rest knelt on the floor, arms outstretched towards the heavens as they prayed for the healing of their clansman.

Kahtar approached, his eyes moving to the young doctor whose fingers were busy inside the hole in Honor's back. He noted the long tube attached to Honor's upper arm. It ran across the length of the table into the arm of another warrior, whose own blood now flowed into Honor.

The doctor glanced up at Kahtar briefly, his eyes immediately going back to Honor's wound while defending. "The prayers of the clan weren't fast enough. He almost bled out before the Old Guard found him. A transfusion saved his life."

Before Kahtar could speak, the deep baritone of an Old Guard informed. "We found him, in the street, with this injury."

"Was there any evidence of the assailant?"

"He was alone," was the reply.

"Did he summon you?" Kahtar put a hand on Honor's arm. It was cold, his face too white.

"It was providential."

Kahtar glanced at the Old Guard's eyes. They were solid black, no whites, no discernible pupil, impenetrable. Asking why the Old Guard might have been alongside a country road was futile. They did not explain themselves. Neither did they investigate crime scenes.

"Did someone go to the scene?" he asked the cluster of his warriors lining the room.

"Squire and Consider are investigating." Welcome Palmer, the young doctor, answered him. "They were on duty here when Old Guard brought Honor. I told them they should go, that you wouldn't mind."

Distracted, Kahtar looked sharply at the doctor. Like all the Palmer men, Welcome's eyes were emerald green, and he had the dark hair and striking features of his family. Kahtar didn't particularly care for the Palmers. Not that they were dishonorable, but most of the Palmer men were involved in the sciences, few were warriors. He had no use for them. Welcome Palmer, though not a warrior had always seemed very like one. Kahtar could respect him, though not when he overstepped his bounds.

"I didn't think that you would mind me releasing them on this particular occasion." Welcome's expert fingers moved over Honor's flesh, the wound vanishing as it healed slowly beneath them.

Kahtar scanned into his rookie. The bullet had torn through Honor's flesh brutally, nicking his left pulmonary artery. It was miraculous that the Old Guard had found him. Miraculous that Welcome Palmer's maverick skills had kept life in him. Welcome would be in for grief from the head of the clinic, where traditional methods of healing were preferred, not blood transfusions, even if it meant death. Kahtar allowed his heart to slap against Welcome's.

The young doctor nodded his head slightly in his direction, indicating acknowledgment of the gesture. It was a cool truce.

Even on the verge of bleeding to death the kid had something to say, Honor's second voice sounded faint and weak as it whispered inside Kahtar's head.

"*Was the car yellow?*" Hope swelled in Kahtar's heart and prayer for healing burst from him towards the warrior. The prayer settled over the young man as a tangible thing. The prayers of Warriors of ilu were powerful, more powerful than a bullet. This time.

PARALLEL PARKING WAS embarrassingly beyond her skill level. It seemed a shameful deficit in a woman with three degrees, almost four if she could only have kept her opinions to herself in graduate school. Unable to resist looking, Beth peeked at the house and experienced, however briefly, stunned confusion. The yellow convertible ended up parked with one wheel on the curb and the back-end too far into the street. A thrill tingled through her as she clambered over a door without bothering to open it. She ran towards the house.

Stopping in the front yard she soaked it in. It was exactly like the 1935 postcard except it was in color and 3D. A three story Victorian, 35 Pearl Street, the home of her dreams towered. Heels sinking into crabgrass, hands clutching two fistfuls of hair, she drank it in. Snowball bushes, untamed lilac trees bursting with seductively scented blooms, Old-English ivy hugged an entire wall, the porch, a soft dove grey, embraced the enormous welcoming house which had been expertly painted half a dozen hues of gentle blues.

With tears in her eyes, for the first time in her life, Beth White felt at home. It made no sense. She'd never paid a whit of attention to where she lived before, but this place had called to her like a living thing.

Rushing back to her convertible she hauled out a giant silver handbag and dug through it, locating the old postcard. How could anything so random feel so right? She'd unearthed the postcard wedged between the pages of an encyclopedia at a rummage sale, at a defunct church in a terrible neighborhood. Dad would have had a coronary if he knew she'd even stopped in the place.

Turning the postcard, Beth held it up to compare with the actual living house. It could have been taken today. Dancing on the sidewalk she hugged herself. Maybe, just maybe, this was meant to be. What were the odds that librarian had even known where this house was? All the postcard said was '35 Pearl Street' handwritten with the flourish of a fountain pen. The house might have been in any one of thousands of obscure locations, in one of many states. Yet not only had the librarian known where it was, she'd known it was for sale.

Scrambling the contents of her purse, Beth fished out a wooden box. Dashing up the limestone sidewalk, she pounded across the porch. Opening the box she produced an antique lever lock type of key. Certain it opened every door in the house, like any good skeleton key, she jammed it into the keyhole and burst through the door.

Home!

This part felt a bit anti-climatic. The pristine façade had pushed an idealized view of what the interior would hold into her imagination. Reality was abrupt as usual.

Dust and cobwebs covered every surface. It might take a hazmat team to clear them out. Ancient, crumbling wallpaper hung in loose sheets on the walls. Filthy chandeliers dangled from the ceiling, but not one light switch or electric outlet was in sight. Upon closer examination the light fixtures all appeared to have been designed to hold candles, but 1935 wasn't that prehistoric! Weird.

Racing from window to window to look at the view of the neighboring park, and peering over the tops of the trees lining the river below, an anomaly struck Beth. There were no power lines in this section of the village. Retracing her steps, she marched back to the front windows to look, and studied the house next door. It had the appearance of a nouvelle restaurant about it, though oddly there was no place to park. Even odder, there were no power lines to it either. Behind the restaurant an alley stretched, revealing the backside of shops on Main Street. Only one had a sign above the back door and it appeared to be a fine furniture store. The sloping roof was covered in solar panels and a generator sat outside the back door.

Oh well, Beth decided, she was all about being green. The zoning board would have answers and then, after she found someone willing to shovel the half foot of dust mites out of this house, she would finally have the shop she'd always dreamed of. The last six years had been a sacrifice towards fulfilling this dream, now it was just a matter of opening shop. How hard could that be? Patting the door on the way out, she unashamedly spoke to it.

"You are a dream come true."

DIGGING THROUGH HER trunk crammed with random treasure absolutely necessary before the moving truck came, Beth tugged out a wooden board. The sign wasn't very big, two feet wide by one foot high. Dad had painted it a creamy white that hinted at yellow, the name of Beth's shop was burned into it in scroll lettering, Sweet Earth. For some reason, as she stood on the wide front porch, Beth couldn't bear the idea of hanging it up. Maybe the color wasn't right or maybe because it wasn't in the postcard, but it didn't belong. I'm getting to be such a freak, she thought propping it up against the wall, outside the front door.

"Hey, you!"

The voice belonged to a young woman wobbling up the slate walkway from Pearl Street. Dressed in an old-fashioned waitress uniform in the only shade of pink that Beth would call ugly, the woman plodded along in a pair of outlandish glittery pumps. Stopping at the foot of the steps, she looked up at Beth.

"I'm Brenda Blake. I work at the diner, Cliff's." Smoothing the awful dress with both hands, she wheezed a smoker's laugh, "Obviously, right? Heard you were looking for help."

The bleached blonde clomped her way up the stairs, exposing miles of dark roots and a pierced eyebrow. Beth caught a whiff of cigarettes and started to formulate a polite rejection, trying to let her down gently.

"I don't want to get off on the wrong foot with other businesses in town, hiring employees from other restaurants."

Brenda cackled, "Other restaurants? There's only Cliff's. I get you though, but I'm on flex time at Cliff's on account of my girls, and I wouldn't leave there. We're family, well the kind you wish you had, you know? I can work here whatever hours you want. I need the money."

That frank statement, and loyalty to her current employer, won her points in Beth's eyes. Beth knew she should ask about Brenda's girls, their ages and names, but she didn't bother much with polite conversation, especially not when there was something else that needed clarification first.

"What do you mean about other restaurants? That place right there is a restaurant." She pointed to the smaller one-story house on the lot next door.

Brenda glanced over at it. "No, it's not. Why do you think that?"

That was a very good question.

"It looks like a restaurant." *No. It is a restaurant. I'm sure it is.* Though as yet she hadn't seen a single person go in or out.

"Just looks like a house to me, like an old people's house. Besides, this town can barely tolerate Cliff's coffee shop. I think they'd be happy to have a perfect looking ghost town. Surprised you got a permit to open."

Worry prickled up Beth's spine. "I don't, not yet."

"Well dang, girl, good luck with that. Can't imagine why you'd want to move to this fun-forsaken town?"

"Why do you live here?"

"Hiding from my ex. There's only one road in and one road out, and I think the cops in this place would give you the chair for even speeding. It's safe here."

Beth waited. Though she thought Brenda was probably right, there was another reason. She could sense it in the woman.

Brenda grinned at her. "And the cops are hawt."

Beth wanted to roll her eyes. The woman had children for pity's sake. Hot? The image of the hulking Police Chief flashed to mind. Touché. Her eyes were drawn back to the restaurant next door, just a house, according to Brenda. She was definitely getting weird. Brenda seemed a bit weird in her own right, but that kind of weird was easily cured. Some coaching on polite conversation—along with kinder hair dye—and she might make a fine addition to Sweet Earth.

"Come on inside, Brenda, and we'll talk. I'm Beth White. How old are your girls?"

HONOR MONROE REMEMBERED nothing. It was infuriating.

"How can you not remember? Within minutes of when I left, you were shot point blank in the chest!" Kahtar said.

"I realize that." Honor's cheerful demeanor was not easy to crack. "I'm lucky to be alive." Positioned carefully in a plush bed with pristine white sheets, just hours after being shot his bare chest showed only a very faint scar right in the middle of his breastbone. The prayers of the clan's warriors were strong combined with Welcome Palmer's skills.

Stalking around the good sized bed, Kahtar clutched the remnants of Honor's bloodied shirt. There was a hole in it as large as his hand.

"Fortunately the Old Guard happened on me. What are the odds of that so far from the Arc? It wasn't my day to die."

In frustration Kahtar looked at the doctor leaning patiently against the window seat. Welcome shrugged fit shoulders covered by a black t-shirt, with the slogan *Got Christ? He's kosher* on the front. Kahtar found it disrespectful. Welcome moved to the bed and leaned over to kiss Honor on the forehead. His green eyes slid slightly out of focus briefly as he scanned inside the warrior and then looked up at Kahtar.

"He's going to be just fine, except for a really nasty scar from the exit wound, afraid his back will never look the same again. He should stay here and rest a day."

"He doesn't remember what happened!"

"That's not unusual, he almost bled to death. In time it might come back to him."

"Sorry, Chief." For the first time, Honor Monroe sounded genuinely upset, not because he'd been shot, but because he couldn't answer his Warrior Chief's questions.

Kahtar went to his side and impulsively tried to pat Honor's thick spiky hair down. He was a good kid, with a good heart.

"Sometimes the mind blocks things out." *I wish mine did.* "We'll be wearing armored vests for a while."

Honor smiled, his bright blue eyes lit up at the thought.

Kahtar dropped his hand and warned, "You'll take the day to rest here before you can don yours. Understand?"

"Absolutely, Chief."

In the tradition of the clan Kahtar leaned down and kissed him briefly. Then in an old gesture he'd kept since the beginning, he pressed his thumb against Honor's forehead.

"I love you, Honor. I'm thankful you survived."

"I love you too, Chief, but you never answered, was the car yellow?"

WITHOUT HONOR MONROE'S story of what had happened, the Willowyth police force, which at the moment consisted only of members of the clan, was left to deal with forensics. It was a warrior specialty, no samples or vials or rubber gloves necessary. A group of a dozen warriors dressed in their navy police uniforms stood alongside the rural roadway, scanning and categorizing all available evidence with just their minds. Squire Askins and Consider Drake stood side by side reporting verbally to Kahtar. The two were an odd pair, one pale and thin and the other dark and stocky. They worked in tandem.

"There were two men, both fairly short, around five foot nine or ten inches." Squire Askins squinted as he simultaneously scanned the evidence, apparently reenacting the crime scene in his mind from bloodstains, fiber particles, and DNA embedded in the road and weeds.

Consider Drake shot his partner a dirty look. "Five ten is hardly short."

"When we're talking to almost seven feet of Warrior Chief, I'd say they were practically petite." Squire smirked at all five foot seven inches of his best friend. Squire had exactly one inch on Consider. He turned his attention back to Kahtar. "These guys didn't stick around, Chief, I'd say they got out of their vehicle, weapons drawn and shot Honor without a word of warning."

Running a hand over his cropped hair, Kahtar frowned without really focusing on the men. They'd both demonstrated an uncanny ability with their talents many times, and he knew their hypothesis would be impressively accurate. The fact that it didn't make much sense was irrelevant. The thought of drug trafficking wafted through his mind a split second before Consider Drake shot it down.

"I don't sense any drugs, though I suppose it could have been well wrapped in plastic. Someone threw a cigarette out of their car over by that patch of Queen Anne's lace, but I'd guess that was yesterday. Judging by the tire print in the grass right there, whoever shot Honor was driving an SUV. We should all memorize the pattern in case it shows up again."

Squire Askins piped up. "Chief? Judging by their gait I'd almost say they were related. They walk in a similar fashion."

"Gang members?" Kahtar prompted, scanning the faint markings of dusty footprints in the soft tar of the roadway.

"I don't think so, not gang members. No self-respecting gang member wears superstore cheap shoes like these." Consider Drake sat down on the road with his short beefy legs spread and stared at the places where the footprints were invisible to the naked eye. They still left a ghost of a mark in the mind of a scanning warrior. "Though I see what you mean, Squire. It's almost like they step precisely the same distance with each footfall. Odd."

Kahtar waved a motorcycle around the crowd of police. The driver stared at him so long he drove right off the pavement and had to swerve to right the bike, his sudden acceleration sprayed gravel back into Kahtar's face. He spit a stinging mouthful into the grass, moving towards his car.

"Find me if you discover anything useful. Everyone on police duty is to wear their vests—everyone—I know it is hot and I know they're half plastic—no exceptions. Until we find out what happened to Honor we're not taking any chances."

CHAPTER
THREE

INSTEAD OF TURNING left into his driveway, Kahtar made an abrupt right. The police car bumped up a dirt road, where weeds grew tall on either side of the rutted roadway. At the end of the narrow road it took a moment to turn the vehicle around, and then he punched the gas, scanning in all directions at once, including straight up into the heavens. Trees blocked the bulk of his little game, but it wouldn't do to have any eyes in the sky watch him vanish.

Knowing all was clear, he shot back across the road and just before reaching his driveway he threw the car into neutral and shut it off. A roar of air rocked the police car as though it had been dropped out of an aircraft at terminal velocity. Kahtar shot right through the opening of the veil that hid his house from the rest of the world. Momentum took the car almost a half mile, most of it simply at a slow roll from the gentle downward slope of the drive.

Home sweet home. The complete absence of 21st Century noises was a balm to the soul. No aircraft, no traffic, not even a cell phone signal could possibly penetrate the veil. Weather, however, was another matter. The same oppressive humidity that he'd endured all day in his polyester blend uniform, pressed just as uncomfortably inside his little pocket of paradise. It took less than a minute to yank his uniform off and toss his shoes into the trunk of the car. By the time Kahtar pulled on a simple cotton blouse and leggings, the familiar canter of his dog, followed by his enthusiastic panting, echoed down the drive.

Wolves, the name he gave all his dogs for the sake of simplicity, crashed into him as the warrior walked barefoot to meet him. The dog was a huge eighty-pound behemoth of brown, red and grey shaggy fur with a Border Collie face and mismatched eyes. He looked more like a mixture of coyotes than any wolves. Cradling him like a puppy, Kahtar scratched his belly and the dog gnawed wildly on his upper arm, teeth chattering with excitement. Kahtar scanned the dog, lamenting the fact that canines lived such short lives and grumbled, "Ach, Wolves! You've got fleas again! Get lost!"

The dog raced away as Kahtar approached the log cabin he had built with his own hands. It stood two stories high with a sloping porch wrapping all the way around, a large stone chimney jutted from the middle of the roof. The corners of the cabin were jointed and squared off, not a single nail had gone into the finely crafted home. The green swell of an open field and several old outbuildings were visible behind it, and the smell of fresh cut grass greeted as welcoming as the sprawling front porch.

Dropping into one of the giant Adirondack chairs, Kahtar waited less than thirty seconds for his dinner.

Two dark haired boys banged out the front door. They both had long hair and too pretty faces. Without bothering to look directly at them Kahtar knew they were brothers, and judging by the green eyes they were Palmers by blood. Despite the heat of the day they wore the thick quilted tunics, hose and high boots of a plebe. Both nervous, they were over attentive to the needs of the clan's Warrior Chief, hurrying to bring him drink and food and almost dumping his plate in his lap.

Usually Kahtar gave plebes grief, but he was simply too tired today. He bowed his head over his plate, offering thanksgiving for the food and hoping that it was edible. Twelve and thirteen year old boys weren't famous for their cooking skills. While he shoveled mushy vegetables, rice, and chicken into his mouth, the two plebes waited anxiously in the doorway. Wolves galloped up the porch steps and sniffed his bowl of food suspiciously, glanced towards his master looking for mercy and then sucked the food down in three loud swallows. Deciding that Wolves had the best approach, Kahtar followed suit and then told the boys to return to the Arc.

Closing his eyes, Kahtar listened to their footsteps as they raced across the yard and did as he bid, their exit both silent and instant. Then, only the sound of Wolves running in circles in the field out back, chasing imaginary rabbits, remained. He muttered another prayer of thanksgiving for the solitude of his veil. The hustle of twelve thousand living in the confines of an Arc had long ago appealed, but for a long time now he had preferred not to get too attached to his clans. Soon enough he'd have to get used to a new one anyway.

TRYING TO SLEEP that night in the oppressive heat wasn't working. Scenes from what may have led to Honor's being shot kept flashing through his mind, like the distant lightning flickering outside the veil. When thunder began to rumble within the veil, Wolves started scratching at the front door and whining. Kahtar turned on his side and held a pillow over his exposed ear. His bedclothes were fresh and their clean smell made him remember that morning, before Honor had wiped every other thought out of his mind. It seemed so long ago now, but the memory came back clearly.

The woman, Beth White, danced into his head just as rain began to fall inside the veil. Refusing to allow forbidden thoughts to take any form, he closed his eyes and breathed the clean scent of rain, wondering if the woman had any idea what rain was supposed to smell like. For some inexplicable reason, he really hoped she did. Sleep came easy then.

Longinus's sandals soaked with the blood of his kinsmen and mixed with the dust of the road. It made a gruesome mud that caked and dried and made the sandals as heavy as his heart. Disguised with the weapon, helmet, and cloak of a Roman Centurion, he plodded a path over a hill where few dared trespass. The red cloak was far too short and the metal helmet squeezed his head, biting against his exposed ears. Small groups of people, mostly women, huddled at the bases of ruined trees sobbing and wailing in grief. Consumed with their own misery they paid no attention to him.

So close to the walls of the city the pain and suffering of these wretches provided him safe passage. The remnants of the Centuria searching for him were unlikely to come here. It was a place even hardened soldiers avoided. Two similarly dressed real Romans stood arguing nearby, debating ways to torment one of their victims and not paying any attention to him. Longinus heaved woodenly onward. If the Romans noticed his unusual size or ill-fitting clothing, they showed no sign of it. He held the stolen spear reassuringly in his hand and kept to the path. There were only two of them and he would kill them only if forced.

The call of Longinus's people sounded faintly in his mind, wordless voices beckoning, whispering for his return to the safety of the Arc. It was time to leave this dark place and he wanted only to make his way down the hillside to them. Heart aching, Longinus moved past the cruel despair of wailing strangers, their pain pressing against him like the dark clouds gathering overhead. The Romans ignored him until he was close enough to touch them. Then one of the soldiers turned towards him and ordered, "You! Halt!" Longinus' hand slid down the shaft of the spear and he turned to face them, but both soldiers returned their eyes to their victim.

"Just check for a pulse," the darker of them said, a Tribune.

"I'm not touching him," the other replied. With barely a glance at Longinus, the Tribune motioned to the bloodied mess of a man bound in the tree and ordered, "Check him for signs of life."

"Do you need us?" The second voice of one of his warriors spoke into Longinus' mind. He replied silently with a firm negative. To prove it and hasten his escape, he stepped forward. Longinus didn't raise his eyes to the body hanging in the twisted old olive tree. He had seen enough inhumanity today. Sensing an odd mixture of both death and life in the ravaged flesh above, he hefted the spear higher. It would be a kind-

ness to dispatch the man. Surely his people would not object. Mercy was not killing. Plunging the stolen spear brutally upward, through flesh and muscle, forcing a path past bone he pierced beneath the ribcage of the soul hanging there.

Unwilling to lift his eyes to the sight of this victim of scourging and torture, it wasn't until blood and water ran thick and hot down his arm, splashing into his mouth, that he glanced up. And then the realization of what he had just done burned into his very being with blazing clarity. Longinus began to scream.

Where am I? Am I blind? Dark sat on him. How did I get here? Longinus wanted to touch his eyes to be certain they were still there, but his body was shaking so violently he couldn't feel his limbs. A cloak wrapped around his neck so tightly he could barely breathe. And blood…he felt it trickling down his face, over his lips, warm and salty. It was not his. Awareness of what he had done seared through him. His dishonor scorched lava hot in his veins, and the memory burned into the core of his being. There could be no atonement. Anguish formed a scream in his throat, but all that came out was a strangled sob. The pain in his heart should have turned every atom of his being to ash. He welcomed the pain. It was all the penance he could offer.

Clarity came to Longinus in drops. It was night. He was not blind. The blood was actually sweat and it was all his. There was no cloak, only bedclothes twisted around his neck. Without the use of his arms or legs, he managed to turn, escaping the choke hold of damp sheets around his throat. He could breathe. Awareness of his limbs arrived slowly and he cautiously moved them in the strange bed. Memory synapse gelled. I am not on the hillside. I have not been called Longinus for millennia. Where am I now? Who am I this time? He sat up. Kahtar, I am called Kahtar this time.

MOONLIGHT FLOODED HER bedroom on Pearl Street and Beth sat straight up, wide awake. After a moment she slid to the edge of the bed and felt around the floor with her toes until she located her slippers. Debating exactly what had roused her, besides hunger—which wasn't unusual. It felt as though she'd been laughing really hard and she tried to remember what she'd been dreaming. It was vague, but it had involved friends that she didn't have, and food, really good food that, in this little village, was as elusive as friends. Thudding across the hardwood floor in fuzzy, heeled slippers, she shoved the lid off a cooler and stared at the sad contents.

The ice had melted and a container of strawberries floated in the water, she snagged it and crossed to the window. The late night rain had left stifling humidity in its wake and not even a breeze stirred the hot air. Kicking a long leg out the window she maneuvered onto the fire escape and tiptoed around the south side of the house to peek at the small house next door. She caught a whiff of something wonderful. It had to be a restaurant. As a matter of fact, she was fairly certain it had starred in her dream about food.

In the moonlight she could tell that the restaurant's hedges had been trimmed, and wondered when that had happened. Her own grass had become a sea of yellow dandelion, though she liked the overgrown look of her flowering bushes. Clusters of snowball flowers glowed creamy in the pale light, ghosting bright against dark leaves. Dropping soggy strawberries into her mouth, Beth breathed the scent of lilacs and joy settled through her so intense that her eyes watered.

"Thank you," she whispered into the night, wondering again why she was so happy in this place. Why she had spent an insane amount of money to buy this behemoth of a house sight unseen in the middle of Nowhere, Ohio? Where winters had to be miserable and even springtime was stormy and hot, and good food existed only in her dreams! Leaning against the newly painted wall, Beth slid down until she was sitting on the metal fire escape, propping her feet on the iron railing. The feeling of following her heart instead of her head taunted her. She'd fallen in love with both a house and the idea of running a business in a place that Brenda had dubbed a "ghost town". Closing her eyes against the moonlight, enveloped in the scent of lilacs, Beth willingly allowed her dreams to pull her back to laughter and good food, away from common sense and logic.

The dull metallic thud of a slamming dumpster lid woke her up. Beth scrambled to her feet, tugging her big t-shirt to make sure she was decent. An older man stood in the alley behind the furniture store, and though she waved at him, he didn't notice her. Peeking over at the restaurant, that supposedly wasn't, she found it blank and empty as always, however, a new row of daffodils now ringed the red tulips rioting around the house. Really? Who planted flowers before dawn? She'd been hoping to spot the landscapers, her grass needed cut and she wanted to hire someone. In the middle of crawling back inside the window, Beth noticed her own grass and stopped, one foot inside and the other out. Then she hurtled through the window and dashed through the labyrinthine rooms of the huge old home.

Slamming out the front door Beth looked around in disbelief. Her grass had been cut, not a single dandelion remained, and hundreds upon hundreds of purple crocuses now grew thick all along the front of the house. Those flowers had absolutely not been there yesterday. Squatting beside them, Beth tugged on a plant and it lifted easily from the earth. It had definitely been freshly planted. Standing abruptly she jogged through the damp grass in her slippers, racing to the house next door. Determined to get answers she stormed right up to the front door and started pounding on it. Not a sound came from inside, not even the echo of her own banging. Beth stood, still hammering away, when Brenda teetered up the sidewalk in her sparkly pumps.

"SEEMS TO ME you'd be glad they did your yard work for free."

"Maybe I should," Beth griped, "but I'm not. They trimmed the flowers off the bushes, and why would they do yard work at night anyway, and why would they ignore me when I knock on their door? I know they were in there."

"I don't get you. They're probably at work or afraid to open the door the way you were banging." Brenda opened a bottle of lotion. "Wow, this is nice. Where on earth do you get all this stuff? More important, who do you think is going to buy any of it?"

"The restaurant next door would be interested in a lot of things I have, if they would stop ignoring me. It's rude."

Brenda plunked the bottle back on the shelf. "Oh my gosh, would you stop? You should open this shop downtown or in Beechwood, it's too upscale for Willowyth anyway." Meandering towards shelves stacked with tiny paper boxes, she started to open and sniff the contents.

"It will all work out." Beth said with confidence. She felt that truth deep in her heart even while she had absolutely no idea how on heaven or earth that was ever going to happen.

Brenda turned to grin at her, her hair looked terrific thanks to the box she'd taken home the day before. "Kind of like, 'If you build it, they will come'? Good luck with that." She dropped the box she'd been examining. "Oh gross! What is this stuff?" Turning from the shelves, she covered her mouth with a hand, gagging.

Laughing, Beth hopped up and rescued the discarded box, folding the wax lining closed and putting it back on the shelf. "I know, and if I told you about this tea you'd think I was nuts."

"I already think that," Brenda mumbled through her hand.

The comment hurt slightly, especially since Beth knew Brenda wasn't kidding.

"Nobody would put that near their mouth, Beth. I work in a coffee shop so you can trust me on that."

Squaring her shoulders, Beth insisted, "It's one of those things only guys can appreciate. Like hunting or NASCAR."

"I love NASCAR," Brenda stated firmly, but Beth looked into those pretty brown eyes and knew it wasn't true.

Brenda looked away, focusing on unpacking a crate of honey and stacking it neatly on a shelf. They were quiet for a few moments. Beth walked around the big room and tried to force the windows open a bit wider, inviting air and daylight in and biting her tongue over Brenda's tiny white lie. She couldn't help but wonder why people lied so casually and without cause.

Behind her, Brenda snapped out angrily. "My ex loved NASCAR and I still watch it!"

Beth turned to face her. "What's wrong, Brenda?"

The woman rubbed her forearm and for the first time Beth noticed she had a man's name tattooed on it, a small homemade tattoo, done in ink as though she'd been branded.

"He's back in the area, my ex, shacked up with some nineteen year old right outside town."

"Tell the police, you said yourself they're vigilant. They'll care if there's someone in town who might cause trouble."

Brenda straightened her shoulders and flipped her hair back. "Right. If I sent the cops after him—ha! You wouldn't understand. Heck, I wish I didn't. Just stay out of it because you have no idea what you're talking about. People like you have it so easy! Wish I'd had a rich, cushy life like yours—no worries, cool cars…."

"You know nothing about my life."

"I know that your big problem today is that someone landscaped your yard without your permission."

THE DEPARTMENT OF Public Safety didn't look much different than the Department of Motor Vehicles, except there wasn't the long line of people with varying degrees of frustration and despair written on their faces. This room was empty but for the woman behind the counter. She sat in a cubicle decorated with hundreds of blank forms taped all over the walls, and Beth stood in front of the counter, trying her very best to feign respect in a land where paperwork reigned.

"I brought you a jar of honey from my shop, thought you might like to sample something from the place that you're—assisting—in getting all the paperwork straight for." She could hardly say that the woman had helped, in fact the bored, non-descript woman with the hostile expression had been anything but helpful.

"I'm diabetic." The woman stared Beth down as though she would accept nothing short of a cure from her.

"You're not diabetic." The statement slipped out, as they so often did. A drop of truth in your face, take that, liar. *Why would anyone lie about such a thing?*

"Excuse me?" Eyes narrowed and Beth knew she was in trouble. That didn't matter though, because here it came. Why had she expected anything to be different in Willowyth? How could anyplace be different once she got there?

"You're not diabetic. Why would you even say that? It's not a pleasant thing to have! All you have to say is you don't want it, you don't have to lie!"

"Are you calling me a liar?"

Uh oh, Beth bit her lip, but the woman had asked. "Yes, I am, only because you're lying though!" *Smooth and I'm sure that permit application will be tossed before you walk out the door.*

"Excuse me, Miss? Is everything okay in here?" A ginger haired man in a spectacular suit touched her arm politely, pale blue eyes glancing towards the woman behind the counter. "Big wheels move slow, eh, Marge?"

"I just work here, you know! I don't make the laws!" The woman behind the counter glared at both of them, Beth felt a stab of regret when she saw the woman's chin quiver. Why couldn't she learn to control her big fat mouth? Why did she have to provoke the woman even if she was a liar?

"I'm sorry!" Beth apologized, pity stabbing her heart. She had hurt the woman.

"You should be!" The woman lashed out. "You don't come around here calling me a liar! Who do you think you are? I don't take bribes and I do so have diabetes. You're not a doctor!"

Beth was thankful when the gentleman in the suit tugged her out the door of the office, and closed it firmly. It didn't stop the words from whipping out of her mouth though, and she shouted them, angrily. "It doesn't take a doctor to spot a liar!"

"Whoa, been at it with Marge for awhile? Trying to get a permit around here can be frustrating for even the most patient of us." The man's disapproving expression made it clear he did not see Beth as the most patient.

Covering her mouth with a hand, she took a deep breath. *Let it go, just let it go!*

"I'm sorry, that was rude. I'm Beth White." She peered down at the man, inescapable given her height and heels. Professional and smooth, he wore his hair wavy, and an elegant silk tie peeked from beneath his jacket, in a shade of green that only redheads could get away with.

"Sherman Kelts." Shaking her hand, he smiled a perfected smile. "You're new in town."

"Yes. I'm opening a shop off of Main Street."

Pale eyebrows lifted in surprise. "Really? What kind of a shop?"

Beth displayed the jar of honey still clutched in her hands. "It will be like an old fashioned general store with only natural products."

"I see." By his tone, Beth decided that Sherman Kelts did not see. "And you don't even have electricity yet?"

She looked at him in surprise, wondering how he knew that, and he grinned, displaying very white caps.

"I'm a lawyer, Miss White. I can recognize every permit application the state has from across a room. I can help you get that permit. By law they can't deny you a basic permit like that. As a matter of fact, you can go right ahead and get started on the work. There isn't much they can do about it."

CHAPTER
FOUR

THE WEIGHT OF his mesh tunic hung familiar and soothing against his torso. Chainmail was new since Golgotha. New was good. It helped Kahtar focus on now. Passing through the edges of the misty veil, an unnatural cold wind kicked up. It felt good after the humidity of the day. Air rocketed over him at the entrance to the Arc, and the flesh of his face pressed into his skull, moving back towards his ears as he forced his way forward. It felt as though the wind and clean air passed through every molecule of his being before the Arc opened and allowed his entrance. Only members of his clan, Cultuelle Khristos, could enter their Arc. Even Covenant Keepers from other clans could not penetrate. Such was the nature of an Arc.

Inside, paths forked in several directions. Kahtar took the well-worn one leading to the cave. The sky spread cerulean blue, and there was no hint of humidity, fields of tiny purple and white wildflowers yawned and bent in the gentle breeze. Only the hum of insects and his footsteps followed. Trees far taller and thicker than any left in the Northeast spread blossoming branches towards the sun. If his veil was clean, the Arc was pristine, a bit of heaven on earth. The hearts of his clan thrived within the Arc and the faint touch of them seemed to hover on the air. It soothed, and if he were any other man Kahtar would never want to leave.

Kahtar turned slightly sideways at the narrow cave entrance. The chinking sound of his chain tunic jingled as he maneuvered broad shoulders effortlessly through twists and turns, descending through the passageway into the depths of the main cavern. The familiar earthy clean smells of guano and burning oil filled his nostrils.

The Mother and Elders of Cultuelle Khristos waited for him in a side chamber, lit with the shimmering light of Old Guard and the faint flicker of candles. The Elders sat on a long, curving wooden bench perched upon a stone plinth. A chubby little Elder, Abigail Adit, sat on the very end, her sausage-like legs encased in stockings, and her orthopedic shoes barely touching the ground. Her sharp eyes took him in with a faint hint of impatience. The Mother, leader of Cultuelle Khristos, rose graceful as a dancer to glide to his side and demand the traditional kiss.

It was time to discuss clan security and Kahtar had absolutely nothing to tell them about how Honor Monroe had been shot, and on top of that he was late. Sometimes being Warrior Chief didn't feel so much different than being Police Chief. Kahtar pulled away from The Mother's kiss a bit sooner than was polite.

"Everyone who isn't warrior should retreat to the Arc."

At his announcement a wall of protests echoed through the cavern, Abigail's loudest of all, drowning out everyone else's words.

"Warrior Chief? If you had your way, none of us would ever step foot outside the Arc. You are blind to the purpose of Cultuelle Khristos."

"Abigail." The Mother reprimanded gently. "He is doing his job."

"That is the only occupation worthy of significance in his mind! Time will teach you, Warrior of ilu, not all battles are won at the point of a spear."

Kahtar bristled, time had taught him much. Yet it was her unknowing use of the word spear that cut. He hadn't touched one in over two thousand years. The Mother sensed his agitation and her heart reached to brush lovingly against his, soothing, calm and cool as the pools of water dotting the cave.

"Abigail and many of Cultuelle Khristos are willing to take their risks in the outside world. It is their choice," she said.

Abigail grumbled, poking a dimpled elbow into the Priest at her side.

"As though we could shut down Cobbson Compound and retreat to the Arc like it was the flood!"

Father Wixen nodded in indignant agreement, though Kahtar knew for a fact that the old Priest had never stepped a foot outside the Arc and into the world of Seekers in his entire life.

"There is no sign of who shot Honor. He still remembers nothing and even with the evidence Consider and Squire have accumulated, we have found no trace of the assailants. It could happen again," Kahtar warned.

Despite his chain mail and a sword dangling from each hip, The Mother slipped an arm around his waist, and hugged. Kahtar remained in position, legs firmly planted, arms slightly bent and hands open, Warrior of ilu. Yet he felt the touch of her heart, felt the touch of every heart in that chamber, even Abigail's. Though he held himself apart from his clans, he loved them all.

ANOTHER LATE NIGHT storm had Wolves scratching at the front door of the cabin. Kahtar ignored him. Sitting on the steps to the main room he again tried to shake off the memory of when he had been called Longinus. For the third time this week the old shade had descended, hotter and more painful than death by fire. Kahtar's hands were still shaking, thighs weak. He took deep, calming breaths, trying to distract himself by scanning through the dark.

Every Covenant Keeper endured shades. They all experienced the random dark memories from the lives of those who had gone on before them. When a Covenant Keeper died they left their pain behind, and that pain took the form of shades. Yet this shade came from his own past, this shade followed him through time, Kahtar's own personal purgatory. Unlike most shades, it wasn't someone else's pain. He'd earned this.

Sitting on the stairs he'd fashioned with his own hands and sensing the hundreds of weapons lining the walls around him helped. He'd been injured or died at the wrong end of each and every weapon that covered those walls. Instead of those painful deaths stirring gruesome memories, somehow sitting there surrounded by his own painful mortality helped dissipate the hold of what he had done. Surely, somewhere in all that pain came some measure of penance, however miniscule.

A familiar light shimmered in the room downstairs, glinting off the hundreds of weapons hanging from floor to ceiling, illuminating wicked looking bits of metal in the glow. In a flash of soundless lightning, a man appeared solidly at the bottom of the stairs. Wolves yelped outside the door and scampered away. An Old Guard, glowing from his inner light, stood in the front room, shimmering and looking like what surely had been ilu's prototype for man. Like all Old Guard, his ancient eyes were completely black. Kahtar hurried down the steps to face the man. The Old Guard's face was wrinkled with age, his hair peppered with grey, but he stood as solid as a granite mountain and as impenetrable.

The Old Guard stood unnaturally still, not even moving his mouth when he spoke. His second voice flooded the Warrior Chief's mind with what Kahtar always thought of as white hot ice.

"Come."

Within minutes Kahtar was dressed in a fresh uniform and at the side of the Old Guard. Together they flickered away, an act Kahtar had engaged in so many times over millennia that the transportation gifting had almost become his own. Fast as light he blinked out and became nothing, and then he was back, standing in an unfamiliar doorway. The smell of must and vomit mixed with the oil and tar of the nearby railroad tracks. The narrow old house perched on a crumbling cliff over a trickle called the Chagrin River. The entire row of worn out houses was asleep, the only sound a far off train. A fellow clansman, Allis Drake, was kneeling in the tiny kitchen next to an unconscious woman. He looked up at Kahtar, one hand continually stroking her blood soaked hair, as though to offer comfort in lieu of the healing he was forbidden to give.

"If I'm not permitted to heal her, she will die," he said quietly, distress and anger etched into his kind face.

Kahtar scanned within the young woman, she'd been beaten almost to death, but she might survive if they were quick enough. He turned his scan outward.

"There is an ambulance four minutes away, she could make it." Her cell phone wasn't far from where she'd fallen. He retrieved it and dialed 911. As soon as it was answered he sat it on the floor beside her. It was all he could do.

The only light in the room was from an open refrigerator and the flickering brilliance from the Old Guard. A quick scan of the premises revealed that no weapons had been used, other than the culprit's own two hands. That husband or boyfriend was sprawled over a torn and stained recliner, drugged, drunk and incoherent. Vomit splattered down his out of shape torso, tattoos covered a good deal of his flesh. Kahtar wasn't amused by the stupid marks. The symbols were a mixture of Japanese and Chinese—none of which were spelled correctly. The woman's dried blood covered bruised knuckles. A collection of women's names, scrawled in homemade tattoos, lined his wrist. All but one had a vulgarity tattooed over her name. If the list was accurate, the woman by the front door would be Denise. Kahtar wanted to kill him.

The perusal had taken only seconds. He moved towards the man. Despite Kahtar's size and the paper-thin construction of the house, his footsteps were silent. Glancing to the Old Guard for approval, he reached for the man.

The Old Guard turned his head slightly to the right, request denied. Old Guard rarely permitted the killing of a non-Covenant Keeper, a Seeker, and apparently this man's life had purpose. Kahtar hid his scowl. *What purpose this? Beating a woman to death?* But he had to obey. He waited, knowing the Old Guard had summoned him for a reason. The solid black eyes shone strangely in the glow from the refrigerator. The

Old Guard was so big that the tip of his sword, barely jutting past his back, touched one counter and a studded leather strip of his skirting rested against the other. His ice hot second voice was brief.

"He need only be alive and aware."

There was no satisfaction in destroying a man's body, but neither did it bother Kahtar. It was his duty to obey Old Guard, and he did so without conscience, making certain the abuser would spend the rest of his life needing the help of a woman for even the simplest task. He scanned within the man, whispering his healing chant and using the healing skill he'd been gifted with to ruin instead of repair, methodically injuring nerves in the man's back and neck.

Expert medical care might recognize something peculiar, but likely he wouldn't receive that. Likely he'd be given debilitating drugs for a muscular disease he didn't have. It took less than thirty seconds to satisfy the Old Guard.

On his way out the door Kahtar knelt beside the woman, knowing Allis Drake's frustration at being forbidden from healing her with his gifting. Putting a large hand on her bloody skull he longed to fix it, the swelling in her brain could be reduced in seconds, but she was a Seeker and he was a Covenant Keeper and he was following the way and his feelings did not matter. Quickly he leaned forward and kissed her forehead, rising swiftly he went towards the Old Guard.

Allis went outside to his squad car, to wait for the 911 call to be traced. Kahtar regretfully flickered away at the side of the Old Guard, praying for the woman to survive, wondering when he'd started feeling that obeying the way could ever be wrong. It was strange, in all his time he never remembered feeling it before.

CHAPTER
FIVE

FLAGS FLEW ALONG Main Street after the Memorial Day parade, and groups of people headed home. Kahtar drove slowly around a corner and parked his vehicle in the spot reserved for the Police Chief. A group of his warriors, dressed in the pressed cotton slacks and polyester blend shirt of the police force, stood outside the station conversing with Seekers.

Kahtar opened the car door. A woman's shrill laughter punctuated masculine voices. Unfolding his body from the squad car he noted the lone woman standing in the group chatting and laughing, her high-pitched shriek familiar. Kahtar ran a hand over his short hair.

A couple warriors glanced towards him and it took only one meaningful glare before all the men dispersed to their duties, including the Seekers. Only the waitress Kahtar recognized from the corner coffee shop remained, smoking a cigarette. She waved to him, laughing out her shrill greeting and Kahtar waved back. Avoiding eye contact he walked towards her. The woman had begun to take up post outside the station during her coffee breaks, flirting with the warriors. She exhaled a cloud of smoke from the side of her mouth.

"Morning, Chief. Cliff's baking some of those strawberry pies you like."

"Is he?" Kahtar stepped a bit too close, and she took a small step back. Her name was Brenda. Her husband had left her to raise two little girls on her own. As she lifted her cigarette to her lips, he noticed the homemade tattoo on her wrist for the first time, 'Stan' in indigo blue. Eyes sweeping over Brenda, Kahtar instantly took in chipped teeth, a telltale scar on her upper lip, the pert nose that had healed almost imperceptibly crooked, and the way she held her cigarette in her left hand because the right arm bent at an odd angle. The woman was lucky to be alive. Brenda had her troubles. Kahtar knew she could barely afford the flat she rented over someone's garage on Second Street. Still, she risked his warriors' lives by attempting to ingratiate herself with them. Seekers and Covenant Keepers did not belong together, and his duty was to ensure that never happened.

Kahtar edged closer, invading her personal space, and Brenda looked up at him, soft brown eyes widening in surprise. He'd always been distant but very polite to her. Meeting her eyes, her frightened gasp was audible. He was being mean, but forcing her out of the little town would be cruel. At her income level, she'd have to move to the city, and life would be rough there for her girls. He glared down at her, keeping a fake smile pasted on his face.

"I like pie." The simple comment was filled with as much innuendo as Kahtar could manage, the remark made his own skin crawl. Brenda muttered something incoherent, dropped her cigarette then dashed back around the corner. He'd grossed himself out, but found consolation in the fact that Brenda never had to worry about being beaten again. Stan's days of hurting women were over.

LATELY THE WILLOWYTH police force consisted entirely of Warriors of ilu. Despite that, they ran the station like any police station in the state. Red tape and bureaucracy reigned. Warriors weren't designed for the pencil pushing tasks necessary to run the police force, but there was no choice.

Conformity had become necessary in order to blend. Internal Affairs always hovered and occasionally a Seeker rookie would be placed with them, so the warriors kept their guard up, playing their parts well while in the station house. Today's conversation consisted of typical police business. Boxes of fresh doughnuts stacked the front counter, four coffee pots filled with fresh brew sat on a table in the tiny waiting room. Notices with updated regulations were stuck to the wall. Kahtar filled a cup with java and piled doughnuts on a plate. He had no intention of eating or drinking either. The food wasn't clean, but they'd all had to force a bite of doughnut now and then or sip the coffee, for the most part the coffee went down the drinking fountain drain and the doughnuts got flushed.

Kahtar pushed the door of his office open with a foot. *Kent Costas, Police Chief* stenciled in gold and black lettering glistened on the frosted glass. Normally he detested his office at the station, though on any given week he put several hours of face time in. Today he was anxious to use the rickety computer to check on the status of last night's victim. Plopping the plate and mug on the edge of his cluttered desk, he dropped into his chair.

Kahtar found all he could on Denise, serious but stable condition.

Thank you, ilu.

Then he glanced at the little clock on the monitor, ten minutes had passed, and he sighed. The monotony of the station seemed to invite the unpleasantness of shades to descend. All the men complained about it. Determined to avoid them, and keep his mind occupied, for some twisted reason Kahtar got on Wikipedia and searched 'Longinus'. For two thousand years the shade had followed him. He knew a legend had sprung up from that day, knew that somehow those there had learned his true name that day, but over the ensuing centuries he'd ignored it. Yet today, on a whim, alone with a computer and no witnesses, he impulsively reached into the past.

He found it. Some of the stories were expectedly convoluted. Still the details of that day survived surprisingly accurate, especially considering the amount of time that had passed. Leaning close to the machine he started to fish around in cyberspace, wondering if there were paintings of Longinus that might even be similar. He felt certain those at the foot of the tree had gotten an eyeful of him that day, and despite his odd repeating existence, he always looked exactly the same. Gazing down at his big hands on the keyboard he flexed them, had anyone ever been as familiar with a pair of hands as he was? A memory stirred and Kahtar no longer saw the keyboard.

A boy's hand, pink and small engulfed in the black hand of his warrior father.

"Baba, why is my hand the wrong color?" the little boy's voice quavered. His father, wearing the vivid colors of clan leader, knelt in the dust, looking into his eyes. Strong, ebony fingers combed through his son's long hair, it slid through his fingers the color and texture of dry savannah grass.

"ilu has his reasons."

The memory came sharp. It had been seconds later when he'd remembered. His past had dropped like it always did, the realization of his endless history roaring through him, like a tornado, a hurricane in his head. When he stopped screaming, when he opened his eyes to gaze into the dark, worried faces of his clan, he knew why his hand was the wrong color. I am, again.

The door to his office banged open so hard that the glass rattled, pulling Kahtar rudely from memories of an Arc in the Serengeti. Honor Monroe stood grinning in the doorway of the police station in Willowyth, the picture of health.

"Chief."

Obviously there'd been trouble in town, nothing tickled Honor like action and apparently being shot hadn't changed that, he already had his bulletproof vest in his hand.

So young.

"911 over on Pearl Street," said Honor.

"Where? The only life on Pearl Street is Cerulean Blue. Who'd call 911? They don't even have a phone." Despite his argument, Kahtar got to his feet and moved.

Honor Monroe ran in front of him, shouting, "It came from a cell. Consider heard the recording, said some guy is threatening someone's life."

THREE SQUAD CARS seemed overkill. The men doubled up piling into vehicles, and jockeying for the opportunity to drive. One barked command in Kahtar's second voice and they fell into order like the well trained Warriors of ilu they were.

"Stop smiling." Kahtar hurtled through town in his vehicle, scanning the short distance to Pearl Street while griping at Honor Monroe. Sitting in the passenger seat, with his spiked hair sticking up in all directions Honor wiped the smile off his face, but even his frown looked thrilled. Scanning ahead, Kahtar couldn't sense anything unusual from Cerulean Blue. Hidden inside an abstract, the public had no access to the eatery. Unfortunately even millennia of experience hadn't given Kahtar the skills to scan inside the thick cloaking of an abstract, so he couldn't be certain nothing had happened.

Honor's right hand opened and clenched over his hip, as though worrying the hilt of a sword that wasn't there.

Kahtar snapped at him. "And kill the siren, what's the point in announcing we're coming? There are three plebes sitting inside Cerulean Blue, eating their lunches outside the abstract, they'll probably run outside in broad daylight if they hear us."

"You can scan that from this far?"

"There's a reason I'm the Warrior Chief, Monroe. Wear a vest anyway."

Honor's reply was muffled as he hurried to don the vest in the confines of the squad car, but Kahtar was fairly sure he'd muttered the word 'cool'.

They pulled onto Pearl Street and Kahtar realized there were people in the old Victorian, next to Cerulean Blue. He noted the line of vehicles parked along the usually quiet street the same time his warriors did. Communicating only in second voice the warriors raced across the yard, mounted the steps silently and then stood outside the door with weapons drawn. Kahtar had no idea who or why people were inside the old abandoned house. Though the half dozen people inside seemed to have no weapons, this anomaly so close to Honor's shooting struck Kahtar as far too curiously coincidental. Kahtar did not believe in coincidence.

Almost expecting to find assassins, they attacked. Kahtar kicked and the antique door came off the hinges. It slammed against an interior wall and glass crumpled with a faint tinkling sound and his men poured in, weapons drawn.

The room filled with shouts of protest and a handful of men ran back and forth in confusion, but in times like this Kahtar shone. In the midst of chaos he could access a situation in a glance, it was his particular gifting—gestalt. What he saw made him point his weapon in the air and shout to his men in second voice.

"Draw up." As one they obeyed. The tumult in the room continued for several moments while workmen with tool belts, and one lone businessman, in a suit, ducked for cover. Within seconds they were under tables or behind a counter. Kahtar's warriors remained standing, and one lone woman. Beth White stood staring at them in disbelief.

The Orphan of the Inquisition he had threatened to arrest, if he ever saw her again. He certainly had not expected to ever see her again. Yet here she stood, right in the middle of his territory, staring in wide eyed wonder at the half dozen police holding guns in the air. The statuesque woman wore heels that put her eye to eye with the bulk of his warriors and she fearlessly made only one comment.

"What on earth?"

Kahtar suddenly felt excessively foolish, obviously something had gone very wrong, but Beth White had not shot Honor, and nobody's life was in danger. Several large blueprints were scattered over a countertop and Beth held only a charcoal pencil in her hand. She looked amused when she met his eyes and without meaning to he stepped towards her, her too friendly heart already flip-flopping against his. He refused to know how appealing it was.

"Somebody called 911."

Beth's brows arched as though considering that, but she didn't argue, taking Kahtar at his word. She stooped neatly to look under the mismatched tables, addressing the cowering men with calm politeness.

"Does somebody have their cell in their pocket maybe?"

The workmen crawled out as one, and several hurried to check their phones until the culprit popped up from behind the long walnut counter and shamefacedly admitted.

"I was sitting on it—but I didn't ask for the police!"

Consider Drake piped up. "I heard the call, there was shouting and somebody said 'They were going to slaughter them …' and then it cut off."

Men Kahtar recognized as local electricians and plumbers, started to laugh. Beth grinned at the abashed culprit, the only man wearing a suit.

"Sherman made a booty call," she teased.

The soft faced, grey suited man swore, placing the phone in the inside pocket of his suit.

"Lawyers have their own vocabulary, and I meant I was going to slaughter the town in court if they didn't approve Beth for wiring—legally they have to." Looking around at the police, his pale eyes narrowed in suspicion. On a silent signal from Kahtar his men all immediately holstered their weapons, and two of them started to help a carpenter trying to put the door back on its hinges.

Sherman continued to eye them grimly, addressing Beth and feigning calm. The Lawyer lifted a piece of paper off the counter and fingered it. Kahtar noted the city's seal on the letter and also the sheen of sweat on the man's forehead. Sherman's continually darting eyes and rambling betrayed his nervousness.

"This town is notorious for over-reacting. If they thought this house was really uninhabitable they wouldn't have issued a Certificate of Occupancy. If they didn't want an occupant they shouldn't have let it go for back taxes, either, though I'd hardly call half a million back taxes! This letter is sheer bull!" Dramatically Sherman waved the paper before plunking it back on the counter. "Beth, you promised whoever gave you the best news got lunch, and I'd say that's me."

Beth, statuesque and polished, grinned at the man. Before she could reply, Kahtar interrupted with a growl.

"I'm afraid Miss White won't be able to keep her promise. She's under arrest."

CHAPTER
SIX

THE LOCAL LABORERS, who'd spent the morning trying to overcharge her and exaggerating the already substantial work the house needed, were suddenly on Beth's side. The Police Chief himself slapped handcuffs over her wrists and led her across the room by her elbow, but now she had five new supporters who followed, shouting angry protests at him. Despite the cop marching at her side, Beth's eyes kept returning to the door the brute had kicked down. The relief she felt over that intact door made no sense and she wondered why virtual strangers were more upset about her arrest than she herself.

When her new protectors quieted in unison, Beth looked around curiously, trying to see what had caused their silence. One look at the grim faced Police Chief and she had a good clue. The two carpenters became preoccupied with examining the doorframe again, and even the electrician began helping them. Chickens the whole lot of them, afraid to even look at the Police Chief—like he was a Gorgon for heaven's sake. The plumbers had gone back to the counter to roll up blueprints and Beth looked towards them.

"Excuse me? Please start on the wiring and get gas to the water heater? I'm not paying any of your quotes though. How about you give me the same rate you give Cliff? I know it's under the going rate…"

The Police Chief gently nudged her towards the door and she tossed back.

"But since you practically tried to rob me I'd say it's fair!"

Only Sherman stuck with her, dogging the big cop's steps and holding in his paunch as they moved through the door and down the porch steps.

"Excuse me, Chief? I'm Sherman Kelts. Surely this is overkill? Is this about her parking tickets? It's hardly a criminal offense to ignore those, everybody does. I haven't paid one myself in ten years."

Easily darting past the man, the Police Chief expertly moved Beth along in front of him, one hand firmly on the small of her back. He didn't reply. Sherman Kelts raced behind him fussing until the cop opened the back door of his patrol car and put a giant hand on the top of her head, shoving her just slightly less politely into the back seat. He tucked himself into the front and shut his door firmly right in Sherman's pink face.

Beth piped up from the back of the squad car.

"That was rude. Did you know he's a lawyer?"

The Chief's good-looking partner caught Beth's attention. His dark eyebrows shot up in mock surprise and he commented with a friendly grin, "Uh, oh." The man swiveled completely in his seat and gave her such a welcoming smile that for a moment Beth forgot she was being arrested and felt like they were old friends. That would be if she had any old friends. Smiling blue eyes glanced towards her arms, which were uncomfortably wedged between her and the seat.

The cop apologized. "I'm really sorry about the handcuffs. Twist around and I'll take them off. Are you Clan Huron?"

Before Beth could even open her mouth the dark haired cop spun around, facing forward, looking straight out the window. The Chief glared in his direction. Something about his expression suggested a shouted reprimand though not a word had come out of his mouth. Beth could see from the side view mirror that all traces of the nice cop's smile had vanished. Odder still, the cop then immediately slumped against his seat and closed his eyes. It was the worst acting she had ever seen, like a kid trying to get out of school and pretending to be sick. What the heck was that about?

The Chief was watching her in the rearview mirror and he offered up his first words since he'd slapped the handcuffs on her.

"He has a problem with his blood sugar."

Beth snorted, for pity's sake what was wrong with this guy and why on earth did they let this nut be the Chief of Police, for that matter what was up with his pathetic little sidekick?

"He does not have low blood sugar, what is your deal? Why did you do this? Sherman will have half his law firm on this in the next few minutes. He already thinks he has a thing for me. The last thing I need is to be rescued from jail by Sherman Kelts!"

There was nothing about this that made much sense, but she wasn't angry about being arrested, she was angry about the impending attention of Sherman Kelts. He'd spent the whole morning bragging about his law firm, his house, his condo in Mexico and a recent trip to Europe, the whole time with his eyes glued to her legs. Meeting the Chief's gaze in the rearview mirror Beth had the distinct impression that Sherman's attention bothered him too. That made no sense, but it felt true just the same.

The Chief, if she remembered correctly, was Kent Costas. Glancing at the steely eyes in the mirror, still looking at her, she had the oddest sensation that wasn't really the man's name. His big hands were squeezing the steering wheel as he began to recite her Miranda Rights. She stared at him through the mirror the whole time, but he avoided meeting her eyes again. Everything about him; his voice, his posture, his wacky partner still curled up against the passenger door, told her they were lying to her. She listened to the Police Chief's voice, analyzing it for truth and found none. Every perfectly delivered word sounded like a veteran actor, and halfway through his speech he tilted his face so all she could see was his mouth. He knew she knew.

When he pulled up in front of the police station, parking right by the front door, she informed him, "You forgot to tell me why I'm being arrested, Chief."

There was a very pregnant pause during which, for some absurd reason, she felt certain that he and the cockamamie sidekick were somehow talking about her.

"Driving without a license."

"Look, I don't want to provoke you, but would you mind clarifying? You arrested me at my house, where you kicked in my door, put me in handcuffs and now I'm supposed to believe you arrested me for driving without a license two weeks ago? If I were a vindictive woman, I would let Kelts, Phelps & Associates have a go at you. As it stands right now, I can hardly wait to see what this is really about."

Several officers arrived en masse to escort her from the car. Once she'd been taken by immigration, customs and DEA officials from an airport in Asia, and there had been less of them hauling her off. What was going on here? It definitely had absolutely nothing to do with her stupid driver's license. The men clustered around her, not like they thought she was a dangerous criminal who would run, but like they were escorting her down the red carpet and thrilled to be doing so. A combination of the absurdity of this situation, and the fact that there was something absolutely spectacular about these men, made Beth smile at them, their faces remained solemn but their eyes betrayed enthusiasm. Despite whatever the whacked chief had going on, and she didn't know why, but she sensed that there was about nothing these guys wouldn't do for her, so when the Chief moved out of earshot she asked them for her purse.

"SORRY, CHIEF." HONOR Monroe opened one eye. "I've never met an Orphan of the Inquisition before. Do they all do that unchecked thing with their hearts like she does? I thought she wanted to join with me! Are we going to initiate her into the clan?" His last comment was wistful and Kahtar turned to glare. Honor yanked his door open, and slid out and onto the pavement.

By the time he got to his feet Kahtar was standing next to him, hissing. "Do you not understand the laws of the clan, Monroe?"

"Of course. I'm sorry, Chief."

"Guard her. Somewhere where she can't see you would be a good idea."

"What am I guarding her from?" Honor reached to unlock the strap over his pistol and it took effort for Kahtar not to roll his eyes. The woman had definitely disoriented his rookie.

"From us, Monroe, from the warriors here who will react even more idiotically to the touch of her heart than you did. I sincerely doubt you'll need your gun for that."

"Sorry, Chief, of course." Honor scampered towards the door where the lone jail cell was roomed and vanished through it.

ARRESTING BETH WHITE was simply follow through on Kahtar's previous threat. The moment he'd seen her he'd known his course of action, he did not make idle threats. It had been his job to chase her off and he'd failed. That was going to be remedied. The problem was what he'd learned in the minutes since his men led her off to her cell. Beth White had not only somehow managed to buy a house in town, a house that should never have been for sale, but she was planning to open a business in it and that could never be allowed.

While compiling a mental list of how to dislodge the unwanted Orphan, one of his warriors found him pacing his office and handed him her rap sheet. Miss White had been arrested dozens of times.

No wonder she took it so well, she's used to it.

In Asia she'd been arrested for trying to bring seeds from poppies through Customs, in Japan—detained for inciting a near riot? Tanzania for disorderly conduct…. Kahtar rooted through the papers, quickly taking in the information.

The door to his office banged open in the customary Honor Monroe entry, and Kahtar opened his mouth to condemn, but then the tall blonde in question appeared and he shut his mouth in surprise. She stood in the doorway, in her too short dress, shoes with five inch heels giving her at least an inch on Honor Monroe who was staring at her star-struck, but following protocol.

"Chief Costas? Beth White has a driver's license," said Honor.

"And a lawyer whether she likes it or not, but apparently that was a good thing today." Beth watched Kahtar with interest as she spoke, and he was careful to keep his face blank.

A voice piped up from the hallway behind her, Squire Tupper arriving for his shift.

"Well hello there! Are you Clan Huron?"

Squire's curly red head barely had time to become visible before Honor shoved him further into the hallway and slammed the door shut.

Looking through the frosted glass of the door, at the silhouettes of the departing officers, Beth asked frankly.

"Who is Clan Huron? I've never even heard of anyone named Clan but apparently I'm her doppelganger. That's who you thought I was too, didn't you? When you stopped me for almost speeding the other day?"

"Don't you mean when I told you next time I saw you I'd arrest you? Did you forget that part, Miss White?" Kahtar glared at her, but it didn't seem to faze her. She smiled up at him and there was nothing sarcastic in her look. It was disarmingly sweet. They needed to get rid of her quickly, but suddenly he wasn't worried about the attention that Beth could bring to Willowyth. That she might discover too much about them seemed a bigger tragedy, because if that happened, her life would be over.

"Being arrested for not having a license seemed a bit irrelevant once I got one—do you need to see it?" For a moment she fished in her big silver bag and then waved the laminated square as she pointed out. "Not that it matters because this was just an excuse wasn't it? Were you so determined to find a perp this morning that you settled on me? Do you have a quota of dangerous criminals to fill? I am being the bigger person here, Chief Costas. I hope you realize that. I'm not into frivolous lawsuits but, I assure you, Sherman Kelts exists for them. That is who I called with my one phone call, and now I'm going to have to deal with him. So the way I see it, it is only fair that you have to deal with me, as this whole thing is your fault." She crossed the room and took a seat in front of his desk.

"What are you doing?"

"I want to speak with you. You owe me that much. Your officers were actually going to send me to County Jail!" Crossing her long legs she dropped her purse onto the floor where it tipped and several items spilled out.

Standing beside the door Kahtar tried to ignore the images that Beth's heart stirred within his own. *Safe Harbor, Warm Shelter, Home Plate.* Resting his hand on the door handle he reminded himself that she needed to leave. Beth White didn't belong. In his peripheral vision he saw she was looking at the half dozen artfully arranged doughnuts on the plate at the edge of his desk and she glanced at him doubtfully, looking back at the plate, and at him a second time.

"I'm busy," he told her. "You can take your license and leave. I apologize for your inconvenience."

"You're not busy, and that was the most insincere apology I've ever heard."

"What do you want?"

Beth looked at the computer screens and smiled. They were all covered with images from his morning search. He'd forgotten about them. She'd driven the past completely from his mind.

"Lover of religious art work? Oh, are those statues of Saint Longinus? The one at Saint Peter's Basilica is inspired, have you seen it?"

"What do you want?" Again the words were clipped and rude.

Beth leaned back in her chair and examined him. Clear blue eyes slid from top to toe and back again. Kahtar was used to being looked at. He was a giant, even among his own. What he was not used to was being seen. Beth White looked at him like she knew him—and knew him well. He crossed the room then, to hide behind his desk, pausing only long enough to close the screens on the computers. There was something unsettling about having those images juxtaposed next to him under Beth's knowing gaze. When he met her eyes he had the feeling she had seen too much anyway.

"I've asked you repeatedly what you want, Miss White?"

"Despite the enthusiasm of Mr. Sherman Kelts, and Kelts, Phelps and Associates, I'm not going to get a license to operate my business in town." Tugging at her ear she looked into his eyes as she spoke to him, not many people could hold Kahtar's gaze, Beth apparently was one of them.

Though expert at hiding his emotions, he knew Beth saw the surprise in his eyes, because she continued.

"I'm right aren't I?"

"I really don't know what you're getting at. How am I supposed to know about licensing for businesses in this village?"

"This isn't a professional question, I'm asking for your personal opinion. I bought 35 Pearl Street because I need to open my shop in it, I've spent six years preparing to do this and I will do it."

Her statement had the certainty of someone on a mission and he found himself silently rooting for her. Then he pressed his hands onto the desk in front of him so hard that something inside it cracked.

No. She can't be here! She is not one of us and she is an exposure danger so close to the Arc!

"And you're telling me this because?"

"Because I think they're stonewalling me, I think that the village doesn't want my business here. Look I'm not Walmart. I'm willing to follow all their nitpicky laws and don't get me wrong, I'm not even complaining about them. Those laws allow you to have this lovely little village instead of a pile of strip malls. All I need is a license, but I have reason to believe no matter what I do they aren't going to issue it."

Kahtar found it impossible to meet her sincere eyes. She was absolutely right. She would never get a license to operate her business. Settling on staring at the smooth brow above the candid gaze he kept his voice bored.

"Were you hoping I'd go arrest the city council because you can't get what you want?"

"I was hoping," she scooted to the edge of her seat, "Chief Costas…" She said the name as though she knew perfectly well it was an alias. "That we could discuss nepotism in this city, surely you've been around long enough to know if it goes on."

He looked into her eyes then, and fought the faint touch of connection he felt when he did it, forcing his gaze to remain cold and his heart to ignore the way Beth's heart bounced against his heart like laughter.

"I'm not a lawyer, Miss White."

"No, but you can tell me if it's true. Does the city only issue permits to the in-crowd around here?"

Kahtar's eyes darted immediately away from her penetrating, honest ones. He settled for staring at a wisp of the summer blonde hair that framed her pretty face.

"Oh, I see, of course. You're one of them. I don't know how I missed it before. So was he, wasn't he?"

Kahtar's eyes were drawn back to hers as though he no longer had control of them.

"That handsome officer that showed me in? The one with good manners and the blood sugar problem? He's part of the in-crowd too."

Kahtar couldn't help it, his heart sank. This Orphan of the Inquisition was drawn to them, to the town, to her own people, and they were giving her the cold shoulder, and it was going to get a whole lot worse for her very quickly.

It is for her own good, she can't live in both worlds and we can't have her so close.

Despite the truth of that, remembering his duty he forced her bouncing heart away from his, certain she had to feel the rebuff even if she didn't understand what it was.

Beth White held his eyes for several seconds before they grew cold too. That sight made him inexplicably sad. Silently he apologized to her, wishing it were different. She scooped her bag off the floor, brusque.

"Sorry to have bothered you, Chief, it won't happen again."

CHAPTER
SEVEN

SHERMAN KELTS PICKED Beth up from the police station in his Jag-You-Are as he called it. He announced she could pay him back by treating him to lunch.

At the Bistro of his choice in downtown Cleveland, Beth watched as Sherman actually sniffed the wine cork. Deaf to her protests he insisted on filling her glass to the top with the shockingly expensive beverage.

"You'll love it. Just taste it."

"I don't drink."

"Wine isn't drinking." Sherman took a large mouthful and swished it around like mouthwash. Beth decided Sherman seemed like the sort of man who could have a perfectly happy lunch with very little response on her part, quite possibly none.

Settling comfortably into her cushioned pew, Beth ignored her lawyer and the wine. She ate her organic salad, quietly thrilled to have found what her mother always called real food. Sherman ranted about retribution for her false arrest. Beth occupied her mouth with chewing to keep from arguing, almost thankful for his soliloquy.

After a hopeful examination of the dessert tray, she settled on a Buy Local Fruit Compote. The waitress, a pretty redhead appropriately named Kelli, lifted the glass dish straight from her tray, setting it on the table in front of Beth. Several blueberries rolled over the edge, and Beth nabbed them off her lap, popping them into her mouth.

"Mmm, organic."

"Organic is a gimmick. Just a way to get you to pay more," said Sherman.

"Actually no it isn't," said Beth. Kelli winked at her and turned away with the luscious tray of desserts.

"For the price of that fruit, you should have gone with strawberry shortcake. Now that's dessert—homemade cake and ice-cream. Killer fattening though. Looks like Kelli might be a big fan, if you know what I mean." There could be no doubt that Kelli had heard every word, but she continued smiling at the couple at the next table.

Unable to stop the truth tumbling from her lips Beth glanced pointedly at her lawyer's paunch while he shoveled in a double choco-late cheesecake.

"Kelli and I both know exactly what you mean, and I couldn't disagree more. You're very observant of the perceived faults of others, but you seem blind to your own."

"Don't take it personally, Beth. You could eat everything on that tray without a worry."

"Thank you, Sherman. Perhaps I should."

Holding his fork and a hand out defensively, he said, "I didn't mean to say that you're too skinny. Though women look better a little underweight and that's a fact."

Beth motioned to Kelli, who rolled her eyes a bit and returned. She slid the check across the polished antique table. Beth immediately slipped her credit card into it, handing it back to the gorgeously curvaceous waitress. Counselor Kelts continued stuffing his feet in his mouth until the woman returned to whisper that the card had been declined.

The same was soon true of all three of Beth's credit cards.

While Sherman submitted his take on the wisdom of purchasing a house beyond one's means, Beth rooted in her bag, thankful to locate enough cash to keep her out of any further debt to Mr. Kelts.

"You can't be serious." Kelli shoved the extra fifty back at Beth.

"Don't worry, I actually can afford it. Besides, you earned it," Beth said.

"Thanks." Kelli stuffed it into her pants pocket, and nodded towards Sherman. "I'll use it to buy more cake."

ON THE FREEWAY, heading back towards Willowyth, Sherman had the audacity to ask if Beth came from money. Her opinion of him couldn't get much lower, but she answered frankly, she never really had any choice in that matter.

"No. My parents were both in the military."

"Really? You don't have that look about you, you know, military brat. How did you come up with the cash for Pearl Street?"

Clenching her bag with fists Beth fought it, tried to resist answering the nosy question. It was no use. Whatever filter the rest of humanity had, she had been born without it. Always, all her life, she'd answered questions with brutal honestly.

"I worked in international stocks after university. I was really good at it."

"Did you now? Can't imagine anyone leaving that kind of work for running a gift shop in rural Ohio…."

It wasn't a question and Beth's hands unclenched. She didn't care what he could imagine, and she bit her tongue rather than point out that she most definitely was not opening a gift shop. Hoping to avoid hearing any further questions she rolled down her window. The wind blew loudly into the car, dimming Sherman's voice as he droned on about poor business prospects.

"Why'd you do that?" he protested. "I have air-conditioning!"

Beth leaned towards him, almost relieved to answer this honestly, no longer caring if she hurt his feelings.

"I'm trying to drown out your personal questions. I don't want to answer them. I think they're inappropriate and rude. Ours is a business relationship only." The world was full of lawyers and she'd happily find a new one.

After a moment Sherman Kelts used his controls to roll up her window.

"Well, I thought we were becoming friends." His eyes went to her legs.

Beth moved her big purse down her lap to cover them. It isn't easy to get dresses the right length when you're six feet tall, and she knew exactly what Sherman Kelts was interested in. Her fists balled up again.

"What the…." Sherman groused as a State Trooper pulled alongside the Jaguar, lights flashing. The trooper motioned for him to pull over.

"I was not speeding. What's this about?"

AT LEAST THIS time Beth got to ride in the front seat of the police car, but twice in one day riding in any part of a police car seemed like setting a bad precedent.

"Thanks for driving me home, Trooper Blake, I appreciate it."

The State Trooper nodded at her, making polite conversation. "No problem. I don't often have a good reason to get off the highway. This is a nice area. I've never been here before."

Peering out the window at Willowyth's tree lined Main Street Beth had to agree with his assessment. Already, just a couple miles from her new house she felt the strange anticipation that the house on Pearl Street incited in her. An odd thought occurred to her.

"Can I ask what made you pull Sherman Kelts over? I mean, were you planning on impounding his car when you did it?"

The State Trooper touched the brim of his hat briefly, responding a bit elusively.

"Everything is automated anymore. You can't get away with not paying tickets."

"Seems to me he got away with it for a good long time. I mean he said he hadn't paid any parking tickets in ten years."

"He'll be paying now and just between you and me, I've never seen anyone get away with not paying tickets for ten years. I don't know how he kept his registration current. He's in a lot of trouble." The Trooper glanced over at her and said a bit dryly, "Even if he plays golf with the governor."

Beth grinned at him. Sherman certainly hadn't taken having his vehicle impounded very well. Standing alongside the freeway he'd tried every threat he dared and dropped names without a hint of shame.

"I have reason to believe he was lying about that," she told the officer then pointed at her street, "Turn right there. My place is the big house at the end." It was impossible to keep the pride out of her voice.

"That's not your convertible in front is it?"

"What? Yes it is, why?"

The Trooper looked over at her, tugging his sunglasses off, sympathetic brown eyes took her in.

"Looks like this just isn't your day. Someone put a wheel clamp on it. You parked facing the wrong direction."

BETH TOSSED HER Smartphone onto the bed and dropped to the floor. On her knees she fished beneath the bed and pulled out a shoebox. Despite her Dad's admonitions never to do it, she always kept a lot of cash on hand. Good thing because there was a big orange hunk of plastic bolted to a wheel of her car, and the release fee to get it off was astronomical. Apparently parking facing in the wrong direction was quite the crime in Willowyth. Trying to look on the bright side, she decided that at least they hadn't arrested her for it, not yet anyway. According to the ticket on the windshield she had twenty-four hours, the penalty was left to her imagination. Good thing City Hall was only a couple blocks away.

FLASHING LIGHTS FLICKERED in the rearview mirror of her boot-free car, and Beth yanked the wheel, her tires rubbed the curb as she pulled over. Slamming into park she grabbed her bag and found her license and registration right on top. Four new tickets, all moving violations, in…she glanced at the clock on the dashboard, thirty-four minutes. That had to be a record. Subtlety definitely wasn't how these people worked. It was almost funny because subtlety had never been her strong suit either.

Four minutes later, another ticket in hand, Beth watched the squad car make a U-turn and pull off Pearl Street. Smiling she drove to the end of the street, and then steered her car up and over the curb, parking right in the middle of her front yard. Brenda sat on the front porch waiting for her, her look of incredulity clear in the headlights. Well, Brenda already thought she was nuts. The tickets didn't bother Beth, however, that wheel clamp thing did. She was going to avoid that. Gathering up her four tickets, she dug out a handful of money and using a fat black magic marker she jotted a note right across the front of a ticket.

Brenda hissed after her, questioning, but Beth marched across the yard and then jammed the tickets into the screen door of the house next door. There was really no reason for it, common sense told her that the house could very well be owned by a nice elderly couple, as Brenda often speculated. Instinct told her that the Police Chief would know what she'd done by morning. Grinning she headed back to her house, ignoring Brenda's comments about terrorizing old people. If this was day one in the campaign to rid the village of Beth White, she best be ready for round two.

CHAPTER
EIGHT

AFTER THE WEEKLY celebration, hundreds of members of Cultuelle Khristos stood inside the cave. They blocked paths and prevented thousands from making much headway as they tried to leave through the lone exit. Happy voices sounded through the enormous cavern. Many darted in and out of smaller chambers and children ran screeching, their voices amplified to an almost painful level. Warriors assigned to the mundane duty of traffic cop half-heartedly attempted to direct the exiting masses. Most simply took the time to join in the general mayhem of the typical Sunday afternoon.

Kahtar skulked around the edges dressed in his traditional leggings and chain mail, with a sword at each hip. Preoccupied, he allowed the melee around him to take its natural shape without his usual interference. Today his mind kept wandering to how to rid the clan of the threat that Beth White posed, while simultaneously trying to block out the memory of the way Sherman Kelts had looked at the Orphan of the Inquisition. Every time the picture intruded into his head, he reached to grasp the hilts of both blades at the same time and wondered if, just this once the Old Guard might approve the assassination of a Seeker. Tonight he would have to do penance for his little daydream about beheading the lawyer, but for now he was rather caught up in it.

The familiar huffing and puffing that signaled Elder, Abigail Adit's approach, echoed up the tunnel behind him interrupting his little fantasy. Hoping to dodge her sharp tongue, he sidled towards the front of the passageway but she snapped in his wake.

"Don't you even try. I can feel the vibration when you walk, Goliath. I need to talk to you." The middle-aged woman approached, faded red hair wound into a tight bun, dressed in her usual drab olive green dress. Kahtar recalled the style had once been popular among Seekers many decades past. A gold chain hung around her neck attached to a pair of glasses. She shoved them onto her nose for emphasis from time to time. In the dim light of the tunnel Abigail did just that, huffing up to his side. At barely five feet tall, standing next to Kahtar, the Elder looked like a fat little girl playing dress up.

"What's this I hear about there being an Orphan in town?"

"What did you hear?" Probing those sharp little eyes of hers, Kahtar could read nothing in them.

"Huh." Abigail slapped some papers into his hand. "If you didn't have the plebes scared witless you'd have gotten this sooner. Really, Kahtar, you have some of those boys wetting their beds at night."

Instantly he recognized the traffic tickets and knew who they'd been issued to, he could scan Beth's DNA on the paper. Several bills were folded between them and he counted two thousand dollars. Flipping a ticket over he read in bold black print, *Chief—Can I run a tab?*

Kahtar whispered a word he never said.

"Why does she call you Chief?" Abigail demanded, hands on the area where her hips would be, if they had been discernible from her general fleshiness.

"I am the Police Chief."

"Are you certain that Orphan doesn't know you're also the Warrior Chief?" Ferociously, Abigail slammed her glasses further up her nose.

"Kahtar?" The Mother of Cultuelle Khristos glided attractively to Abigail's side. Anwyn Glorianna D'Aval, the ideal of feminine strength and beauty with dark red curls resting against an ivory neck, looked more like a statue of a water nymph than the leader of their clan.

The quick intelligence in her dark eyes swept Kahtar's face and she murmured, "An Orphan of the Inquisition is in our village?"

"Yes." Kahtar answered both of the women at the same time.

Abigail almost bounced with excitement, peering at Kahtar through what he knew was just plain glass in her spectacles. The Mother's blue eyes lit with interest as she too peppered him with questions.

"How unexpected. How old is he, and where did you find him?"

"It's a woman and she's twenty-four years. The day Honor was shot I'd stopped her for speeding."

"A woman! Imagine! Remind me what is speeding?"

"Driving her car too fast," Abigail explained impatiently.

"Of course. She drives?"

Abigail interjected with authority. "Remember that is how they all travel, Anwyn. I think we should keep her!"

Kahtar had never seen Abigail enthusiastic in all his years. The thought of keeping Beth like a stray pet was almost laughable, but his eyes went to The Mother's face trying to read her serene features.

"Keep her? You know nothing about her, Abigail! Her people might have been wandering without guidance since the Spanish Inquisition. Do you even sense her heart clearly, Kahtar?"

"Very. That has been a problem. Early on, before word spread, several of our warriors approached her asking if she is Clan Huron, me included when I first met her."

"Oh dear, so her heart is that recognizable as Covenant Keeper?"

"It is strong and a bit uncontrolled."

"Oh! Exceptional. Kahtar? Remember the Council voted that we would consider welcoming Orphan children? I wish she were a child, still, twenty-four is young for one of us…does she function well in the outside world?"

It was a question he hadn't expected. The difference in the way their minds perceived a situation often intrigued him, but the images of Beth in her yellow convertible, and Beth with the electricians and carpenters flashed through his mind.

"Quite well." Even as he answered Kahtar wondered if he could be wrong about that, then he brushed the idea away. Beth White with her business savvy was better off in her own world.

The Mother looked sad as she thought. "If she is at home with the Seekers, then she would never function in our world."

"Never is one of those words that don't often apply to Human Beings." Abigail's voice echoed loudly as she argued with The Mother.

Kahtar and Abigail rarely saw eye to eye. "Yet never is a word that often applies to Covenant Keepers," he said.

The Mother nodded. "We never break the laws of being and that is difficult enough for those of us born to it. Abigail, isn't it better to allow the Orphan to live outside, than risk her life trying to follow our laws?"

"I stand by what I said." Abigail glared up at them, "and Orphans belong with their own." The stodgy little librarian huffed away, and The Mother shook her beautiful head.

"You realize Abigail is right of course? The problem is her own aren't part of our world either. We could hardly expect the Orphan to give up her family and friends. She'd likely forfeit her life by breaking a law, and I doubt it would take very long."

Kahtar opened his mouth to make a comment. He wanted to point out to The Mother that few clans had ever tried welcoming an Orphan into their fold, that their rare Christian clan was unusual to consider even an Orphan child. He had centuries of anecdotal data to back that up, but of course he couldn't mention that fact. The Mother waited patiently, watching as he struggled to put his thoughts into words. But the words never came to light, that conversation never took place, because an Old Guard flickered to his side and took him from the cave in a blinding flash of light. The next thing Kahtar saw, as he shimmered back into being outside the Arc, were grey waves washing the shore of Lake Erie.

IN THE SPLIT second it took to fully reappear, Kahtar knew exactly where he was. Standing outside the Arc, forty miles west of the entrance, bright June sunshine seared into his eyeballs after the dim cave, but he could scan. This was an area where warriors always kept watch because it marked a boundary in their territory. This bit of land abutted dozens of veils, and the Arc. While he knew where he was, it took a moment to understand why he'd been ferried away with no explanation. The Old Guard at his side didn't wait for him to understand, his scan seared through Kahtar's head forcing him to scan along the landscape, forcing the Warrior Chief to sense what lay on the pebbly shore of the giant lake.

For a microsecond Kahtar took the information in like the old soldier that he was. Facts: a dead woman washed up on the beach, waves crashing against her and rhythmically shoving her naked body further ashore. Kahtar automatically took in physical attributes first, noting that she was thin, with blonde hair, and then fear gripped him.

"No!" The word escaped and he raced over the rocky beach to her side with his heart seizing painfully, fearful of recognizing her features. They were bloated, almost beyond recognition, her nose missing, but he knew her. Kneeling beside her Kahtar gently brushed her blonde hair back. Long wet strands slid through his fingers, tiny pebbles too big to be called sand, dropped off in clumps. Flies had already begun to gather, clustering over most of her available flesh, lifting off only when another wave washed them away.

"She is not Covenant Keeper. She was an eater of dirty food." The Old Guard spoke and he too crouched beside the woman. The sword strapped to his back should have dug into the pebbly shore, but it didn't, the end jutting downward simply wasn't there anymore. His large sandals didn't even disturb the rocks as he shimmered on the shore, never completely taking solid form. The Old Guard used a flickering backlit hand to brush flies off the body, it lingered on the woman's throat and, where his flickering hand had touched, the flies did not return.

"She was strangled, her windpipe crushed and broken before her body was given to the water."

"Sweet El, take her in your arms." Kahtar spoke the prayer out loud, almost ashamed as both relief and regret washed through him. "Her name is Brenda. She was a waitress in the village."

Honor Monroe flickered into being at the side of an Old Guard and made his way down the beach. The Warrior of ilu dropped his cloak over Brenda's nakedness and he stooped over her, gently picking stones from her hair with Kahtar. For several minutes they were silent, their hearts regretful. Brenda Blake was not clan, but she lived in their village. They were Warriors of ilu, protectors of Covenant Keepers, but they were also Police Officers and they had failed this young Seeker.

Kahtar finally looked into Honor's blue eyes, detesting what he had to order him to do.

"We can't risk an investigation and publicity. Have her cleaned and bury her on the north side of the lake—someplace where she will never be found. Have someone arrange financially for her daughters, something substantial that provides for their college education."

"Chief?" Honor stopped pawing the dirt from Brenda's hair to stare at Kahtar in surprise.

"I owe her. I thought she was safe. This should not have happened in our village, even if she isn't one of our people, we should have done better by her."

BY THE END of the day all the warriors could learn of Brenda was that she hadn't been seeing anyone, and that her girls were being tended by a friend from the coffee shop—a friend frantic with worry and adamant that Brenda would never have left her daughters. Dressed in his police uniform and leaning against a wall in the police station Kahtar spoke low to his warriors.

"See to it that the girls' guardian will acquire a home somewhere in the south. I want all trace of Brenda Blake out of here by tomorrow."

"Her friend's not going to leave while Brenda is missing." Squire Tupper pointed the fact out and Kahtar glared at him.

"Then leave a false trail to Brenda down south. Get her and those girls out of here. I want no publicity over the fact that Brenda went missing in Willowyth. We can't afford any extra attention here. We'll have enough of that from our stray Orphan."

The looks that his warriors shot at him didn't go unnoticed, these lies were dishonorable and they all felt it.

"Hey, Chief?" Consider Drake wandered up the hall from dispatch, a piece of paper in his beefy hands. "Apparently Beth White called in to report that Brenda Blake borrowed her car and didn't bring it back."

Kahtar straightened up. "I'm just hearing this because?"

"Because dispatch didn't put it through to us, they told her that we don't investigate late fees associated with borrowing, but that if she wanted to report it stolen that they'd forward the information. I only found out now because I ran an illegal search on 911 recordings."

RIGHT IN THE middle of her front yard, Beth's yellow convertible had been parked crooked. A ticket stuck to the windshield stated she didn't have enough rubber on her windshield wipers. Standing beside the car Kahtar scanned it to a microscopic level, Brenda had been in it. Motioning with only a nod at the vehicle he went towards the house. Consider Drake and Squire Tupper hurried across the small roadway to examine the vehicle more thoroughly.

Not bothering to knock for police business, he decided scaring Beth a bit could only help. The shop smelled clean though it looked shabby inside, the floor uneven beneath his feet. The original peeling wallpaper had been left untouched and crates and boxes were stacked everywhere, goods piled randomly on every available surface. Nothing had been repaired or modified, but the old wood-work had been polished to a gleam and reflected the late afternoon sunlight streaming through sparkling clean windows. Despite the mess something hinted at purpose in the sheer randomness of the piles of mismatched items.

Kahtar stepped silent. A talent honed instinctively from count-less years as Warrior of ilu. Beth's shop struck him as both the cleanest and messiest place he'd ever been. Not a single chemical or plastic fume touched his scan. From what he could see all she'd done besides dump a truck load of stuff inside, was to polish and scour the place. There was new shelving, but even those weren't permanently affixed to anything, just random freestanding shelves filling every room in the house. He scanned the rest of the house in an instant, basement to attic, noting with disappointment that all she'd done was clean, so they couldn't fine her for building without a permit. What caught his attention most were microscopic traces of Brenda all over the place, apparently she'd been there many times.

Beth stood with her back to him, dressed in jeans and a white t-shirt, wiping down tall wooden cabinets with lemon oil. This looked to be the planned check-out area, an antique cash register rested on the counter. Beth's blonde hair swayed in a high pony-tail, brushing against her shoulders as she rubbed. In canvas sneakers with no heels, Kahtar sensed her to be barely six feet tall. Even unaware of his pres-ence, her energetic heart romped in place, reminding him of when Wolves had been a puppy and used to chase his tail. She jumped when he purposely stepped on a board that squeaked, and then her heart cantered straight for his. Braced for impact, Kahtar was aware of the fact that he was refusing to enjoy something impossible not to enjoy. Not pausing in her work she scolded.

"You scared me, Chief Costas, you walk like a ghost! Are you here to arrest me for cleaning on a Sunday? I assume you got my note."

"You reported your car stolen."

"I reported my car lost. Let me guess, I'm going to be arrested for filing a false report?"

That idea had potential. "I'm interested in how you lost your car."

Beth waved an airy hand focusing on wiping down her cabinet. "I got it back—you probably noticed it out front." Glancing at him she suddenly stopped, her eyes alert and knowing. "What's wrong?"

"Nothing." The woman saw entirely too much.

Setting the rag down and leaning across the counter towards him, she stared into his eyes without blinking. He could not remember a time, outside one of his childhoods, when any woman had voluntarily moved so close to stare into his face, but it felt natural with Beth.

"Why are you here about my car now?" she demanded.

"I just heard about it a few minutes ago." The inquiry had inexplicably shifted.

Those knowing eyes watched him and he fought the urge to move away, sensing it would betray him in some way, besides standing so close to that heart felt right. Something warned him this woman could read a face well, even his own usually inscrutable face, so he didn't pull back.

"Yeah? When I called they were a bit snippy, it surprised me. Your force seemed so professional and polite, when they arrested me without cause. Even when they issued me twenty-two tickets in the past thirty-six hours."

Twenty-three. He wondered if she'd gotten the IRS audit notice yet. "Dispatch is answered by county and then transferred to us."

"Chief?" Beth stared into his eyes as though measuring his reaction to her next words. "Why are all the local cops men? It's weird in this day and age."

"Are you interested in applying?"

Chuckling she went back to wiping her cupboard and Kahtar stood a moment, considering leaving rather than stir any suspicion, and then risked another comment.

"Who borrowed your car?"

"One of my new employees—and I only called because I got worried about her." Again Beth turned to stare into his eyes. "Why are you asking? Something is going on isn't it?"

Adopting his best blank stare he said, "I'm just following up, glad your employee brought your car back."

"Now that you have me thoroughly worried. She didn't bring it back, but you know that."

"How'd you get it back?"

"GPS coordinates. I found it in the driveway at her house. There were less than fifteen miles on it."

"Why'd you give your car to someone who wouldn't bring it back?"

"She doesn't have one and she was going to take her girls to the zoo this weekend. You are scheming, Chief, but you're not nearly as good at it as you think. The thing is are you trying to get me to tell you something about her or just looking for new ways to torment me?"

"Trying to get you to tell me something about whom?"

"Brenda. Brenda Blake." This wasn't proving to be difficult at all. Beth answered every question with unusual candor, despite the animosity she had to feel towards him.

"I don't report idle gossip, but don't count on Brenda Blake showing up for work in the morning." Both statements were true, even if they were misleading. Something warned him not to try to lie to Beth.

She put her hands on her hips. "Seriously? Did she run off with one of your cops?"

"I'm not going to gossip with you. Just be glad you got your car back." Instinct sent him towards the door. If he stirred Beth White's suspicion about Brenda Blake, she just might bring her lawyer friend in. He considered his questioning a success when the enthusiastic bouncing of Beth's heart followed him out the door. She suspected nothing to upset her.

CHAPTER
NINE

CRAMMING A CARDBOARD box full of items, Beth wondered why she bothered. Brenda had left without a word, it was rude. Tucking some candy into the corners for the girls, she grinned. Kent Costas was unhappy, hopefully that meant his officer had married Brenda. The woman had been obsessed with those cops, though Beth couldn't recall a particular one. She'd assumed Brenda had liked them all. She looked at the address in Charleston that Cliff had given her, and decided to hunt up sunscreen for her impulsive ex-employee.

Beth decided she'd have to go get a cashier's check for Brenda's wages, because apparently identity theft had emptied her checking account.

Surely they're not really going to keep my money.

A worrisome thought intruded that maybe it really had been identity theft, if that were the case she probably should be handling everything differently. By differently that would mean actually doing something about it. Beth eyed the pile of mail sitting on the mahogany counter. So far she'd ignored the closed accounts, missing money, and incoming piles of citations and notices, listening to her gut instead of her brain. If somebody really had robbed her electronically, four years of commuting between Frankfurt and Amsterdam might have been for nothing.

Not for nothing, I've got this place.

Digging through a pile of silk scarves she lifted out several bottles of sunscreen.

I'm an idiot. Dad will have a cow if he finds out what is going on.

Impulsively Beth dropped the bottles on the counter, grabbed a trash can, and brushed the entire pile of mail and tickets into it. It was highly unlikely her father would think to ask her if she was being run out of town on a rail, or had been robbed of everything she'd worked for in a period of twenty-four hours.

Beth was surrounded by lies and she knew it, there was just no way to explain it to anyone without sounding insane. *The entire village is plotting to oust me, but they don't mean any harm.* Jamming sunscreen into the box she laughed out loud. *With the exception of Marge at the Department of Public Safety who definitely would like to see me harmed.*

DRESSED IN HER favorite yellow dress, Beth took a seat on the top step of Sweet Earth's front porch and slowly folded a paper bag shut. It was 3:00 a.m. and the brown paper bag crinkled loudly. Strange how much noise electricity usually makes. She never noticed that until it wasn't around anymore. It would be nice, if she didn't need it!

Beth yawned so wide her jaw cracked, and she rubbed it, wishing she drank coffee because she was most definitely not a morning person. Leaning forward she hugged her knees and wrestled the next yawn into a very unattractive hiccup-burp sound. It seemed to her the best defense against this village's offense was to turn enemies into friends. If not friends, at least business partners and she had experience with those. The globe was crawling with contacts Beth had made over the years. If the people running this village really thought fining her and taking her money would make her go away, that might be a really good thing. While they waited for her to pack up and leave, she and her business partners would show them just why they needed her.

To Beth's surprise the gardener didn't show up, but a little boy moseyed around the corner of the house dressed in some sort of weird superhero costume.

"Have you had breakfast yet?" At the sound of her voice, the poor kid jerked straight up in surprise and conked his head against the stair railing. Beth raced down the steps and knelt in front of him to check his forehead.

"Are you okay, Buddy? Sorry I scared you."

"That's okay!" The kid rubbed his chest and grinned at her.

Beth pressed her fingers against his forehead, his skin felt warm and she fought the urge to hug the little guy. With his mop of black hair and bright green eyes, dressed in the silly costume, the kid was almost unbearably cute. She laughed when he reached his arms around her and hugged tight. Less than a minute later, he perched on the stairs with her, sharing fat slices of her Mom's homemade bread spread with strawberry jam. The loaf should have been breakfast the next couple of days, but the kid polished off the entire loaf and then ate the entire jar of jam by digging in it with the butter-knife and shoveling it into his mouth. Beth gave him a wooden box with a dozen jars of the jam to take home, instructing him to tell his Mother to share it with friends, because she had crates of it.

Following the boy across the wet grass, Beth stood on the front porch of the house next door, when two young men came outside. Judging by their expressions of surprise and the fact that they rudely shoved the little boy inside, Beth garnered that they both knew who she was and weren't inclined to stay and chat. Shoving her paper bag into the arms of the nearest fellow, she smiled at him.

"Good morning. I wanted to share some of this tea, if you like it and want more you can have all you like. I have plenty."

As though unable to be completely rude, the burly fellow kept the package but told her bluntly, "We're not interested in buying your tea."

"It's a gift," Beth was unable to completely keep the hurt out of her voice. "Besides I can't get a permit to run my shop, and since I've accumulated so many nice things, I'm just going to give it all away. These things have a shelf life and I want to share them. I'm not interested in making money I'm just interested in…" Beth considered for a moment, trying to put the elusive thought into words for once, "being here."

The two men glanced at each other and then without thanking her they backed through the doorway without another word.

Well. At least the little boy had been nice.

MOVING HER LIPS silently, Beth mentally rehearsed exactly what she was going to say, berating herself mentally. *You will do this, and you will keep your big fat mouth shut.* Tote bags and her big purse weighing her down, arms loaded with heart shaped fabric boxes she had to back through the door into The Department of Public Safety's office. Marge sat behind the counter and her little eyes narrowed, her mouth set in a firm, definitely uncooperative line.

Just do it fast.

"Good Morning, Marge! I know you say you have diabetes and I want you to know I'm not here to ask for anything, so please don't think this is a bribe. I can't get my permit to open shop and so much of my stock is perishable, so I'm giving it away." Beth twisted to reveal the silk covered boxes better. "I'm hoping that some of the people who work here might be interested in these chocolates, they're Ugandan, organic, the best I've ever had—quite expensive on the market but free today. Can I PLEASE leave these boxes here for whoever wants them?"

Marge's eyes went to the colorful boxes with interest then flickered back to Beth suspiciously.

"It's not like I can stop you."

Beth dropped the boxes of chocolates on the countertop and bolted. She made it halfway down the hall before blurting, "You could if you really wanted to, liar." She hoped Marge hadn't heard her.

"Who you calling a liar?"

Beth swiveled towards the masculine voice, dropping several tote bags and her purse. An unfamiliar cop stood there, staring at her with a frown on his tanned face. He'd asked her a question, so of course she had to answer.

"Marge." Motioning with her chin towards the door to the Department of Public Safety.

Brown eyes glanced in that direction and he tried to bite back a smile while grudgingly admitting, "She does lie."

Then to Beth's surprise the cop squatted down and started to gather her stuff together. She watched him critically, taking in the fact that he looked almost like a bodybuilder except that he was graceful. When he stood with her things, she felt skinny as a walking stick next to him.

"I'll carry them to your car," he offered, seemingly unabashed to carry the colorful totes and giant silver pocketbook past interested onlookers.

Beth took the opportunity to proceed with her campaign, and told the cop what her shop sold and invited him to come by.

"I don't really have hours, but drop by anytime you see my car out front. I'm Beth White, by the way."

"I know," he admitted frankly.

Beth glanced at his badge that bore the name, 'A. Drake.' They stood by her car and his soft brown eyes studied her so intently that she blushed and added.

"Bring your wife or your girlfriend if you like. I'm sure I carry something you'd be interested in."

"You mean that?"

"Of course I mean that, anything you need, stop by."

"That's all right. I think I have what I need now, thanks." A. Drake slid Beth's pocketbook back onto her shoulder and walked away.

Beth watched him curiously as he slid into his squad car, not so coincidentally parked nose to nose with her car. It wasn't until he gave her a friendly wave and started to drive off that she realized with absolute certainty that he'd pocketed her cell phone from her purse.

CHAPTER
TEN

WAKING BEFORE 4:00 a.m. shaking and sweaty from the shade of Golgotha, Kahtar ran the wooded paths behind his pond. Wolves's barking chased him, but the dog couldn't stay focused long enough to run with him. Breakfast was then charred venison, gummy oatcakes and freshly picked strawberries. Those nice berries might have saved his plebes from a caning, but did nothing for their self esteem when he told them exactly what he thought of their lack of skills.

An Old Guard met him in the huge old barn in the back field. From the moment Kahtar stepped into the dark, dusty confines of that barn he battled for his life. Old Guard did not play games. They tried to kill him, and he fought back with everything he had. They started with spears—the type that had been around as long as he had—they were the one weapon he refused to touch. He had not held a spear in his hand since Golgotha, and today he used a metal pole to defend himself against one.

The Old Guard soon grew bored and exchanged their weapons for claymores. Kahtar managed a brief moment of fleeting pleasure by scoring a small mark across his Old Guard's cheek with the sword. The scratch faded almost instantly, and the man laid him down with the flat of his blade right across Kahtar's back, smacking him to the ground as he had threatened to do to the plebes earlier. Moving on they graduated to gladiator scissors, which they strapped to one hand. The weapon had a razor sharp blade attached and they both held a katara dagger clenched in their other hand as they circled. Kahtar had been named after that dagger in this repeat. He felt it was his duty to win the round with his namesake. He felt an affinity to the name Kahtar. He'd been named after many weapons, but Kahtar was a new name, and new was always good in his book. He wondered if anyone had any idea how many different variations the name John had evolved into over the centuries.

When the Old Guard grew bored of besting him, the man simply flickered away in a flash of light, letting his gladiator scissors and katara dagger drop to the dirt floor. Kahtar put the weapons away, hanging them on the posts and crossbeams where hundreds of other weapons waited for tomorrow. Limping a bit as he made his way over the dark field to the pond, he wiped blood that trickled into an eye. The cut was deep and eventually he gave up, letting it run freely. Plebes had run his bath in the shed that served as his bathroom. All of Cultuelle Khristos had indoor plumbing except Kahtar. After all his time on earth, something about putting a toilet inside a house still seemed wrong to him.

In the dark of the shed, his plebes managed to heal the wound above his eye. Three of the boys pressed fingers to his forehead and whispered their healing prayers. Kahtar felt the sting of the wound as it closed. The lads were honorable, if inept in most other areas. Honor and faith were necessary for healing.

Preparing for the day, he wondered if Beth White had any aptitude for healing, and if she'd ever thought to try. Few women could heal well. They had a far greater gifting than knitting bones and flesh. Standing in the black of the shed over a bowl of water, and lathering soap on his face, he used a straight blade to shave. It wasn't necessary to see to shave that face, it wasn't necessary to even scan. He knew that face—every dimple, divot and curve. For thousands of years, in every repeat, he grew into a man wearing that exact same face and he shaved it.

THE FIRST LIGHT of daybreak painted the sky pink, and the dark shape of Wolves raced across the field in front of him, barking an enthusiastic greeting. Christian Moore waited for him, trying to shoo Wolves away with a folder and failing. The balding man in the grey suit retreated up the porch steps to escape the dog's dirty greeting. Kahtar whistled one sharp bark and Wolves slunk off into the woods with his tail between his legs.

"Thanks, Kahtar, I'm working at the bank today and that dog stinks. I think he rolled in something."

"Good news or bad?" Cutting straight to business Kahtar sat on the porch steps, accepting a mug of tea from one of his plebes and offering it first to his kinsman.

"Ah, no thanks, I ate breakfast with my wife who was kind enough to cook this morning. She tends to take pity on me the mornings I need to be in town." Taking a seat on the stairs below Kahtar, right in a wet spot, Christian opened his folder.

"It's bad news. Don't get me wrong, I've put plenty of obstacles in her path. Financially and legally I've squirreled up everything with Beth White's name on it, from the IRS down to the music she buys online. It will take her years to straighten it all out. Kelts, Phelps & Associates will be no help. They're under enough strain of their own thanks to us."

Nodding, Kahtar smiled. There were so many ways to win a battle. Christian pulled out a piece of paper and frowned as he stared at it.

"The problem is she has enough inventory and access to cash that these things won't stop her anytime soon. Just yesterday she bought two new cell phones with money from an account I hadn't known about, and from what we can see she's moving along, planning to open for business."

"We'll see about that." Setting his mug down, Kahtar stalked up the long driveway, towards his vehicle.

"WHAT DO YOU mean she's giving it away?" Sitting in his office at the police station Kahtar stared blankly at the rookie, trying to make sense of his words.

Dark haired Honor Monroe wistfully fingered a cardboard box of tea, repeatedly lifting it to his nose for a whiff.

"I was next door to her shop, at Cerulean Blue for breakfast, and they were talking about it. She'd given this tea to them and it is divine. It is really good, clean but somewhat addicting. I've never had anything like it before."

Kahtar glared, and Honor cleared his throat.

"Anyway she'd told them since the town wouldn't give her a license to open her shop, she was just going to give things away."

Consider Drake lumbered forward—strong, compact, and extremely hairy. His police uniform only enhanced his thug-like appearance.

"She's following the way instinctively. It's inspired. Like she knows that we don't use money. I think she just knows—you know in her heart—that is how it is supposed to be."

Kahtar leaned forward to pluck the box of tea out of Honor's hands and reminded Consider.

"She's not part of our clan, and you don't follow the way by adhering to one rule." Lifting the box to his nose, his mouth watered and he almost groaned. *Brack tea. Where on El's Sweet Earth did she find brack tea? Even the Old Guard can't get it anymore.*

"Honor? Why did she give you this?"

"She ran into the street to nick a cat that almost got hit on Main Street. So I gave her a ticket for jaywalking. She rolled it up and tossed it on the sidewalk. Then she told me to give her one for littering, and I'd probably get promoted."

Kahtar closed his eyes and asked, "Did you?"

"Yeah, I know it sounds cheeky, but she is so candid it wasn't even sarcastic. Then I was getting in my cruiser and she waved me down, came running over. She had a big bag of stuff, said thanks for arresting her so politely the other day and that she thought I'd like this."

Kahtar looked from Consider to Honor, both obviously champions of Beth White.

"How nice. Let's ignore the fact that you accepted what could be construed as a bribe, Monroe. Do you think she'd fit in with our clan?"

Both warriors nodded, watching him with sudden interest.

"How would that work? Would we just brew a cup of this and invite her over? Mention that we belong to an ancient cult and how'd she like to be part of the club?"

"Well why not, Chief?" Honor's blue eyes were bright. "Surely she has shades as well as any of us. She'll know it's true."

"Oh I'm sure we could make her believe us, at least eventually. I could stab you, Honor, and she could watch us heal it—or even more convincing—we could stab her and then heal it. That would surely win her loyalty, make her want to spend her life living in a cave, and hiding out from the rest of the world."

Consider made a sound of protest, but Honor covered his own mouth with a hand, thoughtfully rubbing. Consider argued.

"We are her people! Once she understood that, those bonds would hold her as well as they hold all of our clan!"

Leaning forward Kahtar drove his point home.

"Loyalty, good point, Consider. What of her loyalty in the world outside of ours? Do we make her choose us over her family?"

Honor Monroe was rubbing his hands over his thighs now, thoughtful.

"Consider? Chief's right. What if she accidentally broke a law? For all we know she already has a Seeker boyfriend."

"She doesn't." Consider was adamant, one hairy fist pounded the desk. "Why do you think she wants to be here? She senses us! Her heart leads her!"

"You both need to realize that this is all irrelevant. The Mother wants her out of town. Our duty is to make that happen." Putting the box of Honor's tea in a desk drawer, Kahtar gave his orders. "No one is to step foot in her shop. I don't care if she's giving away land in The Fortunate Isles."

Honor put in, without quite meeting Kahtar's eyes. "So Christian Moore's effort didn't work? What are we going to do? Force her out of town with parking violations?"

Kahtar snapped, "No, stop issuing tickets. I'm afraid that Miss White isn't afraid of us. Boys, we're going to change that."

Consider whispered, "Ah, no." Despite his feelings he stood, ready to obey.

Honor lamented. "There is no honor in this, Chief."

"Follow her. Next time she's driving someplace remote, notify me."

THE SHADE FROM Golgotha had just ended when they came for him in the middle of the night. Old Guard stood shimmering and silent while Kahtar hurried to put on his uniform, breathing deep, trying to shove the shade from his mind.

I am Kahtar, not Longinus. This is not Golgotha. Focus, focus.

It wasn't helping much, and there was no way to hide his shaking hands and swollen eyes. Trying to focus he flickered away and then back into being at the side of an Old Guard. The first thing his eyes lit on was light from faux gas lamps, illuminating a small park right in the middle of a campus. Villa Nova sprawled right outside town, a small Christian University founded by the clan in the mid 1800's. The hum of electricity and distant airplanes was the only sound this late at night. Half a dozen Warriors of ilu, dressed as the local police force, skulked around the perimeter of the parking lot. Consider Drake moved almost soundlessly to his side, did a double take when he saw Kahtar's tearstained face and then ignored it.

"It's a student, Chief. Dead."

The last vestige of Golgotha got swept away in a wave of new horror. Scanning outwards searching for evidence, his scan ripped through his warriors. Their pained protests cut through the night air.

90

Consider gasped, "Over there, Chief, that convertible at the edge of the lot."

Looking down at the young male student killed on the campus sickened Kahtar. The boy was maybe twenty years old. A tall, thin lad who wore his blond hair long, his neck had been expertly broken. Objects from his life surrounded him, a guitar case in the back seat of his nice sports car, books on philosophy and religion scattered the floor of the vehicle. For several moments Kahtar just scanned, checking for information, looking for any sign of drugs or alcohol in the car while simultaneously searching the perimeter of the school for anyone or anything out of place. The campus was empty. Few students stayed for summer term and those that did were either doing homework or sleeping. Kahtar's scan bit through the warriors nearby. Consider Drake staggered to the edge of the lot and vomited before Kahtar finally stopped.

Honor Monroe moved to the dead body, and just like he'd done with Brenda Blake, he put a hand on the boy's long hair and smoothed it.

"If you want me to make him disappear, we don't have much time."

"No. It will draw more attention if he disappears. This boy is almost as clean as a Covenant Keeper. Make it look like an accident. You'll need help. Old Guard?" Summoning the help of one of the faintly shimmering shadows of light, a flash of light shot over the boy and then both the light and the boy vanished.

"Have one of the clan discover his body, maybe Abigail. She spends enough time in the library here—nobody would question it if she found him. And call in experts from county to investigate. It's protocol," said Kahtar.

"There is no evidence, just like Brenda's murder."

"There is little to link the two, but I don't believe in coincidences, most especially murderous ones."

CHAPTER
ELEVEN

SEVERAL BOXES OF donuts crowded the beige Formica counter top. A dozen of Lake County's Sheriffs stood in the main room of the Willowyth Police Station, tearing through boxes of Dunkin Donuts and drinking coffee. Kahtar stood with them, a Sequoia in a room of Oaks and Maples. He clutched a local newspaper in one hand. The headlines read that there would be a candlelight memorial service for Douglas Jeffries, seminary student at Villa Nova, on the campus green that evening. The by-line explained the tragic details of the boy's freak accident on the stairs outside the shower room. The fact that his parents were expected to sue the university filled all of page six and half of page seven.

After a week of investigations and speculation, Kahtar couldn't wait for the talking heads to leave. Lying was exhausting and a waste of his time. A burly Detective, who surely had once played football, commented to Kahtar.

"The parents aren't going to get anything suing. It was an accident. That kid slipped over his own two feet going down three steps. They weren't even wet."

Filling his mouth with coffee Kahtar just nodded. The action had been repeated so often during the past week that he was beginning to appreciate the dark brew that Beth White had sent with a note stating "mine is better".

The ice hot touch of an Old Guard's second voice crept into his brain and only years of discipline kept his shudder at bay.

"Come."

Politely maneuvering his way through the throng of detectives, Kahtar hurried to obey. Shoving open the emergency exit at the back of the station he stepped into the empty alley. Windowless back walls of the surrounding shops and dumpsters greeted. A hand snaked out of nowhere and grabbed his arm, yanking him into oblivion like a child tugged at the side of a merciless adult. Shimmering into being again at the side of the Old Guard, he shivered to find himself deep inside the cave.

DRESSED IN HIS police uniform, Kahtar stood inside the cavern Cultuelle Khristos used as a courtroom. It took a moment to orient. It felt like he'd dropped a hundred floors inside a high-speed elevator, entering the Arc at the side of an Old Guard was unsettling.

Elders and warriors filled the room, and the faint comfortable touches of familiar hearts reassured. He took a step forward, regaining his equilibrium. Low anxiety and the absence of fear meant the warrior on trial had not passed the point of no return.

Kahtar looked at the warrior accused of a crime and did his best to hide his surprise. Allis Drake stood within a circle of Old Guard and the Old Guard didn't shimmer. They stood solidly surrounding him, weapons drawn, their black eyes locked on the accused. Kahtar tensed, his mind flitted briefly over possibilities and settled on the most likely. Allis had helped the woman they'd left dying on the floor of her dilapidated little house. Was Allis the reason that Denise had survived? Kahtar reviewed the battered woman's injuries in his mind. It seemed the most likely law for Allis to break. The man had more heart than discipline, not a good thing in a Warrior of ilu.

The Elders of Cultuelle Khristos sat shoulder to shoulder. As a group they nodded formally to their Warrior Chief, but none of them really focused on Kahtar. Their attention centered on Allis. The Mother approached Allis. In the flickering light of the torches she looked almost like a young girl. Her white gown swept over the cave floor. She bent towards Allis and took his hand, leading him outside the circle of Old Guard to sit at a bench with her.

Oaths were not necessary in a court of ilu. Honesty was a given, rules and sentences familiar. The Mother addressed him almost casually.

"You have gone with a woman who is not one of us? I would ask you why but it doesn't matter, Allis. You will give her up. Never see her again. Do I have your word?"

Kahtar's heart sank into the pit of his stomach and a hundred curses flitted through his mind. The phrase 'sick and tired' did not even begin to cover how he felt about Covenant Keepers falling in love with Seekers.

Unable to hold The Mother's eyes, Allis's head dropped into his hands, the pain in his heart shared by his entire clan. It was huge, and familiar to Kahtar, he had sensed it many times before. So many men succumbed to women forbidden to them. Without looking at the faces of the other warriors in the room Kahtar knew that half were sympathetic. They understood. The other half were furious that Allis would risk exposing them all. Kahtar knew without looking, because that was always the way.

Perhaps The Mother understood Allis's dilemma, perhaps not. She never elaborated or explained. She obeyed the way and her words were firm.

"You have no choice, Allis. If you do not give your word you will both go into The Mists together. She cannot be part of our world. If you cannot leave her be, that will be her fate."

"Denise is not well, she would die there."

Kahtar wanted to groan, to shout at Allis that he had known the woman less than two weeks! How could he give up everything for a woman confined to a hospital bed? How did he even know her well enough to love her?

The Mother replied calmly. "Likely you would both die, Allis. It is not an easy life and eventually you would cross paths with a clan much less understanding than ours. How many laws would you break by then?"

Allis cried as he gave his word. The Mother looked up at Kahtar. They both knew Allis had to leave. Despite the strength of his honor, he was still only a man. They could all feel his shaky resolve as the touch of his aching heart brushed their own. Kahtar went to his side and squeezed the warrior's shoulder, trying to impart strength.

"Land or sea, Allis?"

Not even bothering to look up, his shoulders heaving in silent sobs, Allis struggled to answer.

"It doesn't matter. Send me where I'm needed most."

"The Middle East then. You will be missed."

The Mother leaned towards him and put a hand under his chin forcing his head up. Tears were running down his cheeks, dripping onto his police uniform. For a moment she leaned her forehead against Allis's and she whispered to him in a voice so low that Kahtar barely heard it.

"Don't be ashamed for feeling, Allis. Be ashamed for acting when it was forbidden. I love you." She kissed his lips, lingering, a farewell gesture and Allis wrapped both his arms around her and held on for a long time.

When Allis finally rose, Kahtar put an arm around his shoulders and led him away. As they traversed the path out of the cave he wanted to tell Allis that time would heal his pain, but he couldn't. Kahtar had no idea if that was true. He'd never loved a woman like a wife. He felt sorry for Allis, but thankful no one had to die, thankful that the Old Guard had stopped the warrior before he'd betrayed his entire clan and joined with a Seeker.

BETH'S CELL BUZZED with a text and she opened her eyes and dug it out of her bag to look, 11:54 a.m. and the incoming text didn't identify the sender. She dropped the phone back in the bag and rolled out of bed. Crossing to the bedroom window, she tried to force it open wider. What she wouldn't give for air-conditioning, or electricity to run a fan for that matter. At least she finally had gas hooked up, so while a hot bath was a possibility it didn't even appeal, it was disgustingly humid. The pretty silk sheers she'd hung over the window had no breeze to billow in, but she plunked back on the bed appreciating that shade of blue next to the peeling old flowered wallpaper.

Digging in her purse Beth pulled out the cell, realized it was the wrong one, and rooted another moment for the right one. She figured if the cops were going to steal phones from her, she'd save time and she'd bought two. Going without electricity was one thing, going without a phone another entirely. Her tunes were on here. Officer A. Drake would hear about his thievery next time she saw him. It wasn't really even the phone. Dang it, he'd taken her best music. She wondered why the hijacked iTunes account and her missing gadget seemed more personal than her vanishing money.

Nobody messes with my car or my phone. We all have our lines in the sand.

This phone was an upgrade, so after fiddling with it for a half hour, Beth found herself almost forgiving the theft. Then she realized the incoming text had been from her Dad.

Dang! I lost my contact list. A. Drake is a jerk!

There were four messages from Dad. He wanted her to come for dinner after church on Sunday. Mom didn't text. She hated technology of any kind. Beth replied, telling Dad she'd be there, and that she loved them both.

At one in the afternoon Beth still sat in the baggy concert t-shirt she slept in, paying for and downloading songs that she already owned. Except iTunes had inexplicably locked her account, and she couldn't go without music. She hauled herself off the bed to cross the room. Dropping her purse over her desk chair, she plunked into the chair to fiddle with her laptop. It took a full minute to get a satellite connection so she could confirm deliveries of incoming goods for that afternoon, and the battery sat at half power already.

The day looked to be shaping up nicely, coconut oil and fresh spices would be on time. Then she clicked on her international bank account, the balance now stood at zero. She slammed the lid down and crossed the room to her closet. Rooting for a lightweight dress, she wondered why she wasn't afraid. There had been times in the past when people had frightened her, intimidated her, she was hardly without fear.

It's because they're not bad. Even if they steal? When do good people steal? *I don't know, but it's a good thing I transferred half the money out of that account yesterday.*

WITH THE HELP of Old Guard, Kahtar reappeared in the alley behind the police station. He took a few minutes to compose himself, disoriented from the trial at the cave and escorting Allis away. The Drakes would be bereft, Kahtar dreaded when Consider found out what his brother had done. Scanning into the police station he debated what his story would be for his disappearance. The investigators were still inside, still drinking coffee. Intestinal trouble seemed like the best excuse. After all, he hadn't been gone that long.. As soon as his hand reached for the back door he felt the familiar pressure on his upper arm as an Old Guard grabbed him again, and the door vanished.

Instantly Kahtar reappeared on a highway on the west side of town. Before his eyes even adjusted to the change in venue or he scanned, he knew why he was there. He felt it.

The death of one of his own bore down on him. The weight of the hearts of his surviving kinsmen told him before his eyes or scan found Consider Drake and Squire Tupper. Consider would never know the fate of his brother Allis, because Consider Drake and Squire Tupper were both dead.

Kahtar wondered why, after all his years, the deaths of those he loved still burned as intensely as it ever had. Shouldn't time have dulled it? Shouldn't all the death he'd known have made him calloused? It hadn't. It cut through him like a blade. Consider lay in the middle of the asphalt roadway, recognizable only by his stocky build and hairy arms, his head no longer recognizable as human. Most of it splattered across the road in an obscene arc, a macabre rainbow of blood, flesh and bone. Moving forward, unable to feel his feet, Kahtar assessed the situation dutifully. Reading the evidence like a story, he tried to reenact the crime like Consider and Squire had always done.

Consider had stopped a vehicle, had opened the door of his squad car and stepped out of the driver's door. The door still stood open, and Consider's electronic notepad lay next to the car. Two bullets had been stopped by his vest, but they had laid him flat, long enough for the assassin to approach and shoot him point blank in the head. Kahtar could sense bullets lodged in the asphalt road. Squire's body still sat in the passenger seat, slumped against his seatbelt. He'd taken a single bullet through his right temple, fired through the windshield of the car. His head was turned towards his partner, a look of horror on his face. Kahtar pushed away the fact that Squire had seen his partner shot and turned his mind back to the facts of what had happened. There had surely been two assassins. Caught by surprise Consider never had time to sound a battle cry. Squire's horror had slowed him only seconds before death took him too.

If Consider and Squire were still alive they would have pieced together more details, but their giftings were gone forever, with them.

A warrior moved forward to meet Kahtar, his voice cracked.

"We were on a loop, three cars five minutes apart. Honor and Willet had driven past here right before it happened."

"Why?"

"Chief?"

Kahtar looked towards the thin warrior with the pale face, *so young,* his hands were shaking and he was trying not to look at the bodies of his friends. Francis Snickerbacher, the name floated into Kahtar's mind, new to the force, fresh from the Arc and unused to life among Seekers. *Unused to sudden death from a gun.*

"Why did Honor and Willet drive past here? They were to be shadowing the Orphan."

"Yes, Chief, they were, and Ansel and I were following behind them to take the next shift, but we came upon—this…" Francis's voice trailed off and he motioned towards the murder scene of two of the most talented Warriors of ilu that Cultuelle Khristos could boast.

"This took place in the space of five minutes." The young warrior's voice shook.

Kahtar gripped the man's shoulder. It felt slight.

"Notify Honor and Willet of the deaths. Beth White will have the evening free of us. The entire clan will meet at the cave tonight to grieve our loss."

THERE WAS NO difficulty in tending to the remains of Consider and Squire, in twenty minutes almost no sign of the shooting remained. The two best friends rested on limestone slabs in the cool humidity of the cave, with only their grieving families at their sides, until nightfall, when the entire clan would gather with them for the last time.

There was no difficulty in giving orders, and issuing commands to secure the village as best could be done, before all gathered for the Gloria Tribute. There was no difficulty in temporarily shoving aside the emptiness that two of his best had left in their wake. There was no difficulty in shoving aside the heaviness of knowing he had failed them, it was neither the first nor last time he would fail. It was not the worst failure. It was another failure in millennia of failure.

The difficulty was in going back to the police station and finishing his day. The difficulty was in making small talk and drinking still more coffee and pretending to see to paperwork and mundane tasks. The difficulty was in pretending to be what he was not.

IN THE FLICKERING torchlight the cave, a sea of white, waited. Women moved slowly in flowing white gowns, men stood in white tunics and leggings, even the Old Guard of Cultuelle Khristos dressed in a white version of their usual gladiator skirting. Kahtar's quilted tunic shimmered pristine white, his blouse beneath it matched perfectly, his double balteus gleamed silver, belted on his hips and a blade dangled from each side. The tears of the clan over the deaths of two of their finest washed through his heart, a river of sorrow, and he cried with them. This was the time to grieve their loss. Every member of Cultuelle Khristos seemed to fill the cave, thousands stood as one.

Consider Drake and Squire Tupper lay upon limestone tables, both clad in the traditional white of a funeral. Consider's face gone, his thick, muscular build diminished in death, the thick hair on his arms and above the collar of his snow white blouse the only identifier of who he had been. Squire's head remained turned to the left, a small bullet wound barely visible through his thick red hair. Hidden was the fact that most of the left side of his face had been blown away with the exit wound. Consider's family enjoyed no illusion as to the fate of their son, yet his father stood at his side, lovingly smoothing grizzled hair over the ghoulish skull. The sight tugged Kahtar's heart more brutally than the death of a perfect angelic child might. This is the fate of a soldier, a sacrifice given willingly. Don't turn away from what he suffered for you. Look and know. Kahtar's heart seared with that knowledge.

As one Cultuelle Khristos prayed and cried for their loss into the night, and eventually the ceremony took a turn. The clan's own grief was set aside, and as one their hearts turned to the two men they loved, gone on now.

A dozen young girls dressed in the blue-grey dress of Avalon filed out to surround the bodies. They sang, and the hearts in the cavern swelled with joy, the loving touch of the girls' hearts reached through the crowd encompassing all, absorbing pain and birthing hope. Now was the time to let Consider and Squire go, departing earth armed with the joy that they had made. Their pain had gone. It would become a shade now, a shade that would stay on earth to haunt those left behind. Their joy, they would take that with them, it was their reward. Kahtar's heart swelled with that thought and he sang too, tears running down his face. Forcing his focus on the joy of warriors moving on, as so many warriors he had known over his existence had done. They all went on eventually. Everyone did, except him—he alone was trapped here, forever repeating again and again. It was his fate, his life, his legacy. Every being in the cave would die and take their joy with them, except him.

It came to Kahtar then, while the voices of Cultuelle Khristos were raised in joy, with the touch of so many hearts pressed against his own. Revealing itself in a split second, a moment of crystal clear clarity descended and he understood. Loose ends came together making sense. Images flashed through his mind, while joyful singing echoed through the great cavern, but he no longer participated or heard it.

Glancing at Honor Monroe, he remembered the warrior shot through the chest, it had been the day Kahtar had stopped Beth White. His mind flashed to Brenda Blake, killed while she sat in Beth's yellow convertible in the driveway of her home, her body dumped in the lake. The young boy from University, Douglas Jeffries, slumped over the wheel of his cream colored convertible, his corn silk hair hanging over his face. Driving down the highway in the evening the slight boy surely could have been mistaken for Beth. Consider Drake and Squire Tupper had been shot to death moments after Beth White drove past. The connection seemed so clear. How had he missed it? Someone was hunting Beth White.

CHAPTER
TWELVE

THERE WAS NO moon, but light from gas lamps shone faintly through the dark of Pearl Street. An Old Guard left Kahtar in the thin woods behind Beth's shop, still clad in his white funeral tunic with his weapons dangling from their sheaths. To his left, a black SUV had been parked where Pearl Street dead-ended. Faint light reflected off the shiny paint like moonlight on water. The front bumper rested carelessly against the guardrail. The tires were the same tread that had been left in the dirt off the roadway where Honor had been shot.

One hand went automatically to the hilt of a blade and then Kahtar stepped deeper inside the trees to obscure the bright white of his clothing, his mind racing. Whoever wanted Beth had found her. For a moment he considered that the problem of Beth White would be solved tonight if he did nothing, but judging by the fate of Brenda Blake and Douglas Jeffries, she was in mortal danger. Kahtar moved then, a silent white streak across the back yard, sliding around the edges of flowering snowball bushes, thick with huge clusters of the unscented white blooms. The smell of fresh cut grass seemed to grow stronger with each footfall.

Ghosting around the corner of the house, he scanned inside, sensing unfamiliar scans moving towards him. Warriors! Strange

Warriors of ilu were who had been hunting Beth? These scans were not of his clan.

Clarity flashed again. The image of Consider Drake sitting in the middle of a highway, and Squire's comment, "… I see what you mean, Squire. It's almost like they step precisely the same distance with each footfall. Odd." Who besides Warriors of ilu were trained to such exacting precision? How had he missed it?

The strange scans neared and Kahtar ducked down, crouching against the stone foundation of the house, closing his eyes and forcing his own scan over himself. It was disorienting, it felt like a stroke, as though the left and right side of his brain had swapped places. Shoving his cloaked scan forward, towards Beth, felt like running without breathing. His scan moved slowly now, impervious to detection. Grabbing the bottom of the porch railing, he pulled himself up and over, landing silent and moving towards the front door.

Kahtar could sense three warriors inside the shop, and they all had guns. Two of the men stood near the front door, weapons at the ready. The third approached Beth with his gun held loosely, pointing at the floor. Kahtar could sense that he was a burly, muscular man, short, but with shoulders like a gladiator and arms like a gorilla, strong. His voice carried the thick brogue of the Germanic language spoken in Lowland Scotland, his words clear as they drifted through the narrow window above the front door.

"Elusive ya are, Beth. Were ya not expectin' to see me agin? Or Doric?"

One of the henchmen near the door grunted, whether it was a greeting or acknowledgement of his name Kahtar couldn't tell.

Beth sounded angry. "How dare you just walk into my house! Why did you come here, Berwick?"

With his knife, Kahtar began to work the lock on the door, listening.

"Yer my declared. I tole ya that."

"And do you remember what I told you?"

"Ya doan understand. I—we need ya to build our Arc."

Kahtar's stomach clenched as he worked his razor sharp knife against the metal of the deadbolt.

"You need me to build a—Berwick! Why do you have a gun?"

Only millennia of experience kept Kahtar from breaking the door down.

"Ta protect ya."

"To protect me from what?"

The lock clicked open and before the warrior in the entryway could turn towards the sound, Kahtar silenced him forever. Lowering him quietly to the floor, Kahtar moved into the first room. Every window and flat surface held faux candles casting faint circles of battery operated light. Standing in the main room, the squat warrior named Doric was picking through barrels, lifting colored cubes to sniff. Examining a pale blue square, he took a small bite out of it before Kahtar reached him. Then Kahtar's hands slid under Doric's arms to wrap behind his head, with a quick jerk Kahtar shoved the man's head forward, the snap of his neck barely audible.

Oblivious to the drama in the shadows, Beth shouted at Berwick. "You come here with a gun and bodyguards to protect me? You're the only thing I need protection from!"

Berwick's brogue grew thicker as he argued with her. "Dis village issa clan, yer'na safe 'ere amongst such Cove'nt Keh'pers. I kin offer ya an Arc."

Beth turned her back on Berwick, reaching for something on the shelf behind her. Kahtar glided to Berwick's side, silent in suede bottom boots. He reached for Berwick's gun at the exact moment Beth turned with her cell phone in her hand and gasped. Instantly alert, Berwick jerked the gun up and attempted to turn, momentarily leveling the weapon straight at Beth. Kahtar reacted without a single rational thought. Foolishly he put his left hand over the muzzle of the weapon, attempting to jerk it away at the exact instant that Berwick fired. The bullet burned right through the palm of his hand and blew an exit wound out the back as large as most men's fists.

Beth screamed, but Kahtar focused, knocking his head against Berwick's, hard. Kahtar's right arm slid under Berwick's, grabbing his head Kahtar twisted, straining to break the man's neck. Kahtar's left arm hung useless at his side, momentarily numb even from pain. Berwick was strong, he resisted, struggling to break the grasp with his right hand, his left hand swung the gun. Beth jumped instantly into the fray, both hands locked around Berwick's left arm she managed to pull the gun point blank against her own chest. If the man had ever wanted to kill her, he would have surely done so then. Kahtar used a knee, momentarily lifting the man off the ground as his knee slammed into the man's groin area.

Like a machine Berwick kept to his feet, Beth tugged with all of her weight on his left arm. Berwick shoved her to the floor so hard that she hit the ground with an audible thump and slid several feet. His gun hand free, Berwick fired and a bullet went through the inside sole of Kahtar's boot and into the floorboards. The flash burn seared the inside of his left foot, but the bullet went shy of any real damage. Kahtar braced for a second shot, but Beth prevented it.

Back on her feet with her zebra print cell phone clutched in one hand she knocked it against Berwick's elbow, smacking his ulnar nerve so hard that the man grunted even though his neck was bent almost to the breaking point. The second bullet missed both Beth and Kahtar, splintering the hardwood floor. While Berwick's left hand loosened reflexively from the assault to his funny bone, Beth grabbed hold of the gun and jerked, simultaneously lifting her left leg and jamming the long heel of her shoe against Berwick's knee with one hard kick. The gun dropped and a smile flickered briefly on Kahtar's mouth, vanishing completely when Berwick hit Beth with an upper cuff, and the sound of her teeth slamming together mingled with the sound of the gun sliding across the floor. Back on the floor Beth scrabbled backwards, grabbing something off the floor. Propelling herself away from both men, Kahtar sensed her clutching the cell phone again. With the gun no longer a threat, he now had to contend with both Berwick's hands struggling to break his grip. Again kneeing the man in the groin, Kahtar wrapped his right leg around Berwick's and used his greater height to his advantage.

"Don't call 911, please, Beth, I need you to trust me." Kahtar warned as he twisted Berwick's neck brutally.

The wide blue eyes stared at him as she slid a finger over the screen, bringing it to life anyway. Keeping his voice calm and conversational, while he fought to kill a man in front of her, he said, "Beth? That call will go to county before any real help can come. I can never explain what happened here. Please, do not make that call."

With one of his own massive arms wrapped around the Scot, his other hand hung limply at his side, blood dripping down his beautiful snowy white clothes. Beth's eyes were wide as she took in his clothes, the swords hanging at his sides. They flashed to the heap that was Doric in the shadows at the far end of the long room. Then her eyes lighted on Berwick's face. Even in the dim light it was a dark shade of purple and she shuddered.

"Oh please, don't hurt him. You're killing him."

"Yes." Kahthar's comment was calm, unemotional.

Beth's reaction was without doubt, very emotional. Lurching across the floor she nabbed the odd wooden gun and pointed it towards both Kahtar and Berwick. Loosening his hold, Kahtar moved, Beth's finger trembled against the hairpin trigger. In tandem the two warriors tried to move out of her line of fire, briefly united. Senselessly the gun followed them, certain to cut right through Berwick and at least halfway through Kahtar if she fired.

"He has no gun now. Don't you dare kill him! Police don't kill when there is a choice!"

"Stop it, Beth. There is no choice! He killed two of my men today!" Struggling too late to reclaim his hold on Berwick. The smaller man brought a short heavy leg up, stomping on the bullet wound in Kahtar's foot. The giant warrior chief found himself instantly on one knee, right in front of Beth. The shaking gun with the hair trigger, pointed right at his chest. Berwick rounded the counter and crashed through shelves and barrels, racing towards the far side of the house and up stairs.

Kahtar would have followed immediately—except Beth's hand fell limp into her lap, a finger still on the trigger. The barrel now pointed right into her own thigh. The thought of the damage that could be wrought to that leg made Kahtar risk reaching with his intact hand to move the barrel, and he lifted Beth's finger off the trigger. The weapon slid harmlessly to rest between her legs.

Kahtar reached over her head, to a display of brightly colored silk scarves, and grabbed a handful. Moving to the edge of the counter on his knees, he used the scarves to gather bits of the bloody mess that had once been part of his hand. Scooping gore from the polished floorboards he tried not to get bits of wood splinters with it. Then sitting on his heels he pressed the mess against the back of his left hand and tied the scarves tightly around it all. Blood oozed through immediately, but he turned his attention to Beth who, despite her shaking hands, had managed to snag her cell phone and was again trying to dial 9-1-1. With his good, but bloody hand, Kahtar nabbed it and tossed the phone. It bounced across the floorboards.

Beth's look was far more angry than fearful, and he stated calmly, "I told you not to call."

"You're hurt, and Berwick will get away."

"Berwick didn't leave. He's on the second floor. He needs you too much to leave."

The expression on her face was one of confusion and disbelief.

Using his good hand Kahtar grabbed one of her trembling hands and hauled her to her feet. He focused on covering Beth with his own inverted scan. It hurt. His head pounded, but at least she had disappeared momentarily from Berwick's mental radar. Leaning, he picked up the gun with the dangerous hair trigger.

"I can't let him leave here alive. He's too dangerous."

"Oh no, oh no, you're mob, aren't you?"

Unable to help it, a laugh escaped, just one short bark. Beth glared; her blue eyes confused and angry.

"I'm not a mobster."

"You're something like that. An assassin? I see what you did to Doric…." Her voice broke, her eyes darted to the shadows at the far end of the room where Doric's feet were visible beside a barrel.

"I belong to a cult. A clan."

"You sound like Berwick. You're freaking me out."

"Because you know I'm telling you the truth?"

Beth crossed her arms tightly over her flat chest, tucking her hands under her arms, the knowing eyes fearful. Kahtar sighed.

"I need you to do something for me, and I want your word that you won't leave this house or call anyone, especially not 911."

"I'm afraid to trust you."

Appreciating the candid reply, he gave her one of his own.

"You have good instincts, Beth, but you're going to need to trust me starting right now. I give you my word I won't lie to you again. Not ever."

Knowing eyes darted back and forth, studying his expression.

Tugging one of her hands loose, he knew he was taking away her life almost as coldly as Berwick wanted to. He pressed her palm flat against his chest, for the first time ever allowing his heart to respond to hers. Relief flooded through him. This was an action he hadn't even allowed himself to imagine. Beth's heart moved against his and a warm awareness of her slid right through his body. He closed his eyes and bit back a groan. It felt better than he could have ever imagined. No heart had ever touched his entire being. The pain from his injuries vanished. There was only Beth's heart and his, the heat of a warm glow moving through his entire body. Covenant Keeper to Covenant Keeper.

Spring rain, fresh air, sanctuary. I could love her.

Beth leaned towards him and put her head against her hand resting right on his chest. She whispered, "It's not the house. It was never the house. It's this. It's you. I thought this feeling was the house."

"Did you? No wonder you wouldn't leave it." He wanted to hold her there, to believe she had come for him. "It's not just me. There are many of us here, people like you and me. Right now we need your help as much as you need ours."

Beth lifted her head up, but for several seconds she kept her hand pressed against his chest, finally moving it almost reluctantly. It hurt him when she moved it, and Kahtar wondered if it hurt her too.

"I need you to go upstairs now, into the attic. Be quiet and lay flat on the floor, under the west window. If anyone comes up without identifying themselves—shoot them."

In the darkness he positioned Berwick's gun properly in her hand. "There are only three shots left, so don't miss."

Instead of listening, Beth moved closer. The touch of her heart pressed against his stronger, trusting, curious, welcoming the response he gave her. The top of her head bumped into his chin and he could smell the citrus scent of her shampoo. The urge to kiss her forehead was strong, as though she were one of his clan. She was as good as, now that he'd taken away her choices. Bending forward, he allowed his lips to brush her hair when he spoke.

"Hurry."

"Chief Costas, I can't shoot someone."

"My name is Kahtar Constantine…if Berwick takes you, Beth, every day you live you will wish you had."

"I can't see anything in the dark." Her words shook. She believed him.

Kahtar turned her towards a staircase and pushed gently. "You can feel your way in the dark. Go as fast as you can, but move quietly. Berwick is in that room with all the candles, on the second floor. Don't let him hear you pass." Beth didn't ask him how he knew that. By the time she made it up a flight of steps, Kahtar could sense the Scot already assembling weapons from tools he'd found.

Once they engaged, Kahtar wouldn't be able to hold his scan over Beth, but with luck the heavy oaken beam beneath the attic window would hide her presence from Berwick's weak scan.

CHAPTER
THIRTEEN

UNFAMILIAR WITH THE back staircase, Beth ran fingertips over the wall to orient herself, and she tried to move quietly up the stairs. Her heart thundered with fear passing the second floor, knowing Berwick hid there, and she rushed upwards unable to imagine shooting a human being, even him. Kahtar's words echoed in her mind, *"If Berwick takes you, Beth, every day you live you will wish you had."* Goosebumps rose on her flesh though it was a humid, muggy night and Kahtar's cryptic words about clans and cults suddenly bothered her much more than when she stood in his capable presence. He'd been telling the truth.

Beth reached the third floor, her bedroom was just down the hall and in her purse was the other new cell phone she'd bought. It would only take a minute to grab it. Pausing in the dark hall she listened intently. Years of listening to music far too loud had left a persistent hum in her ears. She couldn't be sure if it was distant shadows of old songs in her ears or the movement of Berwick. Her fingers gripped the gun but she knew it was useless in her hands. She didn't have what it took to pull the trigger, but that cell phone could link her to the saner world outside.

That new phone tucked inside her purse, hanging on a chair in her bedroom, seemed a talisman against clans, and cults, and creepy stalkers. It could be a lifeline to policemen who didn't change their names in the night, and never wore swords. She raced down the twisting hallway into her bedroom and dug it out. She almost turned it on before thinking better of it. It would make noise, cast a glow. Beth ducked low, hurrying past a window where the night peered in.

Trying to listen for movement, she skittered down the hall towards the attic steps. She knew Berwick had found her a split second before he thundered out of the shadows and knocked the cell phone to the floor. He grabbed her and hoisted her up like a child, tossing six feet of grown woman over his shoulder. In panic she did shoot the gun. All three bullets dislodged blindly into the dark hall. Then she heard a grunt and sensed the faint touch of Kahtar's heart before he fell. She'd shot Kahtar.

Berwick thundered down the black hallway like a bull, and Beth screamed at the top of her lungs, smacking him in the head with the empty gun and kicking him, focusing on using the sharp heels of her shoes. He hit her, hard. She'd never known until then that seeing stars could be a literal thing. Beth went limp, and Berwick raced into her bedroom. In seconds she knew he was planning to go out the window onto the fire escape.

She waited until he had one short leg out the window before she did something her mother had once told her could stop any man. Reaching into his trousers she bravely fished down nether regions, grabbed a handful and twisted, hoping she'd gripped the right part. Simultaneously she bit his nose, hard, ignoring the horror of flesh and blood in her mouth. Berwick dropped hard, his crotch ramming against the window sill and Beth felt bones in her hand break. Then he dropped her, and she fell onto the hardwood floor, her head slamming against it so hard she saw stars again. Scrambling to her feet she tore the iron curtain rod down and hit him as hard as she could, whacking and kicking until he toppled outside the window onto the fire escape. She slammed the window down and locked it, knowing that the glass wouldn't stop him for long. She raced back into the hallway.

"Come here!" Kahtar's voice a groan. She obediently headed for it in the darkness, almost passing him, but he grabbed her foot and yanked her straight to the floor. She didn't realize she was crying and gagging until he put a huge hand over her mouth.

"Silence!" he demanded, and she fought vomit rising. It was no use. She had what might be a part of Berwick's nose in her mouth and the vomit came. Kahtar let her go and she retched onto the floor.

"Stupid girl!" Ignoring his own bid for quiet, he shouted at her. "He sensed the phone! I couldn't cover the stupid phone! Don't you EVER disobey a Warrior Chief! Never!"

Beth had no idea how Berwick had sensed a phone, but Kahtar didn't have to tell her that he was referring to himself when he said Warrior Chief. The anger in his voice hurt her. It dug right into her heart, pushing away every nuance of joy he'd put there earlier.

"Fool!" he continued to rant, but his voice sounded weaker, "and don't you dare call 911." Then he let go of her ankle and slumped over.

Beth reached to touch him in the dark, trying to find his injury, her hand slid over his chest, and she couldn't even sense the newfound touch of his heart in hers. Fear bit through her, terror that he was dead. Her fingers found dampness, blood. She'd shot him in the stomach, and she had no idea what to do about it. His shirt was a heavy quilted material and instinctively she pressed on the wound, but more blood seemed to ooze through, hot and thick between her fingers. Kahtar's mouth was by her cheek as she leaned over him, and she felt his breath on it.

Thank you, thank you, Jesus! Tell me what to do!

Then she felt around in the hall, it took several long minutes to locate the cell phone, during which the terror of Berwick possibly crashing back in almost drove her to panic. *"Don't you dare call 911"* echoed into her mind as soon as she ran her fingers over the screen, bringing it to life. She dialed 411 instead, forcing her voice to remain calm.

"Hello? Can I get the number for the Willowyth Police Department? No, it's not an emergency."

BETH'S EYES ADJUSTED and she recognized him when the bad actor, with the alternative hairstyle, showed up. He raced down the hallway and knelt in front of Kahtar.

"Hey, Beth," he greeted her like an old friend. "Ooch, he's not good but he'll be all right. Move your hands, I've got it."

The man's hands pushed hers out of the way. Terrified of what would happen when she moved them, she obeyed, her lips moving in a silent prayer. *How did he get here so fast? It's only been seconds since I called!*

"Do me a favor, Beth? Go down in the basement for a few minutes."

"What?" *Go down in the basement?* "Why?"

"Please, Beth? I need to get some help with this. He's lost a lot of blood."

"I know what you are. I know he's Kahtar, he's the Warrior Chief…."

"Do you?" The voice sounded cheerful, "Well, I'm Honor Monroe, Beth. If you know all that you ought to know that an Old Guard can't help me transport him with you here. So if you'd head down to the basement—that would be a big help."

THE FOOTSTEPS ON the basement steps scared Beth, the weight sounded like Berwick's. She'd been sitting on top of the brand new, never used, washing machine for hours now, listening to the police walk back and forth upstairs. Not a single one of them had spoken to her when she'd passed them to come down here. She wondered if they realized it had been her stupidity that had hurt Kahtar.

Then there he was, trotting down the steps with a scowl on his face, dressed in his police uniform, and Beth sat staring, wondering if she had somehow hallucinated the entire night. Kahtar didn't say anything as he crossed the basement, but when he reached her, he put one finger under her chin and closed her mouth for her. She glanced down. He'd used his left hand and there was a huge ugly scar on the back of it—bigger than her entire palm.

"Let me see your hand," he demanded.

Beth automatically put her left hand out.

"The other one," he spoke patiently, like he was speaking to a slow child.

Fearfully Beth offered her right hand, she didn't know how many bones were broken, Berwick was a heavy man, and she was pretty sure she was going to need surgery because all four fingers were useless and it hurt beyond description.

"This will hurt." Kahtar told her without pity, and then he used both his huge paws to encase her hand and she screamed. Tears filled her eyes as he forced the hand flat mumbling something and holding on tight, while she struggled to dislodge herself.

"It would hurt less if you wouldn't fight, Beth."

Finally surrendering, silently plotting eventual reprisal, she stopped trying to escape. The pain was magnificent and she squeezed her eyes shut while it burned. Pain seared through her in waves, and tears ran down her cheeks. After a moment she became aware of the sound of Kahtar's voice, praying in a language she'd never heard before. She peeked at him and his eyes were closed, when he finally dropped her hand he told her, "There is nothing to be done for the pain, but it will fade soon. You can use it now."

In disbelief Beth stared at her hand, though swollen it looked almost normal. Tentatively she bent a finger, then another, then all four, repeating the motion several times. When she looked up at Kahtar he again reached his left hand up and used a finger to close her mouth. Then he grabbed an old wooden chair and throwing a big leg over it, he sat on it backwards, facing her.

"I'm tired. I lost quite a bit of blood. I suppose I can't give you too much grief. You got me on a technicality with 411. Normally we don't use any means of technology that could risk our exposure—but there's really nothing normal about this situation we find ourselves in with you. I understand you didn't know how to get help otherwise, but

Honor was already on his way. Don't look for ways around my orders again, Beth, you risk the entire clan when you disobey me."

Beth's mind crowded with questions. *What, how, why, when?* Then she thought to make sure her mouth was shut properly, it was, mostly. She swallowed.

"I'm sorry I shot you."

"You should be sorry for a lot more than that. Why did you go for that stupid phone in the first place?" Without giving her a chance to answer he continued. "The entire clan is in danger with Berwick on the loose! He killed two of my best men yesterday! It was Berwick who killed that boy at University."

Beth gasped, she'd read about it in the newspaper, but it said he'd fallen in the locker room, a freak accident.

Kahtar sized her up a couple of moments and added, in a gentler voice, "Berwick killed Brenda, Beth."

For several seconds she didn't understand. "He killed Brenda? My Brenda?"

Kahtar nodded, his fierce eyes looked sad, and tired.

"I don't understand. Berwick went to Carolina after Brenda? Why?"

Kahtar glanced briefly at the floor and she suddenly understood.

"You lied to me? Brenda never went to Carolina? She never ran off with one of your officers?"

"No, Beth, Berwick killed her the day she borrowed your car, threw her body in the lake. We found her washed up on shore."

Pain lit through Beth's heart, closing her throat, and tears welled up in her eyes again. *God, no, please? No.* Thoughts of Brenda filled her mind, her lectures on how to run and not run the business, her guileless lack of sophistication, her daughters. *No! No, please, her daughters!*

"I'm sorry, Beth. I assume Berwick had been hunting for you, and when he found her...."

"But, why'd he hurt her or the boy?" Tears ran down her face and she didn't bother to wipe them away. Douglas Jeffries had been planning to be a missionary. She didn't know him, but he had been engaged to a girl from her parent's church.

Kahtar looked reluctant to explain but he said, "Berwick is not the kind of man who takes disappointment well. Brenda got in his way when he wanted you. Douglas Jeffries drove a cream-colored convertible. He was tall and thin and had long blonde hair…."

Beth covered her face with her hands and started to sob.

THE FRIENDLY WARRIOR, Honor Monroe, was her guard, though no one had actually told Beth that. It was obvious though. He simply sat on the edge of her bed, playing with her old iPod, one bud in an ear and his eyebrows moving further and further up his forehead as he listened to her songs. Beth sat at her desk. Honor had hung the curtain rod, slightly bent, and the blue sheers brushed the floor. The window over the fire escape was still closed and locked. She wanted to shut every window in the big house just to be safe, but Honor had dramatically told her he would rather face Berwick than heat stroke. A faint breeze wafted in through the open window on the far side of the room. Beth kept an eye on it, though she knew logically that short, squat Berwick certainly couldn't scale the house—at least not in broad daylight.

They'd taken her laptop off of her, and both cell phones, leaving only the old iPod Shuffle. If Honor found those tunes shocking, it was a good thing he wasn't listening to her newer stuff. Rearranging nail polish and make-up on her desk, Beth kept darting glances at Honor in the nearby mirror. He looked normal. Cute.

"You would kill Berwick if he showed up?"

Honor glanced up at her, looking surprised at the question, blue eyes ringed with dark lashes met hers in the mirror.

"Of course."

"Without a trial? You'd just kill him?"

"Beth, he killed four people in town and shot me."

"I shot Kahtar."

The brows shot up even further.

"Did you?" Then he chuckled. He had an awesome smile, kinda like her Dad's. "I'd assumed Berwick did it."

"It's not funny. I didn't mean to."

"No, of course not." The smile vanished.

"And you just believe me?"

"Shouldn't I?"

She turned from the mirror to face him in person. He leaned forward slightly, as though quite interested in what she had to say.

"I don't lie, but how do you know that? How do you know, for sure, that Berwick doesn't have…extenuating circumstances? Or for that matter that he committed all those murders?"

"We know." His answer was supremely confident and he stuffed a bud back in his ear. The pretty eyes turned back to her iPod.

"Even if you know," Beth interrupted him, "Who made you judge, jury, and executioner?"

Honor's blue eyes were very sincere and serious when he replied, simply, "ilu—God."

"So you do believe in God?"

The blue eyes went round with surprise.

"Beth? Of course, we're Covenant Keepers. Our clan is Christian even, just like you."

"How do you know what I am?"

Honor smiled broadly.

"I've followed you to that Catholic Church enough the last weeks. You go on Wednesday nights too. And you believe in God don't you?"

"Yes, but I don't kill people."

Honor tugged the earbud from his ear. "You believe in penance and justice, don't you?"

"Thou shalt not kill. I believe in that."

His blue eyes met hers. His were dark now. He looked agitated.

"You cannot claim moral high ground, not when you live a life built on the blood and sins of soldiers who kill for you. Besides, the commandment is Thou Shalt not Murder. There is a difference."

The truth of those words cut through Beth like knives. After a couple quiet minutes, during which Honor Monroe continued to stare at her, she decided not to ask him any more questions. She didn't want to know the answers. As a matter of fact, all she wanted was to get out of this place and never see this house, these men, or Willowyth ever again. Turning her back on him, she picked up a bottle of nail polish and started shaking it.

AS SOON AS Kahtar stepped foot back in the house on Pearl Street, Honor's second voice gave report from another room. *"She stopped talking about it. I thought she'd ask questions, want to understand."*

"It doesn't matter, Honor. She'll know everything soon enough, she's part of our clan now."

"I'm glad. Call me selfish, but I'm glad."

"You're very selfish." But so am I. Mostly, he thought.

A pile of disabled laptops and cell phones sat on the counter in the main room, right where Kahtar had grabbed the muzzle of the gun and taken his first bullet of the night. Beth White's contact with the outside world was now over. Scanning to sense her location, Kahtar moved down a hall. His regulation police shoes made a very faint sound on the hardwood floors. He found her in a smaller room, jammed with shelves of cooking implements. Honor stood at her side inexplicably helping stock shelves. Side by side the two were unpacking and arranging tiny sacks of spices. Honor's shelf was covered in neatly arranged rows of tiny bags, color coded, blue orange yellow, blue orange yellow. Beth reached over and messed them up. Honor repaid by rubbing his hand over her neat silky hair, trying to rumple it. They looked like a happy couple. The touch of Beth's heart romped playfully past, and Kahtar ached for it to notice him. What were they doing? And why waste time stocking store shelves? There would be no store. There would be no Beth. Not in this world, not anymore. The desire for her attention soured. This was his fault.

"I need you both to come with me. Beth, you'll want to pack a suitcase."

Turning towards Kahtar, she automatically took a step back, bumping right against Honor Monroe, who wrapped his arms around her and held tight. Beth's eyes went almost automatically to Kahtar's left hand and she opened and shut her newly restored right one. *This must be very strange for her.* Yet why did she snuggle against Honor? That warrior hugged her tightly as though reassuring her and it ticked Kahtar off. Honor healed and was healed the same as he did, Honor was as much oddity as any of them.

Not quite, you're a much bigger oddity, and she senses it even if she doesn't know why. And so does Monroe.

Unable to stand the sight of their embrace Kahtar turned away.

"Hurry up if you want to take any of your things with you. You won't be coming back."

IN THE END, they didn't get Beth out of Sweet Earth as planned. That she might simply refuse to cooperate hadn't occurred to the warriors of a clan where cooperation was paramount. Not until later in the day, when the nearby furniture shop closed, was Kahtar satisfied that they would be safe from the eyes of Seekers. Then he forced Beth out. He carried her bodily and put her into the back of his squad car while she shouted in protest. Shutting the door on her he tucked and adjusted his rumpled uniform, glaring at Honor.

"Thanks for the help, Partner."

"I just can't, Kahtar."

"You're the one who said you're glad she's part of the clan now. This is what it looks like when you force someone into a cult. Did you think she'd be glad?"

"There was no choice anyway. You said Berwick would have forced her into theirs."

"Berwick would have killed her. Beth would have never cooperated with him."

"So there was no choice! They just wanted her because they need a woman to build an Arc! You can't force a woman to do that! We will give her a home, not force her to—"

"What are we doing, Honor? Wouldn't you call this force?" Beth's furious shouts were muffled from inside the police car.

They slid into their seats, and Beth put both her feet on the metal divider and kicked like a two-year old. She had good lower body strength. Kahtar hesitated to leave; concerned she'd attract attention on Main Street. With both warriors ignoring her, Beth screamed in frustration. Honor turned to apologize for what had to be the hundredth time that day.

"I'm sorry, Beth. We don't have a choice."

"Yes you do. There is always a choice!"

When they ignored her truthful comment she shouted. "At least let me bring my laptop! I have work to do!"

"Chief?" When Kahtar didn't comment, Honor opened the car door and hurried back into the shop.

"This is kidnapping!" Spitting the words from behind him, Beth at least quit kicking.

"Yes." Twisting in his seat to look at her, Kahtar wished he hadn't. The angry look of betrayal and distaste flared clearly in those honest eyes. That welcoming heart now tucked down like a beaten puppy, like something sweet and gentle that should never have been harmed.

"I promised to tell you the truth, Beth. Is there anything you want to ask me?"

The knowing eyes glanced at his hand, but when she looked at him she only asked, "When can I have my life back?"

"Never."

Tears slid down her cheeks, but she didn't say anything.

"Will you answer a question for me then? Truthfully?"

One pert nod, but she looked out the window so he knew she was reluctant.

"When you moved here, and started setting up your shop without your permit—without hope of getting a permit…"

"I'd have gotten one."

"No you wouldn't have. Not ever. This entire village is run by my clan. When you came here, didn't we make it clear we wanted you to leave?"

The clear eyes looked into his then, and she nodded.

"This is why we didn't want you, Beth. You don't belong, even though you're one of us. Of course convolutedly that's exactly why you wanted to be here, do you understand that? You wanted to be with your own people."

"I'm not one of you." Again that glance at his left hand, the scar visible as it dangled over the steering wheel. "I don't even know what you are!"

"Same thing you are, a Covenant Keeper. We're direct descendants of those who made a covenant after The Fall of Man, those who survived inside an Arc on Mount Ararat."

"I must be insane. How can any of that be true?" She whispered the words.

"You're not insane because you believe me. You know you aren't, and you know you are one of us."

"I know I'm being treated like a prisoner." Those knowing blue eyes held his, accusing.

"You are now. You should have gone when you could."

"Why can't you let me go now?"

Studying her frightened face, Kahtar wished he'd burned her house down. She'd have left then. She'd have lost interest in the elusive draw she felt towards them. Some part of him had allowed this to happen, had wanted her to stay every bit as much as Honor Monroe had, as all his warriors surely had. Beth's eyes darted back to his hand as he turned it back and forth. It had taken many warriors' prayers for the bones to reform, for the muscle and tissue to reassemble usefully. It had taken a couple hours for the gunshot to his stomach to be repaired, the prayers of Warriors of ilu held great healing. Again he held his hand up in front of her.

"I can't let you go now for several reasons, Beth. For one, you've seen too much."

"Nothing I care to repeat, and who would believe me if I did?"

"There's that, but that is the least of the reasons. You wouldn't be able to stay away now, even if you tried."

"Watch me."

Kahtar smiled faintly at the determination in her voice, but more than anything it made him sad, because he wondered if maybe she could ignore the siren call to go with her own. Perhaps she could deny it, and he sighed. The sound escaped before he could stop it and she pressed the point.

"Please? Let me go. I'll get in my car and leave right now. You can believe me, I don't lie."

"I can't, Beth."

"Why?"

"For the most important reason of all, it's against our laws, and we do not—ever—make exceptions to our laws."

The eyes went back to the window, and she went completely silent as Honor slid in, her laptop zipped neatly into its zebra print bag. The ride to the far side of town was silent.

TURNING ONTO HIS driveway, Kahtar hit the gas. The car shot through the foggy veil that hid his property from the eyes of the world. If Beth noticed the unusual buffeting crosswinds that rocked the car, she made no comment. Hunched in the back seat she didn't even look out the window. After driving right to the front door, Kahtar immediately opened her door to let her out. Looking up at his enormous two-story cabin, she glanced at him.

"This is your house? You're keeping me prisoner at a house?"

"Yes."

Silently she examined the huge cabin. Trying to see from her perspective, he wondered what she had been expecting. There was no way she could know she was his clan's first prisoner. Covenant Keepers didn't take prisoners. Beth's eyes studied the rustic cabin with the log walls and wood shingled roof. They came to rest on the wide wrap-around porch with its homey and comfortable Adirondack chairs and welcoming benches. When Honor told her to go in, Beth turned her back on the house and crossed her arms, refusing.

Going to the trunk, Kahtar tugged Beth's suitcases out. Four suitcases, a garment bag and two small toiletry bags were what she'd considered 'basic necessities'. They were all covered in the same bright turquoise canvas, with her initials hand tooled into the leather handles. This adjustment would not be easy for her. Tugging three of the suitcases into his arms, with the garment bag draped over his shoulder, Kahtar headed for the wide porch steps.

Honor grabbed the rest of the bags and the two men marched up the porch steps. Stubbornly refusing to cooperate, Beth stood at the foot of the stairs, looking at the surrounding woods and fields. The crazed barking of Kahtar's dog approached from the field behind the house. Looking over the neat summer dress that hugged Beth's form, baring thin arms and far too much of her long legs, he warned.

"That's my dog, Wolves, he's not mean but he's an idiot with no manners. He also tends to roll in manure."

Smoothing the yellow fabric of her dress Beth skipped up the stairs in her heels just in time to duck behind the safety of Honor, as Wolves, tongue lolling and mismatched eyes rolling, hurtled up the stairs and against his master.

"Kahtar! Your front room!" Honor Monroe's second voice warned. Pushing the frantically thrilled dog reeking of something dead, off his legs, Kathar turned to see what was wrong with his front room. Beth stood in front of one of the many curtainless windows lining the porch. An expression of horror on her face as she studied the hundreds of old weapons hanging inside. They covered every wall and even the chimney of the stone fireplace, glinting wickedly in the light. Several old torture devices were on display, freestanding about the

room like modern art from a horror museum. Dozens of varieties of harpoons were grouped together and a few stragglers were propped against windows, sharp points inches from her white face.

Beth turned, resolutely, to face the two warriors. Those knowing eyes darted between their faces as she asked, her voice frightened.

"Are you planning on killing me and burying me here?"

Honor's mouth dropped open, his bright blue eyes more horrified than Beth's. Those clear, summer sky eyes of Beth's were on Kahtar's boring for truth. *She believes we brought her here to kill her, but she still believes I would tell her the truth about it.*

"No, Beth—I promise I am not planning to kill you, nor is Honor."

"Torture then? Or brainwash?"

Honor interrupted, both his hands in the air, careful not to touch her, keeping his distance. As straightforward as Beth's questions were, she looked terrified.

"Beth! Of course not, now you're being ridiculous. We're not going to hurt you."

"Not hurt me? You've held me prisoner in my own shop, not allowed me to make a phone call or get on my computer. You kidnap me and bring me to a house loaded with weapons from the pit of despair. We're out here in the middle of nowhere, so no one would hear me scream."

"Beth! Come on! Do I look like I'd hurt a woman?" Honor kept his hands up, looking affronted by the accusation.

Beth stared straight into Kahtar's eyes.

"You look like you'll do whatever it takes to satisfy your agenda, what is your law for a woman who knows too much?"

Honor opened his mouth and then closed it when Kahtar held a hand up to silence him.

"I did not bring you here to kill you."

"But you would, wouldn't you? If I don't adopt your mantra?"

Opening his mouth to answer truthfully, it hit him that the truthful answer wouldn't be pleasant. In all his time he'd never seen an adult Orphan adapt to clan life, if she didn't adapt the clan would have no choice but to send her away. There was a place for those who didn't obey. It took discipline not to look at her outrageous shoes at that moment, to answer calmly.

"What happens depends on you now." That was true, evasive, but true.

"You said you'd tell me the truth." Those knowing eyes watched him, waiting. Honor stood beside Beth in agony, hardly able to bear the truth.

Staring back into those eyes at that moment, with Wolves slinking and whining at his feet, something happened to Kahtar, something new and unexpected and terrifying. He couldn't tell Beth the truth, because he didn't know the answer. For the first time in his existence he didn't know if he could fulfill his duty—not if it ever meant hurting this woman.

Those clear eyes turned away. "Don't trouble yourself, soldier. I understand your silence."

I doubt that, Beth White, because I surely do not.

CHAPTER
FIFTEEN

IT WAS IMPOSSIBLE to enter that cabin. The wicked weapons crowding that room made Beth's legs weak and her stomach churned with fear. They weren't planning on killing her, but they were a cult and there were a lot of them. They had some sort of…she looked at her right hand. It was fine, slightly swollen. They had some sort of abilities. The memory of the hole in Kahtar's hand made her feel even sicker, and she'd never actually seen what her bullet had done to his stomach. *What are they? Oh, my God, please help me, how do I get out of here?* Why hadn't she left?

There had been so many clues that something was wrong with the town, and the way they all acted, it wasn't normal. They had wanted her to leave, and she hadn't. She was an idiot. In all her life she'd never been more frightened. Honor Monroe handed her the old iPod shuffle, and Beth jammed the buds into her ears and turned it on as loud as it would go, sinking blindly into a porch chair, she closed her eyes, but nothing could shut out what she'd seen in that house.

THERE WAS NO doubt that Beth was terrified, and near panicking. Scanning the goose-bumps on her arms and accelerated heart rate convinced Kahtar not to force her into the house. Sitting on the front porch, eyes closed and listening to music, she appeared to be pretending to be elsewhere. *She honestly thought we were going to kill her.* Wolves, waste of fur that he was, seemed to sense her anxiety. His flea bitten hide now stretched right over her fancy shoes. To Kahtar's surprise Beth didn't object, despite the bits of dead minnows stuck to the dog's fur. Honor behaved as attentively as the dog, taking a seat right next to Beth and patting the back of her hand every few seconds.

Kahtar went inside to change into his usual tunic and leggings, grateful to shed the polyester blend of the police uniform. The natural fabrics that he'd worn for centuries felt good against his skin but he briefly hesitated before walking back onto the porch, concerned about upsetting Beth more with the unusual dress. Finally he shoved open the screen door, she'd seen him in his bloodied white funeral gear—it wasn't likely anything else he wore could horrify her more than that.

To Kahtar's surprise, Beth was now holding Honor's hand, eyes still closed and headphones still on, she didn't move as he approached, other than to squeeze tighter onto Honor's proffered hand. Sitting on the porch steps, in the fading light, with a pile of soft cloths Kahtar quietly wiped down one of his swords. When the last vestiges of daylight faded, he lit a lantern and went back to his task. When he felt Beth stir, keeping his eyes on his task as he cleaned dried blood out of a filigree hilt, he said, "The water closet is the first shed past the back corner of the house, you can't miss it. Take the lantern."

There was no need to look up to know her reaction to an outdoor toilet, but he thought allowing her the small freedom might be reassuring. When her heels clicked past him with Wolves following, he shot Honor a look, warning the warrior to keep his seat. As soon as Beth and the lantern faded from view, Honor's scan followed her. It left a dark shadow of pain in its wake as it brushed past him. The kid had no finesse when it came to scanning.

"Stop it, Monroe—give me a break and allow her some privacy. She's not going to run off in the dark, I expect her break for freedom at first light. Go put her luggage in the house."

"In your room?"

"Of course not!"

"It's the only bed."

That was true, Kahtar didn't get overnight guests. He'd have to get her a bed, but in the meantime he motioned with his head to the main room. "The sofa is very comfortable, it's dark now and she won't see the walls."

Honor scanned the walls of the great room with his mind. Kahtar felt the focused sweep over the various swords, pole arms, axes, clubs, and chain weapons. A shadow of the touch reflected painlessly onto him while it raked over the hodgepodge of armament.

"She knows they're in there, Chief. Orphans have shades don't they? Even I don't want to sleep in there."

It was true, unpleasant experiences did tend to stir up shades. Like vultures nipping at the wounded and flapping off so another could take a bite, they could be relentless.

"Just grab a blanket off the couch then, it's going to be a warm night. She can sleep in the hammock down by the pond. You can head back to the Arc. Someone will be coming for the night shift."

"Chief? I'd like to stay on with her if she's going to run. Willet or Briggs would probably tackle her."

Knowing his sardonic look was lost in the darkness Kahtar insisted, "Go home, Monroe, and wash up. Take the morning shift. No one is going to tackle her. When she runs, we're going to let her."

"Chief?"

"Let her run, where's she going to go? She doesn't know how to get out of a veil."

"You don't think she could get hurt?"

"Those heels she wears and Wolves's stench are the only dangers under this veil."

WHEN BETH PUSHED the door open from the water closet, she saw Honor trudging through the backyard weighed down with her luggage. The dog went for him, barking furiously at his bizarre shape.

"Shut it, Wolves! Beth? I know I'm the big strong man, but give me a hand here? I think the strap on this bag is going to guillotine my hand off."

Heading for him, she couldn't stop the sardonic remark, "That's not a big thing for your kind is it? I imagine someone could glue it right back on for you in a minute."

"Not if Wolves eats it first."

Beth laughed, she couldn't help it. For some ridiculous reason she could picture the whole thing. She grabbed her biggest suitcase and pulled the telescoping handle out, setting it on its wheels. An overnight bag fit perfectly on top of it and she pulled a third bag over a shoulder and headed back to the bathhouse.

"I didn't know they did that."

It made Beth laugh again, she admitted, "And I can carry them all when I have to, though it isn't pretty."

Inside the shed Honor lit lanterns on shelves, cleverly placed mirrors reflected the light around the big room. Honor stacked Beth's suitcases on top corner shelves. Pointing to a door he said, "The bathtub is in there, there is hot water, you'll be able to figure it all out. Kahtar just has this thing about toilets inside, the rest of us are more civilized. Um, I'll wait for you outside if you want to take a bath? Then I'll show you where you can sleep."

"I can't sleep in that—"

"No, you don't need to go in the house. It's just a collection, Beth, honestly, Kahtar's hobby—to coin a phrase that usually doesn't apply to Covenant Keepers. Of course he is Warrior Chief, it makes sense he'd be into old weapons."

"None of this makes sense."

"Hey?" Honor stepped right up to her and hugged her close, it felt good. The touch of his heart sweet and honorable, just like his name. She felt safe with him, and her eyes welled with tears.

"Don't be scared. So many of us wanted you to stay right from the start, we want you to be happy with us. We're good people."

He meant it. She could sense the truth in his voice and she hoped that they really were good people. The problem was, good or bad, they weren't her people. They were a cult. How on earth could that possibly be a good thing?

BETWEEN FIGHTING OFF his shade of Golgotha, to repeatedly scanning towards the pond to check Beth, Kahtar couldn't fall asleep. Beth lay in the hammock strung under a huge old weeping willow, huddled beneath a heavy buffalo blanket. Wolves had circled beneath her, fussing, until she'd hauled him up to sleep against her. It shocked him that she could bear to have the foul dog huddled against her, that she'd even touch him with her bare hands. It surprised him even further when she fell right to sleep with an arm draped over that mangy dog. Two of his warriors stood watch in the night, keeping too close to Beth. Kahtar felt fairly confident they just wanted to feel the touch of her romping heart while she slept. There was no other reason they'd spend the night standing at the head and foot of the hammock, his orders had been strict, to let her run if she chose to.

The shade of Golgotha descended, in full, three times that night. By the time Kahtar's feet hit the floor his head was already pounding. Downstairs he found breakfast early, and instead of his usual slop prepared by plebes, the best cook in the clan had sent a big basket of rolls stuffed with cheesy eggs and meat. Kahtar had time for his usual morning run, the daily beating by Old Guard in the back barn and a bath before he finally sensed Beth stir. To Kahtar's surprise, she didn't try to escape.

PINK RAYS OF light shot through the summer sky and reflected the rising sun in the surface of the smooth pond. The green willows a bower as their branches touched the earth around the hammock. Kahtar made his way to the pond, of course Honor Monroe was already there offering Beth breakfast. She stretched under the thick buffalo robe and accepted a flaky pastry from the young warrior. It was as large as her head. Wolves's nose popped out of the top of the blanket to sniff hopefully.

Honor had dressed for the day in the normal fashion of Cultuelle Khristos. Similar to what Kahtar wore, a sleeveless linen tunic and leggings, the undyed fabric a plain cream color. A sword dangled at Honor's waist and Kahtar noticed Beth seemed to purposely keep her smooth curtain of shiny hair angled to block that fact. Even at first light her hair fell neatly into place, and she behaved as though she often slept in a hammock surrounded by Warriors of ilu. Looking over the wisps of fog curling low over the surface of the pond, at the beautiful green fields and trees surrounding her in all directions, she carefully avoided studying the warriors, their clothing or weapons. Kahtar wondered if she noticed the abnormal quiet and the clean air, but she seemed determined to ignore what she didn't want to know. Beth made polite conversation when he approached.

"This is the life."

"It is." If pretending made her comfortable, Kahtar saw no reason to force reality on her. The fact that her hand trembled clutching the roll, made him wonder if she still feared for her life. Wolves's eyes were glued to the breakfast roll, but he rubbed his head against Beth's chest, as though to offer comfort. Stepping closer, the damp grass wetting his suede boots, Kahtar determined he'd find a way to reassure Beth. Then Honor stepped forward and boldly smoothed that already smooth hair. She closed her eyes and leaned into his hand, and Kahtar suddenly wished with all he had that he'd thought to make the gesture. The thought of Beth's cheek against his hand, her heart pressed against his made the words he was going to speak evaporate from his mind.

Beth bit the roll and her eyes widened in surprise. She sat up, the buffalo blanket dropped to her lap revealing the yellow dress she'd slept in, and Wolves rolled right out of the hammock with a thump.

"Is this meat?" Beth's words came out around the mouth full of food, as though afraid to swallow.

"Yes." Honor explained, "But it is clean meat, not like you're used to."

Chewing and forcing down a swallow, she shuddered slightly. "Is this buffalo?"

Kahtar couldn't help it, the chuckle just shot right out. Four warriors stood at her beck and call, she was supposedly their prisoner but it seemed more like they were hers. Beth's brows drew together at the sound, but she ignored him. Honor tucked her blanket neatly around her and gently shoved Wolves away with his boot, reassuring.

"You mean like this buffalo blanket? No, it's venison."

Doubting that fact soothed a vegetarian, Kahtar headed back towards the house. He told himself he'd lived thousands of years without a mate, and that wasn't likely to change. Beth's heart only danced around the periphery of his now. She'd felt the touch of other warriors now, most notably Honor's. Kahtar's had simply been the first. That was all it had ever been. It shouldn't bother him as much as it did, but like it or not he would put his disappointment aside because duty called, and duty always came first.

APPROACHING HIS FRONT porch Kahtar sensed Abigail Adit before she even shot out of a brief tunnel of dark and light, to step inside the veil. Tripping forward and smoothing her ever present olive drab dress, she crunched over the gravel driveway in her orthopedic shoes, her sharp eyes darted, searching.

"She's not here to get acquainted with the clan, Abigail, technically she's a prisoner."

"Oh there's a brilliant plan. We'll surely win her over by locking her up. I didn't come to see about her though."

"This is the first time you've ever come to my house, you expect me to buy that?"

"I don't really care what you buy, Kahtar Constantine. I'm not one of your warriors so watch your tone, I am an Elder. I came because the Old Guard won't show themselves in front of that Orphan until she's part of the clan."

"Did something happen?"

"Well, they found genetic markers for that Berwick you're looking for, at a storage place in the city. There were several tanks of liquid hydrogen stored there."

"Shades of War!"

"The Old Guard got rid of it, blew it up or something dramatic. It's in the news. The Mother said for you to keep that clan away from here. I think she was pretty surprised that warrior got away from you. It was just the one man wasn't it? Oh, and she said for you to keep the Orphan safe too."

Heading up the steps into his house Kahtar pulled his tunic over his head while he muttered to himself. Abigail clomped up the stairs right behind him, following him to the second floor while he peeled off clothing and even when he stood in the middle of his bedroom half naked.

"The Mother is sending emissaries to Scotland, putting out feelers trying to locate that Berwick warrior's clan."

"Oh for the love of all that is…" Yanking off his leggings he stood to face Abigail. "There are some pretty old Arcs in Scotland they could be really big. We know he's trying to start his own Arc. If they need a second Arc, that means they're a lot bigger than us."

"The Mother has a good reason, Kahtar. She thinks Berwick's a rogue warrior, off to start his own clan without permission. Think about it, what clan needs two Arcs?"

Tromping to his armoire Kahtar tossed a clean police uniform onto his bed, pulled open a drawer, and tugged shorts on. The Mother was an intelligent woman. He would never dismiss her thoughts without reflection.

"So The Mother thinks Berwick's own clan might help us track him down?"

Abigail trotted to his side and shook out his shirt, holding it towards him.

"Catching on pretty quickly for a warrior. Think about it a bit harder. Berwick came hunting this Orphan to create an Arc. Joining with her wouldn't be sanctified in most clans, Kahtar."

"That's true." An Orphan of the Inquisition with a dodgy genetic background wouldn't be welcome in most clans. "So The Mother thinks if we find Berwick's clan, they'll send their own warriors to hunt him and he won't be our problem?"

Abigail sniffed, "Precisely. How many Warriors of ilu would stockpile liquid hydrogen? If we can get their help they will surely take care of their own. At any rate maybe you killed all his accomplices the other night."

Pulling on his trousers he eyed Abigail. Quick and clever in her own right, she had absolutely no battlefield sense.

"A Warrior of ilu does not go into battle with his entire legion in the front lines."

"Oh dear. They'll be nearby won't they?"

"Yes, Abigail, near and well hidden, if Berwick has enough warriors to start his own Arc...."

CHAPTER
SIXTEEN

"IT'S LIKE CAMPING. Surely you've been camping before?"

Honor Monroe was definitely both sweet and clueless. Beth wondered what about her pegged her for a camping kind of girl. Honor plopped a third big Adirondack chair next to the hammock, combined with a small wooden table, he seemed to think she now had all the comforts of home.

"What about when it rains?"

Honor stared off in the distance while he considered that.

"Well, surely you could sleep on the porch those nights? Maybe try not to look in the windows?"

A shiver rippled up her spine at the thought of what was inside that house, a chamber of horrors. The place made her remember a horrible movie with a disgusting dungeon scene, and a woman…Beth blinked and forced it from her mind. She never even remembered seeing such a movie.

"Can't you just put me in jail?"

Honor dropped into one of the sturdy chairs, grabbed her hand and yanked her into his lap. It was briefly startling. Then she sensed his intention from the touch of his heart on hers, as innocent as happy laughter. Beth relaxed against him, resting her head on his shoulder, and closing her eyes. The heart thing kept people honest. She really liked it.

"It's like this, Bethy, we don't have jails."

The memory of what Honor had wanted to do to Berwick instead of arrest him made her eyes pop open.

"You have no jails because you take no prisoners. That's not very reassuring."

Honor wrapped both his arms around her and squeezed, kissing her cheek, and holding her there.

"Everyone usually follows the rules, not because they're being forced to, but because they want to. So we don't need jails."

The memory of the woman in the dungeon slipped back into her mind and she shook her head, trying to knock it out.

"So I'm your first prisoner?"

Honor squeezed her tighter and laughed.

"You are! Congratulations, the very first."

In Beth's mind's eye she saw the woman in the dungeon again. She was being dragged by a rope tied around her wrists, it hurt her. It hurt her so much Beth could feel it. It took effort to push it away, it made her mad.

"Being a prisoner's not funny, Honor! And why do I have to be here? Can't you put me someplace with indoor plumbing?"

"Well here's the thing. Our clan lives inside an Arc."

They were all insane, every single one of them.

Honor started to laugh, so hard and long that the laughter jounced into Beth's own body like she was laughing, it felt good. It made the thoughts of that old dungeon movie evaporate.

"The Arc's not a boat, Beth! That's what you were thinking I could see it on your face! You crack me up! Covenant Keepers live in clans, clans live inside Arcs—at least we have since the flood. Yes, by flood I mean biblical flood. ilu showed us how to build them, they are sanctuaries. I'm not going to describe them, because someday when you go inside it, I want you to be surprised. You can trust me on this though you won't want to come out. The thing is, only my clan can go inside it, but maybe someday you'll—join—the clan…."

Every word Honor spoke she could sense truth in, not only did she sense it, but she almost remembered Arcs herself. Clean skies, and clear water, and fresh air, like old dreams—good ones—images darted through her head. Honor's blue eyes were close to hers as he studied her expression. He dipped his head closer and kissed her right on the lips.

"I love you, Beth."

It was absolutely sweet and perfect and he meant it, but she didn't even try to stop what tumbled from her lips.

"I love you too, but I don't want to."

He looked hurt. "Why?"

Beth couldn't help it, she knew her face crumpled like a distraught child's, her throat tightened and tears started to spill.

"Because I want to go home."

Honor wrapped her in his arms tighter, pulling her close against his chest, he whispered, "I'm sorry, Beth. I'm so, so sorry."

BY THAT AFTERNOON, Beth knew she'd never seen a movie like the one she kept remembering. She'd never have watched something so cruel, so evil. Honor tried to get her to go sit on the shady porch and eat lunch and she refused, drooping by the edge of the pond, she waved him away. When he went to lunch without her, she wished he hadn't, because other dark memories that didn't belong to her started to haunt her.

Beth knew she was a big baby to curl up at the side of the pond and cry, but she could feel these dark stories racing through her mind: A mother stood on the edge of a cliff, clutching a baby in her arms, a toddler held onto her skirts screaming as a band of men approached on horseback. The woman threw the baby off the cliff, took the toddler's hand and jumped to their deaths on the rocks below. Beth felt the woman's agony. It ripped through her own heart. She saw the helpless baby drop and her throat ached with pain, and horror churned in her heart.

Maybe it's my hormones, from the stress.

Trying to logic her way out of it didn't help much, because she sensed that every thought from crazy to hormones wasn't true. Curled up and crying by the pond she tried to force the shadowy daydreams away, tried to focus on other thoughts, boring things like all the inventory at the shop that was going to go to waste.

She didn't hear Honor come back until he cried, "Sweet El! Shades! Ah, Bethy, Sweet Bethy! They're just shades. Come here." He sat beside her in the grass and pulled her from the fetal position, straightening her hair and wiping tears off her face.

"Surely you've had shades before, Beth? Dark memories that aren't yours? Bad dreams?"

Beth felt foolish because she couldn't stop shaking. She'd had bad dreams when she was little, but Dad always helped her with them. He used to tell her, 'Change the channel, Bethy, just change the channel.' Shades? From somewhere deep inside her that word was as familiar as Arc or Covenant Keeper.

"When we die, a Covenant Keeper I mean, we leave our pain behind. It stays here on earth, where it was created. Those of us still living can sense that pain, especially when we're upset, tired, or sick. We all endure shades, Beth. They suck."

If she wasn't so worn down she would have laughed at that understatement. It helped though, just knowing what they were. Wolves squished his stinky head between their bodies as Honor continued to hug her, practically decapitating the dog who didn't even try to pull away. The dog's phenomenally gross breath blew against her face, making her eyes water, but Beth scratched his neck. He quivered with joy, pressing against her. The dog helped, but she needed to get away from here, away from shades, Arcs and Covenant Keepers. She needed to be free.

THE BLACK SUV was the exact make and model, right down to the tire tread, as the one that Berwick had brought to Beth's shop. Kahtar stood outside an ocean of corrugated metal and cinderblock sheds on the outskirts of the town of Euclid, and scanned into the storage facility, his mind digging deep. This facility covered three acres. Whatever Berwick kept here might be in any one of the many bays jammed with miscellaneous items. Scanning hard and deep, Kahtar searched for signs of Berwick's genetic markers. An Old Guard grabbed hold of his arm in broad daylight and they flitted so quickly into one of the larger bays, that Kahtar was barely aware of the change in venue.

Metal barrels were stacked in the dim space, and the smell of death greeted them.

"Seekers." An Old Guard supplied, his flickering light revealed three dead bodies slumped together on the floor.

Kahtar and the Old Guard stepped towards the dead men at the same time. Kahtar's gifting of gestalt instantly took in the scene as he moved forward a step. The men appeared to be melting into the floor. Water from recent rains had dampened the concrete floor near the closed garage door. Kahtar didn't even have time to register danger as his foot stepped onto damp concrete.

WELCOME PALMER, AT just twenty-six years old, was considered accomplished even among his own clan. A gifted healer, the young doctor had spent years in medical school, living among Seekers while earning his official degree. The clan had not been supportive when the young healer had left to attend medical school. Yet time and again Welcome's skills had proved invaluable, and today Kahtar had good reason to be thankful for the doctor's stubborn independence.

Sitting on the edge of a comfortable bed in just his drawers, Kahtar's police uniform lay neatly cut to pieces beside him. Welcome's handsome face hovered just inches from Kahtar's big leg as he wiped a clear liquid over horrible white splotches on Kahtar's feet and shins.

"Good thing you got here when you did, Warrior Chief, we would have had to amputate."

This repeat seemed to want to cost him a limb. This made the second time in days he'd almost lost one. Losing both feet and part of his legs would have been difficult to take, though it wouldn't be the first time he'd had to live without them. Still it made him wild to catch up with Berwick. The man fought dirty. An Old Guard flashed into being beside them, Welcome didn't even look up as he worked, his lips silently moving in prayer. The healing itch was agony deep inside bone. Forcing his gaze towards the black eyes of an Old Guard, Kahtar wondered how many times in his existence these men had watched him cry. Countless.

"Abigail contained the spill using a tesseract," was all the man said. Then in a dazzling burst of light the giant vanished.

"No one else was harmed?" Welcome asked, a frown above his green eyes.

"It was just some of the Old Guard and me. They ruined their sandals, but of course it didn't affect their flesh like mine."

Welcome glanced up at him, then around the procedure room. Just the two of them remained, but his friendly voice dropped lower when he commented, conversationally. "Hydrofluoric acid normally would do quite a bit more damage than this."

"What do you mean? This isn't enough for you?" Tears continued to run out the corners of Kahtar's eyes, he didn't bother to wipe them away. It didn't seem likely they'd stop anytime soon.

"I mean at the level of exposure you waded through, it should have been absorbed into your tissues and caused cardiac arrest. It should have killed you."

Looking over the spots of dead white tissue on his feet and legs Kahtar considered that. It hadn't even hurt at first, when he had stepped right into it. The Old Guard had moved lightning quick. Even now looking back he wasn't sure what they had done to clean the dangerous liquid off before they brought him here to

Cobbson Compound. They had moved faster than he could comprehend. Considering the strength of his gifting to perceive what was happening around him, it was the first time that had ever happened. Though it wasn't the first time Old Guard had saved his life. A wave of thankfulness rose up in him and Welcome, sensing the prayer, patted his leg.

"It wasn't just the Old Guard reversing your exposure and cleaning you. Your flesh is different than the rest of ours."

Kahtar's heart skipped a beat, his steely eyes bored right into Welcome's green ones. "What do you mean?"

Welcome shrugged. "Your DNA does not match your composition."

"What are you talking about?" Though Kahtar understood immediately, at least partially, what he didn't understand was how Welcome Palmer sensed something no one else had in the thousands of years he'd existed.

"I mean you have the DNA of the Constantine men, but you certainly don't look Spanish, and I mean that the make-up of your flesh has light attributes to it very similar to Old Guard."

Light attributes like Old Guard? That wasn't something he'd ever known. Of course he'd scanned his own body before, countless times.

"What are you saying, Palmer? That I'm an Old Guard hybrid?"

Welcome chuckled at that idea. "I'm not saying anything of the sort. You're different is all I meant. Did you know?"

Well, Doctor Palmer, I've been repeating for millennia. I die and come back again and again and no matter who my parents are, I always look exactly like this. I suppose you might say I've noticed something was off. Kahtar kept his thoughts to himself and remained silent.

"No one cares if you're different." Welcome added those brilliant green eyes of his so loving.

"No one else has ever said anything like this before." Stunned at Welcome's perception, Kahtar couldn't think of anything else to say.

Welcome laughed again, shaking his head of thick dark hair.

"Chief, when I scan within a Human Being I can see light spectrum within cells. It's my gifting. Covenant Keepers and even some Seekers have colorful lights within their genetic makeup."

"I don't?"

"Oh you most certainly have light—it is just white—like Old Guard."

"You know Honor Monroe thinks he can scan color too." The comment was wry and Welcome was grinning by then. Standing up he leaned too close, the physician didn't respect personal space most of the time. Kahtar fought the urge to lean away from those green eyes.

"I noticed it years ago, assumed it was indicative of a gifting you had, but I've never seen you use it."

"What gifting?"

"I thought it meant you could, you know, shimmer in and out like Old Guard do."

It was Kahtar's turn to laugh then.

"That would be convenient." How many times had he died trapped in a sinking ship or chained in a dungeon? The ability to vanish and reappear where he wanted to be would certainly be useful.

Welcome Palmer's too perfect face was serious.

"Well, have you ever tried?"

CHAPTER
SEVENTEEN

DESPITE WELCOME PALMER'S ridiculous suggestion, Kahtar arrived home as he usually did. The police car shot through the veil and coasted to a stop far from his cabin. The walk in was long on legs where pain exploded deep inside his bones with every step. It wasn't the kind of pain that one could ignore. There were painkillers in his pants pocket and despite the fact that taking them would mean spending a night walking the hills of Golgotha, he wanted only to get to his bed and swallow them. Wolves didn't run to greet him and thinking about why that was quickened his step. Beth White. A bed should have been delivered during the day so she could sleep indoors tonight. The thought of her sleeping nearby somehow made the pain almost bearable.

Behind the house, the sun set low in the evening sky. Fireflies already winked in the thicker patches of woods. Wolves made sounds like a cross between a whimpered greeting and his tail being pulled. As though torn between greeting Kahtar and the pain of leaving Beth's side, the dog didn't move from the long feet of the woman sitting on the stairs, not even for his master.

Traitor.

Long and lean, Beth stretched out over four steps, wearing a spotless white sundress and the ever present heels. What made Kahtar pause mid-stride was the fact that she nestled practically in Honor

Monroe's lap. With his thick legs sprawled on either side of Beth, her head rested on his chest. Honor looked blissfully comfortable, a human pillow, one hand carelessly smoothing silky hair.

Suddenly the pain in Kahtar's bones intensified. Wondering if Honor had spent the entire day playing with Beth's hair, jealously welled up in a flash of heat, and he wanted to shout at the warrior. Beth glanced up at him, seeing his expression she pressed against Honor tighter. Two strong arms wrapped around her and Honor casually kissed the top of her head. Without speaking out loud, Honor's second voice filled Kahtar's mind.

"She hasn't eaten more than a bite all day she's upset about her parents, said that they'll be frantic with worry. Guess she usually calls them a few times a week, and they expected a visit today."

Stumping up the stairs past them, Kahtar wasn't inclined to be charitable to Beth. If she chose not to eat that was her problem, he was rude and abrupt when he informed her.

"Don't worry about your parents. They think you're traveling."

Even in the dusk, those clear eyes searched his face for truth.

"Why would they think that?"

"Because you called them and told them you would be. As a matter of fact, you'll call your Dad every single day. Imitating voices isn't even an unusual gifting for Covenant Keepers."

There was some satisfaction in the fact that Beth pulled away from Honor's arms when she sat up.

"My father will know it isn't me."

Kahtar's rude snort made her stand and glare at him. With those five inch heels, Beth's honest blue eyes were nearly the level of his.

"I don't care who is faking my voice, he'll know! He's my father!"

Even as they argued he felt a sense of relief, she was looking at him. Her heart wasn't touching his but the glow of it danced near.

"Today your father talked to you for two hours Beth. His only worry is that you're going to have halo-halo ice cream without him."

The expression on Beth's face changed to one of utter dejection. In one fluid motion she turned and raced away, headed towards the pond in the dusk, Wolves on her heels.

"Chief!" Honor chided. "Why are you taunting her? Isn't the idea to make her want to be part of our clan?"

Stomping onto the porch Kahtar defended.

"At least she knows they're not upset. Both her parents are perfectly happy, they don't expect to see her for months. They think she's shopping for junk for her shop."

Honor didn't say anything. Quietly turning he headed for the pond. Kahtar fought the urge to forbid it. If Beth bonded with even one member of their clan that would be a good thing, but the memory of her in Honor's arms made him want to smash something.

THE NEXT MORNING arrived with pouring rain. It drenched everything within the veil as thoroughly as it did the world outside. It was simply a cleaner deluge within. The atmospheric conditions outside the bubble stirred the inside of the bubble to replicate exactly the same weather. Walking past the room made up for Beth, there was no need for Kahtar to scan to know she wasn't inside. Every warrior under the veil stood on the porch, there were three of them, and the half dozen plebes in the house kept darting to the front door. There could be no doubt that Beth and her untamed heart were on the porch.

As Kahtar approached, the boys hurried back to their tasks. Kahtar barked at them to leave the woman alone or he'd beat them with his bare hands. Pushing open the screen door, he realized he'd have to make the same threat to his warriors soon. Brigg and Willet both stood at attention, their backs to him, staring towards Beth's sleeping form. A flash of lightning revealed Beth sound asleep in one of the Adirondack chairs, Honor Monroe cradling her in his lap like a sleeping child. Beth was so tall that her head and her long legs were dangling off either end of the chair. It took effort not to storm over and tip them both out of the chair. Kahtar raced down the steps to run his miles in the rain and exorcise his own demons about Beth

White. He had no right to be jealous, no claim on her, even captive her heart was free to go where it chose.

RUNNING THROUGH SUMMER rain, Kahtar's mind focused obsessively on one thing, Beth White's heart. Not since the night he'd killed Berwick's men had Beth's heart even skimmed by Kahtar's. When she slept it frolicked closest, around the perimeter, just out of reach from his. Both Willet and Brigg could surely feel it. Both warriors stood far too close as she slept, nothing else could have made them hover so near to watch Honor and Beth sleep. Outside the veil a manhunt was going on, but none of these warriors even tried to get in on it.

Honor certainly felt Beth's heart. His bright blue eyes looked intoxicated most of the time. The thought that Honor might declare to Beth, might join with her and make her a willing member of their clan, should have been a solution Kahtar could appreciate. It wasn't. Racing through puddles in the storm he tried to shove that thought away, telling himself that he'd had no real intentions towards her. For millennia he had existed to be Warrior Chief, not husband, and he couldn't think of one logical reason it should make him so angry that Beth's heart had gone dark to his.

Three hours later, Kahtar ran back up the porch steps and neither Brigg nor Willet appeared to have moved. Honor was awake, his face nuzzling into Beth's hair as she slept peacefully. Without a word Kahtar rushed into the house, pausing only long enough to threaten the plebes. The only comment he made, before he left for the day, was to growl to Brigg and Willet.

"The woman has a bed to sleep in now, and she certainly doesn't need three warriors to guard her under a veil."

Arriving at the cave in a deluge, it occurred to Kahtar that he'd just paved the way for Honor Monroe. Now the warrior would be alone with Beth all day long, with just plebes to chaperone. Honor might take it as encouragement to court Beth. Kahtar should have meant it that way, instead of simply sending warriors away because they were enjoying Beth's heart when he couldn't. Rain came down in sheets, even inside the Arc it was storming. It seemed to cut through him, synchronized with the pain of Beth and Honor nestled together on the porch that he'd spent months building. Somehow that made it worse.

Suddenly, an Old Guard blinked into existence right in front of him. His shimmering outstretched hand kept Kahtar from walking right into him, but Kahtar lost his footing on the wet ground and slid right down with a muddy splash. Cold water immediately penetrated his trousers and he hurried to stand.

The Old Guard didn't smile or offer assistance, stating only what he'd come to say.

"A vehicle with a bomb inside was left parked outside of 35 Pearl Street." Then in a flash of light Kahtar was standing outside Beth's empty shop in the pouring rain, trying not to fall again.

"IT'S A GOOD thing the neighboring shops are empty." A good-looking green-eyed warrior, a relative of the clan's handsome doctor, made the comment. Half the clan seemed to be made up of Palmer men. Kahtar wondered what Beth would think of them when she saw them, and it annoyed him.

Turning his attention from the man, Kahtar looked around the shop. Everything had been meticulously cleaned in the Orphan's absence, and his mind strayed from the bomb that had been planted outside. He wondered why Cultuelle Khristos hadn't had everything in the shop on Pearl Street taken away. Beth was never going to be allowed to run it. Yet not only had they repaired the damage from Berwick's attack, they'd repaired hundreds of little things. Fresh hand-made wallpaper had been hung, worn woodwork sanded and refinished, and more shelving had been artfully installed. Every box had been unpacked and the items that Beth had hoped to someday give away or sell were neatly on display. It occurred to him that Cultuelle Khristos was wooing Beth, just like Honor Monroe.

"Yeah." Brigg made the comment, peering out a window at the empty rental truck still parked out front. "In this weather a stiff wind might have caused that truck to explode. Thank ilu for Abigail and her vanishing tesseracts. We might have been blown to bits trying to get rid of that bomb if it weren't for her."

The Palmer warrior pointed out the obvious. "I thought this Berwick clan wanted the Orphan. Why would they try to kill her now?"

Kahtar interrupted. "They're playing us, keeping us occupied while they search for her. They knew perfectly well she wouldn't be here." Beth was safe under the veil, but suddenly he wanted to get back there and check on her, make sure.

Several Old Guard shimmered into being inside the shop. Kahtar looked up expectantly, but in an unusual move they clustered around a shelf, ignoring the warriors. When they left in a burst of light, everything on the shelf was gone and a pile of gold coins had been left behind. *Brack tea, the Old Guard just bought all of her brack tea.* Maybe Beth's shop would flourish within the Cultuelle after all. The Palmer warrior groaned and Brigg voiced his objection.

"They took all that tea! I've been dying for another cup of that stuff!"

Now that Kahtar thought about it, he remembered there was a box of brack tea in a drawer at the police station. Heading for the door he noticed Beth's car keys sitting on a shelf filled with jars of honey. On her silver key fob a Celtic cross dangled. Picking them up he ran a thumb over the icon almost identical to the one engraved on the handles of his swords. Most of his existence his clans would never have allowed the symbol, but Cultuelle Khristos embraced it. Beth embraced it too, apparently.

"I'm taking her car," He said to no one in particular.

CHAPTER
EIGHTEEN

IF IT WEREN'T raining and Kahtar could put the roof down, Beth's convertible would have been much more pleasant to drive. As it was his head poked uncomfortably into the canvas roof, still he was happy he'd thought to take it to her. Beth could charge her laptop and iPod with it. The box of brack tea sat on the seat beside him and he drove the vehicle under the veil that hid his home, and right up the long driveway despite the fact that he normally didn't allow motorized vehicles to drive the long miles to his house, polluting the inside of the veil the whole way. This was an exception because maybe Beth would be pleased to see it. Maybe she'd look at him with something other than revulsion for a change. She was nowhere in sight and something was obviously wrong when he pulled up to the house and got out of her car.

Honor paced back and forth in front of the house, oblivious to the rain.

"Where is she?" Kahtar growled. He sensed Beth then, a couple miles to the south, wandering through the woods in the pouring rain with Wolves at her heels.

"You told me to let her go so I did. Can I go get her now?"

"No, but you can follow out of sight, stick close enough that you can scan her, just to be sure she's safe. She's two miles to the south-west. Berwick's clan can't get inside, but we're not going to underestimate them." He knew he was being ridiculous, that Beth would be fine inside the veil even in the rain. Before Honor could take two steps he shouted after him.

"Why did she run?"

"I told her that she needed to go inside the house, you'd insisted. I think she expected I'd force her because she pushed me down the steps and took off. Your weapons really upset her."

Nice, Monroe, make me the bad guy. Though it was the truth, he was the bad guy.

"You let Beth push you down the stairs?"

"Should I have pushed her down to stop her? You said to let her go."

Nodding, Kahtar headed up the stairs. Warrior instincts were strong. However briefly, Honor had at least considered defending himself.

"Follow her. Just don't let her see you."

AT DARK KAHTAR put a lantern on the front porch. Warrior, Willet Evans, showed up, seeming to materialize from thin air near a Rose of Sharon tree across the driveway. They were cousins by blood, but as Welcome Palmer had pointed out, physically there was no sign of the relationship. Willet had Mediterranean good looks like Kahtar's Mother.

"Chief? I'm on watch tonight."

Punctual as they were taught to be, Honor slouched back from the woods, soaking wet and water sloshed over the top of his boots with every step he took. Kahtar told him to go home. In the faint light of the single lantern, water ran from Honor's dark hair and dripped into his blue eyes. He looked wretched.

"I think she's lost, Chief, she's been wandering in circles the entire evening."

"She'll survive and be less likely to run off again."

Speaking from his heart, Honor implored.

"She's found the southern edge of the veil. It's cold and miserable back there. Those heels she wears have made her feet bloody. I don't know why she doesn't take them off. The worst part is she keeps drinking water from puddles."

"For the love of…did you scan it?"

"Yeah. It isn't polluted scientifically speaking, but it isn't clean either. It's teaming with bacteria. Apparently she doesn't know any better. I've been getting as close as I dared, praying for healing. It helped some, but she surely doesn't feel too hot."

Willet Evans, hard edged Warrior of ilu, stood in the streaming rain, his thick eyebrows pulled together in a frown over black eyes.

"She'll learn to quit drinking dirty water then, won't she?" Looking towards Kahtar, he reassured. "I'll intervene if it becomes life threatening."

Dispassionate adherence to duty had once impressed Kahtar. Not in this case, the remark struck him as callous and extreme. Honor appeared to be in some agony himself as he waited for his Warrior Chief's verdict. Kahtar leaned to adjust the lantern perched on the edge of the porch. Picking up two sets of car keys he'd left there, he tossed them to Willet.

"Put those inside the house. I'll guard Beth tonight."

Willet moved quickly to obey, but Honor delayed, walking slowly towards an exit in the bushes, not in the least bit reassured, apparently, by Kahtar's mercy anymore than Willet's.

Am I really that bad? But he knew the answer to that question. Obediently Honor moved towards the bushes until he vanished from inside the veil.

THOUGH THE RAIN had increased throughout the day, Kahtar could sense that the clouds to the north were thinning and it would dissipate in the night. Tomorrow would be sunny and warm. Tonight, however, would be uncomfortable and along the windy perimeter of the veil it would be cold, especially for someone soaking wet. The trees that made up the woods under the veil were much older than what now surrounded the countryside outside. This little slice of what used to be hadn't been harvested for wood, beyond what he'd taken to build his house years ago. Racing past woodpiles and ghosting through the large old trees, he found Beth easily in the dark woods. Scanning for her through the forest, her genetic markers were now almost as familiar as the women in his clan.

Wolves's whimpering and Beth's retching would have drawn him even if he hadn't the ability to scan. While being sick in the middle of the forest, she managed to seem every bit a 21st Century woman. Seated on a stump with her soaking hair held over a shoulder by one hand, her legs neatly crossed and her ever present heels carefully out of the way, she leaned to the side gracefully as her stomach tried to rid the unclean water from her body.

Sensing the bacteria multiplying quickly towards agony, it surprised Kahtar when Beth forced herself to her feet and turned resolutely towards the cold wind that signaled the edge of a veil. Despite the dark, rainy night, she was visible with her light hair and white summer dress. The force of terminal velocity blew her hair back, drying it, and pressed the dress against her body. Fighting against the force of the wind Beth struggled to move forward. The movement as she approached the edge seemed curious, but before Kahtar could decide why, she staggered forward another step. The full force of the veil threw her back and he rushed forward, catching her before she landed flat on her back.

"Honor?" Beth reached to touch his face in the dark, running an icy hand up his cheek and over his cropped hair. Recognizing him, she pushed lamely as he lifted her against his chest.

"Don't be picky. You need help. You're sick." Pressing a hand against her stomach he could sense the turmoil inside and prayed silently, immediately the bacteria began to die under his skilled hand. Beth stopped struggling and leaned her head against him with a groan. The rain had stopped, but it still dripped from trees and Kahtar moved quickly, doing his best to keep her dry, dodging between trees as Beth shivered with cold and pain.

"Don't you know better than to drink standing water?" Sensing the presence of parasites mingling with the germs made him angry. How could she be so foolish?

"Wait!" Moaning she tried to look around, craning her head in the dark. "The wolf dog."

"Wolves?" Kahtar glanced back. Wolves was joyously rolling around on the ground in Beth's sick. "He's busy, he'll follow when he likes."

"We're near the road." She whispered. "He's not very smart. He'll run in the road."

"He can't get there from here." For some reason he whispered that back to her. After that she didn't talk, but twice he had to let her slide to the ground until her dry heaves passed.

When they reached the porch, Beth struggled free, walked a few steps and laid down right on the floor of the wooden porch. Kahtar stood there a moment, considered dragging her upstairs and then he went inside by himself. Willet sat on the sofa in the dark, sipping a cup of brack tea. The scent made Kahtar's mouth water. He hadn't had a sip of it in centuries.

"Make yourself at home, Cousin," he groused.

"Didn't think you'd mind. Do you want me to take guard now?"

"No. I'll take care of her."

Grabbing a thick blanket off a sofa Kahtar returned to the porch. Tossing the blanket next to Beth, he lay down on it in his uniform. Uncomfortably soaked through, his feet slid around inside his water filled shoes. Poor Beth looked miserable, curled into her gurgling gut she failed to bite back groans of pain. Trying to be gentle Kahtar pulled her onto his thick, warm blanket and wrapped the edge over them. One hand slid to her belly, and he whispered his healing chant out loud, in The Ancient Tongue. Beth quieted next to him and he knew she was listening to the words, distracted from her slowly receding pain. They were all born with the innate ability to understand the language of their ancestors, though Beth probably hadn't heard it outside her dreamlike shades.

The night air warmed beneath the blanket and with Beth's body heat, Kahtar grew comfortable and tired. When her breathing became even he stopped praying. For several moments he lay still. Beth's heart was tucked down like a beaten dog again, held far from his, but as he lay beside her, he was content and at peace. It felt right. His right arm draped over her and he leaned his face into her damp hair and breathed of her like Honor so often did. A sigh escaped him and Beth nestled tighter against him. Instinct made him pull her close, to feel her against his chest and a thrill shot through him at the contact. Never, in all his time, had he held a woman like this, with intention. He could love her. In fact, he did.

"Honor?" Beth murmured low.

The moment soured, and Kahtar started to pull away, but as his hand slid away, Beth grabbed it and pulled it tighter around her.

"Stay." She whispered, barely audible.

Desperate enough for contact with this woman, whose heart beckoned even when it hid, he did as she asked. As he fell asleep with a sigh of absolute contentment, Kahtar succumbed and whispered into her neck. "Sweet Beth."

"Mmmm, you." He heard as he slipped away.

DESPITE HIS WET clothes, he slept comfortably. Kahtar dreamed about Beth and sank deeper and deeper into a blissful oblivion. Of course it didn't last, always his sins caught up with him. There was no escape from the two thousand year old shade. There was no escape from the hills of Golgotha. It was different this time. A faint, prolonged rumble seemed to follow Longinus in the shade, where he thrust the cursed spear yet again, and blood poured down his arm. In the shade Longinus seemed oblivious to the strange sound but asleep on the porch, Kahtar wasn't. It kept him half outside of the shade, in two worlds at the same time. Blood ran down Longinus's raised arm, still warm it splashed across his lips and the sound changed. The rumbling faded, and it was replaced by a faint roar.

There wasn't thunder, not yet. That thought roused Kahtar, held the shade at bay for the first time ever, and he opened his eyes to a muffled roaring sound, trying to place it, confused as his shade faded.

What does this mean? It took several minutes for his mind to turn slowly from his horrible past.

Under the buffalo blanket Kahtar lay damp, slightly chilled with the warmth of Beth gone.

Her stomach, he remembered. Scanning for her he admonished himself, he'd fallen asleep before tending to her thoroughly. Rising to a sitting position, Kahtar scanned towards the latrine despite the fact that it was an intrusion. It was empty. Then he scanned towards the pond, wondering if she'd gone to the hammock. Tossing the blanket off he rose to stretch, considering his options. If she insisted on trying to escape the veil, he hoped she'd quit drinking standing water. It was then, as he considered the fact that drinking water out of a mud puddle was downright stupid, and that Beth was not a stupid woman, that the sound from his shade clicked into place in his mind.

A car. In surprise he looked towards the driveway, even in the dark of early morning his eyes could make out that only his cruiser sat there. The convertible was gone. Swearing he banged through the screen door, and looked at the iron maiden where he kept keys dangling on the little nubs that jutted out near the eye-holes. Only the cruiser keys were there. His mind raced.

She'd been too terrified to walk through the doorway to sleep in a bed, but Beth had gone into the house to get keys, had taken them right off an instrument of torture. Willet pushed the kitchen door open and with a fresh mug of brack tea in his hand.

"Kahtar? Was that a car?"

"Beth took it! Where the blazes were you?"

"Making breakfast. Call Old Guard."

"They don't do cars or Orphans! You know that! Have them drop warriors along the highway. We have to stop her! Put on one of my uniforms. Hurry!"

Willet's mug of tea hit the floor, spilling the liquid over the floor boards. In the faint morning light it looked dark red, like blood. Horror seized Kahtar. Berwick would be waiting for her, if he found her…*Dear Sweet ilu. Please. Protect her.*

THE POLICE CRUISER didn't move nearly as fast as the Saab, and Beth had a good head start. Flying at top speed out of the veil, Kahtar knew he'd been played. Beth had simply been biding her time, waiting for a chance to escape. Why hadn't he seen it? What about her as he'd tried to force her to leave town had ever hinted at a woman who would mournfully mope? A woman who would wander aimlessly in the woods, stumbling towards an impossible escape? A woman who'd drink dirty water from a mud puddle? Part of him admired her cleverness, he wasn't often had. Another part of him was horrified. Even if Berwick didn't find her before they did, the clan didn't give second chances. Shoving that thought away he focused on recovery and damage control.

A roaring battle cry tore through his head as Willet summoned the clan's warriors.

The point of no return. Every available warrior was now called into action, away from their assigned posts. Beth had gone too far. With the gas pedal all the way to the floor, Kahtar's cruiser screamed towards the highway. This was the opportunity Beth had been waiting for and he had been foolish not to have known it. The image of her moving along edges of the veil flitted into his mind, her head bobbing forward then back. She'd been smelling it! Beth understood how to get out of a veil! How was that possible?

Kahtar had been a fool not to have warned her of the danger, of the consequences of an escape attempt. He'd considered it an impossibility! In frustration he slapped a palm against the steering wheel, scanning as hard and far as he could, but he sensed no hint of her organic composition. His scan cut through trees, cars, houses, and warriors popping into thin air at the blink of Old Guard, hundreds of them in the miles his mind could stretch. Yet there was no sign of Beth White. The Orphan had bested the entire clan, including him, a warrior with thousands of year's experience.

BETH CUT OFF a Mercedes on the freeway, and the driver flipped her the bird, adrenaline still pumping through her body made her hands shake. She surprised herself and returned the gesture.

Why am I angry? Afraid, yes, but angry? Glancing in her mirrors, she expected to see Willowyth patrol cars materialize from nowhere. She exited the freeway, certain the first place they'd look for her would be the highway. Adhering to the speed limit, she wound her way through several streets populated with strip malls. Pulling into the parking lot of a pancake house, she shoved the gear into park. Resting her head on the steering wheel, Beth pressed a hand against her bony chest trying to appease her aching heart. She felt sick, and she had no idea what to do now. There was no way she could involve her parents in this, and she had no idea how far the arm of the cult could reach.

In movies this was the part where you called an old friend. Beth had no old friends. She was a professional bridge burner thanks to her inability to control her tongue. The closest she'd ever come to a friend was…Honor. The memory of Honor Monroe telling her that he loved her sneaked into her head, and she thumped her head against the steering wheel trying to knock the image out.

Concentration camp mentality. This is what cults do. They seduce you. Beth's stomach gurgled threateningly and she darted out of the car to the door of the restaurant. Her escape plan had a couple of flaws, one of which was churning furiously in her gut.

There are many places to have epiphanies, and folded over the toilet bowl in the dodgy ladies room of a dodgy 24-hour restaurant, was where Beth had hers. *Why did I leave?* Because they kidnapped me, because of what they are: Warriors. Covenant Keepers. Shades. She'd run because they'd given her no choice. The truth was that she was the same as they were. She was weird and scary. The truth was she belonged…with them. No. She belonged with him, and he belonged with them. That answered her question about where she was going.

Beth was going to go back. Right now, before it was too late.

It took awhile before whatever nastiness she'd ingested worked its way through her, before she could get to the sink and clean up. Then in her damp white dress with her hair still wet, she pushed open the ladies room door, and walked into the greasy sweet smell of all you can eat pancakes.

Beth's heart almost dropped through the floor. A Warrior of ilu stood just feet away. Before she'd known what they were, how had she failed to recognize them? They'd been in her dreams even as a child. Their posture stiff and alert, like a crouching feral cat. Their arms slightly bent, hands positioned to grab a weapon, attentive, on guard, dangerous. Terrifying. Berwick looked like a molting orangutan even in his custom made suit. How had he found her? He stood flanked by two of what were surely his men, and just on the opposite side of the entryway from her, only a crowd of hungry families separated them. He glanced over at her and nodded and it was the singularly most threatening gesture she'd ever encountered.

Beth reacted impulsively. A man in some type of security uniform headed into the men's room and she grabbed his arm, pointing at Berwick and his men.

"They didn't pay!" The crowd waiting to be seated turned to stare, and the busy host and hostess immediately made their way towards Berwick. Beth darted from the restaurant, her stomach churning again. Her hands shaking, it felt like it took an eternity to get into and then start her car. She exited the parking lot a bit recklessly.

Beth's convertible had just pulled onto the service road when a glance in the rear view mirror showed Berwick running out of the restaurant. He pointed right at her as though he knew she watched, maybe he did, her stomach roiled. She had just a minute's head start to make it back to Willowyth, and banking on the fact that her convertible could move faster than the SUV, it never occurred to her the extent of her problem.

As soon as she merged into the north bound traffic, a black SUV roared past, cut right in front of her, then slowed down. She saw another one coming to box her in seconds before the big black vehicle pulled too close, riding alongside. What Berwick's men didn't know was that Beth had learned to drive in Jakarta. She knew how to get out of a box, slamming on the gas pedal and sliding onto the shoulder of the road, she raced in front of the lead car before he could react and then cut across four lanes of traffic. Beth almost got stuck while driving over the meridian, her tires spun and chunks of mud stuck to her car. When she finally entered the west moving traffic, more than one driver made a rude gesture and horns blared.

"Deal with it!" she shouted back at them. One of the black SUV's tried to follow over the wet strip of grass, and to Beth's satisfaction it got stuck in the mud. The problem was she hadn't gone a mile down the road when another black SUV merged onto the highway and raced towards her.

"For the love of..." Beth darted in and out of lanes, taking to the shoulder to avoid slowdowns. She tried to ignore the hostility and blaring horns she was generating, and managed to inch her way through the rush hour traffic heading into downtown Cleveland. Several times Beth took exit ramps, only to reenter on the next one. It didn't help. Berwick's men had the uncanny ability to find her. The gas gauge pointed to empty, so Beth had to risk getting trapped and caught. She got off in a run-down neighborhood and simply raced in and out of streets, putting as much distance as she could between her and the black SUVs.

PARKED AT AN old gas station, Beth tugged her shoe off and lifted the insole. The money beneath it was wet and she peeled the bills out and tucked most of them into the strap of her dress. The other foot hadn't fared so well, her driver's license and credit card had left big bloody blisters on the sole of her foot. The slightly bent credit card wouldn't work at the pump either, so Beth had to go inside to pay. Stomach still gurgling, she searched the shelves of the mini-mart for anything she dared eat, and emerged with a pint of milk, a roll of Tums and a banana.

Berwick was there waiting, leaning against her convertible. His suit was black, like an undertaker, his ginger hair fuzzy. Unlike the other Warriors of ilu that Beth had seen, he sported patchy facial hair and so did his men who stepped around the shiny black vehicle, parked behind Beth's convertible. She backed inside the store and turned the lock on the glass door. Racing to the other side of the small store, constructed mostly of dirty windows, she shoved out the far door. An ancient Cadillac sat parked right by the door, the engine running and windows down. Beth tugged the door open, slid inside and clipped an old Lincoln Town Car on her way out of the parking lot.

The big Cadillac couldn't manage the kind of speed she needed, but she focused on getting lost in the maze of residential streets. Twisting and turning through neighborhoods, she hoped and prayed that Berwick wasn't making the same twists and turns right behind her.

"Honey? Is you crazy? Stealing my boy's car?"

Beth squeaked; twisting in the car to glance at an elderly woman dressed to the nines in flame orange, including a pillbox hat with netting and sequins.

"No! I'm not crazy, I'm desperate. I'll pay for the car."

"Uh-huh. Why you desperate?"

Beth took a corner far too fast and the car slid, bruising several automobiles parked along the street. Car alarms sounded in her wake, but Beth had to answer the question.

"Because I'm being chased by a gorilla from Scotland and I'm afraid of what he'll do to my—people—if I go back!"

"Mmhmm. That's what you say."

"It's true!" As if to prove it, a black SUV squealed around a corner behind them. Beth clipped more cars as she turned down another street. "I'll pay for those too."

"You know you will. That was my cousin's Buick. Go in that driveway right there, it cuts through to the next street." The click of a seatbelt sounded and the old lady scooted forward, pointing. "Now cut through that driveway, and take the alley to the right."

"Oh my gosh! Put your seatbelt back on!"

"Humpf, don't you be telling me what to do. Take a left. You wanna double back to the gas station and get yer own car? Otherwise there's no telling what Clarence is gonna do to you. You stole his baby, and his Mama, girl. You don't want no part of that."

"They might be waiting for me there."

"Humpf." Beth heard the sound of a cell phone while the lady in orange calmly dialed, she said, "What those boys be wanting with you?"

"They want me to build an Arc."

"Uh-huh. Turn right there, by the house with the Christmas lights." The woman's voice rose as she shouted into her mobile. "Clarence? I'm fine. Shut up and watch your language. Any sign of City Kitty there? Yeah, I know they don't know where our neighborhood is, but you see any shiny black gas hogs full of gorillas? Yes I took my Coumadin, answer the question."

Beth decided then and there that she loved this woman. The woman leaned towards her, she smelled like expensive perfume.

"Yer clear. Take a left there, then a right on the highway and hustle. What's yer name girl?"

"Beth."

"Well, Good Morning, Beth. I'm Rita. It's short for Margarita. See the gas station up ahead? You'd better make it quick. Clarence's liable to go off on ya. 'Specially when he sees what ya done to his baby."

Pulling into the gas station on the right and parking beside her car, Beth hurried out of the Cadillac and opened a back door to hug Rita.

"You saved my life."

"Oh, go on."

Beth yanked the still damp wad of cash from inside her dress and peeled off the largest denomination and handed it to Rita.

"For your cousin's car."

"No wonder those gorillas want you. Is this real? Didn't know money came that big."

Beth kissed her, right on the mouth. By the time Clarence came storming towards them, she was sliding her car into drive. He gave her a gesture that she knew he'd be in trouble with Rita over.

BETH TRIED TO get back to Willowyth that night. It was impossible. Berwick's men seemed to be waiting along the highway. In the closest call yet, she escaped only because one of Berwick's SUV's tried to turn too quickly and skidded out of control, causing an accident. She had a feeling that whoever was driving that black SUV wouldn't be trailing her or anybody else, ever again, and it wasn't a good feeling at all.

THE NEXT MORNING Beth sat in her vehicle staring at a map. There were only two ways into Willowyth and she was certain that Berwick's men had them both covered. Too tired to think straight, but afraid to sleep in her car, she parked her vehicle in a parking garage. Then Beth caught a bus, sat in a backseat and fell asleep. She woke up to a homeless man stuffing a plastic bag on her lap and lamenting the loss of the city's old stadium. Beth got off at the next stop, well aware of the fact that she looked a bit homeless herself. She felt it. In fact, she was.

At the bus stop a teenager leaned against a streetlamp talking on his cell phone. Beth stood watching him until he winked at her and clicked the old style phone shut.

"Hey."

"Would you sell me that phone?"

"How much?"

Beth watched his eyes. "Twenty dollars."

"Right." The kid was slight, dressed in red sweatpants and a flannel shirt, in June. His hair artfully arranged to stick straight up in the middle of his head, Beth decided he was trying to achieve a look she was either unfamiliar with or that he couldn't afford.

"Fifty," she offered.

"I have more than fifty dollars in prepaid minutes on this."

It was one of those old prepaid kinds of phones with no GPS capability, and the kid was a really bad liar. Those were both good things to Beth's way of thinking.

"You shouldn't lie. Life is confusing enough without lies. How many minutes are really on it? I don't care, but I need to know."

He shrugged, but admitted, "Four."

Beth smiled at him and offered the fifty. "Because you told the truth."

"Fifty isn't much for a new phone."

"That phone is a piece of junk and you know it."

"Uh, okay lady." He took the money and headed down the street, glancing back at Beth a couple of times. The bus for the zoo squealed to a stop in front of her and Beth hopped on it.

MONKEY ISLAND AT The Cleveland Zoo fascinated Beth. She came up with a theory that monkey society was creepily similar to the way people had been before the invention of television, before everyone became self-conscious. This was also an excellent way to waste time instead of calling the Willowyth police station.

Just do it. She dialed.

"Willowyth Police, is this an emergency?" The voice reassured in its politeness.

"Naw." Imitating voices did come easy to Covenant Keepers. Beth had always been a bit proud of the talent, when she'd assumed it was just hers. She produced some impressively wet coughing.

"Ah need'ta tawk ta Kent, 'bout Brenda Blake."

There was a moment's hesitation before the officer politely offered, "One moment, please."

Beth counted in her head, three, two…and a familiar sounding husky voice came on the line. "This is Chief Costas."

Beth's mouth opened and then she shut it with a snap and hung up. It wasn't Kahtar. It sounded like him, or very close to his voice, but the lie shot through the phone like a slap.

Maybe I should have asked for Honor…no. I can't ask any of them for help. If I do they'll never believe I want to come back. They'll think I need them because of Berwick. I need to get back on my own. Maybe I could hike in through the farmlands, I could get a compass. Beth turned back to the monkeys. She'd lived in many places, but she'd never hiked in her life, and she wasn't even entirely certain what one did with a compass, so that solution was out. Despite their suits, Berwick's men had looked like they could hike The Grand Canyon without breaking a sweat, and she strongly suspected they didn't even need a compass for direction.

A plan began to form. She needed to buy an airline ticket. If the credit card would work. She'd also need to steal a car, preferably one without anyone's mother in the back seat.

CHAPTER
TWENTY

SEVENTY-TWO HOURS. ONE Orphan of the Inquisition had eluded three thousand Cultuelle Kristos' warriors for seventy-two hours. Oh, Berwick had eluded them much longer, yet the men seemed to take their inability to locate Beth much harder, as though she should be easier to find because she was barely Covenant Keeper, or because she was a lone woman.

They're so young. Kahtar had summoned Old Guard the very first day, pleading his case.

"She could expose the clan."

"That was your risk when you took her, your choice."

"You are pledged to protect this clan."

"Yes. We are not pledged to hunt those who do not uphold The Covenant. She is free to do as she will."

The Mother had summoned Kahtar to her home. Sitting at her kitchen table she'd admonished him in her polite way.

"It is not like you to underestimate anyone."

"We will find her eventually. She bought a plane ticket to Buenos Aires. Abigail will take me there using a tesseract."

"Collect this Orphan and anyone she has exposed us to." The look in The Mother's normally serene gaze was worried.

"She didn't go to her parent's house. She isn't a fool."

"I hope you are right. It would be heartbreak to send a family of Orphans into The Mists. They wouldn't survive a day. This Orphan is the greatest exposure risk Cultuelle Khristos has ever faced, Kahtar. Do whatever it takes to find her and protect our clan."

ABIGAIL WOULD MEET him at the cave. Kahtar needed only to check the data bases at the police station one last time. Surely Beth did not have enough cash on her person to travel around Buenos Aires. Eventually she would have to use her credit card again. So far she had charged nothing since she bought the airline ticket in Cleveland. Nothing had been charged in Argentina though the ticket had been used. Bending over the computer, clicking the mouse futilely, Kahtar wished he had access to airport security cameras. He dreaded following dead ends. If Beth was clever enough to set him up from the beginning, she was clever enough to have left a false trail and this felt false. Brigg shoved his office door open.

"Hey, Chief? You have a call on line eight."

"I'm out of here."

"She claims to be Brenda Blake."

Straightening up, Kahar fixed his steely gaze on Briggs.

"Brenda is dead. Is it her friend? The one who used to work at the coffee shop with her?"

Brigg shrugged. "I don't know who it really is, but she sure sounds like Brenda."

Kahtar grabbed the phone and snapped into it. "Chief Costas."

"Kahtar?" Beth's voice quavered. Shock made him sink back into his office chair and he motioned Brigg away with his hand.

"Where are you?"

"I really messed up. I just wanted to tell you I'm sorry. I know it has to have caused you all a lot of trouble. Tell Honor too, okay? Tell him I'm sorry. I know you won't believe me, but I never lied to any of you, and don't worry about…complications. There won't be any."

Something about the blunt, rushed confession, the shaking voice, made him rise, and grip the phone tighter. She was in trouble.

"Where are you, Beth?"

"At a Marathon Gas Station on the East Side, Berwick is here."

A stream of cuss words began to flit through his mind like ticker tape.

"Are you safe?" It was a stupid question. She'd just given him what sounded like her death bed confession.

The snort was devoid of any humor. "Well, he finally realizes I'm not going to create an Arc with him."

"Where is Berwick?"

"He's outside of my car, pumping gasoline all over it."

"We're coming."

"That's nice of you, but that's not why I called. There isn't enough time anyway, just remember what I said. Sometimes I get so focused on what I'm doing that I don't think far enough ahead. Oh, I…"

The line went dead. Turning to his computer Kahtar banged on the keyboard frantically, searching for the location of the gas station. Running to his door he shouted into the hallway.

"Brigg? Berwick's at a Marathon Station on Superior Avenue. Get Old Guard there." Then he slammed his door shut in the warrior's stunned face. Ever since Welcome Palmer had put the idea into his mind, like the scars from the hydrofluoric acid on his legs, it had lingered. *Your flesh has light attributes like an Old Guard." "I thought it meant you could shimmer in and out like an Old Guard." "Have you ever tried?"* Closing his eyes he focused on fading into the light. He'd gone with the Old Guard so often over the centuries, how many times had he wondered if he understood how to do it now?

FOR A MOMENT Kahtar thought he'd gone someplace else, to a war zone, or perhaps he was imploding. Fire roared towards the sky and explosions rocketed, the force of them blasted him through the air. He'd been in enough wars that he knew he should cover his ears.

The problem was he couldn't feel his arms. The percussion hurt deep inside, reverberating through his skull. The bone behind his ears felt as though it shattered, within moments of arriving he couldn't hear anything, only feel the thunderous booms hammering through him. How long he lay on the grass staring up at columns of orange and black clouds, he wasn't certain. The smoke was so thick and greasy he was almost choking to death. His lungs burned with fumes when an Old Guard yanked him to his feet and stuffed big fingers into his ears, healing them in seconds. Sound came back with a violent roar.

The gas station was gone, the building, the pumps, the vehicles that had been there. Berwick was gone. Beth was gone. The black eyes of an Old Guard stared into his, both of them encased in a tornado of smoke.

"Take me home." The second voice was all Kahtar could manage.

WHEN KAHTAR STUMBLED to his porch steps, blackened and aching, he stared at the buffalo blanket still in a heap by the front door. Just three days ago…his head dropped into his hands and he cried silently, his big body shaking with sobs like a little boy.

THE ONLY EVIDENCE the Old Guard found of Berwick was his skull, it had shot through the air and landed in a ditch between the east and west lanes on the nearby freeway. The jaw was missing. While sitting in the police station the following morning, they'd shimmered into Kahtar's office and put a shoe on his desk. A five inch straw colored pump. Unable to stop himself he'd picked it up, then looked up at the Old Guard.

Clearing his throat he asked. "Is that all you found?"

"No. It is all we retrieved. There is more of her, but we will not bring it to you. She is not clan. A dozen non-keepers were killed. Their own kind is collecting their remains."

"Go!" It made him feel sick, to think of Beth's blackened jawbone lying in a ditch off the freeway. Caressing the shoe he stared blindly, another failure in his millennia of failures.

EVEN WOLVES DRAGGED. The dog slept on the buffalo blanket on the porch as though he too missed Beth. Honor wouldn't come to the house. The plebes moved woodenly, blindly, and Kahtar barely noticed nor cared enough to correct them. Suddenly nothing seemed to matter much, and although it was a sin, he wished for this repeat to end. Perhaps distance would help with the pain. There would be years before he again remembered who he'd been, years of sheer being as a babe and then a boy before consciousness would intrude. Sometimes he didn't survive long enough to even remember, once there had been a gap of twenty years. Twenty years of oblivion from Golgotha, or from remembering this, he would take it gladly.

The best solution for the clan would be for Beth's shop to disappear. The Mother was not happy about Kahtar's solution. An explosion and fire within the village would cause pollution, enough to settle through the veils in the surrounding area, at least in some small proportion. Kahtar was resolute. It was the best way to eliminate too many questions. Besides, a natural gas explosion, with Beth's remains left in the rubble, would give her parents an explanation as to what happened to her. If they came into town themselves, and sensed Cultuelle Khristos, it could start another round of chasing away Orphans. Kahtar left orders for Honor to collect Beth's remains from the morgue downtown, while he took care of the explosion.

AT NIGHT BATTERY run candles lit every window in the shop. Forcing open the lock on the front door and stepping inside, Kahtar tried to avoid looking around. He didn't want to see Beth in the details, refused to scan and feel the mysterious boxes and jars that stacked the shelves. Memories of her would haunt him forever. There was no point in stirring them on purpose. Kahtar decided to focus on his duty and turned his mind to the new gas line in the basement.

There would be an investigation and publicity, but it would be worse if she simply vanished. Galloping woodenly down the basement steps, Kahtar forced his eyes away from the clothesline strung across the basement with Beth's clothes clipped to it. Standing in front of the gas lines Kahtar wiggled the copper tubing a few times, checking to see if it was soldered well, if it could be jostled enough to look defective. Ignoring the fact that an echo of Beth's heart seemed to remain in this house even after her death, the ghost of it leaping in the background as hers had once done, he forced his attention wholly on what needed to be done. It would take awhile for the house to fill with enough fumes for the explosion. Then the explosion would move upwards and out, any damage done here would likely leave evidence intact in the basement. This had to be done properly.

"What are you doing?" An impossibly familiar voice demanded.

Kahtar almost jumped out of his skin, as it was he jerked around so fast he banged his head on the metal cover of the fuse box, catching the corner with his forehead and leaving a gash that sliced right through to his skull.

A click sounded and light from a battery operated lantern lit the basement. Beth stood, perfectly alive, holding a little green lamp by the handle. Stunned, his eyes slid over her neon t-shirt that said "THE RAMONES" across the front, it hung to her thighs, there were silver and pink heeled slippers on her feet and her hair looked perfect as always.

"Are you kidding me? After all I went through you're going to kill me in an explosion now?"

His mouth moved, but it was so dry absolutely no words would come out.

"I mean it's a messy way to go, have I really earned that?"

In shock Kahtar sagged against one of the old oak beams that supported the floor above them, his heart thundering in his chest so hard he thought he might pass out. Gesturing futilely towards her he still couldn't get his tongue, throat and mouth in sync to speak, but he managed to shake his head.

Beth's eyes widened in surprise, she sat the lantern on the floor.

"You thought I was already dead?"

Kahtar nodded. He could manage that much.

"So you didn't come to kill me then?"

She's alive! Biting back a sob of joy he simply shook his head again. His hand was shaking as he lifted it to touch the wound on his forehead, barely aware that it ran from his eyebrow up and over the top of his head. When he realized, somewhere in the back of his brain, that he was bleeding, he held the flesh together to stop it.

"I couldn't find the entrance to your driveway or I would have gone back, but I thought—assumed—you'd all scan me here—or your Old Guards would," said Beth.

His mouth was dry, his voice hoarse but he managed. "You know? About Old Guard?"

"I do have shades. And Berwick did talk a lot."

Mutely Kahtar shook his head again, it was a mistake this time, blood splattered and for a moment he used two hands to try to hold his wound together before gesturing questioningly towards her with a bloody hand, unable to believe that she could be alive. Palm up was the best he could do forming a question.

"How'd I get away? Remember I told you on the phone that sometimes I get so focused on what I'm doing that I don't look ahead? I realized I was doing it again, focusing on saying goodbye instead of on how to escape. I noticed the cigarette lighter while we were talking. So I lit it and rolled out the back window, ran and threw it back at Berwick. He was standing in a puddle of gasoline. I didn't even think really, I just did it....

"The first explosion wasn't as bad as what I saw by the time I got down the street. I didn't realize, you know that the pumps would explode and…I never thought I could kill someone and I didn't realize there would be a chain reaction. That everyone inside the store would…a lot of people died because of what I did, because I didn't stop to think."

Those clear, sky blue eyes were filled with remorse and then tears. A quiver started in her mouth, and moved through her entire body as she fought to master it. This he could help her with.

"Everyone is capable of killing, given the wrong set of circumstances. There is no sin in protecting yourself. It is human nature."

Looking at the floor of the basement, Beth's curtain of hair hid her expression from him, but her tears plummeted all the way to the floor, landing with splashes, like raindrops.

"Sweet Beth." The term of endearment slipped naturally from his lips and he realized it was who she would always be to him. He loved her, and pretending otherwise would be a lie. It wasn't difficult then to walk towards her and wrap his arms around her offering comfort. Countless women had sought safe harbor against his chest, but not a single one had had a heart that pressed against his with strength to equal his own. Beth's heart was there, focusing on his. Briefly he rested his cheek against the top of her head, pulling away immediately when he saw his blood matting the silky perfection.

A handful of blood splattered over the basement floor as he moved back, covering the wet that had been her tears. Ignoring it he continued to reassure.

"It wasn't just the gas pumps that exploded. Berwick had containers of liquid hydrogen in his truck, and in the basement of that gas station. Those people were all going to die by his hand. You only took yourself out of the equation. How did you roll out the back window of your convertible?" Prompting, trying to fill in the holes and distract her at the same time. The pale face and wide eyes held horror and guilt but she ducked to the laundry basket and handed him a dirty towel to press against his bloody forehead.

Then she hurried to confess everything. "I—sort of—stole an SUV."

Blood started to seep into his left eye despite the help of the towel and he pressed against it, hard. "You stole a car?"

"Well, as soon as I left here and got downtown, Berwick was on me. I guess I passed one of his men somewhere. I managed to escape the first time, but my convertible was too easy to spot so I—found something else. If it weren't for Berwick I would have come right back here, but I was trying to dodge them. I thought maybe I shouldn't—you know—bring them back around here. It's my fault they killed so many people here in the first place."

"You are not responsible for Berwick, but why were you were coming back here? I thought you'd run. You bought an airline ticket."

"To show you, your clan, that I could have left, that I wanted to come back. I couldn't get past Berwick. It was like trying to dodge The Terminator when I went anywhere in my car. I didn't know about scanning until it was too late…."

She'd wanted to come back. Why? Kahtar tried to pull that answer from her by staring. Looking away she nervously tugged her t-shirt down, smoothing it over her thighs.

"I realized I didn't want to leave here by the time I got about ten minutes down the highway. I want to be part of whatever I am supposed to be part of here. Remember I told you sometimes I get so focused on what I'm doing I forget to look ahead?" Then she looked up at him and scowled. "How could any of you expect me to want to stay the way you did it? You never gave me a choice. You dragged me off and LOCKED ME UP!"

"We hardly locked you up." They'd done the best they could. Beth didn't know what locked up was. Memories of iron maidens floated through his mind.

"You trapped me inside a veil!"

A faint huff of laughter escaped him as blood soaked the rag at his forehead.

"You knew you were in a veil?"

"Yes, I knew." Her eyes narrowed.

"Remember we were trying to keep you safe from Berwick's clan?"

"You dragged me out of my house against my will!"

"You made me do that, and I told you why at the time. You never asked us any questions. I told you, you could ask me anything."

"After you took me prisoner! All I wanted then was to get away from you!"

More tears splashed from those blue eyes and she crossed her arms, glaring at him. It hurt. Not the gash on his forehead that would not stop bleeding, but the way Beth had shouted 'YOU'. The way her heart pulled away. When you were designed, created, and raised to fight men, terrifying women was a given, but still he wished it could be different with Beth. She surely knew how he felt, and now he knew how she felt too. Again he leaned against the beam in the basement, sagging, feeling sick. Yet there was his duty to attend to. Shoving other thoughts out of his mind he again became Warrior Chief.

"Did you tell anyone about us?" Watching her carefully for the answer, he continued to press the towel against his forehead, but it soaked with his blood and oozed between his fingers, running down his arm. The shade of Golgotha pressed against his mind and he shoved it away, focusing on Beth.

"Of course I didn't tell anyone—they'd have locked me up if I did—which I'd never…. Hey, you're really bleeding badly, Kahtar."

Did he imagine the concern in her voice?

"Should I call the police?"

Ah sarcasm, not too concerned.

"Do you think you could drive me up the street? There's a clinic there. I think I need a doctor." His own voice sounded canned, far away. He needed to get out of the basement before she did have to call 911. Stumping his way up the stairs, barely aware of the fact that he was leaving a trail of blood he moved woodenly upwards, his heart not aching with pain like it had upon his descent, but aching with rejection as they walked through the shop.

"One sec!" Beth pushed him to sit on a rattan bench by the front door, it creaked with his weight, but held. She yanked The Ramones t-shirt over her head and shoved it against his head. The room swam, he couldn't see much, but some deep-seated man part of his brain wondered if he'd have looked if he could have focused.

"Let me grab my keys and some real clothes."

LEANING AGAINST THE wall bought Kahtar time, and photographs clattered to the floor from their post behind him. If memory served they were of paintings of St. Longinus and then, despite his light headedness, the irony wasn't lost on him. Trying to apply pressure to the wound wasn't helping much because he couldn't remember which end of his arm was at his injury. It was a familiar sensation, it meant concussion and on top of that he was bleeding too much now. Thinking of those photos as they continued to bang to the floor he announced, "I'm not a superstitious man."

"Well, you're a man who's just ruined and, therefore, purchased six identical photographs. Oh Heavens, you're bleeding worse!" Beth was there then, her arm wrapped under his shoulders, it felt thin. He could smell her in the darkness, she used lemon shampoo and it was sweet.

"Come on, get up. Lean on me."

"No." Certain that his weight would make her buckle beneath him, he leaned anyway, there was no choice. She was stronger than he would have imagined as she hauled him over the porch and down the steps. Then they were in the convertible, the feel of leather through his uniform familiar though he'd only driven in the car once. The roof was off and Beth's hand pressed something against his forehead. The night air blew over him, at first cooling him, then making him shiver. Beth's voice sounded from far away.

"I'm taking you to the police station."

"No. Go east on Main. There's a clinic on the edge of town..."

"Oh, I've seen it. Cobbson? Kahtar? Stay with me. Oh no, you're bleeding so much! God, please, slow Kahtar's bleeding. Please, slow his bleeding...." Her voice sounded repetitious and echoed painfully in his head with the wind blowing. Her prayers weren't enough and it felt like the wind was blowing the wound open wider, his arms fell limply to his sides, and hot blood surged over his face.

Beth pressed the blood soaked towel back against his face as she drove, her voice shaking.

"Stop bleeding. Please stop."

She sounded panicked, and he whispered at some point.

"Head wounds bleed a lot, 'm okay." Then he passed out.

CHAPTER

TWENTY-ONE

BETH HAD NOTICED the sign for the clinic when she first came to town. She remembered a gated entrance, guarded. The convertible raced down the road, going as fast it could with the gas pedal all the way to the floor. Weren't there any police on duty tonight? After all the speeding tickets they'd given her, all for going less than four miles over the limit, now there was no one. Her prayer faded to a shaky, "Please, please, please." Blood soaked the thick Egyptian cotton towel she pressed against Kahtar's head, it was thick and that meant a lot of blood loss. Too much. It ran down her forearm and dripped steadily off her elbow. Some annoying part of her brain tried to measure how many cups of blood now soaked the interior of the convertible.

"Please, let him be all right. What a stupid way to be hurt! After all Berwick did to him, and he was fine, now he bumps his head! Please, please, please. I snuck up on him on purpose too! I knew he didn't see me! I just wanted to see if I could! If he was really human. Oh, God, he is! Please, please, please!"

The clinic sign was not lit at night, and the compound sat on a stretch of roadway with nothing else for miles in any direction. Something sparkled off to her right, or Beth would have passed it. She slammed on the brakes, the car fish-tailed and the tires squealed as she swerved onto the bricked drive. Several men hurried out of the guard shack as she drove towards the gate, they stepped boldly in front of her car. Blessedly she managed to stop before hitting them and she wondered again if at least some of these people were immortal. Yet the blood sliding down to her elbow told her they were very much human. A guard leaned towards her, in a brown uniform with a name tag that said 'Frank'.

"We're a private clinic 'Mam. Would you like me to phone an ambulance?"

Even by his speech, before he had come into view of her headlights, she'd known he was Warrior of ilu. They all walked the same, enunciated each syllable in a similar fashion, as though they were trying to hide the fact that English wasn't their native tongue.

"Let me in! It's Kahtar! He's bleeding badly."

Several warriors rushed the car then and put their hands on him, muttering in a tongue that was vaguely familiar to Beth. A latent memory poked at her and her brain immediately sought to decipher words.

One warrior shouted into the darkness, "Old Guard!"

Another ran a hand down Beth's bloodied arm and she knew he was searching her for injury. "You're fine. Are you Clan Huron?"

Finally she understood what that meant. A woman from another clan, they knew she wasn't from their own clan. It must be small if they all knew each other.

"I'm Beth White. I'm the Orphan of the Inquisition." Honor had told her often enough, and she hoped it made sense to these men.

They all stilled as one, their uncertainly thick in the air.

Someone whispered, "I thought she was dead."

"It could be why the Old Guard don't come, though."

They did know who she was!

"Obviously I'm not dead! You let me in to see a doctor or I'm driving straight through those gates! Kahtar needs help! You're just going to lock me up afterwards anyway, so don't you dare let him bleed while you fuss about protocol!"

THE CLINIC WASN'T under a veil. There had been no wind as she approached. That clean fresh scent that surrounded Kahtar's cabin was missing, besides there were the blinking lights of airplanes in the summer sky. Still the place was obviously other. A faint hum of what sounded like thousands of whispering fans sounded from what, even in the darkness, appeared to be a mile of low slung buildings. Lights shone from windows that looked oddly curved instead of flat; and strange columns of shimmering lights lit up the garden and hillside. Beth had a feeling that those lights were Old Guard. Something deep in her psyche told her that those lights were alive and powerful. She was starting to remember.

They hadn't allowed her inside the buildings, and Beth had a hunch that they'd only allowed her through the gate because none of them could drive, and they wanted Kahtar to get help as quickly as possible. Strangely no one had stayed to guard her. At least it had seemed strange at first. Until it occurred to her that they could scan her. That came to mind after she'd slid from her perch on top the head-rest in the front seat and walked across some sort of soft paving stones to sit on a marble bench that curved beneath her bottom as comfortably as a cushion.

Are they watching me now? How much can they see when they scan? A shiver slipped up her spine. She should have taken the time to put on underclothes. Then the glass doors of the clinic flew open, and a group hurried out. A bright light lit the great expanse of paving stones and Beth glanced at her car parked on them, they indented like a mattress trying to support a heavy person. The convertible had sunk at least four inches into the stone, the body of the car almost flush with the road.

A voice growled into the night. "Left standing outside? It's rude! I don't know protocol either but manners are simple enough. Beth?"

Blinking into the bright lights and trying to believe the hulking figure stalking towards her could possibly be Kahtar, she slid onto her feet. There was no mistaking that husky voice of his, nor the sheer height and width of the man. The heels of her shoes poked into the paving stones and threatened to toss her back onto the bench. Balancing her weight on her toes she stared at Kahtar as he stormed towards her, followed by at least a dozen other people. His entourage were all dressed in muted colors and soft, comfortable looking fabrics. Dozens more people, all warriors, stepped from behind to surround her, and she realized that they'd been in the shadows watching her the entire time.

Goosebumps shivered over every inch of her in the humid summer night. They were clothed like something out of a medieval movie that had been crossed with Robin Hood's shoes with maybe some Star Trek tossed in. The uniformity of their tunics was so precise that they all appeared the exact same size. Yet the cloth fit their bodies like paint, and it looked very futuristic to her eyes. Every one of those men had a sword in hand. When she tried to step away from them, they followed, moving forward with her. They made no sound. She fought the urge to run.

"Cease!" Kahtar barked, looking completely healthy, not even a scar marred his forehead, though blood still caked his face and glistened wet and thick over his navy police uniform.

"Back off!"

As one, every Warrior of ilu backed away from Beth. For once Kahtar didn't seem like the scariest thing in the vicinity. She balanced on her toes and walked towards him. A strong arm encircled her, pulling her close and she didn't protest the blood that smeared over her already bloodied sundress. He was all right, it couldn't have been but fifteen minutes since it had taken three men to carry him through those glass doors and now he was fine. A sudden shiver slid up her spine as the full impact of that hit her, and he let his arm drop, stepping away as though he'd read her mind.

Kahtar ran his fingers across his healed forehead and told her.

"The giftings of healing these men and women possess is quite strong. Healing a head that has been cleaved open is a simple enough task for most warriors. Even your prayers helped, it was the blood loss that needed a specialist. Did I trash your car?"

Glancing over at it, even deeper in the pavement she lamented, "Not as badly as I've ruined the driveway."

Chuckling, he nodded.

"It isn't made for cars. Someone might want to move that car before we need a helicopter to lift it out. Not you, Beth. I want you to come inside Cobbson Compound—you wanted a choice. It's time you discussed that with the leader of Cultuelle Khristos."

THE ENTRANCE INTO the main building was like stepping into Oz's Sherwood Forest with touches by Dr. Seuss. Blinking in wonder, Beth tried to take it in. The room was lit like day. The light appeared to come from the curved windows though it was dark outside. Flowering plants and greenery hung thick from above and the sound of a waterfall crashed faintly through some trees that appeared to be in full autumn glory though it was early July. On the far side of the huge room, several children played on what appeared to be an ice sculpture the size of a small hill. They raced up one blue white side to slide down the colorful cave-like front screaming with laughter.

Strange dark, geometric shapes were suspended impossibly in mid-air around the room. Beth almost overlooked them, except one sprang to life and branches of light shot out of it in the shape of a tunnel. A soldier in desert fatigue dropped out, clutching a machine gun. Several of the people dressed in soft, muted colors hurried to help him. Their prayers of healing echoing in their wake as they disappeared down a hallway, the bloody footprints left behind caught Beth's attention. The floor was smooth like granite, but without the polished sheen. It was matte and dark, and the blood appeared to seep into it and vanish almost instantly.

Glancing up into Kahtar's steely eyes she opened her mouth and then shut it. A hint of a smile lit his face, and she thought for a moment about the instant when she'd first met him. She'd thought he was the most spectacular man she'd ever laid eyes on. Zeus. For an instant she wondered what he'd say if she told him that is what she called him in her head. Then another of the dark geometric shapes shot to life and the light-like branches shot out of it, stretching six feet into the air before a man appeared from nowhere. His business suit caught her attention more than the unusual garb or the soldiers that seemed to come and go in the large room. Nodding to several of the people, he darted across the large room and hopped into a diamond shaped medallion of darkness, vanishing from sight.

Kahtar grinned at her then. "Any questions, Beth?"

Of course she wondered, but obviously it was a means of transportation. The details didn't really matter to her. Even in this place, this odd new reality, what captivated Beth was a sense of finally not being the strangest person in a crowd. Yes, there were curiosities here, but she—for once—wasn't the biggest one. Smiling at the blood soaked Police Chief beside her she shook her head, fighting back a wider smile at his look of disbelief.

I will not ask questions and reveal myself as the weirdest one of all. Glancing down at her purple sundress, with splotches of blood shining like floral embellishments and her silver and pink heeled slippers she grinned too. Never one to try to fit in, because it was simply impossible, it still felt great to not be the strangest one in the room. Women in saris and Grecian gowns and plain grey sweats milled about at the far side of the room. Warriors dressed in what was certainly their traditional gear, mixed with men dressed in the military uniforms she'd grown up with. A tiny girl, maybe four years old, dashed through the length of the room with not a stitch of clothing on.

One of the warriors broke rank and dashed after her. "Buleeh! Sweetheart! Where's your gown?"

Everyone laughed then, and from the thick depths of a jungle area, a woman floated out. Though she wore a cream-colored Grecian gown, her short auburn hair was a riot of curls, and if she'd worn a business suit she might have been CEO of some top company. Gliding to a stop in front of Beth she took her in with a pair of stunningly attractive dark blue eyes. Her smile revealed one front tooth slightly overlapping another, and the imperfection made her—perfect. For a reason she couldn't fathom, Beth's eyes watered, she wanted to hug the woman. The touch of her heart was unlike anything she could have imagined. It was—home.

Soft hands grasped her forearms and instinctively Beth clasped the woman's arms in response. That heart wrapped around hers and a scent of oranges and cloves seemed to waft from somewhere and knowing it was right they leaned towards each other and kissed.

"I am Anwyn Glorianna D'Aval, The Mother of Cultuelle Khristos, and Covenant Keeper. When you ran, Beth White, you endangered the entire clan. You've returned of your own volition, but how can I trust you never to run again?"

The question was simple and straightforward, but Beth knew there was only one answer she could give. She would be held to her answer, and as long as she lived, nothing would impact her future on this earth as much as her response right now. Kahtar stood just two feet behind her, and she could feel the tension in his strong heart. Something about his heart distracted her, made her want to turn and reassure him that she did understand the import, but The Mother's eyes were locked on hers, searching.

"I give you my oath that I will not run to escape. This clan is my fate. I've dreamed of finding where I belong, but I will need to see my family and take care of my store." Determinedly she added her last comment, noting the interested lift of The Mother's brow as she took in the frank reply.

Ignoring the stir of the other people in the room, the hearts that surrounded her like a warm glow and made her want to dance with them all, to laugh alongside them and know their names and hearts individually. Forcing her focus on this one who called herself The Mother, she waited for her verdict.

"It's not safe to allow the outside world access to your heart. It is dangerous."

"I've lived it my entire life. Mother, I belong in both worlds."

Glorianna D'Aval tilted her head slightly, looking into Beth's eyes, surprise lighting those stunning eyes of hers.

"What is your gifting, child?"

Hesitating, Beth wasn't certain how to reply. Her gifting? Glancing around the spectacular room at the hundreds of people coming and going and the marvels she couldn't begin to comprehend, she had never felt so inadequate in all her days. Kahtar's attractively hoarse voice sounded beside her.

"Truth, I think, Mother. I think her gifting is truth. I hear her speak it, and have seen her listen for it in others."

Dozens of people crowded forward at those words, and Beth felt conspicuous. Flushing she looked defiantly back at them.

"Yes. I do know the truth, and I do speak it."

"Perhaps you do belong in both worlds. What an interesting woman you are, but I cannot promise you that you will be allowed the freedom you request."

"I plan to take it then, although I mean no disrespect."

Despite The Mother's tolerant smile, she felt Kahtar's heart sink at her defiant statement. It was pleasantly distracting, sensing the hearts around hers. Glorianna reached up and patted Beth's smooth hair as though she were a child.

"You have just announced your intention to disobey me in front of a small squadron of Warriors of ilu—it is highly unlikely you'd meet with any success at all, normally. Yet in your case I will offer this much, if our resources can bear the burden and you will not risk our exposure to your family—I will not forbid you spending time with them."

"You have my word. Mother? I would die before I would betray your trust."

Glorianna's eyes grew dark, and a deep furrow bit into the ivory skin between her brows.

"You will die if you betray us, Beth. That is a fact. Learn the laws of being before you attempt this life in two worlds. Perhaps our life looks appealing as you stand right here, you need to know it is not an easy path, but it is one none of us regret. Welcome home, Beth

White—your choice is made, you are Orphan of the Inquisition no longer. You are Cultuelle Khristos now."

Bouncing onto the balls of her feet Beth grinned. Whatever the laws of being, this is where she belonged, and it hadn't cost her parents and whether these people knew it or not, it wouldn't cost her dream of running Sweet Earth either. The Mother smiled back at her, and Beth was certain she was the singularly most beautiful woman on earth. Gloriana D'Aval reached up to caress her cheek, and Beth closed her eyes for a moment, feeling the joy of a small child who has met the approval of their beloved Mother.

"As for your shop, we shall see. I will make you no promises, but I will admit that you seem to have a gift for accumulating goods that many delight in. Your shop has already caught the interest of a good many of the clan. Especially Old Guard. I think you will find they are a very influential ally."

Then shouts of "Bethy, Bethy!" reached her ears and Honor Monroe was there, swinging her in circles so that her slippers slid off her feet and clattered into the crowd of grinning spectators. Not spectators, her clan, and their hearts pressed towards hers and she happily kissed Honor back. Never in all her life, had she ever had a really close friend like him. If only he were a girl he'd be perfect. When he finally put her down, teasing that she was diminutive without her stilts on, she scanned the crowd for Kahtar. Disappointment cut through her as she saw him push through the front doors, not even bothering to tell her goodbye before he left.

CHAPTER
TWENTY-TWO

THE UNEXPECTED TREAT of broad-siding Honor Monroe with the flat of his blade, so hard that the warrior did a face plant into the hard ground, made Kahtar happier than he'd been in weeks. In the early morning darkness, he sensed rather than saw the critical black eyes of an Old Guard on him. They felt disapproving even when Kahtar offered the young warrior a hand up. As though the Old Guard knew he was already planning to whack the dark haired warrior into one of the heavy posts planted in the earth. Perhaps the old Guard did know. Too bad. There was no sin in besting another warrior. No sin, really, in taking too much pleasure in it.

Honor took the hand up, and Kahtar sensed it when Honor tenderly touched his forehead. Kahtar didn't need his eyes to know that dark bruising was already blossoming over his rookie's forehead. Kahtar had no trouble keeping his face expressionless. He knew Honor couldn't scan well enough to read it and it was too dark to see. Honor's intrusive scan brushed over his face twice, trying to, before trustingly or perhaps stupidly raising his blade again.

With Beth White now part of the clan and Berwick gone on, the only unusual threat was that Berwick's people would eventually find them and possibly seek retribution. The Mother's emissaries were still searching the lowlands of Scotland in hopes of brokering a peace. In the meantime life continued on, uneventful and quiet. Everything had changed, but nothing had changed. Beth had found her way back to her own people, but she wanted Honor Monroe. Unrequited love wasn't uncommon and Kahtar was certain he was already over it. As a matter of fact he was intent on making Honor into the kind of man worthy of Beth.

Kahtar found himself in a perpetually bad mood, simply as a result of Monroe's shortcomings. That was how he justified his bad mood anyway. Kahtar hadn't seen Beth in weeks. She had taken residence in an apartment at Cobbson Compound, and all he knew of her status was what Honor Monroe occasionally happened to share. Kahtar refused to consciously consider that these two facts could be a good part of his bad attitude.

Honor Monroe took the bait, swinging his razor sharp blade a hair's breadth too close to Kahtar's face, the tip sliced through his cheek. Winning in battle took sacrifice. Sensing the cut in the darkness, Honor dropped his guard, an apology forming on his lips. It never had time to exit. Kahtar spun on the spot and put the flat of his blade across Honor's shoulders and launched him so that his face hit an oak beam so hard he bounced off, unconscious before he hit the ground.

A bit guiltily Kahtar took the time to fix the man's broken nose before the Old Guard could. Old Guard never bothered with healing noses straight, and as much as he hated the thought, he didn't want to disappoint Beth with a lifetime of having to look at a crooked nose, though he did suspect that Honor was just vain enough to have it re-broken and fixed at the clinic.

Breathing through his mouth, Honor groaned regaining consciousness.

"Thanks, Chief, for fixing it right."

"I didn't do it for you." The comment sounded petty to his own ears and he stood and sheathed his blade.

"It isn't like that between us. She doesn't love me like that."

The words 'I don't know what you mean' almost slipped out of Kahtar's mouth, but he stopped the lie, forcing truthful words out.

"What do you mean?"

Honor struggled to sit up. The first pink light of dawn shone into the barn and he was faintly visible as he checked his face carefully.

"She loves me like I'm her sister."

Giving in to burning curiosity Kahtar dropped to one knee. There didn't seem to be any regret in Honor's voice and Kahtar asked, "But you love her?"

"Of course I do." A faint laugh, "Who wouldn't?"

Jealously crept into Kahtar's voice. "Did you declare to her yet?"

"Of course I didn't. I told you, it isn't like that. She's my best friend."

"Are you not attracted to women?" It was the only explanation he could come up with. Honor didn't take the remark well.

"I might have asked the same question of you, if you hadn't just spent the entire morning spanking me simply for being her friend. I used to suspect she was interested in you too, at first, but I think she has better options now."

This information was unexpected. Leaning forward he gripped Honor's leg and squeezed, trying to see his eyes in the dim light.

"What do you mean she might have been interested in me? Did she say something?"

"No. Call it instinct, but you've completely ignored her for weeks, and at last count she's received thirty-four declarations from clansmen. I imagine she'll find a much more pleasant mate than you could ever make. She's eaten lunch with a different Palmer warrior every day this week. Let go of my leg! You're leaving more bruises! I forfeit! Find yourself another whipping boy!"

"Sorry." Rising, Kahtar turned to go, parting with, "You're still a very predictable opponent on the battlefield."

THE FOOD AT Cobbson Clinic was spectacular, in all her life Beth had never been exposed to enough clean food that she actually wanted to eat. Seated at a tall table in a sunny courtyard rife with fish ponds and landscaped vegetable gardens, she eyed artfully arranged vegetables on her plate.

"Do you like the mushrooms?" The warrior across the table from her was, without doubt, movie star handsome. She'd always assumed that a man had to be photo-shopped to look like that. Perfect face, beautiful mouth—sculpted and the edges turned up just slightly, green eyes that really shouldn't occur naturally in nature—it was tempting to accept his offer of marriage just to have children with those eyes—but really, beyond the fact that he was too gorgeous, she knew nothing about him. The green eyes smiled, and the mouth followed suit, and teeth really couldn't be that perfect outside of a toothpaste ad, could they?

"You do know me. What I mean is that you can sense my heart can't you?"

"Yes-s." Faltering Beth looked at him wide-eyed. How did he know what she was thinking?

The smile grew wider. "It shows in your face, your thoughts, but mostly it is your heart. You have the singularly most appealing heart I've ever felt. Join with me, you'll be able to get inside the Arc then, and we'll begin our hony mone today."

Keeping her eyes down Beth wondered if he was aware that he was so perfect that she'd never consider, ever, marrying him. Pairing off in marriage seemed to be the foremost goal of every unmarried man in the clan. Apparently she couldn't get into the Arc—where most of the clan was—until she got married, and every single man in the clan seemed desperate to help her fix that. Well, most single men in the clan.

All of these men so anxious to get married were a huge adjustment from the men in the outside world. Beth wondered why it didn't seem like a good thing. Maybe it was because it left her feeling like the littlest antelope at the edge of the herd. At least one proposal had come her way each day since becoming part of Cultuelle Khristos and it was starting to freak her out. They all seemed far too confident that she'd have no regrets in marrying a stranger, they'd laughed when she'd pointed that out to them. To make it worse they seemed wholly mesmerized by her, and she was absolutely certain that not one of them had considered what it would mean to take a wife who only spoke the truth.

Living in this little bit of paradise, as beautiful as it was, she found herself hiding in her apartment listening to her less than honorable music as much as possible, and swearing mentally for reasons she didn't really understand. She felt like the only imperfect person in a perfect world, like a fraud that everyone was enamored with, and she both dreaded and anticipated disappointing them. Beth focused on the stuffed mushrooms, wondering if the men would leave her alone if she gained eighty pounds. Wondering how many meals she'd have to eat a day to do it. A voice interrupted her grand plan.

"Take the western boundary for a shift, Palmer, as quickly as you can get there."

The order interrupted Axel's vigilant wait for her impending smack down. Beth would have known that voice anywhere, but it annoyed her that it made her heart skip even while she stared at a plate full of vegetables. It was, after all, the kind of voice that a country singer would kill for, and she detested country music.

"Chief?" Axel Palmer frowned and stood, reaching to squeeze Beth's hand even though she hurried to move it. Unfortunately he was as unnaturally fast as he was handsome.

"What part didn't you understand?" Kahtar slid onto Axel's chair and the warrior hurried to obey, and Beth, refusing to look towards that voice, was forced to look at her latest suitor.

The heart-breaking green eyes bored into hers as he whispered, "I will find you soon, Dear Beth."

"I look forward to it, Axel." The words slipped out unexpectedly and Beth thought for a moment that she'd told her first fib. Then she realized it was true, but only because she instinctively knew it would annoy Kahtar, and suddenly she looked forward to that more than anything she'd done in weeks.

"How do you like the food?" That voice thrilled her, and it was slightly annoyed, and that made it even better. She kept her eyes on her plate until she could look up without betraying that fact. When she did, all the Palmer men melted from memory. This giant sitting across from her, with his steely eyes and military crew cut had a rugged, imperfectly handsome face that had beckoned to her from the first. Those Mount Olympus biceps meant nothing though, it was the way he almost assaulted her with his heart that thrilled. It stopped hers like a mountain stepping into the wind and there was no way she could ignore the enormous strength behind it.

She looked away again, angry because for the first time in weeks she felt perfectly happy, and there was no denying why.

"What do you want?" There was no way she was letting him off that easy, the big jerk.

"Are you enjoying all this attention?" Motioning towards the neighboring tables, he scowled towards one where three Palmer men sat together. When Beth met their eyes, they all three flashed perfect smiles at her and waved.

Frowning she met Kahtar's eyes, feeling almost as annoyed as he seemed to be over the Palmer's.

"Berwick's proposal held more appeal." Blurting, oh lovely, and how rude to the pleasant men of Cultuelle Khristos, even Kahtar looked taken aback, and he rarely seemed to permit any expression to cross his face beyond a glare.

"How do you mean?" For once he seemed genuinely curious.

Shrugging Beth looked through the curved glass into the atrium beyond. From the outside, the secrets of Cultuelle Khristos were hidden. Peering through that glass from her seat, all that was visible within was empty hallways and she knew for certain that there was a waterfall right inside of where she sat, though strangely she couldn't even feel the vibration of the water.

"I mean as repugnant as Berwick was at least he wasn't perfect. Is that glass computerized?"

"Computerized?" Glancing at the window behind him, that revealed a hallway that didn't really exist, he offered, "No, we don't use computers. That is what is really in there. You do realize that no one is perfect, not even the Palmer men."

"What are you talking about? I've been living here for weeks. There are no desks and file cabinets in there! That's the atrium, waterfalls, gardens, and a glacier."

The genuine smile that lit his face made her heart lurch so that she almost lost her balance, perched on top of a high stool with her heels clipped over a bar underneath, she managed to recover somewhat gracefully and remain erect. Chuckling Kahtar moved Axel's juice out of his way and leaned forward to murmur.

"Still not asking any questions, Beth?"

"Seems to me I just asked you one."

"Touché." Motioning behind him to encompass the main building he said, "Everything inside the main building, isn't actually inside the main building."

"What? What does that mean?"

He shrugged, "Try walking into one of the walls sometime. You'll get the idea. Though it's only the main area that is an Abstract, an Abstract means space that isn't really on the premises as it appears to be."

"There really doesn't seem much point in asking questions when the answers are nonsensical. Are you telling me it's a magic room?"

"There is no such thing as magic if you know the science behind it, and I'm sure you'll be able to find someone to give you technical details. As a matter of fact most of the Palmer's specialize in Abstracts. There is a reason so many of them are still single. Ask one of them that question, but I will warn you right now, you'll be sorry you did."

Daring a glance up into Kahtar's eyes, Beth was pretty certain he was jealous of those boring Palmer's. The thought that he might feel something for her, despite his abandonment, was thrilling.

He is a soldier's soldier, a lifer, don't be an idiot. Looking back at her plate she murmured. "Well, even if they aren't, they sure look perfect."

"You look perfect, too, Beth." The voice was pitched low, and there was emotion in it, as though it pained him to see perfection in her.

Looking up into those grey eyes she searched for an outward sign of what he was thinking. "I am far from perfect."

"Are you?" It didn't sound like he believed her. "Do you like living here?"

"Believe me, I am the opposite of perfect, and no," She answered frankly, "I hate living here, but apparently there is nowhere else I can go."

"You could come stay with me. Join with me."

Beth spilled her water in her rush to grab it, and give her mouth something to do besides hang open. It filled her plate with a splash and the perfect stuffed mushrooms floated off in a wave. Kahtar put one large elbow right into the mess, ignoring it, those steely eyes held hers.

"I'm not a Palmer, Beth, and I don't know what kind of a husband I would make. I'd never planned to find out, but I've been around long enough to know you and I—for some inexplicable reason—we go together. I've given it time to pass—certain that it would—but it won't."

Of all the proposals she'd endured over the past weeks, this one was without doubt the only reluctant, insulting declaration. Folding her bare arms across her favorite yellow dress she glared at the gorgeous, flawed giant across the table from her. Angry because for the first time she was actually tempted to accept, and apparently the kind of guy she liked was an idiot.

"A bit short on romance, isn't it, Kahtar?"

"That isn't likely to ever change, Beth. I know nothing about romance."

"Do you know nothing about feelings? I haven't seen you in weeks! You left me here in Dr. Seuss's Stepford, Ohio!" Several people at the other tables looked over at them curiously, and then politely away. "Then you drop by to declare, because the feeling won't pass? Try stuffing your head in the oven, Mr. Darcy."

By the time she managed to wrest her heel off the stool, it toppled with a crash to the patio. Made of the same soft paving stones as the front entrance, her five inch heels sank down as Beth attempted to stalk off and she was well aware of the fact that she looked ridiculous having to yank each leg up to escape the heel-swallowing patio. Three Palmer men looked up with interest, when wrestling to find the balls of her feet she put her hand down on their table. Six of the most arresting eyes she'd ever seen seemed to find no fault with her unnatural writhing.

"Can one of you, please, explain to me what an Abstract is?"

If she was reading them correctly, these three men had just completely fallen in love with her.

WATCHING BETH WALK through the doorway into the atrium, with what appeared to be a herd of suitors, Kahtar sensed as soon as they crossed through the Abstract. The touch of Beth's heart vanished. Maybe he should care that half the people lunching on the patio were darting looks his way. Maybe he should be self-conscious or embarrassed to have been publicly rejected. Off-hand he couldn't remember ever being embarrassed, though surely he had been. Probably thousands of years had just given him time to become immune to the feeling. Too bad all that time hadn't given him any insight into affairs of the heart. Heaving himself off the table, he bent to pick up Beth's stool and almost jumped when he stood and Abigail suddenly stood right there.

The woman only came up to his torso, but those sharp eyes and militant librarian demeanor always unnerved him a bit. Maybe because he'd never met anyone like her, he wasn't sure what to make of Abigail Adit.

"Well out of the frying pan into the fire, eh? For Beth I mean. She'll regret that little maneuver. I like that one. Not afraid to make colossal mistakes."

"What do you want, Abigail?"

"Nothing. Just wanted to make sure, you know, that you're not going to actually go stick your head in an oven."

Turning away from the woman Kahtar was suddenly glad that at least she was keeping her nails on chalkboard voice lower than normal. Maybe he wasn't above embarrassment after all. Deciding to hike the long way around the compound, rather than follow Beth through the atrium, he stalked off. Abigail wasn't one to be ignored though. She huffed and worked those chubby legs trying to keep up with him.

"Do you even know who Mr. Darcy is? Never mind, it's in one of those paper and leather things we call books. You need a primer for this don't you?"

"Oh I think I got it, Abigail. Question is why you're rubbing lemon juice on it."

Chuckling she managed to keep up with him.

"Didn't know you had much sense of humor. I'd say you didn't get it at all though, if you really think she isn't interested in you."

He came to an abrupt halt. Abigail trounced on past him and into a patch of wax beans, spinning on her orthopedic shoes, she returned to him.

"Beth doesn't play games, and I think even you know I sure don't."

"I don't think, you think, like she thinks, my slow thinking warrior. You insulted her and she's mad. Any woman who refers to any man by the name Mr. Darcy is interested. It's one of the laws of physics on this planet. Did you happen to notice her heart during her little tirade?"

"There are few times I don't notice her heart." Not looking into Abigail's eyes made that easier to admit, but she had his full attention.

Bouncing up and down on her brown orthopedics, she tormented first.

"Let's see, I need to use small words so that you understand… oh, glare a hole through me, I don't care. If you had declared, without making it sound like you found it repugnant—oh wait—that's a big word."

"Abigail? Are you saying she didn't mean what she said?"

"Oh no, she meant it, I think she'd preheat the oven for you."

"Could you give me a break?"

"No." Squinting she tried to focus on his face through the August sunshine. "Fine. Declare again. Tell her how you feel without being an oaf—if you can."

The Elder's face was sincere, if amused. Abigail obviously had seen something he hadn't, and she approved. For some reason that was reassuring, even if she didn't know what kind of a repeating, sinful, freak he really was. That thought sobered him. Maybe he shouldn't be trying to join anyway. What could be the point in dragging any woman into his crazy repeating life?

"Kahtar?" Abigail's voice had lost all teasing. It was loving and one surprisingly strong plump hand grabbed hold of his forearm. "She all but accepted you already. Have you never followed your heart?"

*The First Law—Love—It is your purpose…*Since the beginning he'd followed the laws of being. And his repeating wouldn't hurt Beth. It would hurt him more next time, but he didn't care.

Turning to head back towards the atrium Abigail tugged him back.

"Hold on big fella. It won't hurt you to let her suffer by comparison. After a few hours with those Palmers, you'll be golden."

Turning his head to try to bite back a guffaw, he admitted, "No one has ever said that to me before."

"Well don't get a big head, Kahtar, it's only because it's Beth. To any other woman in the clan you look like a work horse next to one of the Palmers."

"Thanks, Abigail."

"Come on, do you care if you're pretty?"

"Today? Yes."

"Then go home and change. You've got some kind of sauce all over your sleeve, and who'd you try to kill this morning? There's dried blood all over you. Do you own any clothes that would be normal to Beth? Not a police uniform either. I think you look creepy in them. Go on, she'll be hours before they let her escape."

CHAPTER
TWENTY-THREE

THE APARTMENTS AT the Cobbson compound were deluxe. Kahtar had only ever been in the men's barracks before. It shouldn't have come as a surprise that Beth had been afforded every comfort. They treated her almost as a pet. The first Orphan of the Inquisition accepted into Cultuelle Khristos, possibly the first adult Orphan accepted into any clan. There was a separate kitchenette in her quarters, a company room with bouquets of flowers, and baskets of fresh fruit arranged on low tables between silk sofas. Even her laptop sat on a polished desk beneath a sunny window, he knew without checking there was no internet service. Contact with the outside world was completely shunned unless necessary for security. The fact that she had a computer at all was a concession he was surprised had been made.

Uncomfortable in the only street clothes he owned, Kahtar wandered to Beth's bedroom to look at himself in a mirror. The apartment was spartan and neat, but the bedroom was a mess, for a moment he stood looking around at what could have passed as a crime scene. Clothes littered the floor. All of the bedclothes had been stripped off the bed including the sheets which were hung over the window shutting out the view of the men's exercise park. Written in lipstick across the mirror over the dresser, was a column of rude words.

Standing there, staring at those words, Kahtar almost forgot to look at himself. Unable to make sense of it, he turned his focus on his image. A red polo shirt, khaki pants and a pair of sand colored sneakers. The shoes seemed to go better than his police issue footwear. Beyond his uniforms these were the only street clothes he owned. As he'd never worn them before, he wasn't certain if they were appropriate.

The door to the apartment banged open and slammed closed. Kahtar heard a chair hauled across the marble floor and sensed it as Beth wedged it under the door handle. Apparently she missed locks. She was muttering to herself, but he couldn't quite make it out until she came rushing towards the bedroom.

"Are you freaking kidding me? Whoever taught them how to talk, should be whipped!" Before he could make himself known, she was in the room.

Beth froze, in an almost comical position, with her legs planted too far apart as though braced for impact. Despite her obvious distress she looked perfect, the summer blonde hair simple and smooth, and her yellow dress leaving all of her arms and too much of her legs bare. Straw colored sandals with impossible heels revealed blue toenails.

"What are you doing in my room!"

"Sorry, I was waiting for you and looking for a mirror." Kahtar motioned towards her lipstick graffiti. "Charming. What does 'bite me hard' mean?"

"It's what you can do. Get out."

"I hope you don't actually say that to any men, because it is rather tempting."

Beth had the grace to flush, and he focused on what he'd come to say. To tell her how he felt, believing what Abigail had told him. Yet Beth did not look like she thought much more of him than she did of those Palmer men. Then it hit him. Her gifting was truth.

"Beth? I think you and I belong together. What do you think?"

The pink mouth opened and closed twice, and he could sense a spot on her lower lip where she'd been chewing on it too much. Her arms crossed, protectively over her chest. That frank gaze sized him up in his worldly clothing. He waited; his body as tense as if being strapped in for torture.

ZEUS WAS CHEATING. He knew she had to tell him the truth and he was using it against her. No one else had dared to, even though she knew they all talked about her gifting. From what Beth overheard, they were all impressed with the fact that she spoke only the truth, still none of them had been stupid enough to ask her how she felt when they declared. Or brave enough. For a moment she pondered stupidity and bravery and wondered where the line was between the two. Then she wondered why she was delaying her answer, it wasn't like she was preparing it, or like she'd alter it to spare either of them. If that were an option she surely might have. The shrug was as involuntary as her reply.

"You're probably right, unfortunately."

"Unfortunately?"

"I hardly know you. You do not know me at all—though nobody around here seems to WANT to know someone before they get married. And what is up with that anyway? Is there some sort of law I missed where everyone must be married? Besides that I promised myself I'd never marry a soldier—and you—you're like the soldier king. On top of that you're the enforcer of all those laws I've been reading about."

The analogy made him smile, "And you're like the clan anarchist, I assume?"

Beth grinned then. "Pretty much, I'm fairly uncooperative by nature. We'd be like the dog catcher trying to live with a bag of ferrets."

Whatever that meant, it made him laugh. "Apparently I'm in love with that bag of ferrets."

"Shut up. Is that your idea of romantic?"

"Isn't there anything about me that you find attractive?"

"Yes. I really like your house…Hey! Did you just roll your eyes?"

"I think I did. Is that the best you can do?"

"For now it is. I'm really ticked off at you, Kahtar. I can't believe you dumped me here like you did. It has been my own personal purgatory."

"I thought you wanted to belong to this clan!"

"With you!"

Something happened to his heart at those words, and for a moment he wasn't sure if it was his first heart attack. It ached like it was bleeding, and he could see his pulse in his eyes for several long seconds. Then he went towards her, to embrace her, but she side-stepped him.

"Forget it. I'd just as soon beat you with a chair right now."

Heart sinking, not sure what, if anything, had been settled he made himself offer, "Do you want me to leave?"

"Heck no, I want you to help me escape."

"You can come live with me."

"Ya know, I'm sorry, but seriously wouldn't you prefer a wife who you knew wouldn't smother you in your sleep? Because I can't promise you that I wouldn't, Kahtar. As a matter of fact, I'm fairly certain that I would."

Laughing, he went to her closet and started to pull out her stylish luggage.

"Not that I wouldn't take my chances, Beth, but you don't even have to join with me. You will have your own room at my house, if you can bear to walk past my weapon collection. Consider it a change in venue. You can always come back here anytime you want."

"So we'll just be living together? Quit rolling your eyes at me! I wouldn't have thought that was allowed."

"You do realize that we were already living together?"

"No. You were my jailer, I was your prisoner."

"Are you going to argue everything I ever say?"

"Probably."

"I've declared to you, publicly even. You have not declared to me. It isn't unusual nor uncommon for any type of partially declared beings to move in together."

"And not get married?"

"Usually they do, but once they didn't." Grinning at her, he added. "So it wouldn't even count as scandalous and nowhere near anarchy if you were the second to do so. Though, you're probably the first to move in with a declared just because you like his house."

Beth yanked a dresser drawer right out of the bureau and dumped the contents into a suitcase, a moment later it was followed by a second drawer.

"It's not just the house, Kahtar. I think I can safely say that I love you about as much as a bag of ferrets too."

KAHTAR FLOATED. BETH had objected that his declaration lacked romance, but he couldn't imagine anything more romantic. Abigail's advice had been golden, as she'd promised. He was glad that he'd taken the time to change into the red polo shirt and khakis, glad that he'd taken Beth's yellow convertible instead of the much faster, planet friendly ways there were to travel from the Cobbson compound to his home. Driving through the village and then down the country road, Beth reached over and took his hand without a word, and he floated. Not daring to question or press, he'd simply wallowed in the moment. It felt good, following his heart.

Passing through the veil, watching Beth's hair swirl in the wind and the ends gather in her mouth it occurred to him that enjoying life as an adult would probably be as good as life could get. Gratitude swept through him. Shutting off the engine in front of his cabin, those knowing blue eyes weren't on his house, they were on him.

"Was that a prayer? It felt like something left you…."

"Yes. You're getting to know my heart if you felt that."

Leaning over the console, jammed with CD's, old water bottles and hundreds of little sticky notes, she kissed him, just a quick peck on the cheek. It was possible that he'd kissed and been kissed by hundreds of thousands of women in his existence, mothers, sisters, clan, and friends, but none of those had ever affected him like that brief touch of her lips. This went through his heart like honey melting into hot tea and he knew then. Everything would be right between them. He would learn how to be a good husband. Beth loved him. Sitting there quietly he wallowed some.

"Don't be so self-satisfied, I haven't returned your declaration yet."

"But you will." Kahtar's seldom used jaw muscles hurt from smiling so widely, it was wonderful.

IN THE MIDDLE of the night Kahtar was rescued from the beginnings of his shade of Golgotha by a strange thudding coming through the wall. Pulling from the memory in a cold sweat, he scanned through the wall. Beth was moving furniture. Slumping against his pillows he smiled. This was yet another first. As the shade that plagued him slid into the past, his future beckoned with a new lure. Beth's bobbing heart cut right through the wall, lightening his heavy one even now. Their quiet evening together had been spent simply, just watching Beth walk into her room had been a joy. She'd enthused over the craftsmanship of the cabin, it felt as though he'd lain every log and board for her alone.

An Old Guard shimmered into the room and Kahtar obediently slid to the edge of the bed, waiting only to be told which uniform to reach for, the world of Covenant Keeper or Seeker.

"The Elders have returned from Scotland, they want you at the cave."

The word 'hurry' was never uttered by Old Guard, it was implied by their mere presence. Reaching for his tunic he sensed the dark scan of this Old Guard as it moved through the wall. The thudding noise stopped, and Beth's tremulous voice cut through the darkness.

"Kahtar? Is everything all right?"

Strange. She'd felt it. "Gangbusters." Shouting through the thick wall he explained, "I need to go out for a bit. I'll be back later."

"Okay. Have fun."

It took effort to keep the smile off his face. Fun was not in the job description but with Beth around maybe he'd have the opportunity to taste it at least now and then.

TORCHES WERE BLAZING in the courtroom of the cave. The stone chamber felt pleasantly cool after the humid August night, and excited voices filled his ears before Kahtar took his place near The Mother of Cultuelle Khristos. The Elders were smiling. It looked like good news had been had in Scotland.

"You'll be pleased, Kahtar." Anwyn D'Aval greeted him with a smile. Seated casually on stone benches with The Elders of the clan, she motioned him closer.

"Berwick's men were rogue. Orange and Father Wixen located Elders from Berwick's clan in the Scottish lowlands. Their Old Guard sensed ours, and they were very forthcoming about their rogue warriors. Apologetic even."

Elder, Orange Stoddard at 130 years old, still dressed like a young Quester in leather trousers and cotton blouse, his long grizzled grey hair tucked back in a pony tail. Orange was good friends with Kahtar's biological grandfather and had called him Son as long as he'd been known as Kahtar. Orange's guarded eyes warned Kahtar that he wasn't quite as comfortable or optimistic as The Mother.

"Son? They were not nearly as welcoming once they learned we were a Christian clan. Yet Father Wixen still invited them here."

Kahtar tensed, glancing at Father Wixen, trusting and kind old Priest that he was, he'd never seen a day of battle in his life. The chubby Elder shuffled to stand, sandals peeking out from beneath the monk-like robe he wore.

"We are the only Christian clan they've ever had contact with. They want to open communication. Most of the clans in their area are secluded. They are small, less than two thousand strong."

Taking in the atmosphere in the cave as quickly as a battlefield, Kahtar knew his opposition would be vetoed. Having the benefit of millennia of mistakes was his past alone. Cultuelle Khristos was far too trusting, a trait he both loved and hated. Time so often annihilated the most trusting, yet this was their path, to minister to their own people as their faith demanded.

"When are they coming?" Kahtar kept his eyes on Orange to gauge his trepidation.

The Mother said, "Late August, after salmon have their first run in Scotland, they have a celebration to coincide with it. They'll come after and they want to meet Beth."

Orange didn't look happy but Kahtar turned away from him, angrily confronting The Mother. "Why? What for?"

The only answer from her was a faint frown. Orange replied, "They are called Clan Berwick, and Clan Berwick is intensely curious about an Orphan of the Inquisition assimilated into a clan. They claim they want to make a formal apology to Beth. I suspect that apology is contingent upon how worthy they find her. I suspect they want to see if she deserves an apology or is responsible for Berwick's death. Despite his sins, Berwick was the second son of their leader."

"That is completely natural." The Mother's voice was soothing. "They will see that Beth is honorable, as are we, they will see that it is Berwick who broke the laws of being, not Beth, and most certainly not us."

Kahtar and Orange spoke in unison. "It is a risk."

The Mother nodded, but a hint of a smile played over her lips. "As is life."

Kahtar's experience was simply frustrating in the face of such childish naivety. Brutal frankness was all he had patience for, and he faced Anwyn.

"I'm certain they do want to examine Beth's worthiness as you say. I'm also certain they come searching for an excuse to cause her harm. Mother, Beth killed the son of their leader! You can be certain they will be searching for a way to condemn our Christianity as being outside the laws of being too!"

Father Wixen huffed, while Orange Stoddard nodded in agreement. The Mother, however, simply put a hand on Kahtar's arm, gently squeezing. Her fingers were cool even through the linen of his tunic.

"Likely, Kahtar, yet what will they see when they look at us? What will their hearts tell them? We do follow the laws of being. We have nothing to fear."

"Sometimes you find what you want to see."

"I know that, and should they prove that dishonorable, I know you will be prepared for that battle should it come."

It took effort to bite back the frustration that filled his heart, and Anwyn grabbed hold of both his arms and looked up at him. Never had he permitted himself to raise his voice to her, but he couldn't prevent the growl from escaping.

"Shall we battle with them in the streets of the village while Seekers and children watch?"

Ignoring the protests of the Elders, The Mother squeezed Kahtar's arms tightly, her heart brushing against his, both loving and authoritative.

"We'll welcome them within a veil with our Old Guard and Warriors of ilu, it will be protection enough should the worst come to pass. Remember, Kahtar, whatever they think of us, they follow the same laws we do. They will not expose us. It was their rogue warriors who endangered us in that respect. Give Clan Berwick a chance to be honorable."

IT HAD BEEN a disappointment to wake late in the morning and find Kahtar gone. Then it was an annoyance to have to race down the stairs, through the great room hung with weapons and other dark items. Dozens of shades flickered at the edges of her mind as Beth passed. She shoved them away in her rush to the privy. Loitering in the bathhouse she dressed for the day, choosing the same blue dress she'd worn the very first time she'd met Kahtar. Unwilling to reenter the house and risk shades, she loitered outside, impatient and hungry. The silence under the veil was strange, no white noise, no hum of electricity. Birds and insects were the only sounds her ears could pick out. It was hot and humid, even on the shady porch. The cabin smelled like cedar and resin and if her stomach wasn't grumbling, and if a cool drink had been handy, it would have been very pleasant.

When Honor Monroe showed up, she dashed across the driveway to hug him. Picking her up, he swung her in circles and kissed her lips several times. It was comfortable, almost like kissing and hugging her Dad. Honor's heart made her think of skipping along a path when she was little. When Axel Palmer and his three cousins stepped from the dark rectangle near the bushes, it wasn't as exciting to see them. Their hearts weren't the same as Honor's, and she wondered why they came when she was living with Kahtar. When they produced a picnic lunch, some enthusiasm kindled at the thought of good, clean food, and she followed them to the pond.

Sitting in the shade of willow trees, near the smooth cool water, felt like a tropical vacation. There was lemonade with ice, fat sandwiches thick with cucumber and cream cheese, tomatoes so sweet that they ate them like apples and playfully argued over the last couple. Awarded both, Beth shamelessly ate them and then helped herself to far more than her share of fresh berries slathered in whipped cream. Bloated, she dropped into the hammock with Honor. When Axel offered her a long, stick-like cookie made of crushed almonds, and filled with a sticky apricot mixture, it took concerted effort to force it down.

It was almost blissful, wrapped up with Honor as he gently swung them to and fro. Insects droned, frogs jumped, Wolves nosed noisily through the remnants of the picnic lunch, slurping down every stray morsel. The Palmers continued to expound upon Abstracts, a topic they obviously never tired of. Beth half dozed on and off, her ears constantly alert for the arrival of Kahtar.

Waking with a start, dusk met Beth's eyes. All four Palmer men waited for her to untangle from Honor and they each spoke their farewells in the traditional Cultuelle Khristo's fashion, with a kiss on the lips. Unused to the tradition, Beth flushed redder and redder as they kissed her. The Palmers waited their turn at her lips before reiterating their declarations without any sense of embarrassment or even competition.

"You know," Honor told her after the Palmers departed, "I wish I could add my declaration to your pile. It's no use though I just want to be your best friend forever."

"If those four were as honest with themselves as you are, they'd see the same thing. Your declaration I can return. Honor Monroe? Will you be my best friend forever?"

"You know I will," he teased, leaning to kiss her mouth again and run his hand once more through her hair. "When I someday find a wife, I hope she'll be understanding, because I'll always want to hold your hand first. Though, I don't think she will be, if we judge by his reaction." Lowering his voice Honor motioned with his head back towards the house. "Kahtar took one look at you sleeping in the hammock with me and stormed up to the house."

WOLVES STUCK WITH her, waiting outside the privy while Beth freshened up, and then running in frantic circles around her as she made her way up to the house. Sitting on the porch, with one big foot propped on the railing, Kahtar was sharpening a knife. Even in the deepening dusk, his scowl was evident, and he didn't return her greeting. Nor did he remove his pile of tools from the chair beside him and Beth was forced to take a chair further away.

Dark descended and still Kahtar didn't speak, nor did he light a lantern. Mosquitoes materialized to chew on Beth's bare arms and legs. Kicking her heels off, she pulled her legs up and wrapped her arms around them, miserably swatting at the insects.

Finally Kahtar broke his silence, gruff, "Why don't you go inside?"

"I don't like to go in there," she admitted, "That room with the stuff…did something bad happen with the clan today?"

"No. They did locate Berwick's clan in Scotland though. Apparently he'd gone rogue and taken warriors with him."

She considered that for awhile. "What is Berwick's clan going to do about what I did to him?"

Running a cloth up the length of a long blade he sighed. "Clan Berwick—as they're called—they want to meet you, to apologize for what their rogue warrior did to you."

"You don't believe that. You're mad because Cultuelle Khristos agreed to it."

Kahtar bristled, and shrugged, refusing to respond, so much for being able to ask him anything.

"Kahtar, if you have something to say, just say it. Are you worried that Berwick's clan is going to hunt me down and kill me or are you mad because I had a picnic with a bunch of guys who think they're in love with me?"

Tension seemed to crackle off of him. He didn't answer and ran the cloth furiously up and down his blade. That answered the question. It wasn't the action of a man worried for his girlfriend's life.

"Look, I can't help it if the Palmers come around, can I?"

"Yes you can!" Kahtar snapped and Beth was suddenly glad there was a spare chair between them. The hair rose at the base of her scalp and she fought back a shiver. When he continued, his voice had lost the sharp edge.

"They're not going to give up until they know there's no possibility of you returning their declaration, and I don't know what Monroe is about. Either he wants me to beat him with the broad of my sword, or he wants to braid your hair and play dolls with you."

"Don't be such a crank! Honor is my best friend. I've never had a best friend before, don't you dare ruin it for me. And I didn't know why those Palmers didn't give up. I'm certainly not encouraging them! Where I come from, when a woman is living with a man that pretty much means she's taken."

"Well, where I come from, it means try harder. Your bedroom is full of flowers and notes from those who couldn't make today's picnic. Tomorrow the Palmers are planning on taking you berry picking and then showing you an Abstract they've created from the mountains near Bhutan!"

"I am not going to Bhutan with the Palmers!"

"It's not in Bhutan it's down by the lake. I thought they explained Abstracts."

Slapping at a mosquito she grouched right back at him. "They lull me into a boredom coma before they ever get to the point."

"Don't worry," he snapped right back. "They'll explain it all again tomorrow!"

"In that case, I return YOUR declaration right now."

He exhaled as though he'd been hit in the chest, but the feeling that rose from his heart made her tear up as it brushed against hers. Dear God how she loved this man, every single part of his very being was for her. Why had she even hesitated?

After several beats he responded drolly, but Beth knew he was fighting to regain control of his emotions.

"That's not very romantic. You'll take me just to avoid the Palmers?"

"Yes." Without missing a beat she tossed it right back at him, giving him a moment. "It's quite an incentive."

The battle lost, Kahtar knocked the chair between them over backwards, and all the tools scattered loudly over the porch. Wolves yelped and took off, taking his rank odor with him. Kahtar's arms wrapped around her, as he lifted her bodily from the chair and pulled her tight against his chest. In the darkness she suddenly liked his ugly sleeveless linen tunic and the ridiculous shorts that looked like short long johns, they were soft against her skin. He smelled like the woods and salt, and she wanted to lick his neck where it pressed against her mouth.

Then he lifted her chin with a gentle finger and kissed her, a real kiss. Beth's stomach dropped out and she attempted to climb him. Helping, Kahtar lifted her until she wrapped her long legs around him and held on with her mouth. It was then that Kahtar's heart moved to the forefront of her consciousness. The strong touch of it, as it towered beside her own, was so intense it was as though she could see it.

It was a wall of granite cliffs, rising into a cloudy day, stretching in both directions so far she didn't know where it might end. There was rest there, home. Briefly she paused, feeling it, knowing him and wondering how there could be so much of him. He was a fortress. Then the lure was too much, she wanted to burrow into the silvery grey mass that pressed against her own heart. It was then that instinct took over, her own heart buffeting against his defenses and she suddenly knew how to use it to claim him.

The touch of her heart against Kahtar's grew stronger and razed over his heart. It seemed to be leaving a physical mark as it moved. It felt exquisite to bite through the hard exterior that was Kahtar and scratch across a great length of his heart. Kahtar's moan of pleasure filled her mouth as she marked him for her own. Shivering with pleasure, Beth stopped, afraid to continue, afraid to know the expanse that was Kahtar. He immediately extricated himself from her, his strong hands trembling as he pressed her gently away.

"And so it is done. I am yours. I love you, Beth, but I need a moment to find my land legs again. Let's say goodnight." Then he hurried across the dark porch and into the house, leaving Beth standing alone on the porch in the dark night, wondering.

CHAPTER
TWENTY-FOUR

KAHTAR COULD SENSE pressure outside the veil as he scanned the skies. Storms had passed in the night, but rays of sunlight now filled the veil. Not one shade had bothered him throughout the night, and he'd drawn first blood against an Old Guard in his morning training match. Scooping food from a pan he breathed deep. Never had he felt so alive, so healthy, so at peace. Being declared felt nothing like he'd ever imagined. It felt right.

Beth raced into the kitchen in the same shorts and t-shirt she'd slept in, her feet bare, exposing vivid purple toenails. It didn't look like she'd slept well. The summer blonde hair looked neat as always, but her eyes were puffy and she didn't return his smile.

"Good Morning, Love." The endearment came naturally, and he tried not to think about why she hadn't slept well. "Do you like toast and sausage?"

Without answering she picked up one of the round slices of meat and gamely took a bite. To his surprise she frowned up at him, blunt. "Kahtar? I didn't mean to accept your declaration last night."

Before his heart could sink through the strata of the planet she hurried to explain.

"I planned to accept it! I just wanted to—negotiate—first."

"Negotiate? What did you have in mind?" Suddenly he felt evasive, wondering what she wanted, and if it was something he could possibly give.

"Well…first of all I need an indoor bathroom. Sometimes women need to use it at night." The look was meaningful, and he got it after just a few seconds.

"Oh. Well, all right, that isn't a problem."

Beth didn't smile though. She looked at her hands and sighed.

"Look, I can't sleep in this house with that stuff in here." A slight motion with her head pointed towards the main room, from their angle, axes and clubs were clearly visible.

"My collection?"

"Kahtar? I know what that wooden pyramid thing is—it was used in one of my shades—on a woman."

"The Judas Cradle? Shades of War, I'm sorry, Beth. I'll move it."

"What would be really nice is if you could move it all. I mean, there's a nice big basement here isn't there?"

Looking at her for a moment, he thought of why he kept all that stuff, wondered if she could ever understand that it helped him sleep at night. Wondered how on earth he was ever going to explain what those weapons meant to him. He forced a reluctant nod, they were only things.

"Is there anything else?"

Sliding into the chair he normally sat at, she piled a gigantic amount of toast onto her plate. After pouring a large glass of bright green, unripe-berry juice she took several large gulps before proceeding. Looking right up into his eyes she demanded.

"How old are you, Kahtar?"

Here it was then. He'd expected it last night, after their hearts had abutted so intimately. Even as an Orphan of the Inquisition he was certain she had sensed the vast experience in his heart, experience that came only with time. As she waited for his answer her heart caressed his, touching the mark she'd left on it—her touch was deliciously intensified in that spot. He couldn't tell her, not yet. Easing into the spindly chair across the small round table from Beth, Kahtar blindly pushed food onto his plate.

"I'm fifty-one, Beth."

Her eyes widened, it was true Kahtar defended himself mentally. That was exactly how old his body was, this time—how long he'd been called Kahtar. If Beth saw more she didn't push, the number seemed to sidetrack her.

"You are my Dad's age!"

He shrugged, playfully apologizing. "Sorry?"

She laughed then and took a few bites of her food before commenting.

"I knew you were a few years older than me. Sheesh, you do realize that I'm only twenty-four?"

His eyes lit up.

"Declarations can be broken, hearts heal given enough time, but I'm afraid you cut deeper than most. We are almost joined already, so there is no going back for us. Besides, you are not getting out of this marriage just because I'm old."

Beth leaned towards him, studying his face diligently, and then her eyes flicked to his hands as though searching for age spots. The scrutiny made him glad that this repeat had been relatively peaceful. His body was completely functional and all appendages were still attached. He boasted few scars and all his teeth were even intact. He'd never been handsome like the Palmer men, but neither was he unattractive.

"Why do you look maybe thirty-four?"

"We age differently—Covenant Keepers. I suppose it is the clean living. Your idea of fifty-one would be my idea of around eighty or so."

Her eyes widened as she took that in. "Covenant Keepers live longer? My shades don't show that, and no one mentioned it."

This conversation was painful for Kahtar. He'd been thrilled to make it to fifty one more time, but he'd never made it much further, they might not have much time together. What would come after he died, he didn't want to think about. He led the conversation in another direction.

"Do your parents look their ages?"

"My parents!" It worked, Beth's eyes lit up. "I miss my Dad so much. Kahtar? I've read the laws of being so many times. They are very black and white. My only question was why you spell ilu with a little i."

"ilu is from the Ancient Tongue, it means The One."

"That's what they said at Cobbson Clinic, I still don't really get why it isn't capitalized. So, the thing about the laws of being is, there are only ten and it isn't like they are difficult to know."

"It is in the implementation where the difficulty lies. You do not want to force this life on your parents."

"No, but I won't! You'll be surprised, they won't ask much. You watch. They never do, especially not my Mom. Please? I'm dying to see them, and it's not like I'd say anything to them."

For once his gaze made her flush.

"Oh really? The speaker of truth won't mention to her parents that—"

"That she's really an alien species and has now joined a cult of them."

Kahtar laughed then, a deep hard laugh. "Covenant Keepers are as human as the rest of the planet though technically we are a cult...."

"Don't change the subject. You're coming with me anyway. They're going to want to meet you, especially my Dad."

Grinning Kahtar drummed his fingers on the table as he considered Beth's request, wondering if he'd ever even consider approving this for anyone besides her.

"Of course they'll want to meet your declared."

"Fiancé. My Dad is going to want to meet whoever kept me from visiting him all summer. You're dog meat because whatever cover story you've fed them, he'll just assume I didn't come home because of you. There's no disguising that truth."

The smile vanished.

"We'll have to discuss exactly what you're going to say, Beth. They think you've been traveling, I don't expect you to lie, but I also expect you to be careful what you do say."

She rolled her eyes at him then.

"I meant he's going to assume I've been off getting cozy with you instead of visiting."

THE SCREEN DOOR banged open and Honor Monroe raced through the house. Startled, Beth watched as he entered the kitchen in his police uniform. He bent over her to wrap his arms under hers and haul her to her feet.

"Sweet Bethy! Congratulations! Kahtar? You too, I suppose you won't be pulling your shift today." Plunking Beth back into the chair he moved two steps to lean down and kiss Kahtar. It was curious to see two men kiss so casually, especially after the rude things Kahtar had said about Honor. Obviously Kahtar truly loved his partner.

"I suppose I won't. Beth wants me to meet her parents."

"Excellent." Honor enthused. Beth noticed when he nodded almost imperceptibly towards Kahtar and knew her declared had given orders in his second voice. On a whim she tried out her own.

"EAT WITH US?" It was strange to use an unused part of her brain, the words vibrated through her head oddly. Both the men looked at her and Honor shivered slightly, then laughed.

"Tone it down a bit there, Screech. You'll have dolphins swimming inland for miles."

Beth laughed, thrilled that it had worked. Honor reached across the table and grabbed her hand, bringing it to his lips to kiss repeatedly then flipping it over to kiss her palm.

Kahtar snapped, "You tone it down, Monroe. That is my declared you're slobbering on."

She narrowed her eyes at him, Kahtar pretended not to see. Honor apologized, but kissed her cheek again anyway then dragged a chair across the room and slid into it, his leg against Beth's as he poured syrup over the heap of food on her plate before picking up her fork to share.

"How'd you know we declared?" she asked, as Honor dived into her breakfast.

Both men chuckled. Honor's blue eyes lit as he forced his food down quick.

"Really, Ducky? Your heart. The Palmers turned straight around before we'd reached the porch, went right back the way we came. I don't think they were in a congratulatory mood."

Rubbing her chest through the thin fabric of the pajama top Beth considered that, flushing slightly at what her heart had done to Kahtar's, wondering how much they'd felt. When she glanced over at him, he was studying her with those steely eyes of his.

She asked, "How far away can you feel a heart?"

Honor piped up before Kahtar could open his mouth. "Oh it varies, not far. You have an exuberant heart, that's why every other man in the clan wanted to join with you. Who wouldn't want to come home to that? I sure would."

Shoveling a huge mouthful of food, dripping syrup, into his mouth he met Kahtar's eyes across the table and mumbled, "Sorry?" He scooted his chair closer to Beth's as though seeking her protection and she glared a warning towards her glowering declared.

"You need to get to work but leave the squad car here."

Honor obeyed immediately, pausing only to swipe a brief kiss over Beth's lips then he was gone.

"Are you a jealous man, Kahtar?" Gazing across the table at him, she tried to read his expression.

"No. I don't think so, Beth. You're the first girl I've ever loved, so I'm not entirely certain, but it's just that...."

"What?"

"I'd like to spend some time with you, holding your hand and talking like you do with him. Honor can be your girlfriend tomorrow."

"Okay." It came out with a silly giggle, "I'd like to hold your hand." Wondering why the truth was making her blush furiously, she looked down at her plate. Honor had poured syrup over everything, and the pile looked vaguely disgusting.

Kahtar reached across the small table and took her hand almost shyly. For long minutes they sat quietly that way. Finally he said, "Would you mind terribly if we went to see your parents tomorrow? We've never had a day just the two of us, not really."

Clutching his big hand tightly she met those steely eyes directly and knew he saw her answer there. Lifting her hand he pressed it against his forehead and sighed.

"I never thought to have a wife. And now I wonder how I never knew how much I needed you."

CHAPTER
TWENTY-FIVE

LONGINUS SENSED HIS *kinsmen calling weakly to him in second voice. There was no point in staying here. Darkness had taken this godless land and sixty of his warriors. It was time to retreat. Bloody, mud-caked sandals slowed his step, and the torment of those around him burned against his aching heart. There was no sin in offering mercy, the man was nearly dead, perhaps he was dead…why could he not tell for certain? Longinus's fingers curled around the shaft, and he shoved the stolen spear up, through flesh, sinew, and muscle, the familiar resistance of bone got in the way, but an expert twist helped by-pass that, and he reached the heart. Then he sensed Him, ilu. In that moment Longinus wanted only to die.*

Kahtar was screaming, his world completely dark, he was blind with agony. Hands touched him and he pushed them away, felt a body give easily under his strength, somewhere in his mind he heard the sound of impact and a protest. It tugged him towards consciousness.

Old Guard? Old Guard know not to touch me. Gasping for air his mind fought to make sense of his world. *Breathe, deep, breathe.*

"Old Guard?" He managed to get the name out, a question, not a summons. Beth's voice replied from halfway across the room.

"No! Just me, I think you might have hurt my hip."

Beth! In seconds he was out of the bed and squatting beside her, scanning. Bruises, just bruises, plenty of them and plenty more coming, there was nothing to be done for bruises. Tugging Beth to stand he rubbed his hand across her cheek.

"I didn't know it was you, I'm so sorry, Beth."

"Am I supposed to think that was because of a shade?"

"More of a bad dream." Heart still hammering and sweat running down his back Kahtar didn't know what else to say.

Shades are unbearable when they're memories of what you've really done. It was worse, tonight, than it had been in a long time, so real, so painful, and after the best day of his life. *Did I think being joined would change my sins? I should tell her. Now.* But he didn't want to, not when her heart was already wrapping his, offering comfort.

"I hate when you lie to me." Beth's voice was teary and something deep in him made him tell her the truth that he'd never told another soul. "It wasn't just a shade, not really, just my own sins catching up with me."

To his surprise Beth's arms wrapped around his waist and she hugged him. The skin from her cheek pressed into his bare chest and she leaned into him, tightening her grip. Maybe it was the moonless night, or maybe it was catching him fresh from Golgotha or even the accepting push of her heart against his in the dark, but he rested his face against the top of her head and kissed it.

"Don't," he whispered into her blonde hair. "Don't be understanding about this. You don't know what I haven't told you. What I am."

"I know what you are."

Knowing full well that he should pull away, he didn't. He held her tighter and allowed himself to feel her open heart as he confessed.

"I'm an assassin, without remorse. I'm a killer without mercy. I'm a sinner, the worst one."

Beth's grip loosened and he immediately let go, stepping back, certain she saw him now in this black night for what he truly was. Even in the dark, she would hear and know the truth, that he was what he said. Wishing he'd told her sooner, wishing he'd never told her. He felt her flush even in the darkness, sensed her hands pressing against her cheeks, waited for her condemnation.

What he got was, "You're naked!"

It was too dark for Beth to see, and taken by surprise and emotion, the fact that he'd been hugging her against his body au naturel hadn't even registered. Standing a foot from her his reply was heartfelt.

"In every way possible at this moment." Though Beth had put physical distance between them, her heart seemed to know no boundaries as it frolicked over his. It was far more intense than any draw of the flesh.

"I came in here tonight to be honest with you, Kahtar. I know how you feel about me. I can feel your heart too. Even when I first came to town and you told me to leave, I knew you didn't mean it, that you wanted me to stay. That is only part of the reason I stayed though, so don't blame yourself for that. You've bared your soul to me tonight, let me bare mine."

Confused, Kahtar took a couple steps back and sat down on his bed. Beth followed and sat beside him, he could sense the long t-shirt she was wearing, and when she turned towards him one of her long legs touched his and she left it there.

"You are the first one to ever really recognize that I have to tell the truth. Besides my parents."

"It is a beautiful gifting, Beth."

"Do you really think so? The Mother said that too, and you both think it makes me so wholesome. If you really knew me you would realize how wrong you are. I am not pure."

"What do you mean?"

"I mean I'm not a good person. I've done terrible things. It would take me several lifetimes to do penance for the sins of just this one. It doesn't feel like a gift to me, telling the truth—it is a compulsion of which I barely have control. The Mother spoke of giftings like they are blessings, yet mine is not and now you tell me yours is killing? These are giftings?

"I was raised a military brat, Kahtar, you are not the first assassin I've ever known—just the first who has ever admitted it to me, but I knew…and despite your self-recrimination I know you do not take pleasure in killing. Perhaps you think that is irrelevant, but I think it is the difference between a soldier and a serial killer, between a man doing what he must and a monster doing what it will."

In the dark night Kahtar swallowed, Beth's words a balm.

Still, she does not know….

"At least you can control it, your gift of killing. Consider what you would be if you could barely control your gifting? It would make you a monster. That is what I am. I am not some pure sweet woman that fate has tossed towards you and your clan. I **am** that monster. Perhaps if you really understood what I can do, you would use your gifting against me."

"Beth, Sweetheart." The endearment spilled from his lips as though he'd said it a thousand times. Wrapping his arms around her and pulling her close he kissed the top of her head again. Her hair smelled like tangerines. Beth shoved away from him, scooting out of his reach to the foot of the bed.

"Don't touch me. This is difficult enough, without you hugging me in the dark without any clothes on. Listen to me, Kahtar. I speak the truth. If you touch me again I will take this off." He sensed it as Beth tugged at her thin t-shirt in the dark. "And I will show you just how impure I can be."

Freezing in place, those words rolled over Kahtar and for a moment he battled against the urge to touch her immediately, before his honor stepped firmly in front of the urge.

"Your honor disappoints me this once."

Kahtar didn't dare move, the air between them snapped to life with desires he'd ignored all of his years on earth. Beth's words had awoken a part of him that he did not truly want to control, not anymore, but he just breathed deep and kept his hands to himself.

At her end of the bed Beth pulled her knees up to her chest and wrapped her arms around them.

"As a child I didn't even try to control myself—I had no self restraint—I spoke it as I saw it. When we were stationed in Alice Springs the doctors told my parents I had Tourette's Syndrome. It's a neurological problem where you can't control random physical impulses. My Dad said they were nuts and ignored them. I was thrown out of more schools, including pre-schools, than you can imagine."

She put her head on her knees then, and a sound escaped somewhere between sorrow and despair. "I used to spit the truth at people, like napalm. I saw so much and just had to share. The magnitude of a lie didn't matter, I covered them all: A cheating spouse, a cheating dieter, a thieving bank teller, a hungry child in Somalia." The sob came through clear then. "They cut off his hand…I was four and I did that to a starving child."

"With no clan to guide you—Beth? Orphans never have it easy, you survived, that is saying something."

"I didn't stop spewing even then, oh it bothered me, the consequences always bothered me, but it was nothing compared to the relief of being able to shoot the little tidbits of truth out of my mouth. Do you feel pleasure when you kill?"

The question surprised him and he managed to out, "No!"

"I do—and do you know what the truth does more often than not? It kills. It kills a relationship, hopes, ambition, careers. You say you've killed, Kahtar? I will match you person for person with the killing I've done using words alone."

"No, Beth. You mistake their sins, the consequences of their sins and claim them as your own."

"Tell that to the child without his hand, Kahtar. He won't believe you either. I still see his eyes. He was beautiful, perfect…. My Dad always said it was because I was gifted that I was home-schooled for high school—I think he just wanted to keep me alive. No one could hurt me one on one. But a bunch of military brats have ways of telling you to keep your big mouth shut.

"So I finished high school in two years on my own, and started at local small colleges wherever we lived. That was a riot, I ruined the careers of a few up and coming drug dealers before I discovered on-line college. Good thing we lived on military bases then—I still avoid Columbia and Mexico City. Then by the time I was ready for university I was learning some decent self control. You know I learned the truth could be politely spoken at least.

"I learned it was better to run out of the room than to say some stuff. I have two Bachelor Degrees and my Masters. I might've had my PhD except that my thesis told the truth. I wrote it on 'The Inevitable Enslavement of a Capitalist Republic'. Dad never knew about that. Every time I think about it around him I almost chew my lip bloody and make myself shut up."

Kahtar wanted so much to take her hand, just thinking of the weight of such a gift and she had endured it not even knowing who she really was, without the support of a clan that would have taught her and helped her. Beth stood up and before reaching the door she turned around, looking towards him blindly.

"So do you see, Kahtar? The sin? When I speak the truth and when I don't...I have wrought so much damage—including bloodshed—including death—for speaking the truth."

Not knowing what to say, he said nothing. For awhile they stayed like that, Beth standing near the doorway looking in his direction and him sitting on the bed, allowing himself the relief of touching her with his scan while her open heart pressed and beckoned to him from across the room.

Beth laughed lightly. "I'm glad I told you—I knew you thought you'd lucked into some kind of perfect woman. I enjoyed that for awhile, the idealized version of me. I wish I was her. I belong here, Kahtar, maybe not with your clan, but with you, and I know you have things you are dreading telling me. I just wanted to—level the playing field—so to speak. You know? I showed you mine now you can show me yours? Only, to be completely honest with you, the light of an Old Guard has been shimmering outside in the yard now and then and I've already seen yours. You really are totally gorgeous, Zeus. The Palmer men have nothing on you."

With that she shut the bedroom door behind her.

CHAPTER
TWENTY-SIX

DRESSED IN HIS khaki pants and red polo clothes early on Saturday morning, Kahtar waited as Beth trotted out of her room in a pretty, modest skirt and blouse. With flat shoes on her feet, she seemed short when she stood next to him. Sensing faint bruises beneath the surface of her skin, regret crawled up his spine.

How will this work? Will she ever be able to lie in bed next to me?

"Beth? Never shake me awake when I'm dreaming like I was last night. I've never been able to control it...."

"I got that, Kahtar. I've seen post traumatic stress before, I'm a military brat—remember?"

Post traumatic stress? Well, it certainly fit. Running the back of his fingers down the length of her sleeve, he barely touched the fabric.

"I'm really sorry. Beth? I'd never...."

"I get it." Interrupting, she patted his arm reassuringly. "I know you're not an abusive man. My Dad used to have something like that when I was little. I wasn't allowed to go in his room at night. Don't stress, next time I'll just sic Wolves on you."

The thought made him smile, but she chewed her lip nervously and worried her fingernails together. Even after they climbed into the car and drove, Beth continued to fidget. Kahtar waited until she worked up the courage to tell him what was on her mind.

"Okay—so here is the deal—of course my parents don't know I'm living with you. I justify it in my mind because it's a different world, right? Besides we aren't, you know, doing any pre-wedding activities they would find objectionable, right?"

Kahtar looked at her, wondering if she'd be able to pull this off. If she'd truly thought through the consequences of what could happen to her parents if she made a mistake.

Beth continued. "So they assume I am living in the shop. I am frankly freaked that they will make a reference to it and I will not lie to my parents of course." She laughed faintly. "As if I could. It's just if they realize where I am living, they'll think...anyway, Kahtar, if that happens, it happens, it's just that my Dad's old-fashioned—"

He interrupted, "I won't mention it, Beth. I'm pretty good at keeping things under wraps. Well, I was until I met you."

"Yeah, Dad says I should have worked for the CIA." She reached for the dial of the radio and then pulled her hand away, thoughtfully remembering that he wouldn't appreciate the music. He smiled over at her.

"Traditionally I should be the one who is nervous. I'm the one who has to pass muster. Any words of advice?"

Beth smiled then, sliding her hand into his in a gesture that was already comfortable and familiar.

"Be yourself—my Dad already knows you are a cop—he's thrilled. You will love him, he is the kindest, most wonderful man." She tapped her heart, and Kahtar smiled.

"Your Mom?"

"Oh Mom is...actually, Kahtar? My Mom is a little reserved."

"That's okay, so am I."

"There it is, turn right there. See the house with the yard art? Dad has a little too much time on his hands since he retired."

That alone should have been a warning. When Kahtar looked back later he wondered why it hadn't triggered at least a second thought. Covenant Keepers were minimalists by nature, even the most bored wouldn't spend hours decorating their front yard with cut outs of bears and fake geese with clothes. He didn't notice though, he noted the fine lines of the 1920's home and the good sized yard. He noticed that sapling apple trees had been planted in the front yard, and that every plant in the flower bed was edible.

Beth's Mom came around the house, she had a bowl of baby zucchini in her arms and watching through the windshield, Kahtar bit back a whistle of admiration. She was athletic and gorgeous, very like Beth but stronger. Dressed simply in blue jeans and a plain white tee, the way her clothes fit revealed powerful core muscles, and ripples of honed biceps and triceps cut beautifully through the flesh of her arms. Her pale hair was cropped quite short, a messy halo around her head and she wore no jewelry, not even a wedding band.

Kahtar felt her heart swell to see her daughter. Beth swung her car door open and stood, introducing him. Motioning at him through the open roof of the convertible, Beth said, "Mom, this is the Police Chief of Willowyth, also known as Kent Costas, and Chief, this is my Mom, Carole White." He shot a smile up at Beth, it was the truth.

To his surprise Carole simply nodded at her daughter. Then she came shyly around the car to wait for him to unfold himself from the convertible. Carole's eyes widened as he stood and she went very still, staring at him. Then she turned on her heel and went back around the house without even a nod in his direction.

Kahtar glanced over top the car at Beth and she shrugged. He perused the family neighborhood, kids riding bikes on the street, a guy washing his car in his driveway, a woman mowing the grass, nothing untoward. It had definitely been something about him. A man's voice shouted a gravely greeting from the backyard. Beth squealed, "Daddy!" and apparently forgetting Kahtar, she slammed her car door shut and darted around the house.

Kahtar shut his door and ambled after her. *This cannot be anything but awkward or*...he rounded the corner of the house and Beth's Mother stood right there, blocking the sandstone path...*dangerous*, his mind finished. Carole White leaned forward slightly and locked eyes with him. *Holy Heavens, she's a shieldmaiden! I have not seen a shieldmaiden since*...it had been centuries.

Beth's mother didn't move, definitely blocking his way, and silently staring at him. Kathar's mind ran through their one-sided introduction, what could he have possibly done to get her back up?

From around the back of the house came a huge hulking six feet six inches of man, his rumbling voice deep, he bellowed, "So you're the reason my girl hasn't been home all summer? I was beginning to think somebody had kidnapped her!" And then Kahtar understood Carole White. Because this man wasn't an Orphan. He wasn't a Covenant Keeper at all. There could be no doubt. Ted White was a Seeker. Beth's mother had joined with a Seeker.

Beth was a child of Blending.

Kahtar's heart almost sank to his knees. How many times in his repeats had he abandoned such men in The Mists, men who would dare…Kahtar couldn't begin to calculate the number.

Beth clung to her father's arm, smiling up at her Daddy proudly. Poking him in the chest she told him to behave, that there were worse things than being kidnapped by nice, handsome men. Flushing beet red, she continued to poke him right in the middle of his breastbone and she introduced Kahtar.

"This is K-Kent C-Costas." Beth fumbled over the alias, forcing it out.

Ted grabbed her poking finger and kissed the tip of it.

"Welcome, K-Kent." Ted stretched out a friendly hand. Carole still didn't budge, firmly wedged between Kahtar and her family. "Hon, you gonna move so I can meet Beth's boyfriend?" Automatically Kahtar shook Ted's hand.

"Sir," he managed, impressed that his voice sounded natural.

Ted said, "Sir? Don't call me Sir! Geez my Dad was Sir. We're an informal family. Just call me Mister General White, that's what I prefer kidnappers to call me."

"Daddy!" Beth laughed. Ted squeezed her in a one-armed hug.

"What, B-Beth?" he teased, holding her against his side he headed for the backyard.

Kahtar followed, waffling with disbelief and barely paying attention to Carole White, who now shadowed his every step. His mind reeled. Why had he not considered this possibility—why had he ever assumed? Because Beth was Covenant Keeper as much as any woman in existence, but still, her father was not. The Laws of Cultuelle Khristos were crystal clear on Blending. Ted White didn't belong. Blending was not allowed.

Kahtar glanced towards Carole White. Ted pulled out a cushioned patio chair for her and she sat reluctantly. Kahtar automatically obeyed when Ted motioned that he do the same. Beth went to work setting the table, sliding dishes and silverware across the glass surface. With a bottle of lighter fluid in hand, Ted turned his attention to an enormous stone grill where flames already shot two feet into the air. Fortunately Ted and Beth kept a running commentary that required no participation on Kahtar's part. From the corner of his eye he could see that every muscle in Carole White's lithe body looked tensed to spring, and he instinctively avoided making direct eye contact with her again.

Tossing cloth napkins around the table, Beth bent to peep at him beneath the shade of the striped patio umbrella and silently mouthed, "I think they like you."

Shades of War.

SITTING NEXT TO her father, Beth seemed blinded by love, seemingly oblivious to Kahtar's anxiety and her mother's strange behavior. Ted and Beth talked and laughed almost non-stop. Ted grilled two gigantic steaks and Kahtar forced himself to consume his, not sure the genetically altered food would stay down. The part of his mind that always took in details was aware of the hodgepodge of foods. It knew what Ted had prepared and what Carole had prepared. His mind took note of Ted's jacket potatoes, unnaturally large supermarket spuds full of fake cheese and some sort of sour cream substitute, bad chives and bits of fake bacon. It saw mushrooms and onions marinated together in some sort of liquid made from a powdery substance. And Kahtar shoved it all down, mixing it with Carole's grilled clean vegetables and fat slices of what he was vaguely aware was probably the best bread he'd ever eaten.

While most of his mind seemed jammed somewhere between panic and stunned disbelief, a small part watched Beth and Carole eat only clean wholesome food, and listened to Ted and Beth's stories, and noticed that none of their tales involved Carole. And when it was blessedly time to leave and Beth dashed inside to use the washroom, the part of his brain that gathered facts and worked on automatic, responded appropriately when Ted White took the opportunity to interrogate.

"What religion are you?"

"Same as Beth."

"She's crazy about you."

"I feel the same about her."

"Hmpf. How did you meet?"

"Well, Mister General White...I stopped her for speeding."

When they departed, Ted White was still laughing about that, and Beth was grinning and waving a happy goodbye to her parents, and Kahtar was never as thankful to have a meal finally end.

DRIVING HOME KAHTAR kept his eyes focused on the road, squinting into the setting sun. Beth kicked off her shoes and pulled her legs up, wrapping her arms around her knees. She shivered slightly despite the summer humidity.

"Whew! Hiding things is not for me, I'm exhausted. I was afraid to say your name, that I'd say Kahtar. I called you Kah-Kent all night. Dad kept hugging me and whispering, 'Calm down, Angel, I approve if you approve.'"

Kahtar forced a chuckle for her sake, but Beth didn't seem to notice it.

"I'm sorry about my Mom. She's never been very social. I didn't think she'd spend the whole night just staring at you though. Gosh, you know I think I was more worried that you'd say something wrong than I would!"

He looked over at her in consternation.

"I told you I wouldn't mention where you were living."

"No, no, not that, I thought you'd criticize Dad's food, or say something about Books of Being or Arcs or Abstracts or something."

Kahtar wished that those were the things he'd been thinking about.

"But you were great, you even ate his steak!" Beth put her head on her knees. "You set a precedent though. He'll probably make you one every time we visit."

Kahtar's stomach roiled and it had nothing to do with that steak. The good-natured Seeker, Ted White, had rocked his world in ways he'd never thought possible. He'd sooner fall on his own blade than hurt the man that owned Beth's heart. Gripping the steering wheel tightly he kept as silent as Beth's shieldmaiden mother, thankful that Beth quietly kept her head on her knees.

CHAPTER
TWENTY-SEVEN

BY NOON BETH knew something was wrong. In hindsight she should have known last night. Kahtar had been too quiet and preoccupied. And this morning no sound of fighting had echoed from the barn in the back meadow. Now that she thought about it, she suspected that Kahtar had left last night, because Wolves had snuck into the house and had been sleeping on the floor by her bed when she woke up. The dog wouldn't have dared with his master in the house. After waking to his odor she'd dragged him down to the pond, and washed him with her own good citrus shampoo. Now he lay beside her on the bank, looking embarrassed to smell so nice. Afraid he'd shake and soak her, Beth scooted further away to lean against the trunk of a big willow.

Maybe this is what it would be like being married to Kahtar. Being married to a warrior wouldn't be any different than being married to a soldier. Smiling, she looked over the pond. Funny how she'd changed her mind about what kind of man she wanted to marry.

The light of several Old Guard shimmered around the pond. Their sparkly columns of light were so bright it was noticeable even in the summer sunshine, and for a second Beth worried that something had happened with Berwick's clan. She was part of Cultuelle Khristos now and Kahtar said Old Guard would protect her. Was there danger? Then she remembered that Honor had said countless times that it was impossible for anyone to enter the veil without prior invitation. Remembering the day she'd tried to find her way back to Kahtar's house alone, she knew that was true. In the other world, her world, this acreage was a thinly wooded, defunct Christmas tree lot. Despite that she shivered, thinking of Berwick. Was Kahtar outside the veil fighting?

Then an Old Guard shimmered solidly into being right in front of her. Wolves, the coward, turned tail and bolted towards the cover of trees on the far side of the pond. Beth stared up at the wall of man that stood in front of her. These beings terrified her, their oddly lit skin flickered from within and she was certain they were not human. Ancient, worn faces sat atop impossibly strong bodies. Black eyes glittered in the face turned towards hers, a sword gripped in one enormous hand and the other hand reached for her. Beth couldn't help it, she screamed and would have followed Wolves's example if she could have.

In a flash of light the sunny day vanished, and though she was shaking, her scream cut off as amazement shot through her. The truth of what this being was went through her as though he'd spoken to her. Overwhelmed, she would have fallen to her knees as she reappeared inside an unfamiliar room, but Kahtar was there and he caught her as her legs buckled, his hands warm on her bare arms. The room seemed dark after the bright light of the sunny day, and her eyes couldn't adjust quickly enough in the dim light to read his expression.

Putting his mouth next to her ear he whispered to her, "I will not leave you, no matter the verdict here. Declared or joined, you are my wife now, Beth."

Through blurry vision she saw he was dressed in full battle gear, like something out of her shades. He was wearing chain mail. She'd never seen any of the other Cultuelle Khristos warriors wear it. Squinting into the room she saw The Mother and what had to surely be all of the Elders. Dozens of Old Guard stood not shimmering, but solidly around the room, and Warriors of ilu, in their strange mixture of future and past clothes filled the space. Sharpening vision revealed the worst. Their eyes were all on her. Heart jumping, her mind raced over the last day, trying to place what law she'd violated.

"Beth White?" The Mother intoned, and all movement in the room ceased. It seemed as though the crowd had stopped breathing. "Why did you not tell us about your father?"

"My father?"

"Your father is a Seeker."

Instantly Beth's back was up, they were upset about her Dad! She straightened and glared. "My father is a wonderful man!"

Gloriana D'Aval came towards her, putting a soft white hand on Beth's lightly tanned arm. "Beth? Your Father is not a Covenant Keeper."

"I never said he was. What is going on here? Are you judging him for the sins of humanity? Because surely we are all culpable there."

"You read The Book of Being, Blending is not allowed. Covenant Keepers do not mix with Seekers. You did not think it was relevant to tell us about your father?"

After a moment, where she stood with her mouth open, Beth finally replied.

"I do not think my mother was aware of the rules, as she has no idea she is Covenant Keeper. My father!" Her voice cracked and anger boiled up and out. "My father is the best man I've ever known! You dare…did you seriously think that in the decades or centuries since my people were lost to Covenant Keepers that my ancestors managed to find only other Orphans to join with every generation? That is a ridiculous expectation!"

Father Wixen was nodding his head, but most in attendance looked mortified. The Mother reached to smooth her hair, but Beth pulled away, glaring at her.

"We assumed your parents were both Beings. This does not change the fact that you are part of our clan, Beth, it is a lifetime commitment."

"Then why am I on trial?"

"We needed to ascertain that you did not hide it willfully."

"Control your anger, Beth." Kahtar's second voice whispered into her mind, and automatically she tried to obey by taking a deep breath.

Her muscles were so tight she hurt. Her eyes and lungs burned from suppressing unshed tears, the dispersion against her Father stung. Unable to control them, tears spilled over, running down her cheeks.

"I never thought of it, I've never considered my father any different than my mother or me. Why would I have? I can sense his heart!"

The Mother bit her lip, a frown line between her brows.

"It was our mistake, Beth. I apologize to you. Of course it occurred to me that you had Seeker ancestors, I simply never imagined one of your parents would be…it doesn't matter." Gloriana leaned forward and kissed her on the lips, both cheeks and then let her lips linger on her forehead. Though Beth received the gesture reluctantly, the tension in her back eased at the contact. The Mother loved her, there was no doubt. This is what she had agreed to. This is what the pain of being Covenant Keeper was. The problem was in The Mother's words, 'it doesn't matter'. They didn't ring completely true. It mattered.

But Beth was acquitted of the charge. The Old Guard in the room flickered and vanished, and Warriors began to file out. The Mother glided to her side to announce she was bringing dinner later, and pudgy Elder, Father Wixen, told her that her genetics were secondary to her Christianity. Kahtar shuffled her out the doorway and Beth realized she was somewhere in the sprawling confusion that was Cobbson Compound. Walking down a narrow hall, she saw Honor.

Beth's eyes filled with tears at the sight of her friend. Honor would understand how much this had hurt. Surely he felt it already, her heart ached with the sting of an implied dishonor but it was nothing compared to aspersions cast against her Dad. Rushing to Honor, both her arms wrapped around his torso, past his sword, and she leaned into his familiar frame, pressing her heart against his honorable one. Honor stiffened, his arms did not return the hug. She pulled back immediately and wiped her face.

"Sorry, Honor, you're on duty. Come for dinner later? The Mother's bringing it."

Honor didn't meet her eyes when he replied, his voice cool. "No." Then he marched past her and disappeared down the tunnel, the familiar touch of his heart cold and distant.

Cobbson Compound became a blur. Beth noticed none of the odd activity in the colorful and strange rooms she passed. Whispered comments drifted to her ears. "Who would have imagined? I'd declared to her myself!" and "Poor Kahtar." That one repeated many times. "Poor Kahtar." Shutting her ears to the cruel words Beth slogged forward, following Kahtar's direction as he nudged her into the main room. Beth's heart burned with pain and anger and she fought hot tears, refusing to allow them in public. Kahtar shuttled her towards one of the dark geometric shapes she'd long been curious about, but she barely noticed what a tesseract was like as she stepped through and emerged in front of the log cabin she'd been learning to call home.

Parked beside the front porch was her yellow convertible and Beth stopped in front of it, unable to force herself to walk up the stairs to the house.

Kahtar's voice was low. "They will get over it, Beth. It was a shock for them. We've never had this situation before. Blending is so forbidden, to them all Seekers are tainted, in their shock they think your bloodline pollutes you in some way. Eventually they'll see your heart for what it is—as much Covenant Keeper as they are, they just need time."

"Do they?" Her voice was ice-cold, but anger burned hot as it coursed through her body. "So do I."

"Love?" Kahtar squeezed her elbow and she pulled from his grasp. "Who told them?"

He looked confused, his eyebrows pulled together and he studied her as though he barely understood her language, visibly straining.

"About your father? I did, Beth. Surely you didn't expect me to hide it from my clan?"

"No. I don't expect you to hide anything, most especially not from me. Why didn't you tell me? Why did you drive home from my parents without a word about this? Why did you vanish last night without telling me there was a problem? I got dragged to my trial by Old Guard! Where you stood with your hand on your blade!"

"That's habit." Mumbling, he briefly touched the hilt of one of his swords as though demonstrating.

Looking away from him, Beth went to the door of her car and opened it with such force that it swung back, banging into her sore hip.

"Where do you think you're going? You're my wife now and Cultuelle Khristos."

"I'm not your wife yet, and I'm going home to my parents. To my father who has been everything to me. I love him, Kahtar. With all that I am I love him!"

"I know that you do, Beth, but you can't just leave like this."

Sliding into her seat she slammed the door shut.

"Yes I can. I need to. I need to be with someone I can count on right now. Someone I can trust. Don't you dare try to stop me, Kahtar. I'll never forgive you if you do." Without looking at him again she turned the vehicle around in the grass, and sped towards the veil's opening, not caring how much pollution was filling the veil with her hasty retreat.

THAT NIGHT KAHTAR stood at his bedroom window looking out at the moonless night, simultaneously scanning the perimeter for a half mile in each direction.

Mosquitoes. Trees. Skunks. Trying to focus on the moonless night was useless, random thoughts kept banging through his head.

Shieldmaiden. Orphan. Seeker. Rotten husband. Beth was right, he should have told her first. It would not have even delayed him to have spoken to her about her father first.

Kahtar leaned his forehead against the cool, dark glass of the window and pressed a hand against his chest. Beth's absence left an ache in his heart, whether she would call him husband yet or not. They were nearly one and the separation was wrong. He stood so long at the window that when he finally moved his body was stiff. It had taken that long for a thought to occur to him. Beth had demanded that he let her go and he had, she had said she needed to be with someone she could count on. The fact that that someone ought to be him struck him hard, and he hurried to change into the clothes of her world.

WHEN KAHTAR SENSED Carole White jogging the dark streets, four miles from her house, he cut his flashing lights and slowed. It was 2:00 a.m. At least he wouldn't have to contend with the Shieldmaiden in order to speak with Beth. He parked the police car down the block from the White's residence, and stepped into a treed lot and focused. Like light he was transported away, and before he could consciously know he wasn't in the same place, he had moved. Instantly he was standing inside the White's tiny house in the dark. It wasn't necessary to scan to sense Ted White, the man's guttural snores echoed down the small staircase. Every step protested his weight as Kahtar slowly made his way towards the tiny bedroom Beth lay in. Even a Warrior of ilu couldn't take these creaking stairs in complete silence, not a single board was solid enough to disguise his progress. Pausing frequently, when Ted White's snores quieted, he eventually made his way to the top landing and into Beth's small room.

Street lights revealed Beth curled up in a tiny twin bed covered in a pilled blanket decorated with flowers and peace signs. An enormous floor to ceiling pile of stuffed animals towered precariously in a corner and some rolled down on Kahtar when he knelt beside Beth's bed. A stuffed unicorn skimmed over Beth's head and fell off the far side of the bed, while Kahtar batted back a blue monkey and plaid turtle. Opening her clear eyes Beth looked up at him as though not at all surprised to see him.

He leaned forward, pressed his forehead against hers and whispered, "I'm sorry. You're right, I should have told you first. I'm not used to sharing my thoughts with anyone, Beth."

Immediately she scooted away, and then patted a sliver of exposed space invitingly. Enticing, tan arms stretched towards him, welcoming him to lie beside her. He knew his surprise was evident when she rolled her eyes at him.

"I meant to cuddle. Seriously? What were you thinking?" she whispered.

Scratching his head he pointed out in a whisper, "If I tried to lay on that little bed I think that the crash would take us down into the kitchen. Come home."

"I can't. We're—my Dad—is planning our wedding. I didn't want to tell him I was mad at you. I think he could tell, but I didn't want him to be mad at you too. So when he asked if I had a wedding dress yet, I said he had to help me choose."

At first Kahtar didn't realize that his mouth was hanging open, when he did he had to swallow a couple times to combat the dryness.

"Wedding?" The question sounded weak.

"Yes, Kahtar, wedding. I know no one from Cultuelle Khristos will come, but I figure we'll have two."

"Two?"

"Yes, one at my parent's church, and then one where your clan comes and watches us join."

It took effort to choke back the sudden laughter, and he fought back the inappropriate visual his odd sense of humor tried to paint.

"Why is that funny?" Beth hissed. "Will no one come watch us join just because my Dad is a Seeker?"

Kahtar gently put a finger over her lips to keep her from saying it again. The outlandish assumption was too ridiculous. Leaning forward he put his mouth against her ear and whispered softly, "We have no ceremony, Beth, Covenant Keepers don't. We simply complete what you started on the porch the other night, the part that neither of us was yet ready for."

Pushing up on one arm she looked at him, whispering low. "You mean having sex makes us married?"

"Joined is the correct term, and it doesn't have to involve sex, although it usually does. When your heart penetrates into mine and mine closes over yours, we are one. For life."

In the night, surrounded by piles of stuffed animals, clad in too small pajamas that had penguins dancing across them, Beth contemplated this. Then she put a hand over Kahtar's heart pressing gently against the polyester fabric and the badge with his alias emblazoned on it. Her heart brushed against his, the touch was sultry like a desert night lit by the moon. The juvenile bedroom vanished from Kahtar's consciousness as Beth's heart again bit through the fresh mark she'd left there just days ago, tasting him. With a gasp and a moan he dropped forward, too much of his weight falling on the bed. It screamed in protest and Ted White's hearty snores snorked to a stop.

Beth mouthed, 'sorry,' and Kahtar fought to control his gasping. It would have been easier to quiet moans of pain from a Malay boot and hot oil, than it was to silence what her touch had just done to his heart. The woman cluelessly had no mercy, and if it weren't for the venue Kahtar would have wanted none at that moment. Briefly he wondered if it would be possible to take Beth with him and travel like light, but as his hand closed around her thin wrist he instinctively knew he did not have that talent.

Ted White thudded out of his bed and banged into the hallway.

"Bethy? You good?" His voice echoed loudly, and Kahtar knew if the man opened the bedroom door he'd lose Ted's respect forever. Suddenly keeping in Ted's good standing struck him as of paramount importance. It occurred to him that he could no sooner vanish in front of Beth's eyes than he could in front of Ted's. The last thing he wanted to do was to seem less normal than he already did to Beth. Although he suspected if he told her he could fly she might take even that in stride. Still she'd already been introduced to enough oddity without tossing more at her.

After our Joining floated through his mind, followed by *coward*, and he shivered slightly.

Beth was watching him curiously, but she called out calmly. "I'm good Daddy. You're not getting up for cookies, are you?"

Ted's footsteps retreated and he grumbled good-naturedly, "Well, not now with my skinny daughter using that tone."

Beth laughed and then, as her Dad creaked back to his room and thumped onto his bed, she whispered to Kahtar. "I'll come home in the morning. If I go now, he'll be upset."

Stubbornly Kahtar crossed his arms, and she gave him a look of exasperation and hissed, "It's only a few hours!"

It hurt physically to be away from Beth now, but there was also the fact that she was Cultuelle Khristos and out in the world, right in the middle of Seekers to consider. No other woman in the clan was allowed this dangerous freedom but his wife. The irony of that wasn't lost on him. Scanning the perimeter in his mind he searched for something, anything, to use as an excuse to make her come home with him then. There was nothing. There weren't even guns in the neighborhood, and even the teenage boys he could sense were tucked comfortably into their beds.

Beth seemed to follow his train of thought because she told him. "Oh spare me, I'm safe. Besides, there's been an Old Guard flickering around here the whole day."

He frowned. He hadn't sent an Old Guard. They rarely followed someone they hadn't pledged themselves to, not without a request, but Beth interrupted his thoughts. Scooting close she put her mouth against his ear and whispered, excitedly, "They're angels! I realized that when they took me. Why didn't you tell me what they were?"

"Angels? The Old Guard?"

"Yes." Beth studied him, her eyes were lit with enthusiasm and even in the middle of the night her summer blonde hair fell neatly over her shoulders, smooth and shiny. "Didn't you know that, Kahtar? They're beings of light!"

Rubbing a hand over his cropped hair he was distracted. "Well, they're beings of light…."

"Angels!" Beth insisted, "right in the middle of the world, I always believed in them but I never expected them to be so—scary—but then I thought about it. Why wouldn't they be? If they'd be anything, they'd be scary!"

Angels? For eons he'd known Old Guard and accepted that they were different, they enforced the laws of being, but they followed their own cryptic laws. The consensus among Covenant Keepers was that they had their own way. Rising carefully, to another deluge of stuffed animals Kahtar batted away a fuzzy angelfish and an octopus while Beth smothered laughter. He could sense Carole White running back towards the house, he had to leave or she'd sense him and he was fairly certain if she saw him near her husband at night she'd attack first and ask questions later. The last thing he needed was a battle with Beth's Mom. Wading through a pile of stuffed animals Kahtar slid out the bedroom door while Beth blew him a kiss. It knocked into his heart physically, real and satisfying and he hoped the sensation would last for the next few hours.

CHAPTER
TWENTY-EIGHT

RETURNING TO THE veil Beth was more environmentally conscious. She entered fast, as she'd seen everyone else do, and let her convertible coast. It was hard to be patient, and she cheated with the gas pedal a couple of times, but eventually coasted to the front porch and shut off the engine. There he was, sitting on the front porch in one of the over-sized Adirondack chairs, rugged, strong and definitely her idea of handsome. Wolves came sailing, pounding over the rolling meadow, his paws sending a vibration detectable through the soles of her thin yellow peep toe pumps. Smoothing her flowered sundress she sat back on her heels and waited for the enthusiastic dog. Kahtar leaned forward and barked an order at the dog, causing him to veer away.

About to protest, she caught a whiff of skunk and groaned, "Sprayed? I just washed him."

"It's hopeless. I've had the plebes bathe him every week since I got him and he always smells. He is the nastiest dog I've ever had. Believe you me that is saying something. Most dogs learn to at least avoid skunks"

"Slow learner?"

"No learner." Kahtar grinned, and patted the chair next to him. Rising, Beth galloped up the stairs and hurried to take her place. Before she was even seated he took her hand and kissed it. "Missed you."

"Me too." A thunderous crash vibrated through the wall behind her and she turned in surprise. Through the window she saw plebes, in their undyed tunics and ridiculous leggings, tugging weapons off the front room walls and hauling them across the large room. Beth popped up to hug Kahtar enthusiastically almost unable to believe he'd really move the god-awful collection.

"Thank you! Oh, thank you, Kahtar!"

"Anything for you, Sweet Beth." His tone was gruff, and there was something underlying in it. While hugging him, enjoying the warm resin smell of the house and the clean smell of his soft sleeveless blouse, she placed it. Fear. He was afraid of not having those weapons inside the house. Settling back into her chair she studied him, the square jaw showed a faint hint of tension, the steely eyes revealed nothing. He was not an easy man to read. Cheating she put a hand on his arm and was momentarily distracted by the sheer size of those biceps—she'd always had a thing for muscular men and Kahtar took the cake. Her heart moved against his as she tried to read him, the furrow she'd dug into his heart drew her but she ignored it, trying to sense everything. Yes, there was faint fear there. He was strangely attached to those weapons.

Surprised she looked into those eyes. "Do you worry about Cultuelle Khristos being attacked?"

Amusement quirked the corners of his lips. "Not particularly. Why do you say that?"

"Well, you keep that huge arsenal right here in the house, like you expect an invading horde—and you had Old Guard practically surrounding my parent's house all morning. They only showed as light but I know my mother noticed something. They even followed me in my car. You know I thought Honor once said that they don't do cars...."

Kahtar dropped her hand, an inscrutable mask dropping over his face, instantly alert he demanded, "Are you certain, Beth? That they followed you in your car?"

"Of course, they were flickering like mad. I mean sometimes I do get ocular migraines, but this was unmistakable. They weren't in the car, but they were all around it."

A split second before Kahtar roared out the words, "Old Guard," they appeared. Shimmering into being by the dozens they stood solidly around the porch and despite the heat of the day Beth's hands and feet went instantly cold with fear. They were always formidable, but this time they were terrifying and fierce. Her eyes went to Kahtar's and she saw fear there too, and knew something was strange and wrong.

"Stop them!" He demanded, and though several new lights flickered to surround her, one of the Old Guard towered over her and reached for her shoulder. His hand felt icy hot as it grabbed roughly, her eyes went to his black leather skirt, noting for the first time a plaid sash that draped over his naked chest. One word flitted into her mind even as Kahtar uselessly reached towards her. "Scottish."

KAHTAR'S HAND MET air, Beth was gone in a flash of light and he roared. Turning he caught only a flash of more shimmering light as every Old Guard bearing the insignia of Clan Berwick vanished. Only Cultuelle Khristos' Old Guard remained and Kahtar shouted at them. "She is my wife! You have no right to separate us."

It was grasping, while the Old Guard surely sensed their connection, by the laws that bound them—and in the eyes of Old Guard—they were not technically joined—not completely. Kahtar did not need to ask what had happened, he knew. Should have known last night when Beth told him that Old Guard had been at her parent's house. They hadn't been Cultuelle Khristos' Old Guard. They'd been Old Guard of Clan Berwick, watching Beth, judging her honor for the role she had played in the deaths of so many of their rogue warriors.

"Beth is not responsible for the deaths of Berwick's rogue warriors!"

One of the Old Guard inclined his head slightly, his black eyes unfathomable, though his body language hinted faintly at concession.

"Take me to her." Kahtar demanded, but he knew already that they would not. They would have taken him already if they were going to. Changing his tactics he looked among the men, eyeing one who had years ago pledged to him. "Where is she?"

In a shimmer of light the man shifted closer. "Orthrus."

Kahtar staggered at the dreaded name, almost dropping to his knees with grief. His voice was a cracked whisper when it passed his lips.

"Why?" But he knew, and for a brief moment he hated every second of his existence. Sick of knowing what was coming based on what had happened, sick of his experience that accumulated day by day, year by year, century after century, never allowing him the luxury of a false hope.

His Old Guard's reply was rote, merciless as they always were.

"She is a product of blending. Clan Berwick has demanded her death. Old Guard will determine her sentence."

The porch shook briefly beneath his weight as his knees buckled, pain and gravity bent him forward, his forehead scraping raw against the wood he'd cut with his own hands.

Take me now, to my next repeat, please, please, ilu in all your forms, do not allow me to remember this. Please. His heart burned briefly, like the fire that had burned him to death exactly twelve times. Then it exploded, wet, bleeding pain like a sword cutting through it. Four times. No, five times. This would make five times his heart had been torn from his chest.

CHAPTER
TWENTY-NINE

ODD HOW THAT the senses don't really work in tandem, not really. The first thing Beth noticed was the smell, a forest primeval—and as she'd never been in one she had to trust her shades for that memory. This was better though, the scent far older than her shades were. Earth, clean earth, warm and rich, pine trees so fresh her fear vanished as she breathed deep, trying to suck the sweet air into her very core. The air she'd known all her life, even the air inside the veil, was filth compared to this. She noticed sounds next, gentle wind playing through leaves in tree tops impossibly high above her, scampering sounds of tiny furry feet, the call of birds and the softest thud of hooves on forest floor.

Air touched her exposed skin, caressing her face, arms, and legs. It washed her skin clean with the touch. Then it was the fact that her heels were slowly descending into the earth that she noticed. Instinctively she leaned her weight onto the balls of her feet. She wasn't afraid to lose her balance, hands twice the size of Kahtar's gripped each elbow to support her. She just didn't want to sully this place with the material her shoes were made of. They didn't belong here.

At last Beth dared to open her eyes, knowing they weren't worthy to see this place, but unable to resist cleaning herself with the light she knew would be here. Unable to focus she searched upwards and saw watery rays of light streaming through towering trees. All of it, the earth, the light, the trees, seemed so alive she could feel them all in her heart. Blinking she felt tears run down her face, burning faintly of poisons from the world she'd come from.

I could die here and it would be joy. All semblance of fear vanished and she blinked the dirty tears from her eyes and looked around clearly. Hundreds of Old Guard moved through the forest, solid and real. The only light came from the sky above, not from these men. Here their translucent skin looked perfect and solid, flawless, and they appeared in the variety of flesh colors of all mankind. They moved gracefully, like dancers, and she saw not a weapon among them. Glancing around she noticed not a single dwelling, not a single man made item of any sort, not a chair or a cup and it was then that she realized that the Old Guard weren't actually dressed as she usually saw them. As a matter of fact she didn't think they were dressed at all. Though they didn't seem naked either, she tried to focus on where their clothes would be, but they shifted and fluctuated in those areas, and she gave up. They simply were. It didn't matter.

One of the Old Guard, his grey hair thick and his brows almost white, watched her closely, his obsidian eyes glinting oddly. When he spoke it was in a language she'd never heard before, but though the words made no sense, she understood what he said.

"She senses the truth here too. Are you terrified woman?"

Beth considered this for a moment, perhaps longer, thoughts crowded into her mind as she struggled to answer truthfully, and for once she was uncertain what the truth was.

He stepped closer. "Time passes differently here. If you consider all your mind takes in now, you will not find the words before those you know on earth have all turned to dust. Answer as you will."

"No, though I should be."

If Old Guard ever smiled, Beth thought they might have smiled at her then. Almost as one they began to come towards her, standing comfortably and looking her over. The men who she was certain had been wearing the plaid of Scotsmen at Kahtar's cabin, wore only their odd shifting flesh here. Where they had seemed hostile moments ago—was it moments ago? Now they seemed only vaguely interested in her.

The Old Guard holding her right elbow leaned comfortably back, as though settling into an invisible vertical chair. Gently he continued to support her arm as he informed her.

"There are laws on earth against blending Seekers with Covenant Keepers. They are not our laws, yet we are sworn to keep the laws of the Covenant Keepers. Your father is Seeker, and that is not allowed among the clan I serve."

Beth looked into the dark eyes briefly. They went on forever and held secrets she didn't want to know. Still she was certain this man saw her as no less than any other Covenant Keeper, or Seeker for that matter. The fact that he understood truth as well as she did confused her. He didn't think her less because she was a child of Blending. It was as though truth was irrelevant here. Then she considered what he had said and realized that in some ways it was, he was simply following a law and it was her who didn't understand the truth of why. Existence as she knew it was small compared to what these beings knew. After a long pause in which the men all waited patiently, she finally answered.

"I am not one of the clan you serve. I am bound by the laws of Cultuelle Khristos."

"Tell me something I do not know, woman. You do not belong. Cultuelle Khristos took you in unwittingly. Aberrations can undermine all. It is a precarious world. Would you have the Cult of Christ cease to exist so that you can continue in the world?"

"No, I wouldn't." Beth knew she was forfeiting her life, but nothing in her would argue the point. If these Angels of God said she shouldn't exist, she wouldn't fight it. This is what it meant to be Covenant Keeper.

They didn't look at each other, but she knew something silent had passed between them, out of her range of understanding. The gist of it was regret. She doubted any of them wanted to end her.

"It's all right." Even as she reassured them part of her thought she must be nuts, and wondered where her survival instinct had gone.

"Please just make this count for everyone else and help Kahtar." Tears filled her eyes, welling over, hot and dirty tears in the clean air of this place. "This will destroy him."

"Destroy?" Another Old Guard straightened. His posture alert as he stared at her, hard. "Hearts heal."

Beth shook her head, "You do not take wives do you?"

They didn't move, but it was as though part of them flowed through the trees like the wind. Her comment hurt them, the very air spoke it, but she wasn't sorry for it, it was true.

"You are not joined with the Warrior of the Ages."

"Semantics." Beth argued pointedly. "He needs me. We are aberrations of the same ilk, imperfectly matched. Please? I know you are not counselors, but please explain to him why I had to go. Make him see it?"

Kahtar was a logical man, he would understand, but he would die too. There was no doubt, they belonged together and now he would be broken. More tears welled up and out, sliding over her lips and dripped off her chin. Dirty on the clean, clean ground, a sacrilege.

CHAPTER
THIRTY

INEXPLICABLY IT HADN'T killed him. His heart hadn't exploded. Kahtar's will to live was gone, but that had happened before and he knew in the next repeat or the one after that, it always came back. This time he wondered though, if maybe it could be gone for good.

The Mother had refused his request to annihilate the men responsible for Beth's death. It was his right to seek retribution, to take the life of every man sworn to uphold the laws of Clan Berwick. It was within his power to accomplish the task too, he was a strong man, a skilled fighter. Surely he could wipe them off the earth in mere days, leaving their women heartbroken in the bloody wake. Standing small before him The Mother had looked up into his eyes, shaking her head, her gentle voice low, but firm.

"Why bother, Kahtar? They are a small dystopian clan. Time will finish them soon enough." And he'd been too sick to argue, to demand their blood, their complete sacrifice for their beliefs. Despite the death of his own heart, the thought of killing their plebes sickened him and he was thankful that The Mother had refused him. Vengeance was exhausting, and he was tired to his soul.

Kneeling by the pond in the evenings Kahtar didn't have the energy to seek ilu, to stretch his arms towards the heavens and let his heart soar in search of his maker. For the first time in his existence he did not have the will to pray. Instead he slumped against the tree where the hammock still swayed; the one Beth had liked to lie in with Honor. Honor who had sobbed like a child when he'd learned of Beth's fate. Suddenly the fact that she was a child of a Seeker hadn't mattered to the young warrior. Kahtar had turned his back on the rookie and walked away. He planned never to speak to him again. The last thing Honor had done to Beth was hurt her, and though it was willfully sinful, Kahtar held it against Honor, refusing to forgive.

Unfortunately time marched heartlessly on, duty waited and he was Warrior of ilu. Gladly he might have sat against the tree by the pond and welcomed death from exposure—many times it had come in the past like that, though never before had it been welcome. Death would bring no peace anyway, just another repeat holding the same pain. After two weeks of grief and despair, of cold silence to Honor Monroe and wearing the same filthy clothing until he was chafed like a godless barbarian, Kahtar began to fake life again. It was, after all, his duty to live. The Mother had sent word that he was not to return as Police Chief but Kahtar did not plan to comply. It was his call as Warrior Chief not hers.

More than a fortnight after Beth was taken, Kahtar mechanically rose before dawn and found his way to the barn, defending himself in his morning fight against an Old Guard, and emerging with painful wounds only partially healed. Wolves didn't run with him, as Kahtar forced his legs along paths in the woods, the dog continued to slink about the veil obviously waiting for Beth, and Kahtar ignored him. Making his way to the bathhouse for the first time in two weeks he was met with the sight of Beth's belongings. Forcing his eyes on what he needed to do, he tried not to see the dresser covered in her lotions and potions. All of her clothing was neatly shoved in drawers and cupboards, as messy as Beth was she'd kept her clothing pristine and orderly, including color-coding every item. Pretending not to see the shades of blue peeking through a partially opened drawer, he gently pushed it shut with a knee as he passed.

The plebes hadn't dared to touch anything, and as Kahtar sank into the bath water, he knew he wouldn't allow them to ever do so. This was all he had left and he wanted it there, but when he climbed out of the tub and grabbed a towel, the faint aroma of tangerines wafted from it. Beth had used it last. It took every last bit of fortitude he possessed to keep moving. Pulling on his leggings and blouse he carried the towel with him, drying his cropped hair with it as he went to breakfast.

Folding it neatly he placed it in his rucksack and went to the table. Shoveling food into his mouth was rote, a skill he'd mastered long ago. The shade of Golgotha hovered as he ate, as dark and painful as it had always been. Maybe it should have been good that something hadn't changed, but this was definitely the one thing where distance would have been welcome.

It was the first Tuesday in August, time to review schedules and rotate his men, but he hadn't gotten verbal updates on happenings within the village in over two weeks now. Despite The Mother's wishes, Kahtar knew all that would keep him going was duty. Heading into his front room he was surprised to see Honor Monroe come through the front door. Regret etched lines into his young face, lines that should not have shown even a ghost for another twenty years. Kahtar stiffened, a hand reaching towards his waist for a blade that wasn't there. The motion wasn't lost on Honor.

"Would my death ease your pain, Chief? I think I would give it to you if there was an honorable way to do so."

"If there was an honorable way I would already have had the satisfaction."

The pain on Honor's face should have moved him. It didn't.

"What do you want?"

Honor pushed his dark hair off his forehead, the usual stiff spikes gone, it hung limp and messy. His blue eyes were regret and sorrow. Kahtar didn't care. He wanted him out of his house.

"Beth's father has called the station for you dozens of times in the past two weeks. We got a call from Chagrin Falls police that he's reported her missing and wants you questioned. Kahtar, they want to talk to you. Ted White has friends in Washington, we need a believable story. A—a body."

Kahtar sagged against the doorway and closed his eyes. Wouldn't it be rich if he ended up in a Seeker prison for Beth's disappearance? He hardly cared, but he couldn't let even Beth's death draw attention to the village.

With his eyes still closed he asked, "Why wasn't I notified he was calling for me weeks ago?"

"The Mother said to leave you alone."

Kahtar sighed and knocked his fingers against his forehead in exasperation.

"And no one thought to have someone call them? Several people are quite adept at pretending to be…" He couldn't get the name out, hadn't said it out loud yet and wondered if he ever would.

Honor hurried to answer, "The Mother refuses to allow anyone to lie so blatantly, to pretend that…she's alive." The last two words were a whisper, an agony to both men. Kahtar turned his head away, squeezing his eyes tightly shut.

"I'll go see her parents. They deserve the truth, what we can give them anyway."

"And the—body?" Honor's voice was a whisper.

Finally opening his eyes he focused on Honor. The young warrior stepped back instinctively, and Kahtar pushed past him without answering.

CHAPTER

THIRTY-ONE

DRESSED IN A fresh, neat, police uniform Kahtar pulled into The White's little driveway. A large riding lawn mower sat in the small front yard, and Ted's sedan was parked in the tiny garage, but a quick scan revealed he wasn't at home. Kahtar hadn't thought to call first.

Carole knelt in the backyard, weeding her vegetable garden. Kahtar knew she'd heard his car when he sensed her stand up and brush dirt off her hands and knees. Within moments she hurried around the house, the look on her pretty, smudged face, hopeful.

As soon as he unfolded himself from the cruiser Carole stopped moving towards him and froze. Taking a step backwards, her eyes riveted on his face, she shook her head.

"No, you. You're wrong. I'd know."

For awhile he simply stood there looking at Carole, seeing only Beth in her and unable to compose himself enough to speak. After a time Carole glanced up at the sky and hissed at him, "Get out of here! Ted will be back soon, I can't have him seeing you. He'll believe you."

"It's true." Kahtar managed to croak. "She's gone on, Carole."

"NO." Carole shouted at him, crossed the space between them and shoved a hand against his chest so hard he stumbled backwards. She was a strong woman. "You get out of here, right now. Don't come back here! I'll think of something to tell Ted, but don't come here again with your lies!"

"I'm not lying, Carole."

"You're not telling the truth either! I'd know!" Carole slammed a fist against her flat chest and it made a dull thud. "I feel her still! She's my daughter, I'd know!"

All mothers thought that. So many times when he'd brought women this news they'd insist they could still feel their children. Surely it was ilu's gift to them. What Kahtar wouldn't give to still feel Beth. His own heart was ravaged, bloodied, useless and irreparable. Carole stood across from him, shaking with anger, her expression fierce—a shieldmaiden defending her last hope. Unable to bear it he looked away from those blue eyes and whispered, "She's in a good place, might we all know such bliss in the end…." Ah, even ruined his heart still felt. Pain really had no edges. It went on forever. Swallowing he continued, "Do you want her remains brought here?"

Carole made a horrific sound, but when he instinctively went towards her she backed away, again fierce and angry.

"YES! Show me! You can't and if you do I will kill you! Now get out of here right now! GO!" She screamed the words, her low voice sounded strangled.

Sliding into the cruiser Kahtar knew then how he would end this time. At the hands of the woman he should have called Mother. Death at the hands of a shieldmaiden would be new. It would take planning to make certain she wasn't punished for it.

CHAPTER
THIRTY-TWO

THE VILLAGE POLICE were busy. A tour bus had gotten lost and wandered in off the highway. Unable to find a gas station, it ran out of fuel on Main Street. Warriors from the police force directed light traffic around it. Several men were working to get it operational and on its way. Unfortunately the fifty-four senior citizens on board had taken to the street. Cramming the coffee shop or wandering through town, exclaiming over peculiarities that caught their attention. Parked across the street from the bus, Kahtar climbed out of his cruiser. He scanned for his men who had gone to get fuel for the behemoth. The elderly Seekers didn't hesitate to verbalize their thoughts and comments drifted towards him.

"I don't remember this place, and I was raised not thirty miles from here."

"They don't even have a supermarket, and Martha said there's no school either!"

"There's one shop down that side street, but it's not even open!"

The remark about Beth's shop hurt, Kahtar hadn't even thought of the place in the past weeks. A rheumy eyed, white haired man trotted towards him with a huge smile. Small of stature, he moved like a man much younger than his obvious years and he stopped short of Kahtar, leaned back, squinting, trying to get a good look at him through cataracts.

"Well, I'll be. You haven't changed a lick in all these years!"

"Sir?" Kahtar glanced down at the man, wishing he could do something for those cataracts. It would be effortless, but the man was a Seeker and it was forbidden, odd how much Beth had changed him in such a short time.

"Mr. Asher!" A young woman called to the old man from the shade of an awning, her coral colored blouse and name tag pegging her as the one in charge of the group. When Mr. Asher ignored her, she ran after him. Kahtar didn't even focus on her, though he knew she was smiling up at him and completely ignoring Mr. Asher. The Mother had been right. It was too soon for him to have returned to police work. Pretending simply took more effort than he had to give.

The woman addressed Kahtar though her words were for the elderly man.

"We don't want to bother the nice officer, now do we?" The tone was condescending to a man of such years and Kahtar bristled to hear him spoken to like a child.

But Mr. Asher informed her. "Hah. Montgomery and I fought together at Normandy! He saved my life!" Turning from the young woman he continued, "Never had a chance to even thank you! Bullet in the back takes the words outta a man, that's for sure. D'ya remember? Ya carried me like a sack of potatoes the whole time, taking bullets yourself. Always said a prayer for you, every day since then, a real blessing to be able to say thank you this side of the grave. I mean it, Montgomery. Thank you soldier, glad to see you made it out too."

The man's words brought the experience back clearly—the storm, the beach, the slaughter. Montgomery hadn't made it out alive, not really. Separated from his clan, with no one to help heal him, he'd died from a belly wound not long after pulling the young pilot from the tangled wreckage of a glider. Coupled with the horror around him, that death had been indescribably painful. Physically there was none of the young flight officer left in this old man, but Kahtar remembered searching through the wreckage of gliders for his people and finding the only survivor, a Seeker. Now, over seventy years later here he was, thanking him from the heart. For the first time in his existence Kahtar felt the touch of a Seeker in his heart. Unshed tears almost choked him. He didn't want to feel their hearts too. He didn't want to feel anything.

"Mr. Asher!" The woman admonished, "You're being silly! Normandy was a long time ago, wasn't it?"

How soon the past was forgotten. "I remember." Kahtar told the man gruffly, not caring who heard him.

Asher smiled while the woman stood behind him shaking her head in disapproval.

"Got married, had five kids, twelve grandchildren and seven greats—so far. Still got that bullet though it never bothered me until a few years ago, shifted they say, right up against my spine now."

Kahtar took the old man's hands in his and held them. Tears blurred his vision as he looked down at Asher and the old man squeezed his hands, his grip surprisingly strong.

"Anything I can do?" Old Asher offered. He didn't ask why Kahtar still looked like a man in his prime. He simply offered help, his heart open and giving.

Shaking his head Kahtar admitted, "I lost my—wife."

Asher nodded, understanding. "Me too, at least we lived to have 'em, eh?"

IN THE KITCHEN Kahtar dug out the last box of brack tea and wandered down to the pond by the hammock. Leaning against a big willow he slid to the ground and sat quietly.

After awhile he lifted the box of tea to his nose, he breathed the scent in, it was rich and dark. Of all the earthly pleasures one could consume, this was the one he'd most enjoyed. In the centuries since it had vanished, he'd remembered it with longing. Beth had brought it back into his life. It would vanish now just like she had, it seemed appropriate, brief interludes of wonderful here and then gone. Lifting the lid off the thin cardboard he saw a note she'd scrawled inside the box. 'Gross Man Tea.' Laughter rose in his throat and died there. Unfolding the wax bag inside, he lifted out the dried, black leaves and crumbled them into the grass—a little at a time. The scent filled his nostrils as he worked, emptying the box.

"Old Guard?" His voice echoed across the pond in a summons. Kahtar didn't look up until he sensed one of them appear solidly in front of him. When he did look up he was certain that the man was staring at the pile of leaves in the grass between his knees, the tilt of his head almost sad. It made him angry.

"Yet you ended her though you found her blameless."

The Old Guard paused, shimmered and affirmed, "Yes."

Even in his grief Kahtar sensed something off in the Old Guard's response. The silent pause of a lie, the kind of tone that Beth had seen through before a word was completely spoken. "You hesitated, what aren't you telling me?"

"Much, Ancient One. Time is not constant."

"What does that mean?"

"She's on Orthrus—time moves slower there."

"Did you end my wife?"

The Old Guard shimmered and replied, "She is not your wife."

"Don't you dare!" Kahtar stood up in one fluid movement and jammed his finger into the Old Guard's chest. His hand passed straight through the man as he continued to shimmer, barely there. The contact felt like burning ice against his arm and he pulled it back instinctively. "Don't give me your cryptic answers! Either she is alive or she's not. You have pledged to me, can you not give me that much? Do I need to ask for her body for proof?"

The Old Guard shimmered, vanishing completely several times before taking a solid form again. "If it is your desire we will return her body when the trial ends."

"When—are you telling me that the trial hasn't ended?"

"Time moves differently on Orthrus, Ancient One. The outcome is inevitable. Your declared perceives it as mere moments. There was no reason for you to suffer this knowledge."

The pieces of Kahtar's heart seemed to snap back together in a split second, hope springing from nowhere, Beth was alive. At this very moment she was still alive.

"Take me to her."

"That is not possible."

"End me with her then, release me from this cycle—I can serve no further purpose! I'm done."

Black eyes stared at him, impossible to read. No mercy shone through, no hostility either. Whatever rules Old Guard lived by did not allow his request, and after a silent moment he simply vanished.

Kahtar shouted in protest, in pain, a wordless howl of agony tearing through him. Helpless fury coursed through his veins. Standing at the edge of the pond, screaming with no hope, roaring until his voice was gone he slid to the ground and put his head on his knees, too exhausted to even cry.

NIGHT HAD COME, when he woke the moon already high in the hazy sky. Shouting had left his throat raw. Wolves came to him, slinking through the grass on his belly, he nosed his big shaggy head onto Kahtar's lap, the familiar foul stench almost comforting. Kahtar dropped a hand onto the dog's body and forced his fingers through tangled fur. Wolves burrowed closer in response, his nails snagging the fabric of the police uniform. The dog's shoulder rested against Kahtar's holster, shoving his gun into his hip. For a split second Kahtar had thoughts that no Warrior of ilu was allowed. Immediately his hand went to that gun, he flipped the holster open, grabbed the gun and threw it into the pond where it plunked and sank. The temptation to be finished was horribly strong.

Not that way, I won't go that way, not by my own hand. Watching the moonlight reflect off the pond he decided when the Old Guard brought her body, he'd bring Carole here. The shieldmaiden could finish him in this place. He could end too, at least for a brief respite. Then—he couldn't think of that now. He'd lose his mind.

Emotionally exhausted, at some point Kahtar fell deeply asleep again and dreamed. Beth came to him then, straddled his lap with long tan legs and held his head against her shoulder. She smelled like tangerines and he cried into her neck, tears wetting her silky hair until it hung stringy and messy, and the reek of Wolves consumed her own fresh scent. Her own tears soaked his shirt and in his dream he asked her why she was crying.

"Because you are and because it scares me now—that I didn't want to come back. I wanted to die there. And because Wolves is chewing on my leg hard, and it really hurts."

Clutching a handful of her soft hair he kept his eyes squeezed tight, willing the dream to last, but she kept leaning away, trying to escape and he knew when he opened his eyes she'd be gone.

"I wish you smelled right." He whispered against her skin, the smell of Wolves was overtaking the dream, bringing reality too close. Beth slipped further away.

"I wish you'd get him off me, I'm bleeding! Kahtar! Why's he biting me?" There was fear in her voice and unable to ignore it, he opened his eyes. There in the moonlight dappling through the draping willow branches, Beth's eyes glowed silvery, and she struggled to slide off the far side of his lap away from the dog. Wolves excitedly gnawed on her left thigh, pinching again and again with his front teeth, his tail wagging furiously. Blood seeped from dozens of tiny puncture marks, and the sound of dog's teeth chattering mingled with Beth's whimpered protests. It was so real.

With one shove Kahtar knocked the dog off, he yelped but made another lunge for Beth. Kahtar grabbed his muzzle and ordered him away in the ancient tongue. Wolves started to howl in protest, crawling on his belly in circles, quivering with joy. Wide-eyed Kahtar ran a hand over Beth's thigh, flesh and blood beneath his hand, healing flowed from his hand and closed the bites instantly. Pulling his hand away he brought it to his eyes, it was covered in blood. He scanned the blood and the woman sitting beside him with one long leg still draped over his lap. Grabbing a handful of her hair he rudely yanked her towards a patch of moonlight, staring in disbelief, unable to believe what his senses were telling him.

"You're real. You're alive?"

"Yes." A soft hand cupped his face, tracing stubble on his chin.

"How?" A whisper was all he could manage.

"I don't know. I just don't know. They really are angels, Kahtar, really terrifying ones."

Reverently he took her face between his hands and stared hard, scanning again, running fingers over her features, trying to be certain this was real. She was exactly as she'd been weeks ago when they'd snatched her off the front porch, even her flowered little sundress looked as fresh as it had that day, marred only by flecks of blood from Wolves' uncontrolled greeting. The dog continued to grovel nearby, his teeth clacking together as he shivered with excitement. It was the stupid reaction of the dog that convinced Kahtar that this was no dream.

Crushing her to his chest he put his face against the top of her head and cried like a little boy. For whatever reason the Old Guard had decided not to end her, this was real. Great heaving sobs shook his chest, his voice growing hoarser and hoarser. For the first time as an adult he completely lost control of his emotions, crying until he was spent.

When Kahtar finally quieted, his voice was completely gone and he was exhausted and weak. Slumped against the tree trunk he simply sat with his arms wrapped around Beth. She moved tighter against his chest, pressing her thin body against his. The air was humid. Frogs and insects had again taken up their chorus along the edges of the pond, and the stench of Wolves intruded, confirming reality. Then Beth's heart pressed against his, and his breath caught and he froze, knowing that this was their moment. She found the mark she'd left there, her heart pressed into it, filling it and erasing the pain of the past weeks. The sensation as her heart slid fully into his was like swallowing her. It seemed impossible to hold all of her dancing exuberance within his unyielding heart, but painlessly his own heart conformed to hers and the sensation was that of expanding, growing, becoming more than he'd been, he knew he would hold her like this forever. Even when he did die, this would go with him into the next repeat. This was now his heart. Several more tears came from somewhere and slid down his already soaked face.

Beth reached up and wiped them away and whispered, "I love you, and now they can't separate us ever again."

His gasp of joy sounded like a sob even to his own ears, but he was far too happy to care if every warrior he'd ever known had been there to bear witness. Together they tumbled onto their sides to rest in the damp grass, Beth stayed wrapped between his arms and legs and he closed his eyes, held tightly to a handful of her hair, and knew no more that night.

CHAPTER
THIRTY-THREE

A REPULSIVE REEK threatened to gag her even in her sleep, but Beth fought to stay asleep, so tired she ached with it. When the stench grew stronger, and brushed wet against her cheek she ignored it, tried not to allow her consciousness to speculate on what could be so disgusting, but then a clicking sound grew louder and something began to pinch at her cheek, hard. She was so tired this made her cry. Then she heard Kahtar shout and Wolves yelp. Reaching up to wipe blood off her cheek she found the wound already healed by his expert skill. Forcing her eyes open she met Kahtar's face, tears in his steely eyes as he gazed at her and then she remembered.

They were joined now! It felt so different, as tired as her body was, she felt his strength as though it coursed through her own frame, shoring her, and she smiled at him shyly. There was so much of him, so much she didn't understand. One thing was obvious though.

"You're not fifty-one."

Smiling faintly he brushed something off her cheek and reached to pull her closer, dragging her through the grass. The buzz of cicadas filled the early morning air and no breeze stirred under the veil. Last night she'd been so disappointed to have been taken away from the Old Guard's forest, but this morning all she felt was joy at being with Kahtar again. He stared at her as though memorizing every pore and she felt self-conscious knowing that he now knew her as well as she knew him, could sense her weaknesses. He didn't look disappointed though, determined maybe. He leaned to her mouth and kissed her, really kissed her, lips and tongue, and her stomach dropped out again and again in a wonderfully new way. Stubble dug and slid over her face, Kahtar smelled like brack tea, tannin, and very faintly of the clean air on Orthrus. Breathing deep through her nose, she melted into him.

Then he stopped, pulled his lips away, took a deep breath of his own and told her cryptically. "I repeat."

Beth's mind now stayed half on that kiss, protesting the distance from his mouth. After a moment her brain caught up. "What? What did you repeat?"

"If someone were to slip through the veil right now and shoot me in the head, in a few years a little boy in a clan somewhere would be going about his day, and suddenly he'd remember this. Our joining last night, and us here in the grass together, even the gunshot. Then he'd start to remember more and more, like a tornado in his head memories would blow through him of all the times he had been alive before. I am that little boy. I am born to a clan. I become Warrior of ilu, sometimes even Warrior Chief, and I die. Then—I repeat. The same thing happens again and again."

Now it was her turn to stare at him. She'd known he was different from the start, even among his kind he seemed other, but immortal? Human Beings were not immortal, even the Old Guard were finite, she was certain of it. Beth felt Kahtar's heart surrounding hers. It was so big, not magnanimous but going on and on. Surely he had been doing this repeating a very long time. For the first time, as odd as his explanation was, she felt as though she understood him and his quiet reserve.

Kahtar looked sad, almost afraid of her and what she would think or say, and this truth suddenly made her sad too. Reaching to rub his cheek with the back of her fingers she whispered only, "I'm sorry."

Lying side by side in the grass with Kahtar's heart encompassing hers, Beth pressed her face against his chest, and Kahtar held her tightly. Then he tugged her back to his mouth and kissed her again. It shot through her, wiping questions away. He tasted so good, better than he smelled, and all she really wanted was to taste him some more. A horrible movement interrupted those kisses like she was swooping downwards, falling away from Kahtar. She snatched onto him, clutching his arm and a handful of shirt and held tightly, dizzy in a very unpleasant way. Bracing herself against it, she tried to keep her bearings as everything began to spin.

"Are you all right?"

"Yes. No. Kahtar? I'm so hungry I could eat Wolves right now. I mean, I hurt I'm so hungry."

Those steely eyes widened in surprise, but he sat up and slowly tugged her to sit, before standing and helping her up too. In no time he hurried her into the house, where the floor looked very crooked and shifted with every step. She half noticed the weapons were already completely cleared from the walls of the front room, the hideous instruments of torture gone. In the kitchen Beth held onto the counters and staggered to the breadbox, but the loaves of bread were molded over and rock hard. Bending to the icebox, she found it warm and full of food that had wilted or dried, and the eggs smelled as bad as Wolves. The fruit that hung in baskets beneath the cabinet was rotted through, and a swarm of fruit flies hovered over what had been peaches.

Beth's stomach made a horrible gurgling sound and the room pitched and yawed. Kahtar pushed her to sit and shoved a glass of water and a shriveled orange at her.

"Just eat it anyway," he told her.

Grabbing it she bit into it like a starved woman, chewing savagely through the hard rind and finding relief in the bit of juice still inside. Kahtar dug through cabinets, searching for food while Beth impatiently gnawed through the tough rind of the orange. The brightly lit kitchen grew suddenly brighter as an Old Guard shimmered into being. Kahtar spun away from the cupboard, moving towards them. Beth flinched; afraid she would be taken away. Before Kahtar could even reach her the Old Guard dropped a wooden bowl on the table in front of her, pushed it close and vanished.

"Eat it." Kahtar told her, and he didn't have to repeat the command. It was a large bowl, filled with a dark sticky resinous substance, a thin wooden ladle jammed into the middle of the thick mess. Lifting as much as the narrow ladle could hold, Beth shoveled it in. It wasn't until she was halfway through the bowl that she tasted the food. Nutty, bitter and cloyingly sweet, she was afraid to look too close, because though she was pretty sure it involved honey and seeds—she also thought she detected insects with wings and legs. Glancing up at her husband, who had taken a seat next to her, she jammed the ladle back inside the bowl, repulsed.

"Try not to think about it. Have you had enough?"

Nodding she pushed the bowl away. She felt better, much better, if she didn't think about what was stuck between her teeth, surprised that what she'd eaten was staying down. Maybe it was too sticky to come back up.

Turning to look at the kitchen counter she eyed the swarm of fruit flies hovering over the peaches, she'd helped pick them herself just a couple days ago. They'd eaten so many she'd gotten a stomach ache, and even Kahtar had regretted indulging so much.

"I was gone longer than a few hours, wasn't I?"

"Beth, you were gone over three weeks." Lovingly he ran a big hand over hers, soft and caressing.

"Three weeks! How on earth? We just stood there talking. I could have sworn it was a few hours, tops. How is that possible?"

Kahtar rose, went to the sink and got her more water. For awhile he stood with his back to her, and she could see that his hand was shaking. He spoke in a hoarse whisper. "I think that the air there hydrates the body, it probably even provides nutrients. Otherwise you'd die of thirst in no time."

He'd thought she was dead. For weeks now.

"Oh, Kahtar, I'm so sorry for what you've gone through—if I ever thought something happened to you...."

Stalking to her side he yanked her out of the chair to hug her so hard he spilled half the water.

"You're alive, nothing else matters." He slammed the glass on the table.

Reaching up she ran both hands over his hair, it was longer than she'd ever seen, thick, the dark blond color detectable for the first time. He squeezed her tightly, and she fit neatly against his body, aberrations of the same ilk, imperfectly matched, just as she'd told the Old Guard. She was home. She wrapped her arms around Kahtar and tried to return his hug. He smelled so good, and her mind went immediately to those kisses. He tasted so good. Then she yawned so widely her jaw cracked and she sagged against him.

"You need to sleep. Shades of Mercy, thank ilu you survived. I doubt the Old Guard ever considered how lack of sleep would affect you."

Then Kahtar scooped her up, all six feet and one hundred forty pounds. Her mind started to swim, remembering when she was a little girl with her Daddy. For a moment she fought her exhaustion, trying to swim towards the thought of her Dad. He must be so worried…three weeks! Then the hugeness of Kahtar's heart, surrounding hers so deliciously, numbed all else, and she remembered something about tasty kisses, and gave in and slept.

MORNING LIGHT STUNG Kahtar's eyes when they opened. The world was different, and it wasn't just because this was the latest he'd ever slept. The brutally honest heart resting inside his heart changed everything. With one finger he traced the curve of Beth's ear, waking her as she lay spooned against him still wearing her sundress and shoes. She was his wife, and there could be no awkwardness in claiming her in every way now. It was time. The thought that they were one made his heart soar.

Then a new realization took his heart to an even higher height, he could barely conceive that Beth hadn't even asked a single question about his odd repeating existence. She hadn't seemed fearful or even curious, just sorry for him. Of course she had been weak with hunger, but even now she rested beside him and her heart percolated within his, content and happy.

Stretching, Beth's bare tanned arms and legs caressed the sheets. She rolled onto her back and sighed, a delightful contented sound. The blue eyes opened, clear and alert and the exact same color as the flowers in her little dress. That summer blonde hair spread silky smooth and neat against the pillow. They smiled at each other, hearts entwined and comfortable as though they woke together every morning. Beth bit her lip and slid a hand under his shirt, resting it enticingly against his bare stomach.

Then Beth's eyes widened in horror and she moved away, sitting up and looking around.

"Is Wolves in here?"

"Of course not."

"Are you sure? I smell him." Trying to politely put a hand over her nose, she gagged. "My gosh! It's my breath!"

"Oh." The smell wafted to Kahtar's nose, he forced himself not to laugh. "Whew. It's the worms in the mash. Worms really reek when they start to decay…."

One of Beth's hands went to her belly, and she gagged. Pointing towards the door, he tried to hide his amusement.

"Just go to the bath house and brush your teeth. Don't worry, you won't be sick."

Feet still clad in the same yellow heels she'd technically been wearing for weeks now, she dashed through the bedroom door. Kahtar grinned as Beth clumped down the stairs. Life couldn't possibly get any better than this. Well, at least not until she brushed her teeth. He swung his legs over the edge of the bed. Today was going to be a really, really, good day.

"I KNOW YOU were laughing at me this morning." Beth scooted to the edge of the pond, tugged off her low-heeled pumps, hitched up her long skirt and stuck her feet into the cool water.

Kahtar stepped out of his running shoes, he wasn't wearing socks. He rolled up his khakis and plopped down beside her. Tossing a curious look in her direction, his big feet sank beneath the surface of the water. Beth suspected he'd all but forgotten their morning. She knew she'd ruined his grand plans by dragging him to visit her parents, but a phone call wasn't going to cut it. Not after her three week absence!

"Over the worm stew. You're not laughing now though, are you?"

"Is that how it's going to be?" There was a tightness around his eyes as he looked out over the pond. "You're going to relish this because it will make me uncomfortable?"

"Maybe a little bit," Beth admitted. "Honestly, Kahtar, why is it so repugnant to you? The ceremony won't be but fifteen minutes. My Dad will be so happy. You saw how excited he got today. We owe him something after putting him through my disappearance. As cavalier as he acted today, I guarantee the last three weeks have been hard on him too. Besides, it's not going to corrupt your belief system to have a little church wedding, is it?"

"Argh!" Thrusting his arms into the air, Kahtar fell back against the grass with a thump. "I am so thankful that you're alive that I would have agreed to anything today. You just cannot conceive how weird a wedding will be for me."

"Weirder than what Cultuelle Khristos has put me through? Weirder than what the Old Guard did to me? I think you can wear a tuxedo and promise to love, honor, and cherish me in front of my parents."

The steely eyes softened, and he smiled faintly, taking her hand he held it against his cheek, rubbing the palm of her hand with his thumb.

"Well, when you put it that way…it's been a long unconsummated day. Ready for bed, Beth?" Despite the sun still full in the sky, Kahtar seemed to think she might have missed the innuendo in his comment because he flipped her hand over and pressed it to his open lips. Beth's stomach flopped in response. Holy mackerel, he was going to kill her. Did he not realize she'd much rather have spent the day doing wonderfully naughty things to him? Unable to stop her mind from exploring some of those things, she felt her face flush beet red.

Kahtar let go of her hand. Though disappointment colored his voice, Kahtar was a man of honor.

"There's no hurry, Beth, I can wait. I want you to be comfortable too. How about you go get your suit and we'll just swim for a bit?" He sat up, staring at his feet moving in the water. Gosh, he was disappointed. This was not going to be easy!

Beth swung one long leg up and used her foot to shove Kahtar right into the pond. Caught off guard he slipped under in his only real clothes. Bobbing to the surface the surprise on his face made her laugh.

"Caught you off guard! You said that was hard to do. Seemed simple enough to me."

"It usually is, but why'd you do it?" As he reached towards her legs, Beth jerked away, scrabbling out of his reach.

"Seemed like a safer way to have this conversation."

"What conversation?" He looked worried now.

"The one where I say 'after the wedding'."

"After the wedding? What do you mean 'after the wedding'..." But understanding dawned in his eyes and he added, "You have got to be kidding me. Is that why you don't want to...why 'after the wedding'?"

"Because otherwise the wedding is just a sham and meaningless."

That he already considered the upcoming nuptials a meaningless sham showed on his face plainly.

"It's like this, Kahtar." Crouching beside the pond, Beth implored him to understand. "You are my husband. We are two odd parts of the same strange whole. When the Old Guard brought me back here last night, nothing could have induced me to wait another second before completing our joining. They can't separate husbands and wives, and I wasn't taking any chances! Yet years ago I promised my Dad—that I would wait...and I won't make our wedding completely meaningless."

Treading water he studied her. Those gray eyes of his were so loving as he watched her, that part of her wanted to tell her Dad they'd eloped, but Kahtar nodded in understanding.

"You made a vow. You have to keep your word. I understand vows." Momentarily ducking under the water he emerged without his shirt, tossing the wet red top into the grass.

"Suit up! I'll teach you how to hide underwater. If you slide under the mud on the bottom, the majority of scanning warriors won't even spot you!"

Regretfully she eyed his Olympian shoulders, something very base stirred deep in her stomach and she stood quickly.

"I don't think it's a good idea. I'm going to go...read or something."

"Beth!" He admonished. "I said I understood. It's not like I'm going to force myself on you!"

"No, Kahtar, it's more the other way around that I'm worried about. I've never been very good with absolutes, and we are technically married now, and—you're gorgeous..." she finished wistfully.

Walking away, he shouted after her, his tone quite pleased, "Really?"

"Oh, get over yourself, Kahtar," she teased, but clutching her pumps she broke into a run before she changed her mind.

CHAPTER
THIRTY-FIVE

TWO DAYS BEFORE their white wedding Beth packed up her car and left Kahtar miserable. Time wasted. He could feel the seconds ticking away—time apart they could never have back. Two days they might have had together—gone forever. It made him almost physically ill. She'd insisted it was mandatory, last minute preparations, time with her parents. She told him to be thankful they'd managed to dodge the traditional wedding rehearsal and dinner. She'd only managed it by explaining that Kahtar's parents were deceased and that even his friends couldn't come to the wedding. She said her Dad was disappointed, but was trying to be understanding. Kahtar thought Beth's Dad had no idea what understanding was in this instance.

On the morning of the wedding Kahtar dressed himself in the intricate tuxedo Beth had left hanging in his closet. It was completely snow white—even to the shiny white patent leather shoes and silk socks. Cultuelle Khristos wore white for funerals. Carefully he dressed in the clothing his wife had managed to secure for him, again feeling the maddening sense of wasting time.

AT THE CROWDED little church Kahtar was quite the spectacle. It seemed like every member of Saint Phillips United Methodist Church had come for the wedding of Ted White's daughter. After Ted himself pinned a yellow rose to Kahtar's lapel, and led him to the front of the church, they were stopped every few steps.

"Welcome, Kent, you're Chief of police over in Willowyth? Where is that?"

"Congratulations! You are marrying into a lovely family."

"Welcome, son." From a myopic older man who leaned far back to peer up at Kahtar. "My, my, aren't you a big fellow? Of course the Whites are giants in and of themselves aren't they?"

A blue haired old woman with red lipstick and beautiful skin patted his hand. "Welcome."

Greetings followed every step he took. By the time Kahtar was shuffled into his spot by his soon to be Father-in-law, his heart felt lighter and he was fighting back laughter. They were a lovely lot. He couldn't have been more surprised.

Then his Father-in-law sniffed loudly next to him and Kahtar realized that the man was fighting back tears. He shot a look at Ted. Though he was a burly six and a half feet tall, he had very little hair left and he'd left his reading glasses perched on his nose since pinning Kahtar's boutonnière on.

Kahtar leaned towards the man and whispered, "I'll take good care of her."

"You'd better."

"I adore her."

"Everybody does. At first. But Bethy doesn't need to be adored. She needs a man who is honest and tolerant." Ted White glared at him through unshed tears as he growled, "Be that man for her."

Ted White looked away and Kahtar looked out over the sanctuary. Part of his quick mind automatically took in physical details, yellow roses and white daises, blue ribbons, the sun shining through the stained glass windows and dancing across the two hundred and fourteen members of the congregation, but most of his mind filled with Ted's reprimand. Tolerance was a stretch for a man with Kahtar's background of black and white laws, but he was here among Seekers, at a church wedding, his church wedding, all for Beth. Honesty…he'd always considered himself an honest man, but he had not been honest with his wife. He'd told her that he repeated, but Beth had no idea what that meant. If he was going to be honest with his honest wife, shouldn't she know everything?

Then she appeared at the back of the church and music swelled, and it wasn't traditional church music. It was one of Beth's punk rock songs that she was so fond of, without the lyrics. Kahtar stared as she walked down the aisle towards him. He fought the urge to go meet her halfway, to tell her everything and be the man she needed. Kahtar didn't realize he'd started to move until Ted White casually took hold of his elbow and kept him in place at the altar.

Beth advanced with a bouquet of daisies, breathtaking in a simple white sheath that hugged her long body all the way to the floor. When she got to the altar and turned to set her flowers down, she revealed a dress with no back at all. The ever present heels brought her level with his nose as she took her place beside him.

Anxiously Kahtar took her hand and spoke in second voice. *"I love you, Beth. I will try to be the husband you need."*

Beth squeezed his hand and glanced at her father through narrowed eyes. For the second time ever she spoke into Kahtar's mind. *"What I need is a man who will rub my feet after this, they kill."*

Her second voice was loud and it reverberated hard. Kahtar noticed his quiet Mother-in-law sitting in the church pew in a pretty pale blue gown, her shorn hair sticking up wildly. She was fighting back a smile. He was certain Carole had heard Beth.

When the Minister got to their vows Kahtar had another moment of anxiety. He hadn't spoken to Beth about this. He could not take a vow he would not keep, not even for her. But it was simple, short, a slight variation of words that had been spoken for centuries. Beth had managed to have them altered just slightly. He wondered that the Minister had agreed.

Kahtar promised to, "Love and honor as long as I am." Beth promised to, "Love, and honor as long as I am." She smiled brilliantly up at him.

From the pews an old woman whispered loudly, "What's all the, 'I am' stuff, mean? Why do the kids always have to change it?"

Ted handed him a ring to put on Beth's finger, but she had known better than to get him one. He slid it on at the appropriate time and her second voice explained, *"It was my Grandmother's—My Dad's Mom."*

"Beth? I wish you had reminded me about rings. I would have gotten you one."

Beth's smile got bigger and Kahtar bent to kiss her freckled nose way before the Minister got to that part.

After that it was a hodgepodge of the misery Kahtar had expected from the start. The people were lovely, but introductions dragged and even Beth didn't know the guests, there was food to be avoided—and he was not the only one dodging it. Both Beth and her mother pointedly ignored it. There was no escaping the wedding cake, a huge confection covered in flowers that had to be fed to each other while pictures were snapped.

Then there were more pictures to pose for again, and at last it was blessedly over. After final good wishes and congratulations the guests slowly filed up the basement stairs, and left. Carole hesitated beside the newlyweds then she quickly kissed Beth, and took Kahtar's hands and stood on tiptoe to kiss each of his cheeks. She stared at him, wordlessly, and he smiled at her.

"I love her, Mother. Don't worry. I will protect her now."

Carole nodded silently and darted away. Ted White bent over his daughter and Kahtar forced himself to walk away and give them time.

When Beth finally found him, she took Kahtar's hand and tugged him towards the parking lot.

"Come on. Let's just go. Nothing is going to make this part easier for my Dad."

So Beth tucked her gown up and crawled into her convertible and Kahtar folded himself into his cruiser and they drove the longest two hours of his entire existence.

CHAPTER
THIRTY-SIX

BETH HAD ONLY one thought on her mind as she threw the car into park, gathered her silk gown in an arm and clambered out of her convertible. Kahtar didn't look at her when he got out of the cruiser. The set of his broad shoulders as he stared towards the pond pulled her thoughts away from the moment she had been anticipating for a very long time.

"Let's take a walk." Kahtar spoke without turning to look at her. It didn't bode well, even his back looked serious and his strong heart as it wrapped around hers felt afraid. More than the night the Old Guard had brought her back. Beth didn't want to cooperate, suddenly afraid too.

Dressed in the white tux with the blue silk ascot with the yellow rose boutonniere, Kahtar looked red carpet, movie star handsome. He took her hand and squeezed it gently, brought her grandmother's ring up for closer inspection and commented, "No disrespect to your Grandmother, Sweet, but wedding rings originated as a sign of subjugation."

Obviously it wasn't an idle comment. He looked tense from head to foot and he dropped her hand.

Following the comment to its logical conclusion Beth pointed out, "But they caught on because they're pretty."

"The first ones I saw doubled as a nose ring for hogs."

"What is it, Kahtar? I know you don't want to talk jewelry."

Rubbing a hand over his face, he started walking towards the pond. Beth kicked off her satin shoes with the six inch glass and silver heels, hoisted the beautiful silk gown over an arm and trailed after him barefoot. The grass hurt, crunchy sharp and hot beneath her sore feet. The late August weather felt broiling, the heat and humidity far too high to be strolling outside in the silk gown. Kahtar stopped by the shade of the pond and picked up a handful of rocks, skipping them over the water as he spoke.

"It was the same with bracelets and necklaces once—they were collars and handcuffs usually. Of course the wealthier men made sure their women had pretty shackles."

"Look, I won't wear it if it bothers you."

"It doesn't bother me, I like onyx." Plunk, plunk, he skipped the rocks towards the far bank. Wolves tore out of the woods and hurtled into the water after them, arms and legs flailing, mouth wide open.

The flat black ring had a filigree platinum band. It looked very modern to Beth's eye as she examined it in the sunshine. Technically it wasn't even a wedding ring, but her Dad had always treasured it, therefore she did too. It could have been brass or even plastic and it still would have been special to her.

Kahtar interrupted her reverie, taking her hand to briefly examine the ring.

"Of course that isn't true onyx. It's from banded lapidary material that comes from Mexico."

Kahtar tossed some more stones in, baiting Wolves to swim frantically from one side of the pond to the other trying to retrieve one.

"The ring looks nice against the silk of your dress. That silk is from the wild Saturniidae isn't it? I remember when all Thai silk was wild. Of course that was long before it was called Siam."

"Kahtar? Why are you playing History Channel?"

Casually he bent and gathered more stones.

Wolves was making hacking noises and slowing, but still determinedly swimming.

"He's going to drown himself," Beth pointed out, attempting to lighten the mood.

Kahtar tossed another stone.

"Not that I particularly care after he kept biting me the other night," she added.

Kahtar didn't smile.

He said, "Wolves was almost inside out with excitement. I think he was trying to lick you. He practically bit off his own tongue. He is the singularly most stupid dog I've ever had—so far—but there might be another dumber one in the next millennia."

Beth let the silk train of her gown drop into the grass, her mouth hanging open in disbelief, before she thought to shut it with a snap.

"Millennia? You're serious? Why on earth do you think you'll repeat that long?"

"Well," the question seemed to give him pause. "I suppose the sun rises and sets every day, you start to expect stuff."

"You've been repeating for millennia?"

"Since the crucifixion I have repeated sixty-four times, I think. Sometimes I don't live long enough to remember, so there are gaps…."

Beth remembered to close her mouth and swallow, it took effort to respond.

"You were at the crucifixion? *The* crucifixion?"

Dropping rocks into the grass, Kahtar wiped his hands over his pristine white slacks. Putting his hands on Beth's shoulders he took a deep breath and pushed her to sit, lowering onto the grassy bank with her.

"Yes, I was. At that time my clan called me Longinus."

"You…" Beth pointed at him, and then her hands dropped weakly into the grass. Taking a deep breath she managed to out, "You're Longinus?"

"Yes, or I was, and, yes, I did what everyone said."

Beth sat, never taking her eyes off his face.

"I've seen terrible torture, but none worse…I just did it. I put my spear right through…if I'd even looked at Him I wouldn't have done what I did. I stood at ilu's feet and didn't know Him. It was unforgivable."

After a moment of stunned silence, Beth whispered, "Are you trying to tell me Longinus was cursed…that you were cursed with immortality for an act of mercy? Like that old legend about the Roman Gatekeeper who struck Him? Is that what you believe?"

"Cartaphilus? You know your legends." Kahtar ran a hand over his head and looked out at the pond for a moment, then turned his gaze back to her, his hand was shaking. "No. Of course I don't believe that. I've been repeating since long before the crucifixion. Far longer. Though I'd done some pretty awful things before then. In fact I've done most awful things."

Beth scooted closer, the silk of her dress dragging over the dark grass as she stared at him.

"No you haven't."

Kahtar frowned.

Beth said, "You haven't done most awful things."

Kahtar rubbed a hand over his face. "From a Covenant Keeper perspective I have."

"Okay," Beth allowed. "How long have you repeated?"

Kahtar swallowed, but turned his steely gaze on her. "I don't really remember the early years, just vague shadows. A long time." His eyes looked so sad.

"Kahtar?" A shiver ran up Beth's spine. "Please don't spoon feed it to me. What are you trying to tell me?"

A smile lit Kahtar's face then, and it was simply impossible to see him as anything but the beautiful man in front of her. Briefly he moved a hand to disguise his grin and then gave up, revealing his honest reaction. "That's not enough for you?"

She smiled then too, but the smile was brief.

Kahtar studied her expression. She felt his heart probing her own as though his revelation could affect how much she loved him.

"I should have told you sooner. You should have known before we joined…."

"It wouldn't have mattered!" Beth protested. "I mean you already told me you were immortal."

"Immortal?" he shook his head. "No. I die like every man dies."

"Kahtar? Look at me." Beth rose to her knees and put her hands on either side of his face leaning forward to look into his eyes, she felt a wave of love wash up and out of her, blanketing him. "I love you. These things can't change that."

Kahtar ran his hands up her silky sleeves and rested them heavily on her shoulders, his expression serious. "I needed to be honest with you, and I was afraid to be."

"Why?"

"Because I don't want you to be afraid of me."

"I'm not. Not at all."

Gently Kahtar brushed her hair back and ran one large hand over her cheek. He whispered, "Why not?"

"Well, I guess anybody who repeats as you call it—would have an awful lot of bad in their past. So I don't see you as some dark person."

"What do you see me as?" he whispered.

Beth pushed her hair over her shoulders and sat back on her heels, thinking.

"A man who got stuck."

"Why would a man get stuck repeating?"

"I'm sure I don't know, Kahtar, but I think you're really off base to think it will just keep right on happening forever. You really ought to live every day like your last just like the rest of us. It could be, you know?"

"That's a nice thought."

"Is it? I guess so—when compared to—stuck. I suppose repeating must be…"

"Tiresome." Kahtar said it in a tone that truly sounded ancient and exhausted, worn and unbearable. It crawled up Beth's back wrong.

"Oh really? Poor you, am I that tiresome?"

Kahtar grinned. "You know, Beth, I think you're exactly what I've always needed."

"I'll bet you say that to all the girls."

Roaring with sudden laughter, Kahtar bent over his knees and slapped a big hand against the grass. Wolves scrabbled up the bank and ran into the woods escaping the noise. After a couple minutes, Beth could hear the dog's howling through Kahtar's near hysterical laughter. Shoving off the ground she rose, glaring at her husband, and turned and stalked back to the house. The man knew how to kill a mood.

IT HAD BEEN a really long time since he'd lost it like that and laughed that hard. His chest hurt. In retrospect, this may have been another first. Kahtar leaned forward and stood, wiping tears off his face. Thankfully Wolves had stopped howling. That stupid dog's hoarsening howl had kept him from following Beth for the last twenty minutes. It had slowly faded into a drier and drier canine gurgle that had left Kahtar rolling in the grass. He looked down at his grass stained tuxedo. Good thing he'd never need to wear it again. What a waste. Scanning over the house, he sensed Beth sitting on the edge of her bed, head in hands. Crying.

"What the—?" Kahtar ran. He crossed the yard in seconds and pounded up the porch steps, slamming the front door open and taking the stairs four at a time. Entering her room, he dropped to his knees and slid across the hardwood floor, stopping beside Beth's lap.

"Love? Why are you crying now?" Stupid question really, so much had happened the last weeks, and then his information dump. Maybe this was her version of hysterical laughter. He'd have preferred the laughter. He leaned his head against her knees.

Beth sniffed. "How many times have you been married?"

Kahtar's neck cracked he lifted his head up so quickly. Married? A faint ghost of the laughter bubbled up again and he grinned. Beth shoved him away.

"You think it's funny?"

"Beth! Slow down. You've felt my heart, you felt all there is to me. It's how you knew I'd been around a very long time. How many wives did you feel in there?"

She frowned at him, a little wrinkle between her brows. Her eye makeup had washed into dark outlines around her eyes, the effect strangely becoming. Kahtar reached up and wiped the excess with his thumbs, waiting for Beth to process the idea.

"But how? How could you have never been married?"

"I never wanted to. I never fell in love." Her fresh tears rolled over his thumbs, and he smiled at her and nodded. "Until now."

Beth took a deep breath, and closed her eyes.

"That is the most romantic thing any man has ever said. I was so afraid you were my grandfather or something."

Kahtar chuckled. "I promise we're not related." Her eyes popped open and Beth leaned forward. Tugging her satin gown up to her ankle, she slid a foot into her fancy shoe, and bent forward to strap it on. Automatically Kahtar helped, lifting her other foot into the mate, and fumbling with the thin strap around her perfect ankle. He glanced up and Beth was staring at him, two patches of bright red on either cheek.

Knowing what she was thinking, he felt his own face flame. "No. I haven't."

"Not ever?" Beth sounded incredulous. "I mean didn't you want to?"

"Of course I wanted to!" he snapped. "I'm a man. Covenant Keepers aren't big on free love."

"Still." Beth continued to stare at him and he knew the red had now reached his ears and hairline.

"Never? Not once?" she persisted.

Kahtar shoved to his feet, and crossed his arms. Apparently embarrassment was still well within his repertoire.

"What kind of gory details do you need, Beth? I've never been married and I've never been with a woman—nor anyone if that is where your mind is going next."

"Kahtar!"

"I've been around a very long time. It's not like the thought didn't cross my mind. Trust me, they all did. I just kept very busy."

"I could never have waited," Beth said. Then she flushed. "Much longer I mean."

"Don't those shoes hurt your feet?" Again kneeling at her feet, Kahtar changed the subject, focusing on the outrageous glass and silver shoes. It had been nice to have Beth nearly eye level during the ceremony, but human feet were not meant to do that. "Why'd you put them back on?"

"I know you're into simplicity." Beth stood, towering over him in her satin dress and heels. "And fashion isn't a Covenant Keeper thing, but I kinda had my heart set on showing you why I picked this dress." Beth crossed the room gracefully, the edge of the dress trailing neatly over the floor. She'd managed to save it from a single grass stain. Kahtar rose and sat on the edge of the bed and tried his best to feign interest in the dress.

"It's good cloth." He tried. "Natural fibers…hand sewn." Beth stopped moving and peeked back at him over her shoulder. The dress had absolutely no back, and dipped dangerously low towards her backside. He rubbed a finger over his chin. She really shouldn't wear stuff like that.

"Yeah," she said. "But I kinda liked that you could do this." Beth shrugged one shoulder and the entire dress dropped off in a neat swish of satin, pooling around her. She stood exactly eight feet three inches from him in nothing but a scrap of lace that couldn't be called drawers by any stretch of the imagination. And the shoes. And nothing else. Watching over her shoulder she mimed closing her mouth by placing one finger under her chin, and Kahtar thought to shut his.

"Kala Empium Fin," he whispered hoarsely. Beth turned around to face him, smiling shyly.

"I LOST TRACK of days, are you certain it has been an entire month?"

Kahtar chuckled, their hony mone time had evaporated, and September already had the early bite of autumn in the air. Beth stood in the yard with her arms crossed, pleading her case.

"Because I've lost the desire to do anything else. Do you really have to go back to work? I'll make a deal with you. I won't go back to work, if you don't."

Kahtar started to laugh. He'd never laughed so much in his existence as he had the past weeks. Dutifully he tugged Beth over to a fading Rose of Sharon tree and pointed at a faint hint of darkness behind it.

"That, my love, is not fair. You're not duty bound to run your shop." Spotting the telltale crease between her brows, he backtracked quickly. "Of course you must follow your heart, and The Mother agreed to let you try, so I'm willing to negotiate options."

The crease went deeper, so he tried changing the subject.

"You said you wanted to see the Arc, this is your last chance for a week. We get there through that tesseract." Kahtar dropped his arms around her shoulders for a quick hug. She was deliciously soft and smelled so good. With Beth firmly in his arms, he nudged her into the diamond shape of flat darkness.

It was a tunnel of dark with veins of light decorating it, but their feet never actually touched the ground, and there was no feeling of movement, though something deep in the psyche understood they were moving. Then it was gone, and they were standing on crabgrass like any yard in Ohio.

"That was amazing." Beth looked back at the medallion of darkness. "If I ask how that is done, how comprehensible would the answer be?"

Kahtar held tightly to her hand and paused to kiss it, wishing he could negotiate a longer hony mone.

"Quick and relatively painless because I don't know. Abigail, she's one of the clan's Elders, is gifted to make them, and it is a very rare gifting. I've only known of a handful of women who could do it in all my time."

"Are we inside the Arc?" Beth looked towards shimmering rows of Old Guard. There were hundreds of them flickering in the bright morning light.

"Not yet, tesseracts can't penetrate the Arc. We enter through the doorway here." The smallest niggle of doubt stirred in Kahtar's chest.

Beth has Seeker blood. He glanced at the Old Guard who shimmered like a row of light around the entrance to the Arc. *Surely they would stop me if it weren't possible.* Part of him wondered, though, if the Old Guard were waiting to see what would happen too. Kahtar's heart sank a bit.

"What?" Beth asked, sensing it. Then she was distracted before receiving an answer. "I can feel it! I can feel the entrance. It feels like silent music." She pulled her hand from his and patted the air in front of the opening to Cultuelle Khristos's Arc. "It's very welcoming and familiar, like I've felt it before!"

Not once in Kahtar's entire existence had he even heard of a Seeker penetrating an Arc. During their hony mone this thought hadn't bothered him. The entire month had been a high of bliss that scrambled his thoughts and tossed his rigorous schedule into disarray. They'd loved and laughed, thought only of each other, eaten when they were hungry, and slept only when exhausted.

Like a moth to a flame, Beth continued to run her hands over the Arc's vibrating entrance. She tucked her hair behind her ears and leaned forward to feel it against her cheek, delighted as a child. She looked diminutive in flat slippers and a plain, soft gown, carefree. Kahtar had been feeling almost carefree himself, until this moment.

Several Old Guard solidified to watch them enter, justifying his suspicions. Beth grabbed his hand and slid through first, melting from view. Before he had time to experience anxiety, he was pulled through with her. Standing inside the Arc, Beth stared in stunned amazement. She wobbled and he quickly put out a hand to steady her. She gaped in wonder at the sensory overload inside.

Inside the Arc, September didn't exist. Cultuelle Khristos called this Caeaur, the time of blue and gold. An ocean of yellow grasses waved in the flat meadow where paths snaked out in several directions. The air crisp and so crystal clear it seemed as though one's eyesight improved instantly. The sky so blue you could taste it, to Kahtar it tasted like joy. The only sound was the rippling grass and the waves of the Great Lake in the distance. Trees several feet thick towered at the edges of the meadow like skyscrapers, a doe wandered nearby, blinking at them without fear. Beth's eyes riveted on a large shape in the distance and widened with disbelief.

"It's a mastodon." Kahtar pointed out the large elephantine shape lumbering towards the lake.

Beth didn't move and Kahtar grinned, certain life could not be more perfect. He rubbed a hand over her back as he explained.

"When Arcs are built they go to a set point in time. The animals that belong to that time are in the Arc. Come on, we take this path."

Still ingesting the scenery, Beth leaned far back to look up at the enormous trees and he had to take her hand and tug her. She tripped along beside him, gawking.

"It's like the Garden of Eden!" she whispered.

"Well, I wouldn't know that for certain," he whispered back, "but pretty close I think."

"Is this what the world used to look like, Kahtar?" Beth stumbled along the path, staring in wide-eyed wonder at the trees and plants, breathing deeply of the pure air and pausing to run fingers over thick wildflowers in every shade of blue.

"Close, the air inside Arcs is clearer and the water sweeter than the outside world has ever been, as far as I remember. You can drink out of the lake in here, or eat the fish raw and it's all good."

Kahtar wrapped an arm around her waist and kissed the top of her head.

"We'll explore later. Let's hurry. I want to show you the cave before everyone is gone."

WINDING DOWN A narrow passageway, Beth went first. Behind her, Kahtar had his hands on her shoulders, his strong heart surrounded hers and she soldiered forward to meet Cultuelle Khristos in their own world. Inside The Cave, as Kahtar called it, it took a minute for her eyes to adjust to the darkness and then the flickering light. Her husband's capable hands guided her forward, over the smooth path. The scent of cave greeted, and though it was the smell of damp underground, it was pleasant, like rich earth, cool stone, and clean water. Sound came next, opening up all at once when they turned a corner, it hit Beth like something physical. Thousands of people, voices and laughter reverberated off cavern walls, water gushed and gurgled and the echo of movement was amplified in the enormous echoing space. The pleasant feeling inside the Arc was stronger in the cavern. It felt like the touch of thousands of happy hearts were drifting near hers.

The cave was a huge underground canyon of space, switchbacks and paths as far as she could see. Beth had no idea caves could be this enormous! White waterfalls and green streams cascaded in the shimmering light. Cave formations glittered and sparkled from every direction.

"Glory is over," Kahtar told her. "We'll try harder to make it next week. Keep moving. Everyone will want to meet you."

"Everyone!" Beth hung back, looking over the sea of people.

"Yep. You're practically famous," he teased, with a reassuring squeeze of her shoulders, and he continued to push her along in front of him.

They passed warriors as they continued down the narrow path. The men deferred to Kahtar, stepping off the smooth surface to allow them to pass, but Beth didn't miss the looks of stunned surprise shot at her. They were still making their way past warriors, when Honor Monroe stepped into their path and blocked their progress. Kahtar stopped, and Beth felt tension seethe from his hands as he tugged her protectively backwards, wrapping his arms over her middle. Honor held his place and stared at Beth, and she patted Kahtar's big forearms.

Honor stepped too close, invading her personal space like he always had. The look in his familiar blue eyes told Beth that he still loved her.

"Thank ilu you survived, Beth. I'm so sorry for the way I treated you at your trial. I will find a way to make it up to you someday."

"You know I forgive you, Honor." Beth almost reached to take his hand before she sensed the reserve in his heart, noticed his formal stance, the way he didn't reach for her, and the distance in his eyes. Everything had changed between them. She kept her hands on Kahtar's.

"It will never be the same though. You're happy I'm alive but uncomfortable to have someone like me here inside the Arc." After Beth blurted, she wished she'd bitten her tongue. Honor looked crestfallen, but Beth shrugged. "It's okay, Honor. It's the truth."

"I want to be your friend again, Bethy." But the way he said her name sounded forced.

"No you don't, Honor, not really. You want who you thought I was, not who I am. Don't be upset, we're still clan, right? I love you too, but I don't like you as much anymore either."

Honor pressed his hand against his chest and Beth knew her words had cut. She was sorry for it. Honor nodded then, taking it like he always did. His parents had named him well. Tears shone in his handsome eyes.

"There it is then. The truth really hurts, doesn't it?" He leaned forward and kissed her lips briefly, then whispered so lightly that barely any sound passed his lips. "I'll miss you forever."

When he walked away, Beth realized with surprise that she wouldn't miss him.

The noise in the cavern was increasing, and Beth leaned against Kahtar and glanced up at him. He nodded at her as the cause of the excitement and her eyes widened in alarm. Her exchange with Honor had surely been overheard. How many of Cultuelle Khristos felt about her the same way Honor did?

Beth looked for truth in nearby faces. Stunned was the feeling she picked up from those nearest her, and Beth knew it was due to the same reason she and Honor would never be friends again. She was a child of blending and they'd never expected to see someone like her in their midst. Beth searched for welcoming faces in the sea of people who were suddenly turning in her direction.

Then one vaguely familiar face stood out in an ocean of curious expressions. In the crowd of identically dressed Warriors of ilu, shimmering Old Guard, and strangers dressed in soft muted fabrics, one person stood out. The woman was short and plump, dressed in an olive drab dress with her red hair wound tightly in a bun. She was stoutly making her way through the crowd using sharp elbows and words, eyes on Beth. Jamming pointy, cat-eye glasses onto her nose she continued forward and Beth gasped, "Kahtar?"

Kahtar squeezed her waist, his chain mail digging into her back.

"Maybe there was a better way to do this," he murmured.

The redhead in the glasses griped, "You think so, Warrior? You brought a unicorn to a petting zoo." She smiled at Beth and mouthed the word, "men," with an exaggerated look towards the heavens.

Kahtar ignored the slight. "This is Abigail, Beth. Abigail Adit. She's a clan Elder, tesseract maker and warrior eater."

"Kahtar and I have a special relationship. He worships me, and I tolerate him."

"Abigail is the sun in her own universe. Prolonged exposure can be hazardous to one's health."

"Kahtar!" Abigail looked impressed. "Banter? It's like you're developing a personality!" She looked towards Beth and a strange second voice tinkled into Beth's mind.

"I knew you'd be good for him."

Ignoring the crowd, Kahtar turned, holding onto Beth's hand. He tugged her back up the path. Unable to resist, she looked back at the crowd watching her. Abigail winked at her. There was no doubt about it. Abigail was the same woman. The librarian at the rummage sale who'd told her about the house for sale in the little borough of Willowyth. Beth twisted to look again, just to be certain. Abigail stood on the path behind them and she put one pudgy finger in front of her lips. In the echoing cavern, Beth was certain she heard her whisper, "Shhhh."

ON THE SHORE of the Great Lake, Kahtar stood in the waves of the rocky beach, water rolling over his boots and buffeting his swords against his legs. Beth stayed dry, perched on a large boulder, arms wrapped around her knees. A herd of buffalo grazed to the west, silhouetted against the afternoon sun. Beth had gone quiet, and he regretted taking her to the cave. Abigail had been right. It had been too much.

"It will be better next week," he said.

From the throne of boulders Beth looked down at him, she looked more confused than upset, but a smile quirked her lips.

"Who do you think you're kidding?"

"I meant you'll get used to the way the clan reacts to you, and it won't seem so bad in time. You can trust that I'll never feed you platitudes."

Beth nodded absently, and Kahtar climbed over rocks to get his boots out of the water. Leaning against the boulder beside Beth, he unbuckled his belt and dropped his swords onto a rock. It echoed so loudly, the buffalo in the distance stopped grazing and looked around.

"The clan simply didn't expect you to be able to get inside the Arc because of your Seeker blood. As bigoted as that sounds, in all my time I've never seen an Orphan enter an Arc either. Don't take surprise for condemnation, Beth."

"I'm not," she reassured, her honest eyes still wide. "Kahtar? How do you feel about arranged marriages?"

"What?"

"Never mind," she said.

"Covenant Keepers join only for love, so I don't think they'd work. Do you have someone in mind for Abigail?" He dropped to sit beside her and threw his arm over her shoulders, grinning.

Beth smiled at him, and he studied those appealing lips, full and soft and daring and talented. Kahtar leaned forward to kiss them but three Old Guard flickered into being along the shoreline, standing half in the water, shimmering. The waves didn't even dampen their legs. Kahtar reluctantly moved his mouth away from Beth's lips. Against his arm, he felt her silent sigh of disappointment and he pulled her closer.

"If we're really going to rejoin the world today, I need to make a trip," Beth said.

"To your parents?"

"That too, but I meant the airport." She must have seen something in his expression because she tried to lighten the mood by adding, "I need to see a man about a horse."

He couldn't believe she'd even try this.

"You're not getting on any airplanes anymore. It's forbidden."

"Don't be ridiculous, how am I supposed to get places? I can't keep the store stocked without some trips, Kahtar." She glanced towards the three Old Guard shimmering on the shore. "And a new order of that brack tea should be ready by now. It can't be shipped, and they only sell to me, so I have to go get it," she ended quite loudly.

"Beth! Are you attempting to manipulate Old Guard?"

She grinned at him, and he struggled to hide his amusement, knowing there was no hope. She read him like a book, and he'd just have to get used to it. Smiling ruefully he shot a guilty look at the Old Guard who may or may not have overheard.

"I'll take care of your travel arrangements and it won't involve airplanes. It is much faster, too. You can't go by yourself though. Don't argue. It's a clan rule." Kahtar shifted, tugging his tunic from under him. The chainmail made a zinging sound jouncing off the rock. The stuff wasn't conducive to romance or sitting on rocks, and Beth didn't wrap her arm around him. He fingered the stuff. It was a bit sharp. Then he noticed her expression, pretty blue eyes narrowed as she stared over at the Old Guard. A shiver rippled through her and he tightened his arm.

"The Old Guard aren't transportation, Beth. I meant Abigail will take you wherever you need to go, and she'll keep you safe."

"Abigail?"

"You'd be surprised. Do me a favor? She'll want to show you the world—"

"I've seen the world."

"That won't matter to Abigail. She'll keep you away just to torment me. Tell her you like to be home at night."

"Kahtar, I can't lie." For a brief moment he sagged.

Then he wrapped both arms around her and tugged her closer. "Didn't you learn anything about teasing me the past month? You always pay."

"I know," she purred. "That's why I keep doing it." Despite the chain mail and the Old Guard standing just yards away, Beth slithered onto his lap and wrapped her arms around him, resting her head against his shoulder. Her hair smelled like sunshine and strawberries.

"Do you really have to go?" she whispered. "Just one more day? It's Sunday."

Kahtar motioned towards the Old Guard and they blinked brightly and then vanished. Beth didn't seem to notice, she snuggled closer, long legs wrapping around his waist.

"You've changed me, Beth," his voice sounded gruff. Beth's arm's tightened around his neck.

"Someone had to," she whispered, and he smiled into her hair. It was the truth.

ACKNOWLEDGEMENTS

Kahtar—Warrior of the Ages was written in the wee hours of the night, in stolen years that I seized from my family and friends like a marauding Viking. The muse demanded and I obeyed. I thank my husband and children for their loving understanding and stoic acceptance that apples and peanut butter constitute a real meal. It takes a village to write a book, and I'm forever blessed by my team.

Thanks to the Ragged Edge writers for the hand up: Ted Dekker, Steven James, Kevin Kaiser, Tosca Lee, Robert Liparulo, and Eric Wilson. It was your light on a tough path that made me persevere.

There is one other person who knows this story almost as intimately as I do. That is my main beta, Lindsay Hodges. For his pedantic nitpicky ways, and steadfast perseverance through rewrites, edits, and changes, I am very grateful. It was a pleasure to be red lined by you. Snaps for my backup beta, Kelsey Keating, who watched this story grow and mature, and read and commented on each version. Your enthusiasm and impassioned opinion fueled me through many a tough patch. You are my shieldmaiden and my next-gen clone. Thank you.

To my Blue Monkey peeps who make the writing jungle an oasis, I thank you for all the encouragement and support: Kelsey Keating, Rachelle Rediger, LaDonna Cole, D. M. Kilgore, Kimberly Robertson, Rob Holliday, Linnette R. Mullin, Frank Lattimore, Heather Burch, Robert Liparulo, Robin Harnist—editor extraordinaire, and Steven James.

To the rest of my Blue Munks, including the newbies, I raise my goblet to you (and know there is something banana-flavored in there with hardly any chunks—just drink it, don't look): Tom Mohan, Ashley Cyare, Jason and Jennifer Fancher, Lydia Paine, Elizabeth Buzard, Emily Dukes, Emily Kunkel, Ed Keelan, Donna Marie Adams McChristian, Isabel Berrios-Brown, Tyler Carrington, Colette StOnge Pedersen (spelt correctly), Gary L. Wade, Ben Wolf, Tracey Lanter Eyster, Caleb Jennings Breaky, Donna Underwood Spivey, Lynnell

Koehler, Natalie Pedersen Pierson, Chris Varble, Amy Machelle, Krystal Travis, Reuben Horst, Brian K. Perry, Tim Ward, Heather Sudbrock, Benjamin K. Gathright, Hannah Travis, Lindsay Harless, Caroline Madison, Britton Peele, Karissa Travis, Catherine Jones Payne, Lahoma McMillion, Cory Clubb, Cory Kruse, Chadd Baltzley, Sarah LeighAnn Thompson, Heather Pond, Dayla Cole, Hannah Lee, Kevin Frasure, Emma Chin, Joey Spicer, Rose Ahonen Corscadden, Greg T. Carpenter, Jennifer Bailey, Katie J. Cross, Britain Vanderbush, Emily Ogle, Laura Custodio, Aleena Korell, Kiffin Irwin, Eli Johnson, Annie Adams, Laura Katharine, and of course the unforgettable, sparkly, and blue Andrea Asay, Devin Berglund, Brandon Blackwood, and Lesa Pascavis Smith. Wimoweh, wimoweh to you all.

ABOUT THE AUTHOR

An entrepreneur, wife, mother, and novelist, S.R. Karfelt enjoys spending time with her muse and living outside her comfort zone. She currently resides in the soaring capital of the world.

Visit her website:
www.srkarfelt.com